A PICTURE IS WORTH A THOUSAND HEIRS

A Regency Era Romance

THE LONDON LADIES' LEAGUE
BOOK III

TRISHA MESSMER

Copyright © 2025 Trisha Messmer
All rights reserved
ISBN-13: 979-8-9897299-4-4

Cover design by The Write Designer
All rights reserved by author. This story may not be transmitted, stored, or performed without written consent from the author. This includes, but not limited to, physical publications, electronic formats, audio books, and dramatic readings. This is a work of fiction. Names, characters, places, and incidents are either the product of the author's imagination or used fictitiously. Any resemblance to actual persons, living or dead, or locales is entirely coincidental.

DEDICATION

To healthcare professionals everywhere, but especially those at Peace Health Riverbend in Springfield, Oregon. Without you, this book would never have been finished. Thank you for saving my life.

CONTENTS

ACKNOWLEDGMENTS

It's probably not often that an author acknowledges those who have helped her finish a book by saving her life. Yet, in this instance, it's true. That being said, first and foremost, thank you to my daughter, Amanda, who hauled my stubborn rear-end to the emergency department. Stephen owes you more than a dinner. Be sure to collect.

Secondly, to the amazing medical staff at Peace Health Riverbend Hospital in Springfield, Oregon. From the moment they wheeled me into the emergency department to the time they wheeled me out to go home, I received exemplary care. I don't have (or remember) everyone's name because sometimes things were a blur, but rest assured, I appreciate you.

But there are more than a few people who stood out. To Dr. Callahan and his student doctor, Maddy, in the emergency department. Thank you for your quick (and very accurate) diagnosis that ensured I got the timely help I needed. Thank you to Dr. Littman, who performed the surgery, Dr. d'Ambrosio, the anesthesiologist who explained everything to me with a dash of (much appreciated) humor, and the surgical physician assistants, John and Gregg, who followed-up regularly to make sure I was doing okay.

During my week-long stay, my daily care was always administered with compassion and patience. To Kimberly and Jess, the ostomy nurses, thank you for your encouragement, your patience, and a shoulder to cry on when needed. To Jona, the physical therapist who cheered me on with each step (and I'm still log-rolling!).

On to the RNs and CNAs. What a lovely group of people. Thank you to Colby, who was my day-nurse for several days during my stay. Dude, you got me hooked on Connections! To Rachel, one of my night nurses, who laughed at my lame attempt to be funny and talk like Yoda (I hope you're writing!). To Sara whose brilliance helped me choke down some of my medication by putting it in applesauce. And to Nat, my CNA, who could teach Tyra Banks a thing or two about "smizing." Even behind your mask your smile was evident, and your cheerful attitude, no matter what you had to do, brightened my days.

These folks work tirelessly and deserve so much more than a simple thanks.

Of course, to my family, whose support is ongoing, but who rallied around me with so much love it humbled me. I felt your love down to my bones. Special thanks to Paul and Amanda, who took turns staying with me that first week, running to the store at almost eleven at night for Mucinex because I was coughing my lungs out (and checking for counter-indications against all my medications—five times is a little excessive Paul, but I understand, since you're a Six), cleaning my apartment, picking up groceries, taking out trash, taking me to doctor's follow-up visits, and all around making sure I was comfortable and resting.

To my newsletter subscribers who reached out to me with support and encouragement, often sharing your own stories and telling me not to worry, to just concentrate on getting well and you would wait for Victor and Juliana's story. I hope the wait was worth it. But know that I appreciated your words more than I can say.

To Peter Senftleben, my editor at PES Editorial. Thank you for making sense out of my scribbles and helping to make it the best it can be (not to mention your understanding and flexibility when I had to reschedule everything).

To Lisa Messegee at the Write Designer for my beautiful cover and for the gorgeous flowers you sent to me at the hospital. Everyone who came into my room noticed them and the fantastic fragrance.

To Jessica Kelly at Gray Cat Publishing and Designs for your eagle-eye proofreading skills. Those hyphens will be the death of me.

To my intrepid critique partners who rushed through this thing in record time (because it was already so behind). Brad, Amy, Jess, and Lisa. Thank you for putting up with me and telling it to me straight when something wasn't working.

To Tori, my cat, who didn't forget me during that week we were apart. She doesn't care about thanks; she just wants treats.

And of course, to you, my dear readers, for your patience. This is the longest time between releases I've ever had. I will work much harder to get the next one to you sooner!

CHAPTER 1

An enormous feather perched atop Juliana's head, the height of which she was certain could dust the ceiling of her room in Pendrake Manor, her brother's London mansion. Her hand drifted upward. She had an overwhelming desire to pluck the ridiculous thing from her hair.

Her entire family had gathered in her bedchamber as she prepared to make her debut into society. Even Simon Beckham, her brother's man-of-business leaned against the door frame.

"Try not to touch it, my dear," her sister-in-law, the Duchess of Burwood, said, her tone kind but firm. Honoria was the gentlest of creatures, but at the moment, her impending motherhood had transformed her into a tigress. "Susan has done an exceptional job fastening it on with the tiara and into your coiffure, but I worry the slightest contact might dislodge it. Your hair is so fine and silky."

And straight. Juliana didn't mind her hair, but Miss Price had grumbled about the lack of curl and the ability to hide the feather's end completely. No doubt used to Honoria's thick red curls,

Honoria's lady's maid found Juliana's plain blond locks unremarkable.

"As soon as you make your bow to Prince William and Princess Adelaide, and we are comfortably at home, you may remove it," Honoria said. "At least until the ball this evening."

"Listen to Honoria," her brother, Drake, said. "She knows about these things." Although her brother—well, half-brother—was now a duke, neither he nor Juliana had been brought up in society.

Her mother dabbed at her eyes with a fine lace handkerchief. "It's such a shame the king has been so ill and won't be presiding."

Simon gave a soft chuckle. "It's probably for the best. Old Prinny would probably pry himself from the throne and chase Juliana around the room." He gave a low whistle. "You look beautiful."

Heat flooded Juliana's face, even though Simon flirted with everyone and, to him, she was only Drake's baby sister.

Drake narrowed his eyes at his friend. "You're one to talk about the king. Behave yourself, Simon."

As Juliana gazed at the people she loved more than anything in the world, she hoped she wouldn't disappoint them. The pressure to be perfect weighed upon her. Honoria and Drake had made such a fuss about her coming out in society even though, at twenty-two, she was well past the age of the other debutantes, but the pressure came not from her beloved brother and his wife, but from within and from her own exacting standards to be, at all costs, good.

She would have much preferred to be out riding at Hartridge House, Drake's estate in Dorset, where only the trees and woodland creatures could witness any possible misstep. Animals didn't judge.

Juliana fought to pull in a calming breath, but Miss Price had pulled the corset so tight her attempt proved unsuccessful. She turned back toward the mirror and examined her reflection sideways, hoping the constricting garment had made her appear marginally—and more fashionably—slimmer.

"Come now!" Drake called her attention back. "It's time to stop admiring yourself and allow others to do so." He held out his arm. "Like the prince."

Was it too late to push them out and lock herself in her room? Why did she have to be presented into society? Even though Drake was a duke, she was simply Miss Merrick, the daughter of two commoner parents.

"It will be fine, Juliana." Honoria patted her hand, her soothing voice making Juliana believe perhaps it would be.

It wasn't.

Two hours later . . .

Seated across from Drake and Honoria in the carriage, her mother's arm wrapped protectively around her shoulders, Juliana fought back the tears.

Humiliated.

Mortified.

Crushed.

One careless step as she backed away from the prince and princess, and her foot had caught on her long train, sending her sprawling for all to see. After a collective gasp, a deafening hush settled over the assembly. A titter of laughter broke the silence and grew increasingly louder as each person joined in. The sound assaulted her ears and brought heat to her face.

Why, oh, why had she ever agreed to this? She stole a peek at Drake and Honoria, and shame filled her at having brought embarrassment to the family.

"I'll never be able to show myself in polite society again." She choked back the sob, hating the emotions flooding her.

"Nonsense," Honoria said, compassion filling her eyes. "Tomorrow, the incident will be all but forgotten."

But in that compassion, Juliana saw the truth. Even Honoria doubted her words. Juliana still had much to learn about society, but one thing was clear, the *ton* loved gossip and took perverse pleasure in people's embarrassment—especially those they considered beneath them.

Juliana sniffed again. "Will you call off the ball?"

Honoria and Drake exchanged a glance, and Juliana's stomach knotted.

"Other than having Frampton turn people away at the door, it's too late to cancel," Drake said. "But I shall remain by your side the entire night. No one will so much as dare to say anything, or I shall wither them with my ducal glare."

Honoria held a gloved hand to her mouth, stifling a little laugh.

Juliana voiced what Honoria no doubt was thinking. "You don't have a ducal glare, brother."

"It's true, Drake," their mother said. "You're about as frightening as a lamb."

"Aunt Kitty, then?" Drake asked.

Tears still in her eyes, Juliana laughed along with everyone else at the image of Drake's Aunt Kitty threatening people with her cane. The woman was formidable.

Later that evening, Juliana prepared herself, hoping the ball would go more smoothly than her presentation at court. People did arrive, but rather than delivering smiles and congratulations, many of the guests either offered comforting words or said nothing at all.

However, there was a small contingent of guests who—although they said nothing to her face—stole glances at her from across the ballroom and snickered behind their fans or hands, whispering in the ears of those who would listen.

One in particular, Miss Lydia Whyte, set Juliana's nerves on edge. She'd met the woman at Drake's house party the previous summer. Since Miss Whyte was approximately the same age, Juliana hoped they might become friends once Drake revealed himself and assumed his position as duke. But the moment Simon had introduced them, Lydia's cold assessment as she raked her gaze up and down Juliana's body indicated otherwise. She'd even heard the woman make a snide remark about her to that odious man, Lord Middlebury.

Granted, those less-than-generous attendees were not among Drake and Honoria's closest friends. Although unable to attend the ball due to the recent birth of their baby daughter, the Duke and

Duchess of Ashton sent their well wishes, welcoming Juliana into society and predicting she would be the diamond of the Season.

Ha! Unlikely. Juliana's humiliating presentation was the least of it. Not only was Juliana a commoner, but she did not possess the qualities attributed to such beauties. More well-endowed in the bosom than most young ladies her age, her one advantage was her mother was an excellent seamstress and could work magic with the fit of Juliana's gowns.

Lady Montgomery assured Juliana that her own come-out had been much more disastrous, and yet she secured a love match with the man of her heart. The truth of Bea's statement shone in her eyes when she gazed at her husband, Lord Montgomery, the same love reflected in his.

Yet, as the evening continued, and the dancing began, her only partners, other than Simon, had been the married men and friends of her brother. Even Drake wanted to dance with her, a faux pas Honoria was almost willing to allow but convinced Drake they shouldn't provide any more fodder for the gossip sheets. Honoria's apologetic glance was hardly necessary, as Juliana quite agreed.

No amount of glittering crystal or lovely strands of music from the string orchestra could make up for the feeling of being unwanted.

Would the evening ever end?

Heaviness settled in Juliana's stomach as she watched the other couples on the dance floor. Her gaze landed on Mr. Victor Pratt dancing with Lydia. Lydia laughed at something Mr. Pratt said, then tapped him on the arm with her fan during a pass in the dance.

Mr. Pratt had been friendly during Drake's house party but not overly so. Respectful would be the word Juliana would use. At the time, Juliana had indulged in some girlish fantasies about him. She couldn't imagine him with someone like Lydia. But of course, she really didn't know him.

He was handsome, for certain. That long blond hair tied back in a queue, giving him an air of rebelliousness, intrigued Juliana. Honoria had described it as dashing, and Juliana agreed. But as one of the few unmarried men in attendance that evening, like the others, he kept his distance.

The dance ended, and he rejoined his sister, Priscilla, and her husband, Dr. Marbry. When he inclined his head to listen to something Priscilla was saying, his gaze lifted and locked with Juliana's. Giving a brief nod, he said something in return, and then he strode forward, stopping Juliana's heart.

VICTOR WONDERED IF HIS DANCE WITH LYDIA WHYTE WOULD EVER end. The woman was relentless, and he knew if he didn't dance with her, she would pound him to death on the arm with that damnable fan of hers. In truth, he didn't even want to be at the ball. He'd been perfectly content wallowing in his dark thoughts until his sister, Priscilla, had appeared at their parents' home that afternoon.

"You *have* to go, Victor. Poor Juliana will need some friendly faces and at least a few eligible gentlemen to request a dance."

Victor's skin prickled at the word *poor*. "Why *poor*? I have a feeling it's more than the fact her parents are commoners."

Their mother sniffed. "Which is more than enough reason not to go, I would say."

Victor shot his mother a glower, but it didn't stop her from prattling on.

"But I heard from Lucretia, who heard it from Lady Easton's maid, who heard it from—"

"Stop!" Victor held up a hand. "You should know better than to listen to a chain of gossip, Mother, especially gossip handed down through servants."

"Gossip, true or not, is hurtful," Priscilla said. "And it's all the more reason to show our support."

Mother sniffed again. "All the more reason to stay home, Victor. I would advise you to do the same, Priscilla."

"No," his sister said adamantly. "Timothy and I will be happy to attend. Honoria is my friend, and Juliana is her sister-in-law. And for goodness' sakes, Mother, Juliana's brother is a duke! You should be more careful whom you disparage."

"Hear, hear," Victor mumbled.

And even though he didn't wish to attend the event, Victor had donned his finest evening wear and was doing his damnedest to make the most of his night at Miss Merrick's come-out ball. If nothing else, annoying his mother would be worth every dull moment.

Lydia tapped him with her fan again. Thank God the dance was almost over.

"Are you listening to me, Victor?"

Trying not to. "Of course. What were you saying?"

Lydia lowered her voice conspiratorially. "During her presentation at court, Miss Merrick tripped on her gown and fell on her—well, her *derrière* in front of the whole assembly." The smirk on Lydia's face contrasted sharply with her feigned embarrassment over saying the word derrière. "I'm surprised she's showing her face this evening. Of course, what can one expect from a commoner?"

"You should be more forgiving of people's misfortunes, Lydia. You may have need of compassion yourself one day."

Once the dance ended and Victor deposited Lydia back with her parents, he joined Priscilla and her husband, Timothy, hoping for more amiable company.

Priscilla tapped him with her fan. What was it with women and those fans?! He wanted to rip them to shreds! "What?" he barked.

She gave him a firmer swat.

"Ow! That hurt."

Timothy, chuckled. "She is vicious, Victor. You should know that."

"I wouldn't have to be if either of you would pay attention. Victor, go ask Miss Merrick to dance. The only eligible gentleman who has danced with her was Mr. Beckham. He's such a flirt; I doubt Juliana even counted it as interest. The man even flirted with me last year at Burwood's house party."

Timothy growled next to her, and Priscilla reached back and flicked her fan at him, landing a direct hit on Timothy's stomach.

"Serves you right." Victor fought back the laugh.

"Please, Victor. It will make the girl feel better. You're young and somewhat good-looking."

"Somewhat?" Victor raised a brow. "Cilla, I think that's as close to a compliment as I will ever receive from you." He sighed. "Very well. But be sure to report it back to Mother. I do so enjoy annoying her."

He strode toward Miss Merrick, whose eyes widened at his approach.

"Miss Merrick. May I have the honor of the next set?" He held out his hand. From the corner of his eye, he saw her brother, the duke, give a nod.

Pink rose to her cheeks. "I would be delighted, sir." She slipped her gloved hand into his as he led her to the dance floor. "Thank you for rescuing me, Mr. Pratt," she whispered. "You are my hero."

Victor's stomach clenched. *Hero?* Surely not. Was the girl reading more into his gesture than intended—a simple dance? He glanced down at the fan dangling from her wrist. Arguing with her might result in an assault with the feminine weapon.

Instead, he smiled as they took their places for the cotillion. Thank God it wasn't a waltz. Women put such store in that particular dance. Victor bowed, and upon rising, his gaze snagged on Miss Merrick's. A shock jolted through him at her blue eyes, bringing back the memory he'd tried in vain to push down. He jerked his gaze away.

Adalyn's cerulean-blue eyes sparkled in his mind, and the familiar dull ache pinged in his chest.

"Mr. Pratt? Is something wrong?" Miss Merrick's voice brought him back.

"Forgive me, Miss Merrick." Victor did his best to smile his apology. He forced his gaze back to hers. No, not cerulean. The slight tinge of violet made Miss Merrick's eyes more of a cornflower-blue. Thank goodness.

A shade darker than Adalyn's almost silver-blond, Victor studied Miss Merrick's hair, appreciating how the candlelight brought out strands of red in her golden locks.

No, Miss Merrick was *not* Adalyn Lovelace. Victor sighed in relief. "You look lovely this evening, Miss Merrick." Something flashed in Miss Merrick's—decidedly—cornflower-blue eyes at Victor's polite comment.

Disbelief?

Distrust?

"As opposed to?" she asked.

What? "I'm afraid I don't understand." He truly didn't.

"You said *this evening*. As opposed to when? Other than my brother's house party last summer, I don't remember enjoying your acquaintance."

"You have a literal mind, Miss Merrick. I simply meant—"

"Fear not, Mr. Pratt. Apparently, even my attempts at humor are falling flat today." She winced. "A poor choice of words, that."

Victor chuckled at her honesty.

She quirked a blond brow at him.

"Don't misunderstand, Miss Merrick. I was not laughing at you, but *with* you. I admire a woman who doesn't take herself too seriously."

A genuine smile crossed her lips, and Victor found he liked her smile, too.

"I understand you are an artist, sir."

"I dabble," Victor said, his interest piquing at his favorite subject.

She smiled again. Yes, he definitely liked her smile. "You're being modest, I fear. Honoria says you are quite knowledgeable. Now that he's a duke, Drake has mentioned getting portraits painted for the family. Perhaps you could recommend an artist or apply for the task yourself?"

Oh, what a coup that would be to paint the portraits of a duke and his family. "I would be happy to offer my assistance in whatever way Burwood sees fit."

"I will be sure to relay your offer to my brother, sir."

When the dance ended, Victor was pleased he'd—for once— listened to his sister and asked Miss Merrick to dance, finding both a new friend and, even more hopefully, an opportunity to apply his skills.

Eager to get to know her better, Victor bowed and said, "Would you care for some refreshment, Miss Merrick? Some lemonade or ratafia to quench your thirst?"

Her eyes sparkled. Yes. Definitely cornflower-blue. "I would love that, Mr. Pratt, and although my brother finds ratafia too sweet, I adore it."

Victor escorted her to the refreshment table, requesting one glass of ratafia and one of lemonade. As a gentleman should, he took the ratafia from the footman and turned to hand it to Miss Merrick. A sharp bump to his arm thrusted it forward, and the ratafia splashed from the glass, the red liquid landing in the most unfortunate area on Miss Merrick's white gown.

Prepared to deliver a sharp setdown to whomever had bumped him, Victor spun on his heel only to discover no one behind him. No. Wait. Several feet away, Lydia Whyte chatted with her mother. Lady Whyte's gaze darted in his direction, her eyes widening as she tapped Lydia on the arm—with her fan, of course—and nodded in Victor's and Miss Merrick's direction.

"Sir. Sir." The footman's call pulled him back to his faux pas.

Poor Miss Merrick stood motionless, staring at the red stain spreading like a watered-down blob of paint.

Victor snatched the serviette from the footman's hand but paused before attempting to blot the liquid. "Um." Poised in front of Miss Merrick's abdomen, the serviette dangled from Victor's fingers.

"Oh, dear," Lydia said, appearing by his side, her voice flush with pity. "What unfortunate timing, Miss Merrick." The glint in Lydia's eyes gave her away. "May I assist?"

"No." Miss Merrick plucked the serviette from Victor's fingers, but due to the location of the stain, even she hesitated to dab at the liquid.

Gasps from around the room drew the Duchess of Burwood's attention, and she and Mrs. Merrick raced to Miss Merrick's side.

"What happened?" Mrs. Merrick asked, while the duchess, Honoria, wrapped an arm around Miss Merrick's shoulders.

"It's my fault," Victor admitted. "The glass of ratafia . . . someone bumped me." Victor shot a glance toward Lydia, who adopted an innocent expression.

Tears welled in Miss Merrick's eyes, dulling the cornflower color to a duskier steel-blue. "If you would excuse me, Mr. Pratt."

As Mrs. Merrick and the duchess whisked Miss Merrick away, Lydia tapped him with that damnable fan. "Pity. Miss Merrick seems to have experienced a series of unfortunate events today."

And although Victor's heart went out to Miss Merrick, all he could think about was he'd probably lost his chance at gaining the ear of—and perhaps a commission for portraits from—a duke. Not to mention Miss Merrick's friendship.

At that moment, he wasn't sure which pained him more.

CHAPTER 2

For two months after her horrendous come-out, Juliana had secreted herself away at Drake's country seat in Dorset, too ashamed to show her face in London society. Drake and Honoria had such high hopes for her, and she'd failed them miserably. She would always be an outsider, the common born half-sister of a duke, struggling to fit in and feeling so out of place. But love for her family and the call to be useful had brought both her and her mother back.

She wiped a bit of blackberry jam from her lips, the sweetness fading as a frown creased her brother's forehead.

"What is it, Drake?" their mother asked.

Both Juliana and her mother worried about Drake since their return a week before. The unexpected arrival of Drake and Honoria's first child, a darling little girl they'd named Kitty, had been a call for celebration, but coupled with the also unexpected marriage of Simon, Drake's man-of-business, the events had set her brother at sixes and sevens.

Drake toyed with a bit of toast on his plate. "I'm neglecting you both. Juliana should be attending routs and balls. As her brother and a peer, it's my duty to see she's well received."

Juliana bit back the derisive snort at the pained expression on her brother's face. "I doubt even your authority as duke could accomplish that, Drake. Besides, your place is here with Honoria and Kitty when you're not in Lords fighting for reform. If Mother and I are invited to a party, she can accompany me."

From the expression on his face, Drake was well aware that any invitation from members of the *ton* would not be directly addressed to either Juliana or their mother. Drake would simply bring Juliana along to any events he and Honoria attended, knowing full well people would be reluctant to refuse a duke.

Oh, there were still a few who would be so bold. Lady Charlotte's brother, the Marquess of Edgerton, had made his distaste for Drake evident on several occasions. Drake said that although the man hadn't given him the cut direct, Edgerton had scoffed at any plans for reform Drake had proposed in Lords. Not that Edgerton invited Drake and Honoria to any events he hosted, so Juliana supposed it was a moot point.

On cue, Frampton arrived with a silver salver piled high with correspondence.

Drake sighed. "Thank you, Frampton." He grinned sheepishly. "Is it terrible to wish Honoria would recover more quickly so she can sift through this—mess?"

"Did I hear my name?" Honoria breezed into the morning room. Although the dark smudges under her eyes remained, she appeared more rested than usual.

Drake held up the pile of correspondence. "You arrived in the nick of time. That is, if you're up to making sense of this."

"Kitty slept an entire four hours last night. I feel like a new woman." She kissed Drake on the cheek before proceeding to the sideboard to serve herself.

As Honoria gracefully nibbled her breakfast, she efficiently worked her way through the pile of correspondence, glancing at each item and placing it in a particular pile.

"How does she know where to put things?" Juliana whispered so as not to break Honoria's concentration.

"Years of training that so far both she and Simon have failed to transfer to me." Drake's countenance fell at his own mention of his friend's recent scandal.

Their mother patted Drake's hand. "I have faith in you, Son."

"He doesn't give himself enough credit, Mother," Honoria said without looking up from the stack of letters. "For example, what about this one, Drake?" She held up the letter, neatly folded and addressed with a precise hand.

"Lady Montgomery?" Drake placed his cup down, his brow hitching. "That would go in the open at once pile."

"See?" Honoria grinned as she broke the seal on the missive. "Oh!" Her face brightened, making her appear even more rested than before. "The musicale! It says Lord and Lady Montgomery are officially taking over from her parents, Lord and Lady Saxton. Oh, we simply must attend. Juliana, you will adore it. It's an annual event, and it will be the perfect opportunity to make your appearance in society again. You will be among the best of friends."

Doubt gave a little groan of protest, and Juliana tried to make an excuse. "When is it? Isn't it too soon for you to be participating in anything?"

Both Juliana's mother and Honoria gave a little laugh.

"We're not as fragile as all that, my dear," Mama said. "We must trust Honoria's judgment."

"It's not for another three weeks. And to be honest, I'm aching to get out of the house."

Drake straightened to attention. "Why didn't you say anything? I would have taken you out in the carriage for some air."

"Because I knew you enjoyed coddling me. I'll confirm with Ashton before I send our reply, but all I have to do is sit, enjoy the music, and applaud."

"You are a wonder," Drake said, and leaned over to kiss her. "Before you arrived, I told Juliana I was failing in my duties to get her out into society. And here you have solved the problem for us."

Honoria laughed. "In fairness, Bea and Laurence have solved the problem. I merely opened the invitation."

Apparently, they were going to a musicale.

Whether Juliana wanted to or not.

RECLINED ON THE SOFA IN HIS FATHER'S DRAWING ROOM, VICTOR propped himself up on one arm and glared at his sister. "I am *not* sulking. And don't you have a husband to annoy? It's bad enough with Mother back in London. I don't need you to badger me as well."

"Did I hear someone mention me?" His mother swooped into the room, further darkening his already dreary day.

Priscilla stifled a giggle behind her hand.

Ha! She laughs now. How quickly Cilla had forgotten their mother's machinations to secure a duke as a husband for Cilla. Or perhaps not. Victor's mood was too bleak to parse it out.

Pinched between her thumb and forefinger, the piece of paper his mother waved in the air caused his stomach to tumble. *Another invitation.* Victor plopped back against the sofa with an audible, *"Ough."*

His mother narrowed her eyes, and his stomach tightened further.

Pushing Victor's legs off the sofa, his mother sat in the vacated spot. "This arrived moments ago. The Saxtons are turning over the reins for their annual musicale to Lord and Lady Montgomery. I suppose it's because of that expensive piano Lord Montgomery purchased from Lord Nash."

Victor reluctantly straightened, ignoring the irritation bubbling in his veins over that rake Nash's name. "And they're inviting *you?*" Victor should have been ashamed at the condescending tone of his voice, especially when his mother flinched. However, he was too absorbed in his own problems to worry about hurting his mother's feelings. And mentioning the blackguard who had stolen the woman Victor loved right from under his nose didn't help. He snatched the invitation from her fingers and turned the parchment over, noting his father's name on the address. "You're opening Father's correspondence now?"

"He was preoccupied with a letter from his estate manager in Lincolnshire. No doubt some crisis with the sheep."

Cilla groaned, and it was Victor's turn to stifle a chuckle. His sister had told him how she'd nearly gone mad exiled in the countryside as she was for several years after her disgrace with the Duke of Ashton.

His mother ignored her and continued to ramble on with her pitiful excuse for pilfering her husband's mail. ". . . and I just happened to notice Lady Montgomery's precise handwriting peeking out from beneath the pile of letters. She's such a strange creature with all her talk of science; I didn't want to bother your father with her nonsense."

"Hmm," Victor mumbled.

"Bea is not strange, Mama," Cilla said. "She's brilliant. And because she's my husband's sister, I expect you to speak of her more kindly."

"Hear, hear," Victor said, that time a bit more loudly.

His mother raised an eyebrow. "Such disrespect from my own children."

Victor hoped the crisis in Lincolnshire would necessitate his mother's return to the country. His father was much too busy arguing for reform in the House. "Respect must be earned, Mother."

"Which I have by giving birth to you both. Twenty hours of labor for you, Victor, and eighteen for Priscilla."

Cilla blanched, her eyes widening comically. Her hand drifted toward her abdomen. *Was she . . .?*

Victor shot a glance toward his mother, who remained oblivious to Cilla's reaction, and instead snatched the invitation back from Victor's grasp.

"They won't turn me away if I'm with your father—"

Cilla mumbled, "Bea might."

"And of course, you must attend, Victor. You've been moping around here far too long. It's time you settled down, chose a bride, and married. Your father won't live forever."

"Father is hale and hearty, Mother," Victor argued, too reluctant to agree with what he knew in his heart to be right. He did have to marry—someday. As his father's heir, it was Victor's *duty* to produce his own heir. And he would need a respectable bride for that.

"I understand Miss Whyte is still unattached," his mother said. "Why have you stopped calling on her, Victor? She is equal in rank to us, and her mother told me her father has increased her dowry. Lord Whyte is most eager to have her married by Michaelmas."

"It's no wonder, Mother," Victor said. "Lydia flirts with anything in trousers."

Cilla nodded. "That's true. I worried during the duke's house party last summer that she would get her hooks into the duke."

Victor shuddered at the thought of a match with Miss Whyte. She would probably beat her husband to death with her fan. "Which one? The real one pretending to be the man of business or the man of business pretending to be the duke?"

"Such a scandal," his mother said.

Victor held his tongue, but the thought formed, nonetheless. *You're one to talk.*

"The real one pretending to be the man of business. It didn't take me long to see that Honoria had feelings for Burwood—Mr. Merrick"—Cilla waved a hand—"goodness, it's still confusing. Her husband, the duke. The way Lydia threw herself at the poor man, it's a wonder Honoria didn't pull every blond hair out of Lydia's head."

Victor chuckled. "Her Grace is not you, Cilla. I don't think I've ever met any woman as unassuming as the Duchess of Burwood. But I am very happy she has found happiness with Burwood. He seems an excellent man, not to mention an accomplished horseman."

"Why do men put such store in horsemanship?" When Victor opened his mouth to explain, Cilla waved it away. "But truly, I am thrilled for her as well. Honoria has been a remarkably good friend to me."

"Still, you both would be wise to avoid that household altogether, even if he is a duke," their mother continued. "*The Muckraker* reported yet another scandal. This time with the pretender, Mr. Beckham. I was, however, shocked to learn of Lady Charlotte Talbot's part in the incident."

"Why do you read that rubbish?" Victor shook his head. "Most of it isn't true."

Cilla grimaced. "I'm afraid in this instance, some of it is true. When I called on Honoria to meet her daughter, she confirmed that Mr. Beckham and Lady Charlotte were married and left on their wedding trip to Wiltshire."

Their mother huffed an exasperated sigh. "One less eligible woman for you, Victor. Now, *she* would have been a feather in your cap. Sister of a marquess." She *tsked* and shook her head. "What a step down she has taken! A plain *mister*."

"A very wealthy mister, from what Honoria says," Cilla added.

Victor enjoyed watching his mother's eyes widen at that particular bit of news. For the most part, he was grateful his mother's fascination with gossip had disrupted her mission to find him a wife. His heart wasn't ready for that quite yet. For a multitude of reasons, he and Lady Charlotte would have made a dreadful match, the least of which would have been that Lord Nash would have been his brother by marriage.

Victor simply couldn't countenance that. It would be torture having the man flaunt his happiness with Miss Lovelace—err, Lady Nash Talbot—in Victor's face. Did they go by their honorifics in America, or were they known as Mr. and Mrs. Talbot?

No matter, he supposed. But the fact that a woman as kind and good as Adalyn Lovelace had thrown him over for a despicable, no-good rake like Nash Talbot still galled. Victor thought he and Adalyn had formed an attachment. He'd done his utmost to treat her with respect as a gentleman should, and what did it get him? A broken heart.

His unenthusiastic courting of Lydia, mostly to appease his mother, but also to put Adalyn out of his mind, had dwindled to sporadic calls, which was unfair to both of them.

As his mother droned on about the importance of securing the family's title and family line, Victor stood. "If you'll excuse me, Mother, I have an important meeting."

His mother's teacup clanked to her saucer. "With whom?"

With myself—in silence. "Since I've reached my majority, Mother, I no longer have to provide you with an account of my appointments."

He almost laughed at the indignant expression on his mother's face, but to carry his lie, he found the strength to suppress it.

Cilla placed her tea down, rose, and joined Victor. "I should leave as well. I promised Timothy I would be at the clinic this afternoon."

Their mother gaped. "But didn't you just arrive? I don't know why you feel the need to lower yourself and *work* at that clinic! You both will be the death of me."

Making their escape, Victor swept Cilla from the room. Once outside of his mother's hearing, he gave his sister a stern brotherly examination. "Cilla. Are you . . .?"

"Am I what? Avoiding Mama? Yes."

"No. Are you . . .?" He waved a hand in a circular motion around her abdomen.

His sister laughed. "Men. So fearful of one word. Am I expecting? Pregnant?"

Victor grimaced, and Cilla laughed even louder.

She caressed her stomach. "I believe so. Timothy instructed me to sleep in today and rest."

"But, Cilla, that's wonderful news."

Tears welled in his sister's eyes. "We have been hoping for so long."

"Sometimes the best things are worth waiting for."

And as Victor escorted Cilla from the house, he wondered if that was true for him as well. But where was the woman waiting for him who would erase Adalyn Lovelace from his mind?

CHAPTER 3

F lanked by Drake on one side and Honoria on the other, Juliana pulled in a fortifying breath as they waited in the entrance of Lord and Lady Montgomery's London townhouse. Juliana had instantly liked the outspoken redhead and her more reserved husband when she'd met them at Drake's house party the previous summer. And Honoria assured her Bea would not stand for anyone mistreating a friend.

"You're in for a real treat, Juliana," Honoria leaned down to whisper. "Susan told me she heard it from Lady Montgomery's maid that Camilla Somersby will be singing this evening. What a magnificent voice. It's a shame she and Dr. Somersby were unable to attend the house party last year. They might have saved me from the humiliation of singing that embarrassing song."

Drake's lips twitched upward. "I doubt Simon would have allowed anyone else to sing that particular piece. That, my dear, was intended for us alone."

Wedged between them, Juliana wanted to disappear into a puff of vapor at the lovesick expressions on her brother's and sister-in-law's faces. Although Juliana and her mother hadn't been present for Drake and Honoria's initial performance of *William and Mary*, they had witnessed the heartfelt encore when Drake revealed his true identity—and proposed to Honoria—in front of all assembled.

Ahead of them in the queue, Lydia Whyte stirred a hurricane wind with her fan as she fawned over a gentleman Juliana didn't recognize. "Who is that man?" She inclined her head toward the handsome man with brown hair.

Drake emitted what sounded like a low growl. "Stay away from him, Juliana. That is Lord Felix Davies. Before Simon and Charlotte left on their wedding trip to Wiltshire, he shared some unsavory information about Davies."

Honoria blushed. "It pains me to think I recommended him as a prospective suitor for Priscilla. Thank goodness she saw through him."

"And thank goodness you saw Dr. Marbry's affection for Priscilla and turned down his proposal," Drake said.

Mention of Priscilla Marbry led Juliana's mind to Victor Pratt, Priscilla's very attractive brother. Their last encounter had been bittersweet, their lovely dance marred by the unfortunate accident with her gown.

Would he be in attendance? Effervescence bubbled in Juliana's veins as she scanned the room for Mr. Pratt, trying her best to appear nonchalant even as her pulse raced in anticipation. The long months spent in seclusion at Hartridge House had done nothing to ease the twinge in her heart each time Victor Pratt popped into her thoughts—which admittedly occurred more often than it should have.

It wasn't so much his handsome face, or even his kindness, but something deeper, more profound, that she couldn't name. A sadness in his eyes tugged at her heart, and she wanted to give him comfort from whatever distressed him.

When they finally arrived to greet their hosts, a wide smile broke across Lady Montgomery's face. "Miss Merrick, you came! I'm so glad." She leaned in, grasping Juliana's hand and pulled her close to whisper, "Don't let those gossips win. They are mean-spirited and in dire need of something productive to fill their time instead of stirring up idle and hurtful rumors."

"Thank you, Lady Montgomery. But I'm afraid in my case the scandal sheet reported the truth."

"Call me Bea. Everyone I care about does. And it isn't so much as what was reported, but how it is twisted into something attacking the innocent."

"How true," Honoria said as she greeted Lord Montgomery. "In fact"—she turned to greet Bea—"Charlotte wrote to me suggesting you join our little *club.*" Honoria lowered her voice. "It's to root out the culprit responsible, but we operate under the guise of a charitable foundation. Charlotte is one of our most logical thinkers, but with her away on her wedding trip—well."

Bea's eyes lit up. "That sounds most intriguing. Let me know when you hold the next meeting, and I shall be there."

"If anyone can solve a puzzle, it's Bea," Lord Montgomery said. "My wife is the cleverest person I know."

Juliana had attended several of the meetings since Honoria and Drake's marriage—at least until she exiled herself to Drake's country estate. "Lady Montgomery, that is, Bea, must be remarkable if Lady Charlotte recommended her." It wasn't that Juliana didn't like Lady Charlotte, but she was a difficult person to understand, and other than Honoria and Lady Miranda, Charlotte seemed to have few friends. She barely tolerated Anne Weatherby.

And with *The Muckraker's* attention on Juliana in recent months, she had an even more personal stake in unmasking the scoundrel. They could use all the help they could get.

They took their seats in the second row and reviewed the program a footman had handed them. Murmurs of voices and the pleasant, invigorating mix of sandalwood, cardamom, and cloves drifted from Juliana's right.

"Switch places with me, Victor," a woman's voice said. "I don't want to sit behind Ashton. He's so tall."

Juliana's gaze turned to the right as Victor Pratt, Priscilla Marbry, and Dr. Marbry gathered at the end of the row of chairs.

The Duke of Ashton was indeed in the row ahead of them, and he turned around and greeted them. "Mrs. Marbry, Pratt, Marbry."

He began to rise. "If you prefer, Margaret and I can move to the aisle—"

"No. No," Mr. Pratt waved the duke to remain seated. "My sister is being ridiculous, per usual. It's a musicale, not a play or the opera, Cilla." And yet he entered the row before his sister and took the seat next to Juliana. "Miss Merrick." He nodded in greeting. "I trust you are not so silly as to complain about the height of someone in front of you." His warm smile lit her from the inside out like sunshine breaking through a cloud after a storm.

"I'm simply pleased to be here at all, Mr. Pratt." If she had uttered them earlier, her words would have been a prevarication, but at that moment, there was truth to them.

"As I suspected, you are a most sensible lady."

Both Juliana's heart and her cheeks heated at the compliment. "In your sister's defense, her small stature makes it difficult to see what is happening, and perhaps she enjoys watching the expressions of those performing."

"Thank you, Miss Merrick," Mrs. Marbry said. "I knew I liked you."

"Shh, Priscilla. It's starting," Dr. Marbry said.

Voices quieted, and everyone's attention turned toward the front of the large room where Lady Montgomery—Bea—took her seat by the beautiful grand piano. Lord Montgomery stood next to her and said, "Welcome, everyone, to the first official Annual Montgomery Musicale. Please, sit back, relax, and be entertained. My wife shall start us off with one of her favorite pieces."

Juliana knew little about music other than the silly songs she used to sing as a child, but the beauty and complexity of the music Bea coaxed out of the instrument enraptured her. Curious as to her brother's reaction, she flicked her gaze toward him, only to catch his eyelids drooping. Before Juliana could elbow him in the ribs, Honoria touched him on the sleeve and sent him a censorious glance.

Juliana stifled her chuckle at his mumbled, "What?" Poor Drake needed more sleep. Casting her gaze to her other side, she expected to find Mr. Pratt similarly inattentive. How wrong she was.

As if enthralled, he sat perfectly still, his hands resting on his thighs, his eyes glimmering with emotion. When the final notes ceased their reverberations, the very air around them seemed to still in anticipation. Applause, at first polite and reserved, grew louder, coming primarily from Mr. Pratt. "Brava!" he exclaimed.

If Juliana were honest with herself—which, for the most part, she tried to be—she had been infatuated with Mr. Pratt from the moment she met him at Drake's house party. Handsome and charming, with his long blond hair and sparkling blue eyes, something mysterious had drawn her to him. And although his gallantry in asking her to dance at her come-out ball had been marred by the unfortunate spill of ratafia on her white gown, he had occupied her dreams—both sleeping and awake—for the good part of the last several months.

But at that moment, she saw him with fresh eyes. Not simply an attractive picture with no depth or substance, Mr. Pratt—Victor— was a sensitive man, moved deeply by the beauty around him. And the reality of her discovery slammed into her hard. He was the kind of man she could give her whole heart to.

If only she weren't a disgraced commoner.

VICTOR SWIPED DISCREETLY AT HIS FACE, HOPING NO ONE NOTICED the tears forming in his eyes. Thank goodness Father had convinced Mother to stay at home, regretfully missing the event himself. Both had often criticized Victor for wearing his emotions like a badge of honor.

But he simply couldn't hold it in. He'd forgotten how well Lady Montgomery played. Or perhaps his maudlin mood aligned with the poignant piece. Art in all its forms was his life's blood, that which fed his spirit and nourished his mind.

He'd been reluctant to attend the musicale, remembering he'd first met Adalyn at one of the Saxtons' events. Fool that he was, Victor believed they had a connection when he offered to escort her to the National Gallery. Attentive and charming, Adalyn appeared as enamored with him as he was with her. Things were progressing swimmingly, until Lord Nash had shown up with Lady Honoria and joined them. Was that when Nash began his scheme to steal Adalyn away?

Or had it been even sooner? When Victor thought about it, Nash had also been at that musicale. Had his instincts about Adalyn's interest been that faulty? And if so, how could he trust them?

Victor supposed trying to understand how, when, and why things had gone awry was futile, and although he dreaded attending that evening, hearing Lady Montgomery play had been a balm to his dour mood. Apparently, his sister had her finger on his pulse better than he did. Except . . .

Why had Cilla chosen to sit in the row with Miss Merrick? And to insist they switch places so Victor was right next to the lady? He suspected Cilla was up to her matchmaking machinations. Ever since she had secured a love match with the good doctor, she'd been hellbent on seeing everyone she cared about equally leg-shackled.

He had a sinking suspicion that she'd even played a part in that scoundrel Lord Nash stealing Miss Lovelace from under Victor's nose. It would serve Cilla right if Victor let her think she succeeded in her scheme. What harm would it do to play along and flirt with Miss Merrick?

Confident his face was free of any telltale tearstains, he turned toward her. He half expected a delicately raised blond brow at the emotion on his face he was unable to contain.

Instead, sincerity and understanding filled her cornflower-blue eyes, and she placed a hand over her heart. "I don't believe I've ever heard anything so moving. Honoria told me how well Bea played, but I simply wasn't prepared for . . . for—that." She waved a hand toward the piano.

Victor nodded, desperately trying to clear his emotionally clogged throat. "Do you play, Miss Merrick?"

A pretty blush covered her cheeks—a delicate mix of pink and peach against her cream skin. How he'd like to capture that on canvas. "Not well. I'm trying to learn, but I fear I'm hopeless."

Victor understood the frustration of a novice artist. How many pieces of paper had he crumpled in anger when he couldn't get the lines of a sketch just so, or an expensive canvas tossed aside when his paints blobbed together rather than blended as he desired? "Practice, Miss Merrick, is an unforgiving mistress, but in the end, the reward is worth it. If your heart is there, the art will follow."

The audience settled down, and when Cilla rose from her seat, Victor peeked down at the program and noted Cilla was next to perform. "Whose idea was this?" he whispered to Timothy.

His brother-in-law grimaced. "Bea's. I suspect it's a latent attempt to punish Priscilla for her scheme involving Ashton. Bea has yet to completely forgive her, even though Priscilla is family now. Hopefully, things will change once . . ."

Timothy didn't have to finish his statement. Victor remembered his conversation with Cilla three weeks prior. Children had a way of bringing people together and mending old wounds.

Or setting a final *closed* stamp on one's heart. Cilla had told him that Adalyn and that scoundrel, Nash, had welcomed a son into their family. The fleeting hope that she might come to her senses about her rake of a husband, and return to England, confessing to Victor her error in rejecting him, flapped its wings and flew out the proverbial window.

People—especially women—rarely ended marriages once children were involved. Even Victor's mother had returned from her exile in Lincolnshire, and his father was doing his damnedest to repair their marriage.

No. Victor had to face the facts. If he was going to fulfill his duty as heir to the viscountcy and take a bride, he would have to look elsewhere.

According to his mother, Lydia Whyte was the perfect candidate.

But Victor found Lydia like so many other girls of the *ton* self-centered, shallow, and—boring.

He stole a peek at Miss Merrick. And as he'd done the last time he'd seen her, he unwittingly compared her to Adalyn.

Would he never get the woman out of his mind? She haunted

his dreams and now, his waking hours in the form of Miss Merrick. He tried to concentrate on the piece Cilla performed on the flute.

The polite applause that followed Cilla's performance remained so, not reaching the level of appreciation that Lady Montgomery's had elicited. Victor leaned over to Miss Merrick and whispered. "I'm sure my sister is relieved that is over."

Her gloved hand flitted to her mouth, stifling her laugh, but Victor caught the merriment sparkling in her eyes.

"I dare say she did better than I would have."

"You're learning the flute as well?" Victor's surprise mixed with admiration at her generosity.

She shook her head, one golden strand of hair coming loose and draping down her neck. "I tried, but my attempts were worse than those at the piano. I fear the music teacher is reaching his wits' end. Do you play an instrument, Mr. Pratt?"

"Cello and piano. But only passably well. My mother complained of headaches." He gave her a sheepish grin.

Light and natural, Miss Merrick's laugh lifted Victor's spirits. He smiled at Cilla when she returned to her seat. He would thank her later for insisting he attend the event.

A hush descended on the crowd when Dr. Somersby and his wife ascended the dais next to the piano. Although Victor had yet to hear the doctor play, Timothy insisted the man coaxed his very soul from the violin. And Camilla Somersby's voice was legendary. Had she not been the daughter of a baron, she could have performed on the best operatic stages of Europe.

But as Victor was well aware, people born of the aristocracy did *not* pursue occupations in the arts, especially men in line to inherit. His own aspirations as a painter had not been met with approval or encouragement from his parents.

Victor inclined his head toward the dais. "I understand we are in for a treat, Miss Merrick."

Victor found Dr. Somersby to be an unassuming man, later learning of his Romani heritage. He seemed uneasy at first in front of the crowd but soon became absorbed in his music. And although the accompaniment to his wife's singing was lovely, he allowed her to be the center of attention. When they finished, Camilla encouraged the crowd to demand more from her husband.

The Duke and Duchess of Ashton joined in Camilla's entreaty, the duchess saying, "Play the song you wrote for Camilla!"

A slight flush covered Oliver's swarthy complexion, but he nodded.

And from the first stroke of his bow on the strings, the audience was enthralled.

Victor had never heard anything like it in his life. Gooseflesh rose on his arms and neck. Beautiful and bittersweet, the music held a touch of hope, countering the minor key in the perfect combination.

When the last note faded, hanging in the air like a lover's kiss, no one moved, no one spoke. All eyes were glued to the man with the violin in rapt appreciation. A soft sniffle sounded to Victor's left, and he turned toward Miss Merrick, her eyes shimmering with unshed tears.

Through those tears, she smiled at him, and to his surprise, she reached up and brushed his own tears away.

CHAPTER 4

Had she lost her mind? Juliana pulled her hand back as if Victor's face had scorched her fingers. And although Victor's tears were hot, it was the heat of his gaze that startled her back to reality and the impropriety of her action.

A deep cough sounded beside her, and she spun around.

Drake lifted a castigatory brow, his gaze then flitting to Victor.

Juliana's face burned. Desperately, she searched for something clever to say to save herself from the awkward situation. "It's warm in here."

Ugh. Heat flared anew in her cheeks.

"Perhaps some refreshment, Miss Merrick?" Victor asked, drawing her attention back to him. He glanced down at his program. "Miss Whyte is to play her flute next." Mischief shone in his blue eyes. "If we excuse ourselves now, no one will be the wiser."

"I'll accompany you," Drake said, employing his ducal growl. Really, could her brother be more obvious? He turned toward Honoria. "May I bring you something, darling?"

Honoria shook her head. "I'll join you. A stretch will do me good."

Disappointment mingled with relief that although she wouldn't have a few moments alone with Victor, at least Honoria would temper Drake's protective interference.

Victor made his excuse to his sister, who waved him away as if she couldn't get rid of him fast enough.

Juliana chuckled to herself. Regardless of social class, there appeared to be a universality among siblings. "Is your sister older or younger than you, Mr. Pratt?" Juliana asked as they exited the row and followed Drake and Honoria toward the refreshment table.

"Younger." A grin broke across his handsome face. "And she would be appalled to know you thought she might be older than I. Should I tell her?" He winked.

Would the infernal heat never leave her face? "Oh, please don't. It's only that I noticed she appears to . . . um . . . tell you what to do."

He laughed, the sound deep and sensual, vibrating across her skin and raising gooseflesh. "You mean she's bossy."

Juliana wanted to crawl into the hole she had dug for herself.

Victor leaned down, his breath brushing against her face. "Not to worry, Miss Merrick. Cilla was born bossy."

"Cilla. What a lovely nickname. Drake calls me Jules." She scrunched up her nose.

At the sound of his name, Drake peered over her shoulder. "Since you acted more like a boy growing up, it seemed fitting." His gaze moved toward Victor—thankfully less confrontational than before. "My sister is more comfortable astride a horse than in ballrooms."

Victor's blond brows arched. "Astride? Not sidesaddle?"

Juliana wanted to kick Drake in his aristocratic shins. However, rather than scandalized, Victor seemed intrigued.

"When I was a groom on Stratford's estate," Drake explained, "Juliana helped me exercise the horses. Mother tried to encourage her to ride sidesaddle, but . . ." He shrugged his shoulders. "At the time she was so young, it hardly seemed important to press the issue. But she is an excellent horsewoman, and we've had a special riding habit made for her that ensures her propriety."

Honoria gave a delicate cough. "Mr. Pratt is also an excellent horseman, Juliana."

Juliana slid a glance toward Victor, who brushed off the compliment. "Until I fell off my horse during the fox hunt. It is your husband, Your Grace, who can outride us all."

When Drake squared his shoulders, Juliana fought a smile. It would appear Mr. Pratt knew how to win her brother over.

Honoria squeezed Drake's arm. "Perhaps we could all go riding along Rotten Row. Ashton said I may resume my normal activities now. What do you say, Mr. Pratt? Will you join us?"

Victor blinked, then his gaze flicked toward Juliana. "Well, I suppose."

Juliana wanted to crawl under the refreshment table where they had just arrived. The man no doubt felt cornered into accepting.

"Lemonade or ratafia, Miss Merrick?" Victor asked.

Juliana scanned the room, pleased to find Lydia taking a seat on the dais in preparation for her performance. Still, perhaps it was wise to be safe. "Lemonade."

Victor's blue eyes danced. "Excellent choice." He held up two fingers to the footman serving the beverages.

Receiving the cup from Victor, Juliana lowered her voice. "Do not feel obligated to accept the invitation to ride, Mr. Pratt. If you choose to beg off, I would understand."

"Nonsense, Miss Merrick. Why would I turn down an opportunity to go riding with a duke and duchess?"

Juliana's stomach plummeted to her toes. Of course he accepted because of Drake and Honoria.

"Not to mention," Victor continued, "the duke's lovely sister riding astride her mount."

Oh! Firefly wings lifted her stomach back to its rightful position.

Sour notes screeched through the air as Lydia tuned her flute, and Drake's eyes grew comically wide.

"Ah," her brother said with a nod of his head. "I understand the need to distance ourselves at the refreshment table. Thank you, Pratt."

Victor grinned, sending Juliana's heart fluttering. "My pleasure. Anything to lessen the effects of Miss Whyte massacring Mozart."

Fortunately, once Lydia began to actually play, the notes improved.

Juliana sipped her lemonade. "You've heard Miss Whyte play before?"

"Yes, which is why I'm wondering who invited her to perform. The Montgomerys have better taste."

"Your mother insisted," Bea said, stepping from behind Victor where her short stature had hidden her from view. "Well, I should say your mother and then my mother."

"Then I apologize for my family, Lady Montgomery."

Bea waved it away. "It might work to our advantage. Lizzie, our oldest, is learning to play the violin. Dr. Somersby is teaching her and says she has promise. My hope is she won't be the least talented on the program."

"Will she be playing this evening?" Juliana asked.

"Heavens, no. She's only four. But I expect Pockets, Dr. and Camilla Somersby's adopted son, might be joining our event in a few years. Whenever he's home from Eton, he joins Lizzie in her lessons. He's quite good."

"Pockets?" Juliana asked, intrigued by the odd name.

"Along with Manny, he was one of the children Ashton rescued from that horrible man, Coodibilis. How someone could use children for their own gain is unfathomable." Honoria shook her head. "His name fit him—despicable. And of course, we discovered Miss Fingers—that is Mena—later. All orphans, the children survived on the streets by pick-pocketing."

Ah. The names made sense. Juliana exchanged a look with Drake. "I never realized there was so much excitement among society folk."

Beside her, Victor chortled. "There isn't usually. Except with this lot." He waved a hand toward where Priscilla and Dr. Marbry chatted with the Duke and Duchess of Ashton.

"Speaking of excitement, how are Lady Charlotte and Mr.

Beckham getting along?" Bea asked. "Laurence and I saw them right after that reprehensible report in *The Muckraker.*"

"Did I hear something about *The Muckraker?*" Felix Davies said, appearing as if from thin air. The man was attractive, older than Victor, perhaps in his mid-thirties, if Juliana had to guess. His gaze raked over her, and his sharp, light-brown eyes reminded her of a cat ready to pounce. "Miss Merrick. You look lovely this evening. Recovered from that unfortunate incident during your come-out?"

The reminder stung, but Juliana remained calm. Let him think her obtuse.

Both Drake and Victor took a step closer, almost flanking her on either side. Victor glared at Lord Felix. "Bad form to mention that, Davies."

Although she expected Drake to rush to her defense, elation tingled through her at Victor's response.

Bea squinted through her spectacles. "I don't recall inviting you, Lord Felix."

Juliana suppressed a smile behind her lemonade. If Bea hadn't already won Juliana over with her kindness, her blunt response to Lord Felix's rude remark certainly did.

Lord Felix threw a hand over his heart as if the barb physically wounded him. "Middlebury warned me of your sharp tongue, Lady Montgomery. Luckily, I have thick skin." He waved a dismissive hand. "Miss Whyte invited me to join her and her family to hear her perform."

Victor gave a soft snort. "And yet, you're here at the refreshment table instead of in your seat, enraptured by her melodic rendition of . . ." Victor put a hand to his ear, his brow furrowing. "Whatever that is."

Honoria shifted by Drake's side, clearly uncomfortable witnessing the confrontation. She hated when people argued.

Juliana took her sister-in-law's arm. "Do you need to sit, Honoria?"

Drake snapped to attention, his gaze darting from Lord Felix and Victor to Honoria. "Excuse us, Lady Montgomery."

Victor removed Juliana's empty lemonade glass from her grasp, placed it on the refreshment table, then motioned for them all to precede him back to their seats.

Lord Felix called from behind. "Off so soon? Before I asked His Grace if I may call upon you, Miss Merrick?"

"Over my dead body," Drake muttered.

It would appear that Juliana's desire to enjoy an uneventful night out in society was failing miserably.

Discussion of the orphan children had once again sent Victor's thoughts reeling back to Adalyn. She and—grr—Nash had taken Fingers—Miss Mena—under their wing and to America.

And what was Davies doing escorting Lydia? Victor swallowed a hard lump forming in his throat. Victor wasn't jealous, but Lydia had all but made it clear she'd set her cap for *him*. Or had she? Lydia's association with Davies made Victor question his ability to decipher a woman's interest even more. Of course, he hadn't been a very attentive suitor, their mothers deciding the match had promise and pushing the two together more than from a mutual agreement of the couple themselves—at least on Victor's part.

But Victor's half-hearted courting kept his mother at bay and left him to wallow in his maudlin thoughts about Adalyn.

Victor reseated himself, grateful Lydia had finished torturing everyone's ears. Perhaps she had realized Victor had little interest in pursuing an attachment and decided to invest her time elsewhere.

But Felix Davies? Although Lydia was more often a ninny, more interested in the latest fashion or gossip than in anything meaningful—like art and creativity—to throw Victor over for Felix Davies was an insult equal to the cut direct.

No, Victor wasn't jealous. He was appalled. What was Lydia thinking? Davies was a known rake and a scoundrel. Did all women prefer a scoundrel over a gentleman? Davies was almost as bad as that blackguard Nash.

Damn. Why must he think of *that* man? Thoughts of him inevitably led to Adalyn.

However, if Lydia had turned her marriage-minded machinations elsewhere, Victor would be left without a defense against his mother's nagging.

Victor peered over at Miss Merrick, and a delightful idea popped into his head. Perhaps Cilla's machinations had merit. It might be enjoyable to court the lovely blonde, an added benefit being his mother's outrage over Miss Merrick's common birth. That's if he could stop thinking about Adalyn each time he looked at Miss Merrick. Oily shame squirmed in his stomach that pretending she actually *was* Adalyn would make his efforts more believable. But at what cost?

If he were honest with himself, which he tried to be, even if he didn't always succeed, Victor admitted ladies found him attractive. Most of his flirtations were harmless, and he was careful never to compromise gently bred ladies.

But something about Miss Merrick told him she was not used to the superficial flirtations common among the *ton.* If he imagined she was Adalyn, she might actually believe his pursuit of her was in earnest, and worse—fall in love with him.

Returning his attention back to the front of the room where Lady Miranda played the piano, he curled his hands into fists on his thighs. Could he be such a cad?

He had no intention of breaking her heart as his own had been shattered.

No. He would have to separate Adalyn from Miss Merrick. *Juliana.* He repeated the lovely name mentally to the beat of the four-four rhythm of the music. He would tread carefully with his flirtation, and no one would get hurt.

When the musicale ended, Victor made his goodbyes to the duke, duchess, and Miss Merrick. "I'll look forward to the invitation to go riding, Your Graces. Miss Merrick." His words were sincere, as he looked forward not only to the image of Miss Merrick riding astride but getting to know her better.

Victor bowed and followed Cilla and Timothy out to retrieve their hats and gloves.

As he made his way toward the door, Lydia called from behind. "Mr. Pratt! Mr. Pratt!"

Blast. He'd almost made a clean escape. She had that damnable fan out again, swishing it around like a weapon.

"We barely had time to chat this evening. What did you think of my performance?" She batted her eyes at him, seemingly oblivious that Davies arrived at her side.

"Very nice, Miss Whyte."

Davies snorted. "You were at the refreshment table practically the entire time."

Victor glared. "I could hear quite adequately from there. And you're one to speak. Weren't you there as well?"

Lydia darted a glance toward Davies, then Victor, her mouth pulling into a pout. She slid her hand through Davies's arm and met Victor's gaze as if in challenge. "Lord Felix needs to stretch his legs from an injury. But I'm most disappointed in you, Mr. Pratt."

"Why? You seem to have found a suitable replacement with Davies."

Lydia scrunched her face as if she might cry at any moment, but her eyes appeared tear-free. "Must you be so mean, Victor? Lord Felix and I are friends. You told me you weren't going to attend this evening, and he graciously offered to stand in your stead."

"Perhaps he has other intentions, Lydia," Davies said with a sneer. "I understand Burwood has offered a substantial dowry for his sister." Davies examined his well-manicured nails. "No doubt due not only to Miss Merrick's common birth, but also the debacle of her come-out. A man would need to be paid to court such a walking disaster. Are you in need of funds, Pratt? Is that why you spent so much time this evening toadying up to Burwood and his sister?"

Victor shoved his hat on his head. "I will not dignify that with an answer. Now, if you will excuse me, my sister and her husband are waiting. Good night."

Victor stormed out the door and climbed into the carriage with Cilla and Timothy, settling back against the comfort of the squabs.

"What kept you?" Cilla asked, her tone more annoyed than concerned.

Timothy touched Cilla's arm. "Something's wrong. What happened, Victor?"

"Lydia and Felix Davies happened. Cornered me right when I was leaving. Davies accused me of going after Miss Merrick for her dowry."

"I never liked that fellow," Timothy said.

Cilla snorted. "Yet, both you and Honoria suggested him as one of my suitors."

Timothy drew a hand down his face. "You'll never forgive me for that, will you?"

"No. I've forgiven Honoria because she was simply trying to help. You, on the other hand . . ."

"Will you two stop?!" Victor slammed his hat down on the cushion next to him.

Cilla jumped in her seat.

"This isn't about you and rehashing your bumpy road to realizing you were perfect for each other. It's about me!" Victor's eyes adjusted to the dim light of the carriage compartment, the surprised expression on his sister's face giving him a perverse pleasure.

Pleasure which dissipated when she rolled her eyes. "Oh, forgive me for forgetting the world revolves around you, Victor."

"Now *you* two stop," Timothy said, his tone much calmer and holding a touch of amusement. "In this case, Victor is right."

Cilla elbowed her husband in the ribs. "You're supposed to side with me."

When Timothy didn't respond, Cilla sank down in her seat and pouted.

Even though the three of them were alone in the carriage, Victor lowered his voice and leaned toward Timothy. "Is her *condition* making her moody?"

"I am not moody," Cilla grumbled, crossing her arms over her chest.

"You are perfect, my dear," Timothy said. When Cilla nodded and turned toward the window, Timothy mouthed, *"Yes."*

Thank goodness another level-headed man was in the carriage.

"Is there a basis for Davies's accusation? Your father's estate isn't in trouble, is it?"

Victor wasn't affronted by Timothy's question, it came from Timothy's own experience. According to Cilla, Timothy began courting Honoria because of his family's financial troubles and Honoria's large dowry.

"No." Victor's one word response satisfied Timothy.

Timothy's brow furrowed. "But you have been escorting Miss Whyte about town, and I presumed you had an attachment. Are you now pursuing Miss Merrick?"

"Lydia is a troublemaking gossip," Cilla muttered, still gazing out the carriage window.

Although Victor had some doubts about the young doctor when he'd married Cilla, Victor had to admit Timothy was an intelligent man. He grasped Cilla's arm and gently turned her toward him. "Priscilla, love. Is that why you insisted on the seating arrangements for the musicale? Are you matchmaking?"

"I like Miss Merrick. She has more sense than that ninnyhammer Lydia. And she doesn't deserve the horrible things *The Muckraker* is saying about her. Victor is respectable and passably handsome. So I thought . . ."

Cilla's assertion only confirmed what Victor already suspected.

"Have you learned nothing from your machinations, Priscilla?" Timothy asked, his face clouding with disappointment. "Harry has only recently put that horrible incident with you behind him. You can't play games with people's lives."

"It worked with Nash and Adalyn."

Damn. Why did she have to bring them up again?

"I'm sorry, Victor," Cilla said. "But you and Adalyn weren't right for each other."

"In your opinion." Yet, could Cilla be right? Part of him

wondered if he hadn't romanticized his memory of Adalyn. Perhaps he needed to accept what never could be and move on with his life. Regardless, he needed to end the conversation. "I like Miss Merrick, and Felix Davies can have Lydia. They deserve each other. But it's my life, Cilla, so stay out of it."

Victor turned toward the window, further demonstrating he was finished listening to her arguments.

But if Adalyn hadn't been right for him, what woman was?

CHAPTER 5

Juliana had hardly slept a wink after the musicale. Each time she closed her eyes, Victor's voice echoed in her mind—warm, amused, and maddeningly polite. The attention he'd paid her occupied her thoughts as she turned over each and every possibility as to the reason.

Was his civility because he was forced to sit next to her during the performances? Juliana didn't delude herself, and she had come to know Priscilla Marbry well enough to recognize her intentions.

And yet, Victor had been so kind and attentive at the refreshment table. She countered that with the fact that he had been raised as a gentleman and would do nothing less. But so had Lord Felix Davies, who had been nothing short of rude.

In a moment of weakness, a hopeful thought crept in. Perhaps he'd been genuinely interested. She brushed it off, muttering to herself, "Don't be a cotton-headed ninnyhammer."

A man as wonderful as Victor Pratt would not seriously consider a common-born girl like Juliana Merrick, even if she was half-sister to a duke. People in the aristocracy had standards. Drake and Honoria were testament to that—at least until Drake's true heritage had become known.

Things were so complicated among society.

In the countryside of Somerset where Juliana had grown up, life —courtship—was so much simpler. If a young man fancied a young woman, he simply brought her flowers and took her out walking for several Sundays to determine if they would suit. And if a woman indicated her interest, but the man did not return it, he would tell her in no uncertain terms he considered her only a friend.

Of course, there were exceptions. Juliana's friend Maisie hadn't waited when she'd set her cap for a boy named Jonas. She'd marched up to Jonas as he worked in the field and informed him they were getting married. Four weeks later, when Juliana and her parents attended the ceremony, Jonas stood at the altar, his eyes as wide as a frightened horse as he repeated his vows. Three years later, when Drake had returned to England and Juliana said her goodbyes to her friend to move to Dorset, Maisie had been swollen with her second child.

And Jonas still appeared in shock, but content.

But among the *ton* there were so many rules. Honoria made a valiant effort instructing Juliana, but Juliana longed for the simpler life where people said what they meant without the ridiculous games.

Wouldn't it be lovely if she could confess her feelings to Victor Pratt? Not just that she found him attractive. Of course, he was handsome. But Victor Pratt was so much more than that to her. She would tell him she found him intelligent, intriguing, and interesting. That she longed to see his paintings—and not just to see his finished works, but to watch him paint. To watch his brow furrow in concentration, his eyes sparkle with delight as he brought something to life on a blank canvas.

She imagined she'd caught a glimpse of what that would look like as she studied his face during Dr. Somersby's performance at the musicale. There was an aching pain in his eyes that she found heartbreakingly beautiful, and she wanted to know what, besides the music, had put it there. What emotions lay beneath the surface of his lovely exterior?

Juliana desired nothing more than to solve the mystery that was Mr. Victor Pratt.

"Juliana? My dear, are you quite all right?" Honoria's voice shook her from her musings.

A half-eaten slice of toast dangled from Juliana's fingers, and she placed it on the plate in front of her. "I'm sorry. I was wool-gathering about last night's musicale."

An all-knowing smile crossed Honoria's lips. "No doubt the music captivated you. Speaking of the musicale, why don't we send an invitation to Mr. Pratt to join us for a ride along Rotten Row this coming Sunday afternoon, weather permitting? I realized how much I needed to be out of the house and away from my thoughts about poor Margery and Colin. And riding always lifts my spirits." She gazed lovingly at Drake.

Guilt squeezed Juliana's heart. How could she indulge in girlish daydreams about Victor when Honoria was still coping with the death of her sister-in-law. "Have you heard from your brother?"

Honoria nodded. "Naturally, he sent his congratulations about Kitty, but I worry for him and the girls. He's like an unanchored ship without Margery. I thought perhaps later this summer we might invite Colin and the girls to spend time with us at Hartridge House. A change of scenery might do him good."

Drake squeezed Honoria's hand. "Whatever you wish, my darling. I can't imagine Colin's grief. I would be utterly bereft without you."

Up to that point, Mama had been silent, her gaze drifting between them. "If he wishes to speak of it, I'm a good listener. And having experienced such loss myself, I might be able to provide a thread of hope."

Of course. Her mother had buried two husbands—both Drake's father and Juliana's own, something neither Juliana nor Drake knew until Drake received word of his inheritance while serving in India.

Juliana felt the love between her parents, but learning about Drake's father shed new light on her memories, altering them—if only a little. The times when Papa would lavish Mama with affection, and a faraway look would come over her took on new meaning, even if Mama didn't say as much.

Once, right before Drake had left for the military, Papa had returned from the big house after speaking with Lord Stratford, Honoria's father. Papa had been upset, and it was the only time Juliana remembered him and Mama exchanging heated words. It was also the only time Juliana had seen her father drunk. Drake had stormed off to go riding, upset about something he refused to talk about. Mama had retreated upstairs to her bedchamber, her sobs drifting downstairs to the parlor in their little cottage where Papa slumped in a chair, a glass of whisky dangling from his fingers.

Juliana had been twelve—old enough to know something of great importance had happened.

"What's wrong, Papa?"

He twirled the glass in his hand. "Love," he said, the word slurred.

Love was wrong?

"I don't understand."

He smiled a loopy smile at her, his eyes bleary and unfocused. "Love is a hard master, Juliana. It takes no prisoners, and there are few survivors."

"You're not making sense, Papa."

He laughed, the sound as bitter as the castor oil Mama gave her when her stomach hurt. "Because love doesn't make sense, girl. I know your mother will never love me as I love her. And yet"—he took another drink of the remaining liquid—"I don't care. I still love her. Will love her. Even when both people love each other the same, there is always something in the damn way."

Even with her knowledge of what happened between Drake and Honoria, and Mama's first marriage to Drake's father, Juliana struggled to make sense of what her father had said.

But with her growing feelings toward Mr. Pratt, a sort of vague sense took form. Because Papa was right—something was always in the way.

THE FOLLOWING SUNDAY, VICTOR MOUNTED HIS FAVORITE HORSE and rode to Pendrake Manor to join the duke, duchess, and Miss Merrick for their outing. Gray clouds littered the sky, but enough blue peeked through to give hope the day would still be salvageable. His motives were two-fold. One, of course, to become better acquainted with Miss Merrick. Victor wasn't so dense to not understand the duchess's invitation was an effort to further push Victor and Miss Merrick together, something he was not averse to in the least.

His other motive was—perhaps—a little more self-serving. Very well, a *lot* more self-serving. He'd hoped Miss Merrick would make good on her word to speak to her brother about commissioning Victor to paint the family portraits. But of course, with the further debacle at her come-out ball, she no doubt had put it far from her mind.

However, *if* the conversation veered anywhere near the subject of art, Victor would simply give it a gentle nudge. Not manipulate— he winced at the word—but merely suggest, with all due humility, that his brushes were at their disposal.

Upon his arrival, the butler, Frampton, had Victor wait in the entryway rather than a parlor. "The horses are being brought around now, sir. Their Graces and Miss Merrick are most eager to proceed."

Victor scanned the area, noticing the portraits lining the walls. Quality artistry worthy of aristocrats captured in each and every work of art. The audacity of Victor to presume he could compete with such skill and win the coveted position of portrait artist to a duke.

The thought flew from his head as Miss Merrick descended the long, curved staircase to greet him. Her riding habit of a fine royal blue velvet clung to her curves, and Victor remembered it had been made to allow her to ride astride.

Sure enough, as she took a step, the fabric of the skirt parted, allowing a bit of light to peek through. Although voluminous, the skirt had been divided into two parts, much like extremely loose trousers. How clever! She wore a little matching bonnet on her head, tilted at a jaunty angle, reminding Victor of the one the duchess had worn during the fox hunt.

But unlike the duchess, Miss Merrick's golden hair was pulled back and tied with a blue velvet ribbon, the long locks trailing down her back.

She greeted him with a warm smile. "Drake and Honoria will be down in a moment. They're fussing over Kitty and giving instructions to the nurse." She rolled her eyes. "I've never seen people so besotted with a baby before. You'd think they had produced the first one ever."

Victor laughed. "I suspect you will feel the same when you have your own children someday, Miss Merrick." He waved a hand at her riding habit. "So this is the famous garment that allows you to ride astride."

"It is." She grasped the outer edges of the skirt and pulled, exposing the split Victor had glimpsed as she descended the staircase.

"Very innovative. And I like your hair fashioned that way."

Pink colored her cheeks, giving her a natural, healthy glow. "You inspired me."

Voices drew their attention back to the staircase as Burwood and the duchess approached.

"I'm so glad you were able to join us, Mr. Pratt. Even numbers make for the best rides," the duchess said.

Although Victor would not deign to argue with a duchess, he doubted the number of riders determined the quality of the ride.

Exiting, they mounted their horses and trotted to the park. Burwood and the duchess led the way, with Victor riding next to Miss Merrick. He slid a glance over to her, admiring the expert way she held the reins and controlled the horse. "Your brother was right."

Burwood chuckled. "I'm always right. The question is, about what this time?"

"Miss Merrick has an excellent seat."

Color darkened her cheeks again, and her gaze dipped to her hands loosely holding the reins. "Thank you, Mr. Pratt."

"Would it be presumptuous to have you call me Victor? When we're not in a crowd of people, that is. Mr. Pratt sounds so very stuffy."

Her face brightened. "If you will call me Juliana."

Juliana. It had a musical ring to it that Victor loved.

Inside the park, equipages of various types rolled up and down Rotten Row along with riders on horseback. Luckily, the semi-clouded sky had kept the crowd to a manageable size. Victor tipped his hat, bidding a good afternoon to those he knew.

An enormous barouche carrying the Marquess of Edgerton, his wife, and two sons slowed as they approached. The odious Lord Middlebury lounged next to the boys in the rear-facing seat across from the marquess.

"The poor lads," Victor muttered. The boys not only endured a disagreeable parent, but Timothy had gone on ad nauseam about how obsequious Lord Middlebury was. Apparently, his sister, Lady Montgomery, had narrowly escaped being married to the man. As they grew closer, the boys' sour faces confirmed their displeasure.

Edgerton's gaze snagged on Juliana as they rode past on Edgerton's right. Minding his manners, Victor tipped his hat, but Edgerton turned away with studied precision, facing forward and effectively giving them the cut direct. He must have said something to Middlebury, because the man turned and gaped at them.

Damn. They must have noticed Juliana's unorthodox riding habit.

Fortunately, Juliana must not have noticed their rudeness, or if she did, perhaps she didn't understand the cut, still being unversed in the *ton's* ridiculous insults.

"Who were those people with Lord Middlebury, Victor?" Juliana asked.

Ah. Perhaps he'd been a little too quick with his assumptions. "Lord and Lady Edgerton, and their sons."

Her eyes widened. "*That* was Lady Charlotte's brother?" She shook her head. "That explains a great deal."

"So, you know Middlebury?"

Her button nose scrunched up as if they had passed a pile of horse droppings. Yet the pathway around them was mercifully clear. "From Drake's house party. He cornered me in the hallway and tried to pinch me." Her face reddened.

Leather bit into his gloves as Victor's grip tightened on the reins, and he twisted in his saddle, turning his entire torso toward her. "Did you tell your brother?" he asked, each word clipped and careful, the rage simmering just beneath the surface.

Her blond hair brushed the back of her jacket as she shook her head. "It was the day the truth came out about Drake. Honoria stormed out of the house, and Drake raced after her. I didn't want to add to his burden."

Although Victor admired Juliana's kind heart and concern for others, she needed to be protected from vultures like Middlebury. Courting her might serve that purpose as well.

As other people passed, they received a mixture of cordial greetings, shocked stares, and occasional snickers. The scoundrel, Felix Davies, trotted his horse next to a carriage where Lydia Whyte sat with her parents, her damnable fan fluttering furiously as she apparently carried on a conversation with Davies. Both turned their gazes toward Victor and his friends. Davies leaned in toward Lydia.

As Victor recalled the accusations Davies had leveled at him at the musicale, Lydia held the fan up to her face, no doubt hiding her smirk.

Victor tipped his hat, vowing to be the bigger man. "Miss Whyte, Lord and Lady Whyte. Davies."

Davies shot a glance toward Burwood, whose attention was completely on his wife.

Lucky man.

Realizing the duke was preoccupied, Davies trotted his horse over. "Miss Merrick. Pratt. Out for a family excursion?" He smirked at Victor, his eyes accusing and condemning.

"I could say the same for you, Davies." Victor nodded toward Lydia's carriage. "You're becoming a regular fixture with the Whytes."

Davies waved it off. "Not at all. I'm simply out for a pleasant ride and happened upon them, just as I have you two."

Victor didn't appreciate the lascivious way Davies raked his gaze up and down Juliana.

"Interesting riding habit, Miss Merrick. Quite daring to be riding astride among good society."

"Are you now the judge of what is appropriate for good society, Davies?" Victor asked, the words delivered with more snap than he originally intended.

"Gentlemen, please." Juliana's calm voice cut through Victor's growing irritation with Davies. "Lord Felix, although my method of riding may be unusual here among London's *ton*, where I'm from it is considered sensible."

"Of course," Davies said, his tone countering his agreement.

"Now, if you will excuse us, my brother—*the duke*—will be wondering what's kept us."

Victor almost cheered at the shocked expression on Davies's face at Juliana's couched reminder of whom Davies was insulting. With a jerk of her chin and the jaunty blue bonnet perched on the head she held high, Juliana nudged her horse forward without so much as a by-your-leave.

A grin tugged at Victor's lips. Davies could have Lydia. Juliana exhibited the courage of grace wrapped in steel.

CHAPTER 6

Juliana tamped down the hurt that had risen at Felix Davies's thinly veiled censure. Why had his words stung her? She'd tried to learn to ride sidesaddle, but it felt too unnatural and foreign. But it would seem, even the modiste's elegant riding habit, the design guided by Mama and Honoria, wasn't enough to keep the wagging tongues at bay.

Try as she might to make her family proud, or at least not embarrass them, she failed miserably. How did she ever think she would fit in with society and all their silly rules and judgmental attitudes? People like Lord Felix made it clear she would never be accepted as one of them, not that she needed him to point it out. Like her attempts at riding sidesaddle, pretending she belonged among the *ton* felt alien, as if she were wearing someone else's skin.

Victor had been a dear to come to her aide. But she worried that, like Honoria and Drake, he would also be an innocent casualty of any repercussions. Sounds of his horse rejoining her drew her attention to him.

He leaned toward her and whispered, "That was bloody brilliant."

Both the grin on his face and his words lifted her spirits. "Such language, Victor!" She laughed, hoping he knew she didn't mind at all.

"Forgive me." His own tone implied he wasn't the least bit sorry.

They followed Drake and Honoria, riding in companionable silence for a while when Dr. and Mrs. Somersby approached, accompanied by three children, all of them also on horseback.

Juliana tilted her head in their direction. "Is that the boy called Pockets Lady Montgomery spoke of?" Blond hair poked out from beneath the boy's cap, and one hand gestured animatedly as he spoke to the younger girl on his left.

"I believe it is," Victor answered.

An older girl of about ten-and-four rode on Pockets's right, her dark curls bouncing in rhythm with the horse's gait.

As the family stopped to exchange pleasantries with Drake and Honoria, the girls nudged their horses forward toward Juliana.

"Hello," the older girl said. "You're riding like my papa," she said, a smile in her voice.

Juliana smiled at the child, who sat straight and tall in the sidesaddle. Thank goodness the girl wouldn't receive the derision Juliana faced after she made her come-out into society. "I'm afraid I didn't learn to ride sidesaddle as you are."

"I'm Victoria, but everyone calls me Tori," she said, her incredible blue eyes sparkling. "I like your riding habit. It's pretty."

"Thank you, Tori. I'm Juliana, and I'm very pleased to meet you." She turned toward the younger girl. "And what is your name?"

"Eva." The girl's dark eyes darted up to meet Juliana's, giving her a shy smile before returning her attention to her hands.

Eva appeared to be no more than five or six, and she glanced nervously over to her brother who had remained with the adults. "Pockets." The need in her soft voice tugged at Juliana's heartstrings, and a commotion from someone yelling in the distance swallowed the girl's cry.

"I'll get him for you, Eva." Tori's gaze met Juliana's. "This is Eva's first outing on her new pony, and she's a little uneasy. Pockets calms her."

Tori rode over to where the rest of the adults, including Victor, huddled together on the path. Snippets of the conversation drifted over to Juliana as she caught Simon's name, and Dr. Somersby's enquiry as to his health. Juliana shot a nervous glance toward Victor. Simon didn't want anyone to know about his ongoing fight with malaria. But Victor seemed distracted, his attention turned toward shouts coming from farther down the path.

Dark shadows passed over them, and Dr. Somersby glanced up, his voice a little louder. "Looks like rain."

No sooner than he had spoken the words, than lightning flashed, and a roll of thunder followed.

Shouts in the distance grew louder. "Out of the way! Out of the way!" a man's voice cried. People on foot, in carriages, and on horseback scrambled to clear the way. But Eva's eyes widened and locked on Juliana's, the message clear. The girl was terrified and didn't know what to do.

Eva's horse shifted, its hooves stamping the dirt and its nostrils flaring.

Oh, no!

Well acquainted with a horse who became spooked, Juliana reached for the pony's bridle to steady it. But before she could gain purchase, a man on horseback shot past them.

Eva's horse bolted, taking the girl with it. Without a second thought, Juliana jumped into action, racing after the runaway horse. Hoofbeats pounded behind her, no doubt Dr. Somersby, Drake, or Victor also in pursuit.

Juliana leaned forward, bending low over Sunshine's neck and rising enough to avoid her bottom pounding against the saddle. People gawked and shouted, their faces a blur as Juliana raced past, and Eva cried out for help.

Finally, neck and neck with the pony, Juliana managed to get close enough to grab the reins from Eva's hands, and slow the pony to a halt. Moments later, Dr. Somersby and Drake appeared at their sides.

"Thank God." Dr. Somersby vaulted off his horse and swooped

Eva into his arms, lavishing her face with kisses and hugging the child so tightly, she cried out.

"Papa! Papa! You're crushing me." Yet she clung to Dr. Somersby's neck as if it were a lifeline.

"Well done, brat." Pride shone in Drake's eyes.

Victor was next to arrive, followed by Honoria, Mrs. Somersby, Pockets, and Tori. Every one of them gazing at her as if she'd hung the moon and stars in the sky.

"Huzzah!" Pockets shouted.

"Juliana, that was marvelous!" Honoria exclaimed.

"I wish Manny could have seen that," Tori said.

Tears brimmed in Mrs. Somersby's eyes. "How can I ever thank you, Miss Merrick?"

"No thanks are necessary, Mrs. Somersby. I was simply the closet to Eva." Juliana peered over at the child still clinging to her father. "Are you all right, Eva?"

The child nodded, her face pressed cheek-to-cheek against her father's. A much wider smile crossed her lips. "You saved me."

"You have an admirer for life, Miss Merrick," Dr. Somersby said. "In fact, I believe you have five." His gaze darted to Victor. "Or six."

Uncomfortable with the attention, Juliana brushed off the compliments. "Really, Dr. Somersby, I'm only glad I could help."

"Call me Oliver and my wife, Camilla."

Camilla nodded and wiped the tears from her cheeks. "Whatever you wish, Juliana, say the word, and if it is in our power to grant it, it shall be yours."

"Your friendship is more than enough. I've always wanted a little sister, so perhaps Eva—and Tori—could be my sisters in spirit, much like Honoria is my sister by marriage."

"Hey, what about me?" Pockets complained.

"Well, I have a *big* brother." She peeked at Drake. "But it would be nice to have a brother who didn't tease me mercilessly."

Drake laughed.

"I want a riding habit like Juliana's," Tori said.

Victor, who had been silent during the exchange, smiled. "That's an excellent idea, Miss Victoria. I dare say it was Juliana's ability to ride astride that helped her move as quickly as she did and stop Miss Eva's horse before a calamity occurred."

Oliver and Camilla examined Juliana's riding habit as if only first noticing she was riding astride.

"It does seem more sensible," Oliver said.

"Goodness, such a gallant rescue."

Juliana peered over Drake's head at a somewhat familiar voice. Lord Felix trotted up to them.

Where had he come from?

"I could hardly believe my eyes when you raced past me like a hound on the hunt, Miss Merrick." Lord Felix yawned, the action adding to his bored tone. "Here I was enjoying a chat with Lord Highbottom and—"

"Shouldn't you be with Miss Whyte?" Victor veritably growled the question.

Lord Felix waved it off. "If you're referring to when you saw me with Miss Whyte earlier, I was merely sharing some pleasant gossip for a moment."

"*Pleasant* gossip?" Juliana asked. "Gossip is never pleasant, sir."

"Oh, it's all in good fun. However, dear madam, since you find gossip distasteful, let us hope you haven't provided fodder for those who spread it." His gaze homed in on her position on Sunshine.

Drake moved his horse between her and Lord Felix. "Careful, Davies."

Fat rain droplets dotted the ground and dampened Juliana's clothing. Drake turned his back on Lord Felix. "Come, Juliana, the day has turned foul, but let us hope the rain will wash away the stench."

With Drake in the lead, their little group departed. And although Juliana had no regrets about stopping the runaway pony, she worried she had, once again, drawn unnecessary attention to herself and, by extension, brought embarrassment on her brother.

She turned toward Victor, who appeared deep in thought. "Have I made a muck of it again?"

His head jerked back, a furrow creasing his brow. "What? No.

No. You were magnificent, and anyone who fails to recognize it is a nodcock."

Warmth spread through Juliana's chest and settled low in her belly at Victor's words. As they rode in silence, she wanted some small way to repay his kindness, and she remembered their conversation about his passion for painting.

༺❦༻

TWO DAYS AFTER THE EVENTFUL DAY ON ROTTEN ROW, VICTOR SAT in the drawing room of his parents' home, scouring the scandal sheets for any derogatory reports regarding what had transpired. First, he scanned *The Town Tattler*, snorting with laughter at a particular *on dit*.

Has Lord FD discovered a way to mend his "broken heart" by courting Miss LW? This reporter wants to know!

Victor had no great love for any gossip rag, but although identities were easy enough to decipher, at least *The Tattler* didn't use full names. Unlike *The Muckraker*.

Turning to the aforementioned abomination next, Victor's gaze snagged on the mention of Juliana, his body straightening in his chair.

Reports have reached our ears that several members of the ton *witnessed Miss Juliana Merrick, the Duke of Burwood's sister, in Hyde Park riding astride! Of course, allowances should be made as the "duke" himself was not raised among society and perhaps doesn't understand the proper comportment for gently bred ladies. Or Miss Merrick's common birth could account for such egregious disrespect for good manners.*

Anger flared in Victor's chest that, of all the positive traits Miss Merrick possessed, the repugnant rag singled out her common birth. Not a woman whose bravery had saved a child from certain injury—or worse. Not a woman who children flocked to or was an accomplished horsewoman. No. Her common birth. He crumpled the parchment in his fist the same moment his mother breezed in.

"Victor!" Her gaze swung toward the destroyed gossip rag.

"What is that?" She snatched it from his grasp. "Look what you've done! I haven't read this latest edition yet."

"How can you continue to read such . . . rubbish, Mother? Allow me to save you the time. It holds nothing of importance."

She huffed. "I'll be the judge of that." She pasted on a smile, and Victor's defenses drew to attention. "Now, what brings my favorite son for a call? News of a possible engagement on the horizon?"

"Sorry to disappoint you, Mother. But, no."

With a wave of a hand, she brushed it away. "Come, sit. I'll ring for tea."

Salvation came in the form of his parents' butler with Cilla following.

"Mrs. Marbry, my lady," Digby announced in his pompous tone.

Cilla bussed her mother's cheek in greeting. "Where is Father? I have some news."

"In his study," their mother answered, her brows dropping. "Why? Is something wrong?"

Victor almost rolled his eyes. How could his mother be so clueless?

"Not at all." Cilla turned toward Digby, still standing like a sentinel at the entrance to the drawing room. "Please fetch my father."

When their father entered, Cilla embraced him, and unlike the kiss she gave to their mother, the gesture of affection was heartfelt and genuine. "I'm sorry to disturb you, Father."

"Nonsense. I always have time for you, my dear."

Silence hung in the air as they all took a seat. Cilla practically vibrated with anticipation.

"Are you going to make us all wait until autumn, Cilla? Or are you going to tell us?" Victor's teasing tone elicited a laugh from his sister.

Her eyes sparkled, and Victor had never been happier for his sister.

"Timothy and I are expecting."

After a moment of shock from both their mother and father,

each drew Cilla into their arms. Tears of happiness streamed down Cilla's face, and their father even brushed at his eyes, complaining about dust and how the servants hadn't performed their duties.

Mother grasped Cilla's hands, extending them as she examined her. "The Saxtons must be ecstatic! A boy, you must have a boy for Timothy."

Pain flashed in Cilla's eyes.

Why couldn't Mother simply be happy for her own daughter? Staring point-blank at his mother, Victor said, "I dare say Timothy and Cilla will be thrilled with either a boy *or* a girl."

"Well said," Father agreed. "A healthy child is all that matters."

"Thank you, Father." Cilla hugged him again.

As much as Victor had hoped his father's reminder would silence his mother's misguided opinions, she disappointed him when she said, "Now, we must concentrate on you, Victor. As I said earlier, we need news of an engagement so that you may work on starting your own family. In my opinion, Lydia Whyte is the perfect choice. But there are other options. Perhaps we should host a little soiree and invite the most eligible ladies."

As his mother droned on, considering the attributes of each available woman who might become Victor's bride, only one woman's image rose in his eye.

The woman he lost.

And as happy as he was for his sister and Timothy, the subject of children only brought his mother's scheming to find Victor a bride to the forefront. He couldn't run from his duty forever. When Victor glanced at his father, worry banded his chest at the dark half-moon shadows under his father's eyes. He would speak to Cilla about it and suggest Timothy provide a thorough physical examination.

Was it the trouble in the family's country seat that distressed his father, or something else? Something more—life-threatening?

"Victor! Victor!" his mother's voice pulled him back from the abyss of his dark thoughts.

"What?" His gaze darted up to the footman holding a silver salver in front of him, a piece of correspondence resting in the center.

"Your valet delivered this, sir. He said it appeared important." He pointed to the crest embedded on the wax seal.

The imprint displayed a dragon clutching arrows in one clawed limb. A crown perched on its head, and flames shot from its nostrils.

Victor plucked it from the tray. Sliding his finger underneath, he broke it and opened the missive. His whole body came to attention when he read the contents.

"What is it?" Cilla asked.

"The Duke of Burwood has summoned me." His lips tugged upward. Not only would the request provide reason to defy his mother's admonition to avoid the duke's household, but the nature of the invitation promised an opportunity to pull Victor from his miserable doldrums.

"Find a polite reason to decline," his mother said.

"Mother!" Cilla's voice rose. "Don't listen to her, Victor."

"Aurelia." Father frosted Mother with a glare. "I don't know what you have against Burwood, nor do I care. One does not dismiss a summons from a duke. Victor and Burwood are of the same age. It will be good for our son to have a strong ally and friend when he assumes the title at my death."

Once more, Victor viewed his father with fresh eyes. Something was most definitely wrong.

Victor rose. "I have no intention of listening to Mother. This"—he waved the missive—"is an invitation for an interview to paint their family portraits."

With that bit of news, his mother was the one to throw herself back against the sofa with a groan. "Why must you pursue that messy pastime? As your father has pointed out, you are the heir to a viscountcy, goodness' sakes."

"Oh, Honoria must have been impressed with your knowledge of painting techniques when we all visited the National Gallery two years ago." Cilla *would* have to remind him. He had been the one to escort Miss Lovelace with Cilla as a chaperone, only to have Nash force himself into their company.

The cad had actually been courting Honoria before he turned his sights to Miss Lovelace and began his campaign to steal her away. Victor shot his sister a narrow-eyed glower. Lucky for her she was expecting his first niece or nephew.

Focusing on that happy thought, Victor wondered what truly had precipitated the duke's summons. Even though he'd not found an opportunity to subtly remind her during the eventful ride in Hyde Park, would it be too much to hope that Juliana played a part? He smiled at the possibility. "If you would excuse me, the duke awaits."

CHAPTER 7

After returning to his bachelor apartment where he kept a small studio, Victor searched through drawings and smaller canvasses to provide samples of his work. His hand hovered over one of the sketches he had done of Adalyn, her likeness squeezing his heart and, in turn, reminding him how much Juliana looked like her. He placed it aside, not wishing to draw questions from the duke.

Instead, he selected a few renderings he'd done while sitting in the park, capturing little snippets of people's lives as they went about their business. He chose two completed canvasses—a still life to demonstrate his brush technique and a small portrait of Cilla he'd completed and planned to give Timothy on their wedding anniversary—and wrapped them carefully.

During the brief carriage ride, he ran his hands lovingly over the satchel containing his art. What a coup it would be to be awarded the privilege of being portraitist to a duke, and his skin tingled with anticipation.

But what if Burwood found his work lacking? Victor spiraled with doubt, imagining the disappointment in the duke's eyes as he gazed upon what Victor thought of as his masterpiece. Even worse, what if the duke found his work to be ordinary, lacking any sort of originality or spark of the unique?

The crushing weight of failure paralyzed him, and Victor nearly pounded on the carriage roof to have the driver return him home.

How could anyone understand what his art meant to him? How he poured his very soul into each and every piece. To be criticized. Ridiculed. Made to feel less than.

Victor's throat tightened, and he forced down the lump of fear that had formed.

Although his painting master praised his work, did he really have the audacity to believe he could dare consider himself to be among such exemplary company as Thomas Lawrence, portrait artist of kings?

Before he could raise his hand and give the roof a sound *thump,* the carriage pulled to a stop before the duke's London mansion. Victor wiped his sweaty palms on his trousers, took a deep breath, and exited. His knuckles white as he gripped the satchel's handle, Victor strode toward the front door.

Victor's mind shot back to Juliana's come-out ball. If anyone understood the fear of not measuring up, she would, and Victor secretly hoped she would be a participant in the interview.

The butler greeted him, taking his card and showing him to an empty parlor.

"I shall inform His and Her Grace of your arrival. Would you care for refreshment?" the butler asked.

Victor's stomach roiled at the suggestion. "No. Thank you."

Left alone to wait, Victor rotated between pacing, gazing out the window, sitting on a comfortable wingback chair, and inspecting the paintings hung on the walls—spending considerably more time on the last activity.

In fact, he'd been inspecting a portrait of a surly looking man when the duke entered. "My grandfather."

Victor spun at the duke's words.

"There are several portraits of him here and at Hartridge House, as he lived to be nearly ninety. That"—Burwood nodded in the direction of the portrait—"was the last."

Did Burwood have Victor placed in this room because of that portrait? Was that the result Burwood expected? Although the artistry was exceptional, the subject left something to be desired. Victor stepped forward, inspecting the portrait more closely. "There's a sadness about the eyes. At first, I thought he was angry, but on closer inspection, he appears heartbroken."

At his side, Burwood peered up at his grandfather's likeness. "Now that you say it, I see it as well."

Victor turned toward the duke, who appeared pensive.

"It would align with what Aunt Kitty said about him. That he had regrets about how he treated my father." Burwood shook his head. "What it must have been like for him to realize all of his sons had preceded him in death."

A smile tipped Burwood's lips that didn't meet his eyes. "But let's not be morbid. Come, sit." He gestured to a sofa and the two wingback chairs.

As Victor debated which to choose, Her Grace joined them. "Mr. Pratt. Thank you for coming so quickly." Seating herself on the sofa, the duke joined her, making Victor's choice of one of the wingbacks that much easier.

Before he could sit, Burwood's mother and Juliana also entered. Apparently, the decision regarding who would have the honors of painting the portraits would be a family matter.

The moment Juliana arrived, Victor's nervousness settled. Odd, but it was as if her mere presence gave him the confidence he needed not only to survive the interview but to present himself as the capable artist he believed he was. Her calming effect was unexpected but very welcome.

"First, let's get some particulars out of the way," Burwood said as his mother settled next to Her Grace, and Juliana seated herself in the remaining wingback. "If you insist on formalities, Burwood will suffice, but I'll admit I'm still having difficulty adjusting to the address. I prefer Drake, and my wife agrees, preferring you call her Honoria. If you accept the position, you will be spending a great deal of time with our family, and addressing us by our Christian names will make everyone more comfortable."

"I'm honored. Then you must call me Victor." Victor seated himself and slid his gaze to Juliana, catching the little smile playing across her lips. Had she told her brother of their agreement to address each other informally?

Victor's mind stuttered and reeled back on something Drake had said. "I beg your pardon. Did you say if I accept the position?" He reached for the satchel at his feet. "Don't you want to see my work first?"

"Of course." Drake held out his hand, a slight pink tinge coloring the tips of his ears.

Honoria patted Drake's arm. "What my husband means, Victor, is we are both confident in your ability. I was most impressed with the knowledge you exhibited some years back."

Of course it would be because of the National Gallery.

"Knowledge doesn't always translate to ability, Your Grace— Honoria," Victor said. "Although I'm flattered by your confidence in me."

"Not only your knowledge, sir," Honoria continued. "I recall you studied under the masters in Italy, and Juliana encouraged us to extend the opportunity. She said you were quite modest when pressed about your skill. For the most part, I have found that humble people are often the most talented."

Victor had his doubts about that presumption, but who was he to argue with a duchess? However, his spirits lifted that Juliana had remembered and recommended him. He opened his satchel, removing the sketches first and handed them to the duke.

"What I love to do is catch people when they're lost in the moment. For example, this one"—Victor pointed to the top sketch —"with the young boy crouched down, examining an insect. Simple things that we presume don't mean much, but in reality, do."

Mrs. Merrick leaned over as Drake passed the sketch to Honoria. "Oh! You've captured that tentative reach of a finger so well, Victor. I remember Drake's fascination with insects as a child."

Drake snorted a laugh. "If I recall, you didn't appreciate the dirt I would drag in that resulted from my *fascination.*"

"Oh, and look!" Honoria exclaimed at the next sketch. "A

couple hiding behind a tree. It appears as though he's going to try to steal a kiss."

Victor debated including that particular sketch, but considering the duke and duchess had a love story for the ages, he thought they might appreciate it.

"You can almost *feel* his longing," Drake whispered. He lifted his gaze to meet Victor's. "These are excellent, Victor."

"Well, stop hoarding them!" Juliana rose from her chair and huddled next to Drake on the arm of the sofa.

An image of a family portrait popped into Victor's mind of the duke's family huddled together just so. Much better than the stodgy formal portraits he himself had to pose for with his family, with his arm perched at an odd angle across his father's chair and Cilla complaining about the crick in her neck as the artist positioned her. Hope bloomed in his chest like a spray of watercolor in vibrant reds and golds.

"I have paintings to illustrate my technique and an example of a finished portrait."

The family barely raised their heads as they continued to examine the sketches. Victor handed the duke the still life.

"I've employed a technique for capturing light I learned while studying in Florence, playing off the dark and shadows as well as layering textures."

Juliana hovered an index finger over the painting, much like Victor remembered the boy's careful movements with the insect. "The apple is so lifelike, I want to take a bite." She peered up at him, and Victor's heart gave a *thud* at her compliment. Or was it from something entirely different?

Drake nodded. "My stomach is growling, and we just finished luncheon."

Sketches and still lifes were all well and good, but the true test would be the portrait. Retrieving it from his satchel, Victor drew in a deep breath and handed it to the duke. "This is of my sister. I know it's not typical of aristocratic portraits . . ."

From everyone's widened eyes and parted lips, Victor surmised he had just lost the opportunity.

Juliana gazed dumbstruck at the portrait of Priscilla. Not typical was a massive understatement.

After she had recommended Victor to Drake as the family's artist, Juliana spent time examining all the portraits in her brother's vast home. Other than the one of Drake's father, most were staid and cold, much like that of Drake's grandfather hanging in that very room. The people in them looked—uncomfortable. Although realistic, their likenesses appeared stiff.

But not the painting of Drake's father. A half-smile tipped one corner of his mouth, reminding Juliana of Drake. His gaze held a dreamy, far-away look, as if he imagined something wonderful and —perhaps—unattainable. Mother had pointed out the tiny rosebuds adorning his waistcoat, telling Juliana with a sigh it was what had brought them together. A little spaniel sat obediently at his master's feet, gazing up at him, eyes filled with adoration. Mother told Drake the artist had captured them both perfectly.

Such was the painting of Priscilla. A mischievous glint sparkled in her blue eyes, the technique of capturing light Victor spoke of giving them life. The devious smile playing across her lips supported that which shone in her eyes. Strands of blond hair fell loose against her neck in disarray. But the most unusual part of the painting was the umbrella she held aloft, as if ready to swing at someone and knock them out.

Juliana felt every loving stroke Victor must have applied to the portrait. She understood more fully his remark about passion for one's art, for his work embodied it. Juliana's heart lurched in her chest, a not uncomfortable pang squeezing it, as the emotion Victor had poured into the painting flowed forth and pushed her closer to the already precarious edge of love she teetered on.

Silence settled around them, and Juliana glanced at Victor, catching the furrow of worry creasing his brow. Something more painful twinged in her chest. He thought they didn't like it. Her gaze flickered to Drake, Honoria, and her mother, whose gazes remained latched onto the portrait. If they wouldn't reassure Victor the painting was marvelous, she certainly would.

Before she could open her mouth, Honoria laughed, rather loudly for Honoria, who was typically the model of decorum. "You've captured her perfectly, Victor. This is Priscilla personified."

Drake nodded. "From what Honoria told me about her and my limited experience, it's remarkable. However, I'm afraid I don't understand the umbrella."

"She's wielding it like a weapon," Mother said.

Victor chuckled, the sound brushing against Juliana's skin and trailing gooseflesh in its wake. "Precisely. It's a joke between my sister and her husband."

"Oh! I think I know!" Honoria touched her husband's arm, then exchanged an amused look with Victor.

"It's not my story to tell," Victor said, "but let us simply say Cilla's husband doesn't have to worry about anyone kidnapping her."

The affection on Victor's face as he spoke of his sister tugged on the already raw emotion rushing through Juliana. His eyes locked with hers, and her cheeks flamed at his intense gaze. Were her emotions as transparent as his?

Quickly averting her gaze back to the portrait, she said, "This makes me like Priscilla even more."

Victor laughed. "Because she's a termagant?"

"Because of the portrait. Unlike so many others where I get no sense of who the person really was, I feel like I've received a peek into her soul. Into what makes her truly *her*."

When her attention drifted back to Victor, his mouth hung ajar. "Y-you do?"

"Why are you so surprised, Victor?" Drake asked. "Juliana has put into words what we're all experiencing. What you've captured is real. No. That's not the exact word I want." Drake shook his head and paused for a moment. "Genuine. Yes. That's it."

"I'm flattered, Your Grace."

"Nonsense." Drake waved it off and rose. "Come. I want you to see the portrait of my father, and we can discuss your visions for ours."

"I have the position?" Victor asked, as if unsure of the answer. "Aren't you going to interview other artists?"

"No need. But if you prefer to prove yourself, we could have you start with either my mother or Juliana."

"Wonderful idea, Drake," Honoria said, her gaze flitting between Juliana and Victor. "I suggest Juliana."

Victor turned toward Juliana, his smile sweet. "An excellent idea."

Juliana's pulse raced as she imagined posing in front of Victor while he captured her likeness on canvas.

The fleeting moment of connection vanished as Victor returned his attention to Drake. "Would I have your permission to spend time with your sister? Getting better acquainted with Miss Merrick will help me develop the perfect pose. Although I already have one possibility in mind."

A gleam similar to Honoria's sparkled in Mother's eyes. "I would be happy to chaperone you both."

They reached Drake's bedchamber, where the portrait of his father hung, a wistful expression crossing her mother's features once more.

Victor stepped closer to the large painting. "Hmm. You look like him, Your Grace. There's a playfulness about the eyes and mouth the artist captured. This is much different from the one of your grandfather."

"Call me Drake, Victor. According to Mr. Ford, my Uncle Gyles's—friend, when my grandfather threw my father from the house, he never used that artist again."

"Pity." Victor examined the artist's signature. "I know of this artist. A Scotsman, quite well-known, I believe. He's said to have painted directly on the canvas using no preliminary sketches of his subject." Admiration rang in Victor's words.

"Is that unusual?" Juliana asked, stepping closer to the painting and appreciating it anew.

"Very." Victor's eyes once again met hers, causing her heart to skip. "But I also appreciate his ability to capture that certain je ne sais quoi of his subjects."

Feeling like a ninny, Juliana frowned. "I'm sorry?"

Honoria translated. "It's French. Although it's literal for 'I don't know what,' it's used when speaking about an indescribable feature that makes something unique or special."

"Oh! As you did with Priscilla."

Victor's sweet smile returned. "I'm pleased you think so, Miss Merrick."

Warmth expanded in Juliana's chest and her stomach gave a little flip.

Finished examining the portrait, they returned to the drawing room to discuss the particulars.

Juliana struggled to focus on the conversation, her gaze locked on Victor's profile, his features animated with such joy when he spoke of the creative process and some of his ideas for the family's portraits.

If only she could be the source of such happiness. She sighed dreamily.

"Would that be agreeable, Miss Merrick?" Victor stared at her, no doubt expecting an answer to his question.

If she only had an idea what he had asked.

CHAPTER 8

Surprised by Juliana's lack of attentiveness, Victor reframed his question. Unlike Lydia, Juliana seemed such a level-headed young lady. Perhaps in his eagerness to begin, he had overstepped. "If you have other plans, Miss Merrick, I could return at a later date to begin our session. I simply thought since I'm already here and have my sketch pad . . ."

She blinked, her face flushing and giving her that lovely, natural glow he wished to capture on canvas. "You wish to begin with me today?" Her hand drifted to her head, then her bosom, snagging his attention. "But my hair. My clothes."

"Just some preliminary sketches with ideas. If that is agreeable with you and your mother. And the duke and duchess, of course."

Drake rose and held out his hand to Honoria. "Shall we leave Victor to his work, my dear? Besides, I expect Kitty is missing us, and I would like a few minutes with her before I leave for Lords."

Ah, yes. Their infant daughter. Nervous energy battered Victor's chest at the thought of painting a squirming infant. He'd heard horror stories while studying under the masters in Italy.

He would tackle that challenge later. At the moment, his focus should be on Juliana.

He rose and bowed toward Drake and Honoria. "Thank you for the privilege, Your Graces."

"Remember, Victor. It's Drake." Drake clasped Victor on the shoulder and gave a squeeze. "I expect we'll be seeing quite a lot of each other, and the honorific becomes tiresome." He turned toward his sister and mother. "Keep an eye on her, Mother."

Once reseated, Victor jotted down a note reminding him to capture the glint in Drake's eyes and the playful quirk of his lips that matched that of his father's.

While Mrs. Merrick sat quietly working on a piece of embroidery, Victor retrieved his sketchpad. "Would you mind moving to the sofa, Juliana? Seated across from me would work best. The lighting is perfect there."

Juliana fussed with her skirts as she positioned herself, worry creasing her brow. "What should I do?"

"First. Relax. I'll make some sketches while we get to know each other. Other than your expertise on horseback, tell me a little more about yourself. Your likes, dislikes. What gives you joy?"

An intriguing, deeper blush covered her cheeks. *Well. What might that be about?*

"I'm not comfortable talking about myself."

Definitely not like Lydia. "Don't think of it as talking about yourself, but about the things you find interesting, joyful, or even distasteful if you wish."

She nodded and sucked in her bottom lip.

Victor's heart gave a decided *thump* at her innocent action. *Keep it professional, man.*

"Early mornings, when the sun comes up over the rolling hills at Drake's estate in Dorset. The light is so perfect, the vibrant colors holding a promise of something wonderful. It's the best time for riding. The scent of dew fresh on the grass and birds waking up and singing."

Victor's pencil stilled over the paper, his mind enraptured. "Beautiful."

"Oh, it is," she said.

But Victor wasn't speaking of her description, although it was quite poetic. It was the expression on her face, the wistfulness in her eyes that was simply—lovely. Did she even realize her allure? As his pencil scratched across the rough surface of the paper, he did his best to capture the moment.

Lifting his gaze from the paper, he asked, "Do you have a favorite horse?"

Different from the dreamy look she had before, her face lit with excitement. "I do. Sunshine. The mare I rode the other day."

Victor nodded, sketching another image of her next to the first. He would either decide later which to use in her formal portrait or ask Drake's preference. Although both captured Juliana's spirit, Victor fancied the dreamy-eyed Juliana a bit more.

"Tell me more about Sunshine. Describe how it feels to ride her."

As he'd hoped, the dreamy expression crossed Juliana's face again. "Freeing. Especially if I'm riding where she can run. Hyde Park was lovely, but other than stopping a runaway pony, there isn't much opportunity to allow Sunshine free rein." Her attention drifted to a spot over Victor's shoulder.

"Lord Felix Davies here for Miss Merrick," Frampton, the butler, announced.

What is he doing here? Victor exchanged a glance with Juliana.

Juliana's brow furrowed.

Surprised? Annoyed? Both?

"Tell Lord Felix I'm not at home."

"Now, Miss Merrick, is that any way to treat your admirers?"

Victor turned at Davies's slimy voice.

The cad gave an exaggerated bow. "Mrs. Merrick."

"I instructed you to wait in the entryway, my lord," Frampton said, pulling himself up to his full height.

Davies held a hand to his heart. "Love heeds no one, my good man." He held out an enormous bouquet. "For you, dear lady."

Victor wanted to cast up his accounts.

Frampton snatched the flowers from Davies's grip. "Allow me to put these in *water*, Miss Merrick."

From Frampton's tone, Victor surmised water equated to the rubbish pile.

"Pratt," Davies said, the intonation much like that of Frampton's *water*. His gaze drifted to the sketches in Victor's hands, and his eyes narrowed.

"Davies," Victor volleyed back with as much vitriol as he could muster, each of them sizing up the other.

Juliana's soft voice broke the staring competition. "My apologies. As you can see, sir, I am occupied and, unfortunately, have no time for unexpected callers."

Well done, Juliana. Victor fought his smirk at the perfectly delivered setdown.

"Of course." Davies waved it off, and rather than apologizing and leaving, he made himself comfortable on the unoccupied wingback. "I promise I won't stay long. However, I wanted to put my mind at ease that you have not taken those scurrilous reports to heart."

Victor's stomach clenched, and his gaze darted toward Juliana.

Juliana's brow furrowed. "Reports?"

Feigned concern colored Davies's deceitful face. "Then you haven't heard? Well, I suppose that's for the best. It would only upset you."

Fire shone in Mrs. Merrick's eyes, and she touched her daughter's arm as if to soothe her. "Sir, if you have something to tell us that concerns my daughter, please do so and stop beating about the bush with intimations."

Victor's respect for the entire family grew tenfold. If only his own mother would champion her children instead of trying to manipulate their lives.

"If you insist." Davies pulled the scandal sheet from his pocket and handed it to Mrs. Merrick. "Read for yourself."

Oh, the man was beyond devious. Mrs. Merrick walked right into his trap.

Victor's grip on the pencil tightened, and he had no greater wish than to stab Davies with it.

Juliana leaned over, joining her mother in reading the ghastly gossip rag. Her hand drifted up to cover her mouth and her eyes widened. She locked eyes with Victor. "Did you know?"

Victor swallowed the overly large lump in his throat. "Well . . . I . . ."

"You did. Why didn't you say anything?" Juliana's eyes brightened with a shimmer of tears, but she blinked them back.

"Forgive me, Miss Merrick. I have no desire to cause you distress." He glared at Davies. "Unlike others."

"Me?" Davies's mock offense was laughable. "Unlike *you*, Pratt, I came here because I believe forewarned is forearmed, and I have a solution to this"—he gestured toward the paper in Mrs. Merrick's hands—"unfortunate turn of events."

Victor continued to glower. "Unless your solution is to stop the person spreading these horrible rumors, I doubt Miss Merrick would be interested."

Davies pressed his lips together and gave an audible sigh. "Oh, dear boy. It's only a rumor if the truth of it is doubtful. As we both know, Miss Merrick was indeed seen riding astride."

Blood pounded in Victor's skull. "And yet that *rag* failed to mention her courageous rescue of Dr. Somersby's daughter. Funny how it only reports the negative side of things."

Davies studied his nails. "Which is why I'm here."

Apparently recovered from the shock, Juliana found her voice. "Which is, Lord Felix?"

"To court you. Being seen with a well-regarded—"

"Ha. Well-regarded my foot." Victor mumbled his exclamation of disbelief just loud enough to give Davies pause.

The cad cleared his throat and slid a narrow-eyed glance toward Victor. "As I was saying, being seen with a member of the *ton* will go a long way to quell some of the wagging tongues. Especially if I'm courting you."

Juliana squared her shoulders, determination shining in her eyes. "My brother and his wife are members of the *ton*."

Felix shook his head as if trying to explain something to a small child. "My dear lady. Scandal firmly attached itself to your brother and his wife without any assistance from you. Not only can they not help you, but have you considered you will do them even more harm?"

The urge to plant the man a facer exploded in Victor's chest.

Juliana's brave stance faltered, her shoulders drooping a fraction. "I . . . I have."

"That is, unless you associate yourself with someone who is relatively free from scandal."

Unable to contain his disgust, Victor huffed again. "You sir, are out of line. And if memory serves, you've been in the scandal sheets regularly, Davies."

"As a victim." Davies snapped the last word. "Which makes my proposal to Miss Merrick all the more compelling. I have garnered sympathy from those in society due to my ill-treatment by Lady Charlotte."

The fire flamed in Mrs. Merrick's blue eyes. "I think we have heard enough, Lord Felix."

As if he'd been eavesdropping, the butler appeared at the doorway.

"Please show Lord Felix out, Frampton. We wouldn't want him to become lost," Mrs. Merrick said.

Davies rose. "I urge you to give careful thought to my offer, Miss Merrick." He glanced over at Victor, his gaze again dropping to the sketches in Victor's hands. "That is, unless Mr. Pratt's artistic endeavors are of a more *personal* nature. Which, from the look of them, they must be. They're too—how shall I say this and remain polite?—rudimentary."

Oooh. That did it! Victor shot from his seat. "If you *must* know, Davies, His Grace has commissioned me to paint his family's portraits."

As if in slow motion, Davies's left eyebrow hitched. "I see. Well, then I shall call on you in two days, giving you time to consider my offer, Miss Merrick. Good day." He strode from the room as if he'd been the duke rather than the second son to an earl.

"Oh, Mama." Juliana's strangled voice tugged at Victor's heart. "He's right, isn't he? I'm a disgrace to Drake and Honoria."

Victor averted his gaze when Mrs. Merrick pulled her

daughter into her arms. "Of course not! Drake and Honoria are made of sterner stuff. And you have done nothing to shame them."

But Victor knew the *ton* better than Juliana, and possibly Mrs. Merrick did. "Although I agree with your mother, Juliana, I'm afraid the *ton's* rigid rules leave little room for deviation. People have been giving the cut direct for less." As much as he hated to admit it, Davies had a point.

Although Juliana enjoyed Victor's presence, she wilted with relief when he made his apologies and left them, promising to return the next day to continue their session and discuss ideas for her pose.

She had no intention of accepting Lord Felix as a suitor. Not only did he fail to meet Drake's approval, but his insulting assessment of Victor's sketches angered her on Victor's behalf.

Yet Lord Felix had a point. If a man of good breeding escorted her about town, it might counter the derogatory reports enough to give her time to prove herself among society. The problem lay in the appalling paucity of suitors.

One was indeed a lonely number, especially when the one suitor was Lord Felix Davies.

Could she stomach him long enough to establish a better reputation and possibly attract a more suitable match? Even as she pondered it, one man's face continually appeared in her mind: Victor Pratt.

If only Victor hadn't been so quick to explain the sketches were merely part of his appointment as the duke's portrait artist.

But that's exactly what his relationship with her was, and Juliana chided herself for hoping it was more—*personal*. Which had been the word Lord Felix used. How could she blame Victor for being truthful?

There had to be someone else. Someone more appealing who wouldn't turn his nose up at the common born half-sister of a duke.

Or perhaps she should return to the country and find a nice farmer's son?

She worried about it the entire day, and at supper that evening, stirred her soup aimlessly.

"What is it, Juliana?" Concern furrowed Honoria's brow.

"Should I accept Lord Felix's offer to court me to help repair my reputation?"

Drake's spoon splashed the soup as it fell into the bowl, and a footman rushed forward to blot the liquid from the tablecloth. "I can't believe you're even considering it. Absolutely not. Not after what Simon told me." He lowered his voice and leaned forward. "He struck Lady Charlotte."

"And yet he speaks as if he's a victim," Mother said, shaking her head. "I don't understand men like that."

"But Lord Felix has a point, Mother. How many men have come to call? It's useless trying to be accepted in society, Drake."

Drake and Honoria exchanged a glance, and the hair on the back of Juliana's neck tingled.

"What about Victor?" Honoria asked.

As much as Juliana loved her sister-in-law and admired Honoria's keen sense of observation, it was a different matter altogether when that observation was directed at Juliana. Had her attraction to Victor been that transparent?

"He's only here to paint our portraits. He said so himself. Didn't he, Mother?"

"Well, he didn't say *only*, but yes. I suppose so. But dearest, Mr. Pratt seemed concerned about Lord Felix's interest. Perhaps Honoria has a point, and you *will* be spending some time with him. He seems a very amiable young man." Her mother smiled as she peered down at her soup. "And handsome."

Drake snorted a laugh. "You women. All you think about is appearance. What Juliana needs is a husband who is honest and stable. Someone who will provide for her. One who won't go visiting mistresses."

"Drake!" Mother said.

As if men didn't go on endlessly about a woman's appearance, chasing after the prettiest flirt even if she didn't have a brain in her head. Juliana had witnessed it firsthand among both commoners and the aristocracy. Many a young man's fancy waned the moment she outrode him in a race or bested him in a game of chess. Granted, they were both skills she learned from men, chess from her father and riding from Drake.

So perhaps it wasn't a woman's appearance, but a man's fragile pride that was the issue.

Naturally, there were exceptions. Drake and Honoria, for one. Mutual respect and common interests created a bond between them that had survived years of separation and protests from Honoria's father. Mother and Father were another, and because Mother had always been the intelligent, thoughtful woman she was, Juliana supposed Drake's father had also appreciated Mother for more than her beauty.

Considering further, Juliana admitted she *may* have been too harsh in her judgment, and that how a man viewed women depended on the man himself rather than on the nature of his sex as a whole.

And if that *was* the case, could Victor Pratt be the type of man to give a common-born half-sister of a duke more than a passing glance?

She dearly hoped so.

CHAPTER 9

At the desk in his bachelor apartments, Victor worked diligently, filling out the details of the sketches he had started at the duke's the day before. True, the initial lines were little more than an outline to capture the overall shape of Juliana's face, but Davies's remark that the sketches were *rudimentary* had galled. The man obviously had no understanding of the drawing process. And —Victor assured himself—if Davies had paid the least bit of attention, he would have noticed the detail with which Victor had captured the expression in Juliana's eyes.

He sat back, assessing his work. Many attributed the quote, *The eyes are windows to the soul* to Shakespeare, and although Victor appreciated the man's wit and skill with the pen, he was more likely to believe it had been Da Vinci who had coined the phrase and Shakespeare had merely adopted it, recognizing its truth and beauty.

Because they were the words of an artist.

Regardless of the phrase's origin, Victor acknowledged the truth it held. Eyes brought a portrait to life and provided the viewer a glimpse into who the subject was.

Worry slithered in as he examined the fleshed-out drawings, and he reached inside the desk drawer and removed the sketches he'd made of Adalyn, comparing them to those of Juliana.

Had he inadvertently given Juliana Adalyn's nose or the way her lips parted as if pulling in a breath filled with wonder? Drawn from memory, the image of Adalyn gazed back at him. Gauzy material draped around her shoulders, dipping down seductively and revealing a little more cleavage than was decent.

He had added that detail strictly from his imagination, never having seen Adalyn in anything other than modest attire. Although there had been that gown with the enticing décolletage she'd worn the night she rejected him.

Oh, why did he have to think about that horrible night when the world crashed down on him? The pity in her eyes as he tried to make his proposal crushed his heart anew. How could he have been so blind? Again, he chastised himself for misinterpreting her politeness for interest.

Not expecting company and asking his valet not to disturb him, Victor startled at the knock on the door. "Yes?"

Tierney, who also served as Victor's butler, opened the door. "Apologies, sir, but your mother and Miss Whyte insist on seeing you."

"Out of my way, Tierney." Victor's mother pushed the poor man aside, striding in as if she paid the rents. Lydia followed behind her, the cat-that-got-into-the-cream expression on her face triggering alarms in Victor's head.

He quickly shuffled the drawings under his sketchpad and rose. "Why are you here, Mother?" His alarm grew at his mother's somber expression. Had something happened to his father? And was Lydia's smug expression from the belief she could leg-shackle Victor and become the next viscountess?

"Is Father well?" Victor choked out the words, fearful of his mother's answer.

She blinked. "Your father?" She batted a dismissive hand. "How should I know? He hides from me in his study when he's not at Lords or at White's. I only see him when you or Priscilla call."

No wonder. He couldn't blame his father one bit. Mother was

fortunate Father allowed her to return to London from her exile in Lincolnshire.

"No. I'm concerned about you, my dear. Miss Whyte and I have come to pull you away from this dreary place." She gazed around at his tidy studio, *tsk-tsking* and running a gloved finger over a perfectly clean table. His rooms weren't palatial, but they gave him the space he needed to breathe.

"I'm busy, Mother. I have an appointment this afternoon with the duke, and I must prepare."

"Which duke?" Speaking of windows to the soul, the gleam in Lydia's eyes became predatory.

"Burwood. I was awarded the position as their portraitist. I'm beginning with his sister, Miss Merrick." He placed a hand over the sketchpad, sliding it to more adequately cover the sketches.

Lydia's gaze followed his movement, while his mother gave an exaggerated sigh and said, "Why a duke needs a portrait of a commoner is a mystery."

"Miss Merrick is Burwood's sister, and she is a lovely young lady."

Fear flashed in his mother's eyes. "Half-sister, Victor. *Her* father, unlike the duke's, was a commoner. You would do well to remember that."

With an emphasized sway to her hips, Lydia glided up to him, reminding him of a viper he'd seen once in Italy. She laid a gloved hand on his arm and batted her eyes. At least she didn't wield that damned fan. "Don't fuss with your mother, Victor. Come, let's go to Gunter's for ices. You have plenty of time to get to your appointment with the duke."

Using his thumb and a forefinger, Victor removed Lydia's hand from his person. "No. What don't you understand about the fact that I still have work to do to prepare? I have no time for ices at Gunter's." Unless it was to take Miss Merrick there.

Where had that thought come from?

Lydia pouted, no doubt hoping to persuade him with either attraction or pity.

Ha!

His mother gave an unnatural sneeze and then held a handkerchief to her nose. "When was the last time your maid of all work dusted? It's a disgrace! Allow me to go speak with her at once."

Icy fingers trailed down Victor's spine as his mother moved toward the door. She planned to leave him alone with Lydia!

"Oh, no you don't." Victor followed her out and closed the door behind him. "What is your game, Mother? If you plan to compromise me with Lydia because *she* is your choice for my wife, think again. And I would hope you learned your lesson with Cilla. Do you wish to go back to Lincolnshire and the sheep? Because one word to Father from me and—"

"Cease, Victor!" She huffed another sigh. "I only wish to give you a little nudge in the right direction."

"If, in your opinion, that direction is toward Lydia Whyte, I urge you to reconsider."

An idea, at first no more than a ball of shapeless clay, but punched, pulled, and sculpted by the events of the last few days, took shape. The simplicity of it addressed several concerns at once. With an impetuosity he hadn't felt since meeting Adalyn, Victor said, "In fact, I plan to court Miss Merrick."

"No." The strangled whisper would have been comical had it not been for his mother's alarming appearance as she uttered it. Her skin paled, and she held her handkerchief to her bosom. For a moment, Victor worried he would have to send Tierney to fetch a physician.

He grabbed her arm. "Mother? Do you need to sit?" Opening the door, he led her back into the room. His gaze swung to Lydia standing by his desk and staring out the window. Odd. The view from that particular window was of the neighboring building's brick wall. When she turned toward them, her sickeningly sweet smile set his nerves on edge. He darted a glance to his sketchpad, the tension coiled in his chest easing to find the drawings still resting beneath.

After depositing his mother on the small settee, he poured a splash of brandy into a crystal glass, then handed it to his mother. "I'm sorry. I don't have any sherry."

She pushed it aside. "You *know* I don't drink strong spirits." Her gaze drifted to Lydia, and her brow furrowed.

Victor followed his mother's line of sight, searching Lydia's oddly satisfied expression for what had caused his mother's additional distress.

"Lady Cartwright." Lydia moved from her position at the window to his mother's side. "We've obviously come at an inopportune time. Let's not bother Victor any longer. Why don't we go to Gunter's without him and enjoy a nice cup of tea instead of ices?"

Mother's brow furrowed more deeply, but she nodded and rose. "Very well. Victor, you and I shall discuss your decision later."

Eager to be rid of them, Victor bussed his mother on the cheek. Opening the door wide, he motioned them out. "Enjoy your tea, ladies."

When he closed the door behind them, he pressed his back against it, not entirely relieved. Lydia was up to something; he was sure of it.

His gaze darted back to his desk, and in six long strides, he stood before it. He stared down at the sketchpad completely covering the drawings, unease niggling in his chest. Hadn't a corner of the paper peeked out before? He lifted the sketchpad, trying to remember if it had obscured the sketches completely when he'd repositioned it.

A quick check ensured all the drawings remained, with Adalyn's still on top of those of Juliana.

His body dropped to his chair, and his impetuous announcement to his mother forced concern over the sketches from his mind.

What had he done?

In truth, he hadn't *done* anything.

Yet.

He'd simply said he *planned* to court Miss Merrick.

But the idea was neither without merit nor unappealing. She needed a respectable suitor. At least one better than that cad Lord Felix Davies. And Victor admitted he liked her very much. Spending time in her company would be no hardship whatsoever, and it would fall naturally in place while he painted her portrait.

However, one con niggled at his mind. Would it be fair to Juliana? He had no desire to hurt her.

The clock on the mantle chimed quarter to one. No time to ponder it further, he scooped up the finished sketches—sans the ones of Adalyn—and placed them in his satchel.

He would present them to Burwood, along with his request to court the duke's sister.

And prayed he wasn't making a huge mistake.

❧

Miss Price offered suggestions while Juliana debated over which gown to wear when Victor called. "The pale-rose muslin complements your complexion, miss. Although the blue brings out your eyes."

Juliana had caught a glimpse of the sketches Victor made the day before. Even if most of the sketch was a mere outline, he had captured her eyes in great detail. "The blue, then." She would play to what she hoped was her advantage.

Hardly able to eat at breakfast, Juliana wrung her hands in her lap as Miss Price arranged Juliana's hair in a becoming style. Her stomach fluttered and flipped in anticipation of spending more time with Victor.

Her logical mind reminded her it was only for a portrait, but her heart argued back that Victor *had* danced with her during her disastrous come-out ball. Hope clung desperately to a thin thread between the two. Perhaps spending more time together would allow Victor to come to know her . . . like her . . . maybe love her.

She sighed. Hope was such a fragile thing, more delicate than gossamer waiting to be blown to pieces by the first strong wind.

Once dressed, she tried in vain to occupy her mind before Victor's arrival, eventually wandering into Drake's vast library. Not nearly as large as the one at Hartridge House in Dorset, the room still occupied one quarter of the second floor with floor-to-ceiling shelves of books.

Peace settled over Juliana, the aroma of fine leather of the books' bindings reminding her of saddles and riding. Might that be a reason both Drake and Juliana loved books as well? Murmurs from a far corner of the room drew her attention, and she blushed at the sight of Drake and Honoria in an embrace.

She backed up, hoping to make a hasty exit and accidentally knocked into a table, sending a vase to the floor and the couple splitting apart.

Drake turned, and he gave her a sheepish grin. "Juliana. We didn't see you there."

An errant lock of his hair stood at attention, and Honoria reached up to smooth it down.

A smile tugged at Juliana's lips. Catching her brother and Honoria stealing a kiss had become a common sight both in their London residence and Drake's country seat. "Obviously. I've come for a book as I understood that's what libraries were for, but it appears they may also be useful for other pursuits."

Drake chuckled. Her brother had become bolder since becoming a duke, and he was clearly proud of his amorous advances toward his wife.

However, even the shadows couldn't conceal the blush rising to Honoria's cheeks. "Allow me to select something for you."

The tangy scent of orange wafted in Juliana's direction as Honoria breezed past, examining the books. "Ah. I think this one." She plucked one off the shelf and handed it to Juliana.

Sense And Sensibility. Juliana pursed her lips. "What's it about?"

"Two sisters whose dastardly half-brother has left them and their mother nearly penniless upon their mutual father's death."

Juliana's gaze shot to Drake. "That sounds dreadful. Too bad they didn't have you for a brother."

Honoria's lovesick expression as she gazed at Drake gave Juliana pause. "Something tells me this is a romantic tale."

"Read it and find out." Mischief glimmered in Honoria's eyes.

Book in hand, Juliana left Honoria and Drake, closing the door behind her to give them privacy to continue their amorous activity. She settled into a comfortable chair in her room and began to read, quickly captivated by the story and the sisters. Although she liked them both, Juliana found them to be quite different and gravitated more toward Elinor's clear thinking and contained emotions. She turned the book over, considering the title.

"Ah," she said aloud. Elinor was the *sense* while Marianne was all emotion and *sensibility*. "Clever," Juliana whispered.

Immersed in the story, Juliana startled when the clock chimed half-past one. Wasn't Victor supposed to call at one? She set the book aside, mentally ticking off the number of things that might have delayed Victor's arrival.

Was he injured? Ill? Did something of greater importance pull him away?

Had he arrived and no one had alerted her? It seemed unlikely.

After one last look in the mirror to check her hair, Juliana proceeded downstairs toward the drawing room. The door to Drake's study opened, and he and Victor stepped out. Upon seeing her, the men exchanged a look. Tiny hairs on the back of Juliana's neck tingled. Something had transpired between her brother and Victor. But what?

Drake's tight smile only added to her concern. "Juliana. Good. I was going to send Frampton for you. Mr. Pratt, if you would kindly go to the drawing room to set up, I'd like a word with my sister regarding what we discussed."

What was going on? Had Drake changed his mind about commissioning Victor for their portraits? No. Drake had told Victor to set up. Something else troubled her brother. Juliana's attention jerked toward Victor, whose smile seemed warmer than her brother's, thank goodness.

"Miss Merrick." Victor bowed and left.

"Juliana, come inside."

Her attention fixed on Victor's retreating back, Juliana startled at Drake's words. She followed him in and took a seat in front of his desk. "Is something wrong? What was Victor doing in here with you?"

Drake fell back against his chair, emitting an audible sigh. He suddenly looked older than his thirty years, as if a weight too heavy to be borne had been placed upon his shoulders. "Mr. Pratt has requested my permission to court you."

She blinked, giving her head a tiny shake to clear it. "What?" She choked out the question, unsure she'd heard him correctly. Why didn't Drake look pleased?

"To be a suitor, Juliana. To call upon you in more than the capacity of an artist."

"What did you say?" Joy should have galloped in her heart over Drake's announcement. However, his solemn expression bridled it in. She held her breath, caution keeping tight rein on her hopes.

"I gave it."

She frowned, jerking her head to clear it once more.

He held up a hand. "On the condition of your approval."

His answer did nothing to clear her confusion. Clearly, Drake knew she liked Victor. "Why wouldn't I approve?"

Drake lowered his gaze to some papers on his desk, fingering them aimlessly. "You should have a say in your suitors. I wouldn't want to foist anyone unacceptable on you."

"You're withholding something. Don't you like Victor? Do you not think he's suitable?"

The man with a dukedom thrust upon him disappeared, and the brother she dearly loved reemerged. "I like him very much, Juliana. And, as heir to a viscountcy, he's more than suitable. But my greatest wish is for you to be as happy as Honoria and I are. To find a man who loves you above all else."

Oh. What Drake spoke of was the same dream Juliana bore in her heart. To be loved. Cherished. "And you don't think Victor is that man?" Therein lay the heart of the matter. She stifled the derisive chuckle at her horrible pun.

Drake's serious amber eyes locked with hers. "I don't know. The answer is as honest as I can give you. Time will tell. He's a good man, and he expressed desire to . . ." Drake became distant, as if searching for the right words.

"Yes?" Even to her own ears, the word sounded pitifully close to begging.

"I believe he holds genuine affection for you."

Genuine affection? "What aren't you saying?"

For a moment, he hesitated, then waved it off. "Nothing. I'm simply tired. Kitty kept us awake all night again. I think Honoria has finally agreed to allow the nurse to perform the duties we pay her for." He smiled weakly. "Now, go. Victor and I also discussed two ideas for your portrait, and he's eager to begin. I told him I'd also leave that up to you, although I did make my preference known."

She rose, and Drake stopped her as if finally remembering why he called her into his study in the first place.

"Juliana. Victor requested to speak with you privately regarding his request. I will give you ten minutes alone with him in the drawing room before Mother arrives."

Still believing Drake held something important back, Juliana pondered why Victor wished to speak with her privately. Could it be a declaration of love? Surely not. They hardly knew each other, even though Juliana's affections raced dangerously close toward that precipice. Was it worth risking her heart to have Victor court her? To free-fall head-first in love with Victor Pratt if he didn't return her love? Was genuine affection enough, and more importantly, could she accept it might be all Victor offered?

As the saying went: *nothing ventured, nothing gained.*

"Not to worry, brother. We shall remain the required six feet apart."

Drake's tight-lipped smile returned, and he nodded.

On her way out, Juliana closed the door behind her, praying that she wasn't making a huge mistake.

CHAPTER 10

In the duke's drawing room, Victor placed the blank canvas on the easel and laid out his tools: pencils shaved to a fine point, his palette, some paint, and brushes, his mind circling the conversation with the duke. The man's sharp mind had surely noticed the omission in Victor's explanation, but the success of his proposal hinged upon certain particulars being kept between himself and Juliana alone. He only had to convince her.

She could flatly refuse him.

Rustle of skirts and the sensual scent of jasmine mixed with ginger—surprising for ladies of society—announced Juliana's arrival.

As he turned to greet her, the smile tugging his lips spread naturally upon seeing her. She looked lovely and fresh in her pale-blue muslin. Both wariness and interest shone in her face.

"Miss Merrick." He bowed. "I trust your brother has relayed my request?"

"He has. But he said you wished to speak with me privately." She glanced at the clock on the mantle. "We have ten minutes before my mother arrives."

Victor cleared his throat. "Miss Merrick—Juliana. I believe a courtship between us would be most advantageous."

Her brow furrowed. "Advantageous?"

The argument he'd rehearsed on his ride to the duke's that afternoon suddenly sounded cold and calculating. Not the words a lady wished to hear when a gentleman requested to court her. Yet, he had no desire to lead Juliana astray. He needed to be upfront and honest.

"After Lord Felix announced his intention to court you in order to repair your standing in society, I began to see the wisdom in his words." He held up a hand at Juliana's widened eyes. "Hear me out, please. As much as I dislike Davies, the idea he proposed does have merit. However, Lord Felix is not the best man for the task. I don't trust him."

"And you are? The best man, that is?" The vulnerability in her voice gave Victor pause.

He questioned his approach again. He'd hoped being honest would reduce the chances of the one possible drawback in his plan —hurting her. And yet, it appeared he'd done just that. *Damn.* If only they had more time before her mother would arrive. "I wouldn't say I'm the best man, but I do believe I'm a better choice than Davies."

She moved in slow motion toward the settee, her body falling against the soft cushions, her eyes growing unfocused. "So, this is not to be a true courtship. Not because you have—affection for me?"

Her pained expression made his stomach knot. Oh, he had botched things up. He sat beside her and took her hand, wishing he could call back his clumsy words and start over. "I like you very much, Miss Merrick—Juliana. You deserve to be treated with respect and accepted by the *ton*, and I believe I can help accomplish that. In their eyes, it would be a true courtship, and although I may not be your choice of a suitor, I am respected." *At least more than Davies.*

Her lovely blue eyes became alert and snapped to his. "Does my brother know?"

Victor shook his head. "But he might suspect something is amiss. He asked about my feelings toward you. The way he studied my face, he clearly expected to see . . . ." Victor failed to manage the word.

Juliana squeezed his hand, as if comforting him when he should have been comforting her. "I understand, Victor. However, I must ask. Are you doing this solely as a kindness toward me, or do you hope to gain something from our pretend association as well?"

At Juliana's keen perception, his shallow proposal gained depth, becoming weightier and teasing a promise of something much more than a pretense. He would enjoy spending time with Juliana's sharp mind and kind heart. Might their association turn into something more lasting?

But reading more into his attachment with Adalyn had been his downfall. He had no desire to do that to Juliana nor tread that path again himself.

"Very astute, Juliana. It's only fair I be completely honest with you. My mother has been pressing me to court Miss Lydia Whyte. I have called on Miss Whyte in the past, and no doubt both she and my mother expected an understanding to have developed between us. But Miss Whyte is not supportive of my passion for art. For that and many other reasons, we simply do not suit. I want to concentrate on my painting, on the great privilege your brother has bestowed on me to craft your family's portraits. Courting you would allow me that freedom and, at the same time, assure my mother I am actively seeking a bride."

As honest as he wanted to be, he had no intention of telling Juliana that defying his mother played a considerable part in his choice to court her specifically.

He darted a glance toward the clock on the mantle. Two more minutes at best remained before Juliana's mother arrived.

Juliana cast her gaze to their clasped hands, her brow wrinkling as the edges of her teeth caught the plush curve of her bottom lip.

He needed to give her more. To soften the cold, businesslike proposal. "As I said, I like you very much. And who is to say that as we become better acquainted, a true affection between us will not form? Is it not worth trying?"

Blue eyes locked with his, and his heart lurched at the hope within them. "Very well. I agree."

He prayed again he wasn't making a mistake. He had no desire to hurt the lovely young woman before him. One broken heart between them was one too many. With time running out, he explained how they must present themselves to be believable. "And above all else, we must appear to be a couple enamored with each other."

All things considered, he should have pulled away when Mrs. Merrick entered the room and caught Juliana's hands entwined in his, but instead he smiled up at Juliana's mother, no doubt looking like a small boy who had been caught pilfering biscuits from the kitchen.

The ruse was underway.

FOR THE THIRD TIME SINCE VICTOR'S ODD PROPOSAL, JULIANA TRIED to ignore the aching of her bruised heart and concentrate on his question at hand.

And for the third time, she failed miserably. "I apologize again. What did you ask?"

"Which do you prefer?" Standing before her, he held the sketches up again. One, a traditional pose, showed her seated demurely on a sofa, hands folded in her lap, expression serious—and somehow sad. Elegant and sophisticated, the image matched that of the portraits lining the walls of both Pendrake Manor in London and Hartridge House in Dorset.

In the other, she stood next to a horse, one hand holding the bridle while the other stroked the horse's muzzle. The corners of Juliana's mouth in that sketch curled up, and her eyes held a wistful quality, as if dreaming of a great adventure.

Seated beside her, her mother sighed, reached over, and traced a finger over the smiling Juliana.

Juliana lifted her gaze to Victor's. "Is this a trick question?"

His own lips tipped in a smile, not dissimilar to hers in the sketch. "Not at all. They are simply two different approaches. One formal, one informal. We could also do something of a compromise if you find these too—"

"This one!" She pointed to the sketch with the horse. "The other doesn't even look like me." Her gaze jerked toward Victor, hoping she hadn't offended him. "I mean, it does. You're an exemplary artist, but—"

He laughed. The rich, warm sound soothed her nerves. "I understand what you meant."

Mother continued to stare at the sketch. "It's as if you captured her spirit on paper, Mr. Pratt."

"A high compliment, Mrs. Merrick. I also asked for His Grace's opinion."

The idea of Victor courting her—real or not—had overshadowed the fact that he was also there to perform a task. "Drake mentioned he had a preference, but he didn't tell me which."

"I'm pleased to report his preference aligns with yours, Miss Merrick." Her stomach flipped at the genuine smile Victor gave her. "And mine. I'd hoped you would both choose something a little more avant-garde. However, I did wish to give you the option of choosing something—"

"Boring?" The word popped out. Heat rising to her cheeks, Juliana held a hand over her mouth.

Victor's soft chuckle brushed like a caress against her skin. He had the most sensual voice. "I was going to say classic, but I think your description is much more apt." He placed the sketches down. "However, if we are to include your horse in the portrait, I doubt the drawing room will be the best place for us to begin. I know a spot not far from here, quieter and less crowded than Hyde or St. James Park. My equipment is easy enough to transport on horseback. We could ride there together."

Juliana shot a concerned look toward her mother. "Is the location easily traversed by carriage? Mama doesn't enjoy riding."

Victor's head swiveled toward her mother. "Of course, as your chaperone. Forgive me. I shouldn't have presumed you rode, Mrs. Merrick."

"An honest assumption, sir. Juliana's father taught my son to ride, and Drake took to it as if he'd been born on horseback."

"As has Juliana." The admiration shining in Victor's eyes when he turned toward her warmed Juliana's heart.

A knowing smile graced her mother's lips. "My son informed me, Mr. Pratt, that you have requested to court Juliana. From what I witnessed when I entered, she has agreed. If you can promise to maintain proper decorum, perhaps a footman might suffice as chaperone?"

"You have my word, madam, that nothing untoward will transpire between your daughter and me."

Juliana had no doubt of the truth of Victor's promise. After all, he had no true romantic feelings for her. She recalled his words. *I like you very much.* At best, they were merely friends.

Her mother gave a firm nod. "Good. I'll have Cook pack a light refreshment as well. Juliana, why don't you change into your riding habit while Mr. Pratt packs his equipment? Did you ride here, sir?"

Slight color rose to Victor's face, and Juliana found it quite attractive. "I confess I did. I'd hoped Miss Merrick would choose the more informal pose. So . . ."

Mother wagged a finger at Victor. "Ah. Perhaps I shouldn't allow you two to be unaccompanied except for a footman. You seem prepared to take advantage when the opportunity arises."

Juliana's face heated, no doubt becoming pinker than Victor's. "Mother. He meant coming on horseback."

"Hmm," Mama murmured. "Nevertheless, I shall instruct the groom to saddle your horse and secure a footman to accompany you. Juliana, run along and change. I want a brief word with Mr. Pratt."

Under other circumstances, Juliana would have vibrated with excitement at the prospect of being alone with Victor. Drake's servants exemplified discretion. Simon had vetted them all personally, checking every reference down to the last detail.

So *if* Victor desired to steal a kiss, she could convince a footman to turn a blind eye. Anything more than a kiss would be reported to Drake or Mother, but a kiss—that would remain between her and Victor.

Alas, Victor would not attempt such advances, and any sign of affection would be for the benefit of an audience, not a genuine expression between them as a couple.

Instead of excitement, a niggle of worry crept into her mind as she returned to her room to change into her riding habit. What did her mother wish to speak to Victor about? Had she detected any falsehood in his intentions? Had Drake expressed his concerns? Victor said Drake might suspect something.

Pushing it from her mind, she changed into her riding habit and returned downstairs. Victor waited for her in the entry. He'd already fastened his easel to the side of his saddle and had his satchel with his canvas and supplies draped across his body. The footman her mother had requisitioned as chaperone had a basket with the refreshments attached to his mount.

"It's not far," Victor said, riding next to her and leading them through the busy London streets toward the outskirts of the city. His gaze traveled over her. "Blue is a most becoming color on you. Another advantage of choosing the informal pose. That particular hue of your riding habit brings out the touch of violet in your eyes. If you had chosen the more traditional pose, I would have asked if you had a formal gown in that shade."

Juliana felt her own blue eyes paled in comparison with Victor's, whose sparkled like sunlight on a pool of clear water, with a hint of turquoise whereas hers seemed dulled as if darkened by clouds. "What made you want to become an artist?"

She asked not only to learn about Victor but thought it an easy question to initiate conversation between them.

Yet Victor stared ahead, his expression serious, and she shifted uncomfortably in her saddle.

"I'm sorry. I didn't mean to pry."

When he turned toward her, his smile did not meet those incredible blue eyes. "Nonsense. We should get to understand each other. Understanding each other will ensure our relationship is believable." He sighed. "However, my reason may sound ridiculous."

Nothing that mattered to him would sound ridiculous to her. "You can trust me, Victor."

Time stretched between them. The horses slowed their pace, the gentle breeze brushing against their skin stilled, and even the birds in the copse of trees ahead halted their song. The weight—the importance—of Victor's answer dangled in the silence, and Juliana held her breath in anticipation.

His eyes locked with hers, and her heart fluttered at what she saw in them. "Yes. I believe I can. The easy answer would be that I love art, the process of creating something from nothing. And that would be true—but only the partial truth." He smiled at her. "You are so untouched by the *ton*, Juliana—free from the artifice common among people of my station. Perhaps that's why I like you so much. Many people born into the aristocracy lack purpose. Men languish away their days at their clubs, women their social circles, balls, routs, and garden parties. Their lives are those of idleness and often indulgence."

"I would argue not all people of the aristocracy are so indolent. What of the Duke of Ashton and his clinic?" Drake also came to mind, but she didn't want Victor to think she perceived his words as a personal attack against her family.

"Ah, you are correct to take me to task with my statement. There are exceptions, including your brother and his duchess. But Ashton spent time in America, and your brother did not grow up under the strict scrutiny of the *ton*. But let us hope they will inspire others to follow their example. They are swaying my own father to fight for reform in Lords."

"I'm sorry I interrupted. Please continue."

His expression, although not quite indulgent, conveyed his patience. "When I was young, I would stare at the portraits of my forefathers for hours, wondering who they were and what they had accomplished. Other than a few who had effected changes in the law—which I might add were often for their own benefit rather than the good of all humanity—I only knew them as the first Lord Cartwright, or the second, and so on. Their only legacies were leaving sons to inherit the title upon their deaths. And although I have been reared to follow in their footsteps and sire a son to follow me, I wonder if that is all I am destined for. When I die, will my life even have mattered?"

The pain in his eyes lanced her heart, and she wanted to pull him into her arms and comfort him. Her words would have to suffice. "Of course it will."

The wan smile he gave her conveyed his doubts. "This is why your brother's faith in me is so important. I want to leave something tangible behind that lasts after I die. To use color and texture to evoke thought, emotion. Something people will gaze at years later and say, 'Look how Victor Pratt captured the light in Miss Merrick's eyes, the playfulness of her smile.' I want to be remembered. To have mattered. And that is why I wanted to become an artist."

He laughed, the sound forced and brittle. "I told you it was ridiculous. But thank goodness, we've arrived at our destination."

Contrary to Victor's assertion, Juliana found his answer leagues from ridiculous, and the fact that he trusted her enough to share it gave her heart hope.

CHAPTER 11

At their destination, Victor busied himself setting up his easel, canvas, and paints while Juliana watched. His thoughts flitted like dancing shadows between worry and trust over his confession. Was he wrong to trust her, to expose his heart so fully? Adalyn had been the only other person he'd ever shared his dreams with. And that had ended badly.

It wasn't that Adalyn had laughed at him. In fact, when he'd bared his soul to her about wanting to have his life mean something, she understood completely. Medicine and saving lives being her own admirable ambition.

Victor believed they had connected on a deep level—had a future together. How wrong he had been.

But what of Juliana now that he had bared that part of his soul to her? Had he been wrong again? He hadn't lied when he said he believed he could trust her. Maybe it was because he wanted to trust her—needed to trust her—to trust *someone*. The pressure from his mother to force him into a marriage to Lydia magnified his need to break free and carve his own path.

He didn't want to be like everyone else.

Who better to help him than a duke—and a duke's sister?

Determined to prove his worth with the portrait of Juliana, he placed his hands on his hips and assessed the area, taking special note of how the light filtered in through the trees. "Over here, I think." After positioning the horse, he instructed Juliana to stand at the horse's head. "If you would remove your gloves and bonnet. You have lovely hands, and I want to capture how the light reflects off your hair."

Color rose to Juliana's cheeks, and Victor hoped to capture that as well.

"Do you ever paint from your sketches?" Juliana asked, handing her bonnet to the footman.

"At times. But having the subject before me results in a far superior depiction. For example, here, in addition to the light on your hair, I can see your blush, the exact color and shading on your face."

"Oh!" She raised her hands to her cheeks.

Mixing some paints, he smiled to himself. "Don't be embarrassed. It's lovely. I want to paint you that way." When he returned his attention to her, he tilted his head, studying her and placing an index finger against his lips.

Her gaze dipped toward the action.

Victor wasn't conceited, but he was honest, and he knew ladies considered him handsome. Juliana was attracted to him, which would make their ruse all the more believable. But he'd have to tread lightly; he had no intention of hurting her.

"How should I . . .?" She lifted her hand toward the horse's muzzle.

He stepped forward, palms up. "With your permission, allow me to position you."

After she gave a nod, Victor placed her right hand flat on Sunshine's neck. "To soothe and assure her all is well." The sensation from the warmth of her skin caught him off-guard. How had he not noticed it when he'd danced with her months ago? Had he imagined it? Next, he took her left hand in his, placing it on Sunshine's muzzle, and the same frisson of excitement spread up his arm.

With the positioning of her hands and arms, Juliana's body had angled toward the horse and away from him. He stepped back and assessed her, steadier on the outside than he felt. "Hmm. Can you turn your shoulders toward me?"

"Like this?" Juliana adjusted herself.

"Meglio—better. Just one more thing." Prepared for that same surge of energy, and as gently as he could, Victor took her face in both his hands and turned it forward. Their eyes locked, and Victor's breath hitched. So much for preparing himself. His gaze dipped, fascinated with her seductively parted rosebud mouth.

The pink tip of her tongue poked out, wetting her lips.

Victor suppressed a groan and forced his attention away from her alluring, very kissable mouth and back to her eyes.

Which turned out to be no safer choice than her lips. Her gaze softened, growing unfocused, and as her pupils enlarged, her irises became mere rims of dusky cornflower blue.

Not precisely the expression he *should* capture in her portrait, but one Victor privately burned in his memory. He hadn't had such attraction to a woman since Adalyn. Was it because of Juliana's likeness to the woman who broke his heart?

Regardless, Victor gave a little cough and tore his hands from the softness of Juliana's face, pulling himself back to what mattered most—painting her portrait. "Perfetta—perfect. Hold as still as possible," he whispered and returned to the safety of his canvas and paints.

With his focus back on the task at hand, his mind cleared, and the troublesome—and confusing—emotions retreated. While Victor sketched her rough outline on the canvas, Juliana held perfectly still. Only her eyes moved, her gaze darting away each time he met hers directly. The horse, on the other hand, was a different matter. Juliana did her best to keep the mare still as Sunshine tossed her head and shuffled against the ground.

More to himself than aloud, Victor muttered, "Perhaps including your horse wasn't such a brilliant idea after all."

"Oh, it *was* brilliant, Victor. Sunshine is being difficult. She is a bit headstrong."

Victor did his best to take advantage of the times Sunshine held still, quickly outlining Sunshine's position and as many of the horse's features that he could. Satisfied, he picked up his palette and dabbed his brush into the paint. He'd always found the first touch of brush to canvas exciting, as if a whole undiscovered world awaited him on the white linen surface, and soon he was lost in his art.

A snore sounded behind him, and Victor spun around. Seated on the ground, the footman leaned against a tree, his eyes drooping and his head bobbing, jerking him back awake before he nodded off again.

Victor had forgotten about him entirely. He pulled out his pocket watch, surprised that over an hour and a half had passed. "Shall we stop for a while and have some refreshment?"

Juliana smiled, then whispered, "Should we disturb him or serve ourselves?"

Victor laughed. "He might be offended if we don't allow him to do his job."

The footman startled awake with a snort and rubbed his eyes.

Victor turned toward the drowsy man. "We're ready for refreshment."

The servant hopped to his feet, quickly retrieving the basket, laying out a blanket, plates of food, and a bottle of wine.

Victor poured Juliana a glass of wine, careful to avoid spilling it as he handed it to her.

"Thank goodness it is white wine, Victor."

He laughed at the reference to her disastrous come-out, and nodding, took a sip from his own glass.

The cook had prepared little sandwiches, along with some cheese, bread, and fruit. Victor picked up a slice of orange. "I remember your brother's orangery at his estate in Dorset. Does he transport the oranges from there?"

Juliana shook her head. "There is a smaller orangery at the back of Drake's house here in London, which is fortuitous because if it didn't already exist, I'm sure he would have had one built. The orangery—especially the one on Drake's estate—holds special significance for him and Honoria. I discovered them there once."

She cast her gaze down to the sandwich on her plate, a shy smile breaking across her lips. And from the blush rising to her cheeks, Victor surmised Juliana caught her brother and his wife in an embrace.

An errant thought popped into his mind. Was it wrong that he wanted to steal a kiss from Juliana as they hid among the foliage? "Perhaps you would show it to me when Their Graces aren't—um —using it?"

Her deepened blush indicated he'd not only surmised correctly about Drake and Honoria but also that she understood his desire to imitate the duke and duchess. His pretend courtship with Juliana might prove enjoyable for both of them.

The footman, now fully awake, stood at attention, and Juliana raised her gaze toward him. "I've been so thoughtless," she muttered. "Tobias, would you care for some refreshment?" She lifted the plate of sandwiches.

Eyes widening, the footman—Tobias—stared at Juliana in confusion.

As Juliana offered the plate with an outstretched hand, Victor lightly touched her wrist and shook his head, keeping his voice low. "Although I find your consideration most admirable, servants do not eat with us. It's simply not done."

Tobias's gaze darted from the sandwiches to Juliana, to Victor, then back to the sandwiches. "No. But I thank you, miss."

But the man had been away from the house as long as they had, and the eagerness at which he looked at the sandwiches said otherwise. Victor expected to hear the man's stomach rumble. "When have you last eaten, Tobias?"

"I had a hearty breakfast, sir. His Grace treats us very well."

The man hadn't eaten since he'd broken his fast that morning? Not to mention servants rose well before the masters of the household. He had to be hungry.

Although Victor had been born into the aristocracy, Juliana was the one who exhibited nobility through her actions.

Face flushed, Juliana's head bowed.

Shame, thick and black, coiled around his heart that he had made *her* feel ashamed. For what? Being kind? Caring for others?

Damn the rules of society. He leaned closer, and placing a finger under her chin, lifted it until her eyes met his. "Forgive me. I only meant to guide you to ease your entry into society. There are proper rules of etiquette I urge you to follow when you're among those in the *ton*. But since it's only the three of us, let us make an exception. It will be our secret."

Tears had formed in her eyes, and she blinked them back. "Truly?"

"Yes. Allow me to handle this." Victor took the plate of sandwiches from Juliana and turned toward Tobias. "I insist, sir. Come, make yourself a plate. You can retire over there, and we shall help ourselves, only calling you if necessary." Victor pointed at the tree Tobias had claimed as a resting spot earlier.

Warmth spread through Victor's chest at the man's surprised—but appreciative—smile. But Tobias's gratitude didn't affect him as much as what he witnessed on Juliana's face. Admiration? Trust? Whatever it was, it shifted something inside him, like sunlight breaking through overcast skies.

And although Victor was pleased he had won favor in Juliana's eyes, part of him worried he had paved a way to heartbreak for her.

A whirlwind of emotions raced through Juliana: eagerness and excitement to spend time with Victor, embarrassment over her horrible faux pas with Tobias, and elation that Victor had come to her rescue, salvaging the situation and making her feel . . . she didn't want to say the word.

Yet, it hung heavy in the air before her. How would she be able to keep her feelings for Victor from showing? Each time he looked at her, her heart melted. He made her feel special. Cared for.

Loved.

Juliana wasn't a stranger to being loved. Her mother adored her,

her father had doted on her, and Drake, for all his bluster and calling her brat, wanted her happiness above all else.

But a family's love was different from a man who pretended to be a suitor.

And therein lay the issue. Her courtship with Victor was a pretense, employed to spur Juliana's acceptance into society—and find a suitable husband.

Who wasn't Victor.

Victor, whose kindness outweighed his handsome face. Victor, who had a purpose in life, who aspired to be more than just a soon-forgotten viscount.

Whatever she felt for Victor had grown too big, too risky, and she dared not name it, for naming it might make it real. She'd been teetering on the edge of a precipice for some time, and his kindness had tilted the balance. Was she falling, or simply letting go?

The enormity of her feelings both liberated and restrained her, the juxtaposition of it almost comical if her heart was not at stake. Her affection for him would give credence to their pretense of courtship, but at the same time, she must keep her feelings in check enough so Victor wouldn't discern the truth. She must walk the fine line between allowing her feelings to show enough, but not too much.

And in doing so, she would guard her own heart from being crushed by Victor's rejection.

Stretched out on the blanket, Victor nibbled on another orange slice. He grew pensive, studying her with that penetrating blue gaze of his. "Pretend or not, here we are courting, and you asked why I wanted to be an artist, but I never asked you what dreams you have for your future. Do you want more than marriage and children?"

The piece of cheese Juliana had been chewing seemed to lodge in her throat as she swallowed. "If you knew my dream, you would not worry that I would find your dream ridiculous."

His eyes widened, and he propped himself on one elbow. "Now you must tell me."

She fingered a loose string on the blanket, not daring to meet his eyes. "It's not a very ladylike ambition. I had little hope to pursue it before, but now that Drake is a duke . . . well, it seems impossible. I've already embarrassed him enough."

"You have me too intrigued not to tell me. Please, Juliana. I promise I will keep your confidence."

Deep inside, she knew she *could* trust him—not only to keep her confidence but to not laugh. "Well, since you were so brave to share with me, it seems only fair I tell you. As you're aware, I love horses. When Drake left for the military and until my father died, I continued to help care for the horses on Lord Stratford's estate. When my father died, we moved near an estate where the owner bred horses, and he allowed me to go riding whenever I wished."

Victor waited patiently, but from the line forming between his brows, he no doubt wondered where her story was leading.

"He told me I had a good eye for horseflesh. Once, when I was brushing out the mare I had taken out for a ride, he asked me which stallion I would choose to mate with her."

Heat flooded her cheeks at Victor's incredulous expression, but she barreled forward. "He was teasing me, of course. However, I gave his question serious thought, and, apparently, my answer surprised him. Not only was it a pairing he had considered, but my reasons given impressed him. From then on, he asked my opinion about which stallion to mate with which mare. I became very good at it. Two of the foals went on to become champions. From that moment on, breeding horses became my dream."

"Well, that's fabulous." He grinned at her. "And a most unusual pursuit for a woman."

She tore her gaze away. "It doesn't matter now. At one time before Drake became duke, I thought perhaps I would marry a gentleman farmer who would also share my passion for horses and together . . . well."

Victor scooted closer to her and took her hand in his. "Juliana. Don't give up on your dream. It's still possible. There are many aristocratic gentlemen who put great store in fine horseflesh."

"Ones who would welcome a wife with such aspirations?" She shook her head. "From what I've seen and learned about the *ton*, he would be a most unusual man indeed." She forced a smile in hopes of conveying appreciation for his efforts to give her hope, no matter how false.

They finished their refreshment, conversing on less serious subjects as Tobias cleared the area of the remaining food, plates, and blanket.

Once she resumed her pose—with considerably less touching from Victor—their remaining time flew by. As Victor worked diligently, Juliana occupied herself, imagining herself on Victor's arm at upcoming events. Honoria had mentioned a ball toward the end of the Season to celebrate Kitty's birth. Juliana hoped Victor would still be pretending to court her and perhaps they would share a waltz. Although she struggled at the piano, she had taken to dancing as if she were born to it. The dancing master, who had also worked with Drake, said she had a natural athletic ability, perhaps due to her expertise on horseback.

Shadows lengthened, and Victor paused and peered upward. "We should finish for the day and return. I think I have enough of Sunshine to continue working indoors tomorrow." He swirled one of his brushes in an odd smelling liquid, then wiped it with a cloth. "If that's agreeable with you."

As much as Juliana loved having moments alone with Victor—except for Tobias, of course—spending any time with him, even with her mother present, was better than spending no time with him. "Of course." She gave Sunshine a pat on her neck. "There will be some carrots and maybe an apple for you when we get back."

"She earned them." Victor pulled another canvas from his satchel.

"What is that for? I thought we were finished?"

With a smile that said her question was not as silly as she'd first imagined, Victor held it out, showing her the protrusions on the back edges of the blank canvas. "To protect the wet canvas. Small pieces of wood create a gap and keep the paint from touching the surface. I place the painted canvas surface against the back of the blank canvas. Then I tie it in place with cloth strips."

Oh. He was so brilliant!

Once Victor finished packing up his supplies and the canvas—

which he wouldn't allow her to see—he strode forward, giving a nod toward Sunshine. "Do you need a boost up?"

Although she'd used a mounting block when they'd left, she'd planned to simply place her foot in the stirrup and pull herself up into the saddle. But the prospect of Victor's hands around her waist banished any desire to prove her independence.

She nodded. "That would be helpful."

They stood face-to-face. Victor reached for her, but frowned and pulled back, scratching his chin. "Um. How should I . . .? Perhaps if you turn around?"

"Oh. Of course. I'm such a ninny." Turning, she faced Sunshine, preparing herself for the onslaught of sensations when Victor touched her. Yet, try as she might, her knees buckled a little when Victor's hands found her waist. She sucked in a breath long enough to keep her wits about her and slide her foot into the stirrup and swing into position.

Victor's lips twitched in a tiny smile as he handed her the reins. She jerked her gaze away lest he see the turmoil brewing inside her, but his fingers lingered against hers, and neither pulled away.

They rode back in relative silence, only speaking to greet people they passed. There was no awkwardness between them, reminding Juliana of the quiet communication Drake and Honoria shared with each other.

Was it enough if only one person loved? It was a question Juliana was reluctant to ponder—for she may not like the answer.

CHAPTER 12

The next day, Juliana posed inside Drake's orangery using the branch of an orange tree in place of Sunshine's neck and muzzle. "It feels strange petting leaves."

Victor's delicious chuckle, deep and raspy, scraped against her skin, raising gooseflesh.

"I know, but it's only for positioning. I doubt your brother would appreciate horse droppings in his home should we bring Sunshine inside. Perhaps in a few days we can venture out again." Victor placed his brush down and glanced toward the glass panels in the ceiling. "As it is, we may not be able to continue much longer even now. A storm is brewing, and we're losing the little light we have."

Victor stepped back, his hands on his hips, and assessed the painting. He'd removed his coat and rolled up his shirtsleeves to keep them paint-free, exposing his—very nice—forearms. He had the long, elegant fingers of an artist. Fitting, of course, but all Juliana could think about was how those fingers had touched her face and wrapped around her waist.

Her knees wobbled a bit at the memory. Thank heavens her skirts hid her reaction. Although their courtship was pretend for Victor, her feelings were very, very real.

"Won't you let me take a peek?" she asked, doing her best to keep her tone light. In truth, she was dying to know how Victor saw her.

He waggled a finger at her. "No. And don't think you can use those pretty smiles to sweet talk me into it."

Pretty smiles? Her heart stuttered.

He placed the portrait in his brilliant contraption, then began cleaning his brushes in what she learned was turpentine. "Why don't we pause for a while and see if the clouds clear. Perhaps you can show me how you're progressing on the piano?"

Mother, who had been sitting in a far corner, peered up from her embroidery. "She's becoming quite accomplished, Mr. Pratt."

Although Juliana wouldn't consider herself accomplished as Mother had implied, she'd been practicing furiously, wanting nothing more than to make Victor smile at her attempt at Mozart's *Twelve Variations on "Ah Vous dirai-je, Maman."* Her piano teacher had been ecstatic over her improvement. She couldn't manage all twelve variations, especially those which grew in complexity, but she managed the simpler ones with ease.

Once Victor finished cleaning his brushes and put away his paints, he rolled down his shirtsleeves and donned his coat.

Pity. Juliana rather enjoyed admiring his forearms.

In the music room, Mother rang for refreshments and Juliana took her place at the piano with Victor standing next to the instrument. Taking a deep breath, she focused on the music before her, hoping to calm her nerves and shaking fingers. Thank goodness it started off simply, and Juliana executed the first variation to perfection. Sunshine—not her horse, of course—flooded her chest at Victor's nod of approval.

But the moment she met his gaze, she fumbled the quick, right-hand notes. Victor took a seat beside her on the bench, his thigh pressing against her skirts, which only exacerbated her trembling.

"It helps me to do some finger exercises to limber them up. May I?" He dipped his head toward her hands.

Thinking he meant to play and show her, she lifted her fingers from the keys, only to have him take her hand in his. The same energy as the day before sizzled up her arm, and she inadvertently gasped. Her gaze snapped to Victor's, discovering his own eyes had widened.

He broke the connection, dropping his gaze to her hand and began moving her fingers. One at a time, he stretched and bent them. And with each touch, her heart beat a little faster.

"Excuse me," Frampton's voice broke through her haze of longing. "Lord Felix Davies—"

"Is here," Lord Felix said, stepping from behind Frampton.

"Sir, as before, I requested that you wait in the entry." Frampton frowned, his tone censorious.

Lord Felix waved his gloves in Frampton's face, his lips spreading in a smirk. "But I'm practically family." His gaze swung to where Victor still had Juliana's hand in his.

The smirk vanished, and he took several steps forward. "What's this? I come here in good faith regarding my offer to court Miss Merrick and save her reputation, and I find you two . . ." He waved his gloves again, this time at Victor and Juliana.

Victor's fingers tightened around hers, not painfully so, but Juliana recognized it as a gesture of support.

"Your *services* are neither needed nor wanted, Davies." Victor released her hand and stood.

Juliana already missed his warmth.

"As you have rightly deduced, I am courting Miss Merrick, so you can take your self-serving offer and leave."

Juliana's heart raced at Victor's possessive tone and stance. Pretend or not, Victor portrayed the part of a possessive suitor to perfection.

Mother rose from her seat on the sofa. "Frampton, escort Lord Felix out—again."

Frampton bowed. "My pleasure." Frampton extended his arm toward the door. "My *lord*."

The disdain coloring Frampton's address registered with Lord Felix, who turned on his heel, muttering as he left, "You two deserve each other."

When Victor turned back, he was grinning. "That felt good."

But Juliana had a very bad feeling in the pit of her stomach. Simon and Charlotte didn't trust Lord Felix.

And neither did Juliana.

Two days later, in his bachelor apartments, Victor stepped back from the portrait of Juliana. Even in the quiet of his studio, with the scent of turpentine thick in the air and Juliana's likeness gazing softly back at him, the world felt watchful, as if something waited in the shadows.

He brushed the bleak feeling aside, attributing it to exhaustion. He'd been working on some extra background detail in private in order to utilize his time more efficiently. Victor wanted to finish quickly, hoping to impress Burwood enough to allow him to continue with the rest of the—admittedly, more important—portraits.

Although in retrospect, Juliana's portrait might very well be the most crucial, as it would either win Victor the commission with the duke or send him into the pit of despair should Burwood decide to hire another portraitist.

A lot of work remained to be done on Juliana's likeness, especially her eyes. That particular aspect was something he couldn't work on without the actual subject. He studied the portrait again. Close to what he wanted, but he needed to get it right. The tilt of her head, the easy curve of her mouth. The spark that overtook her, transforming her and making him forget their courtship was a pretense.

Footsteps coming up the stairs drew his attention to the open door of his studio. His valet's voice rose with them. "Madam, allow me to announce you."

Victor angled his easel toward the wall at his mother's answer. "I'm his mother, Tierney. I don't need to be announced. This is urgent!"

Bloody hell. What now? Victor exhaled a heavy sigh. No doubt the *urgent* news was some bit of gossip Victor had no desire to hear.

As his mother stormed into the room, she waved a scandal sheet, confirming his supposition.

"What is it now, Mother? Why must you keep interrupting my work?" Victor wiped paint off a brush, his leisurely motions matching his bored tone. "Has Lady Highbottom been seen wearing a royal-blue bonnet with a chartreuse spencer? How gauche."

Pleased Lydia hadn't accompanied her, Victor finally lifted his gaze toward his mother. And promptly dropped the brush he was cleaning. She looked ghastly. Her color was ashen, somewhere between a dark chartreuse he had teased her about and the color of charcoal.

He raced over, grasping her arm and leading her to his sofa. "Sit." Spinning around, he searched for his bottle of brandy, only then remembering she refused it the last time. He crouched before her, his gaze dipping to the sheet of paper in her hand.

The Muckraker!

Her voice cracked, and her hand shook as she thrust the gossip rag toward him. "How co—could you, Victor? Now you will have to marry her!" She crumpled on the sofa, sobbing.

An uncomfortable thought crossed his mind that perhaps—just perhaps, mind you—he had come by his flair for the dramatic quite naturally.

At least he hoped his mother's reaction to whatever news the scandal sheet held was exaggerated. But the words '*Now you will have to marry her*' put him on edge.

He scanned the piece of filth which began with more sordid gossip regarding Burwood's man-of-business, Simon Beckham, and Lady Charlotte. What followed hit him like a punch to his stomach.

In addition to the scandalous behavior of Mr. Beckham and Lady Charlotte, not only in Swindon but prior to their marriage as well, which this reporter notes occurred in the Duke of Burwood's London home, news has reached our ears that the duke's sister, Miss Juliana Merrick, posed for a portrait painted by Mr. Victor Pratt, heir to Viscount Cartwright. The news would seem unremarkable, as Mr. Pratt is known to be an aspiring artist. However, the reports state that Miss Merrick did so in a state of undress. It would appear that the new duke's home has become a hotbed of scandal.

To make the news more interesting, in addition to painting Miss Merrick's portrait, Mr. Pratt is said to be courting the young—ahem—lady. That a man in line to inherit a viscountcy would stoop to forming an attachment with a commoner elevates the scandal to new heights.

This reporter is curious. Which came first: the commission or the courtship? And is Victor Pratt using Miss Merrick to his advantage? Or simply taking advantage?

Victor's stomach roiled, and he wanted to rip the detestable paper to shreds as he skimmed past reports of babies born prior to their expected arrivals and Lord Felix Davies's purchase of a new gelding at Tattersall's, confirming the gossipmonger directed no more attacks toward him or the duke and his family.

"Lies!" He spat the word, flinging the paper back at his mother.

"Which part? You told me yourself you were going to request the commission to paint the duke's portrait." His mother's gaze darted toward the easel holding Juliana's portrait. "And to court his sister."

She shook her head, dabbing her eyes with a handkerchief. "I'd hoped you said so only to discourage an attachment with Miss Whyte. But now . . . now, regardless of your intention, your honor is called into question."

Victor raised an eyebrow at his mother. "First, there is nothing scandalous about the portrait of Miss Merrick." He strode toward the easel, then moved it away from the wall. "Come see for yourself."

His mother rose from the sofa and inched toward him as if he planned to spring a trap on her. "You assure me there is nothing untoward about the painting?"

"There is nothing to offend your *delicate* sensibilities, Mother. The fact you even ask wounds me."

She grumbled something about young men's desires but stepped around to the front of the easel. Her hand rose to her throat as she viewed the portrait. "Oh, Victor."

"You like it?" The incredulity in his tone surprised him. "You're the first to see it, beside Tierney and me, of course."

Her brow scrunched. "Why is there a horse in the painting?"

Of course, his mother would find fault with *something.* It's what she did.

"She's a skilled horsewoman. Her rescue of Dr. Somersby's daughter on Rotten Row was not simply happenstance. Her exceptional riding along with her cool head and quick thinking saved the girl. The horse speaks to who she is as a person."

His mother's eyes widened. "As a *person?* She's a commoner, Victor."

"She is a lovely young woman."

"So you are courting her in earnest?"

Victor's stomach clenched at the word *earnest.* But to admit to his mother that his and Juliana's courtship was a farce would work against them. His mother could no more keep a secret as rain would cease falling in London. "I am courting her, yes."

Returning to the sofa, his mother pulled out her handkerchief and dabbed her eyes. "Why must you do this, Victor? First that Lovelace woman, and now the daughter of a steward and a seamstress! Do you do this to spite me? To drive me to an early grave?"

Yes, perhaps he'd inherited her penchant for dramatics, but Victor pushed the thought aside. "Keep Miss Lovelace out of this." Mention of her only awakened the twinge in his chest.

Not heeding his warning, his mother continued to rail. "Both commoners! Why must you pursue women who are beneath you when there are genteel ladies available like Miss Whyte who are equal to your station? What attracts you to women of low birth?"

"Low birth?" He couldn't believe the words coming from his mother's mouth. Or maybe he could. "What attracts me are their independent spirits. Their desire to be more than a pretty bauble on a man's arm. I admire their hopes and dreams and—yes, Mother— their ambitions. Their *difference* from the likes of Miss Whyte is precisely what attracts me."

Was it foolish to want someone who would challenge him, who reminded him he could feel something again?

His mother gaped at him, speechless. A rare sight indeed.

Fueled by the horrible gossip rag and his mother's insistence on bringing up Adalyn, Victor continued his tirade. "And *you* are the last person to cast aspersions on anyone. *You* who forced your own daughter to compromise a good man. Not because he was a good man, but because he was a *titled* man. Tell me, Mother, would you still have had Cilla compromise Ashton simply because he was a duke if he had been a man who would beat her?"

His mother bolted from the sofa, her face no longer ashen but crimson. "How dare you?! I will speak with your father about this."

The storm she arrived in blew her out, much to Victor's relief, and he allowed his body to drop to the sofa she had vacated.

Regardless of the innocence of Juliana's portrait, Victor was well acquainted with the havoc gossip could wreak.

God help me if I've ruined her.

He might very well have to offer for Miss Merrick. The possibility landed with a *thud* in his chest. Not because he didn't want to. But because he no longer had a choice.

❧

JULIANA FOUGHT BACK THE TEARS AT DRAKE'S CRESTFALLEN FACE.

Her brother tugged fistfuls of his hair. Spread before him on the table in the morning room, *The Muckraker* taunted them all. "I should have chaperoned the two of you myself. I should have demanded to see the portrait as he worked. I should have——"

"This is not your fault." Beside him, Honoria pulled Drake's hand from his tortured hair and laced her fingers through his, then sent Juliana a commiserating look. "It's no one's fault except the monster behind that horrible paper."

Mother remained unnervingly silent.

"Mr. Pratt has been a perfect gentleman, Drake. He's done nothing wrong." Juliana choked out the words, needing to believe the truth in them.

"Except paint you unclothed."

"He didn't. It's a lie," Juliana said more firmly.

Drake's gaze shot to hers. "Have you seen it?"

Her stomach tightened. Why had Victor refused to let her peek?

She brushed the doubt aside. "Well . . . no. But, Drake, this commission is important to Victor. Why would he risk losing it?"

Drake opened his mouth, then snapped it shut. "I don't know."

Mother wrapped her arm around Juliana's shoulders. "If you trust him, then so should we. However, what is true and what people believe can be two very different things."

"Mother Merrick is right," Honoria said. "We must put our heads together and decide on the best strategy to save your reputation. I will call an emergency meeting of the League. And since Charlotte isn't here, I will invite Beatrix Townsend."

Frampton appeared at the entry of the room and gave a little cough. "Pardon me, Your Graces, Mrs. Merrick, Miss Merrick. Mr. Pratt is here. Shall I tell him you're not receiving?"

Unlike Lord Felix, Victor had impeccable manners and the consideration to take his cues from Juliana and her wishes.

Drake's gaze locked with hers. "We should see what he has to say about this." Drake snatched the gossip sheet, flinging it further down the table.

Juliana nodded. "He has a right to defend himself."

"Send him in, Frampton."

Tamping down the urge to pinch her cheeks and smooth her hair, Juliana pulled in a breath, hoping to calm her frayed nerves. It was not the time to worry about her appearance.

When Victor entered, he kept his attention on Drake. A chill tripped up her spine. Why wouldn't Victor look at her? He carried the large case he used to transport the portrait.

"Your Graces." Victor executed a graceful bow. "Mrs. Merrick. Miss Merrick." Finally, he slid a glance toward her, so brief she could have imagined it, before returning to Drake. "From your expressions, it's clear you have seen the lies written in that abomination of a paper."

Drake's gaze was steely, every bit that of a powerful duke. "We have."

To his credit, Victor didn't flinch, but strode forward, placing the case on the table before them. "If I may?"

Drake held out a hand. "Please."

Juliana would go mad from the curt exchange between the two men she cherished most.

With steady hands, Victor unlatched the case, pulled out the portrait, and removed the protective blank canvas. Juliana sucked in a breath and held it.

Victor turned the portrait around, and a collective *whoosh* sounded around the table.

"It's not finished, and I hate showing you an incomplete work. But I hope this reassures you that Miss Merrick's reputation remains spotless."

"Beautiful," Honoria whispered.

Mother held a hand to her mouth, tears welling in her eyes.

Juliana wondered if the woman in the painting was actually her. She looked so—beautiful. Even amid the turmoil of the situation, her heart stuttered. Was this how Victor saw her?

Drake's voice was brittle. "In reality, yes. *I* know my sister's reputation is above reproach, but as my mother rightly pointed out before your arrival, what is true and what people believe can be entirely different matters. Damage has been done. The question is: How do we repair it?"

Victor straightened his shoulders, his face somber as his gaze locked with hers. "Allow me to offer for Miss Merrick."

How many times had she lain in her bed imagining Victor asking for her hand? But the cool indifference she saw in his eyes at that moment had not been part of her fantasies.

And although she should be thrilled to finally have what she wanted within her reach, it just seemed . . . wrong.

CHAPTER 13

Any hope Victor had that showing the portrait to the duke would end the matter vanished at the duke's icy glare and blunt, but honest, question.

For some reason unknown to Victor, the perpetrator of *The Muckraker* had used him as a vessel to disparage the duke's sister. Logic called for Victor to repair the damage.

Tightness banded Victor's chest as he met Juliana's searching eyes. She deserved better. Not only better treatment from the *ton*, but better than a man who could only pretend. She deserved a man who truly loved her, and only her.

Yet he pressed forward, sorry she would not get what she deserved. He cleared his dry, scratchy throat. "Allow me to offer for Miss Merrick."

Her eyes flared slightly, the sad realization clear in their blue depths that the offer was made out of a sense of duty rather than abiding affection.

Not the best of proposals, but what choice did he have? Every instinct told him to protect her. He needed to be the one to make it right—even if the pain in her eyes shot like an arrow through his heart. In acting gallantly, Victor had never felt *less* gallant.

Burwood pressed his palms against the table, pushing himself up as if a heavy weight kept him in place.

"Come, Mr. Pratt, follow me."

Victor made a quick bow to the ladies and obeyed the duke's command.

Burwood led Victor to his study, where they had met and discussed Victor's request to court Juliana. Had it only been mere days ago?

"Sit." The duke seated himself behind his ornate desk, and Victor sat in the chair across from him. Burwood ran a hand through his hair, mussing his valet's meticulously crafted style. The duke appeared haggard, as if he'd aged ten years, and Victor knew for a fact, he and Burwood were approximately the same age.

"Sir? Are you unwell? Should we send for a physician?"

Burwood waved him off. "New fatherhood, although wonderful, takes a toll, especially when one's wife insists on performing many of a nurse's duties herself. I suspect it's Honoria's way of pushing aside her grief over Margery's death. In addition, arguments for reform in Lords have grown contentious." The heavy sigh he emitted carried all the weight he spoke of. "And now, this."

"I'm very sorry to have added to your burden."

The powerful duke Victor had witnessed moments earlier dissolved into a concerned brother, and much more like the man Victor had come to know simply as Drake. "I'm curious, Pratt. The report in that filthy rag attacks not only my sister, but you. And yet, your defense was only for Juliana. Why is that I wonder?"

Victor blinked. What was Burwood suggesting? "There is no need to defend myself on things we both know to be false."

Burwood nodded. "Yes, that you received the commission before seeking permission to court my sister. But I speak of the other matter."

Victor searched his memory for what other spurious thing *The Muckraker* had said about him.

Moments passed, and when Victor didn't answer, the duke returned. "Permit me to refresh your memory. It implied that you either took advantage of my sister to secure the position as our portraitist, or you did so intending to seduce her."

Victor's jaw tightened. "I swear to you, those are also lies."

His mouth set in a firm, straight line, Burwood studied Victor as if he were a tome written in a foreign language.

An uneasy silence enveloped them, and Victor worried the duke could hear his pounding heart. "As you yourself admitted, the commission as your artist was awarded prior to my request to court Miss Merrick."

"True." Burwood ruffled some papers on his desk. "But, Juliana urged me to consider you. She was most impressed with your *passion*."

The duke's emphasis on the word slammed into Victor. "We spoke of my love of art and particularly painting. I do not deny that. And I did hope to secure the position as your artist. If that was taking advantage, then perhaps I am guilty."

Burwood nodded. "I appreciate your honest answer. However, I'm more concerned with the other accusation."

"That I intended to seduce Miss Merrick?"

Burwood's stare pierced Victor through. "What would lead someone to believe you have painted inappropriate depictions of my sister? From my experience, even the worst of rumors have a basis of truth—even if miniscule."

"Not in this case, sir. I assure you. No one had seen the painting other than my valet, me, my mother, and now you and your family."

Burwood's brow lifted. "Your mother?"

"She arrived with the scandal sheet, most upset as you can imagine. I showed her the portrait to alleviate her concerns." Victor withheld the fact that his mother had insulted Miss Merrick.

"And you trust your valet?"

"Tierney has proven his loyalty to me countless times."

Brow furrowed and lips pursed, Burwood considered Victor's answer. "Then what would have precipitated it? There must be *something*."

"Other than dislike of me or, forgive me, you and your family?"

"Hmph. True enough, but there is bite to this somewhere. It's too specific in the accusation regarding Juliana's state of undress. I feel it." Burwood's eyes widened. "What about your sketches? Who saw them? Were any of them . . . suggestive?"

Victor shook his head, then a chill of a memory froze him. His mind whirled. The sketches of Adalyn. Lydia alone in his studio. Victor's gaze snagged with the duke's.

Burwood straightened in his chair. "What is it?"

"There are some other sketches. Not of Miss Merrick but of another woman, similar in appearance."

That time, Burwood rose. "Could anyone have seen them?"

"I don't know." True, but if he told Burwood his suspicion, the duke would take matters into his own hands. Although Lydia was a flirt and a gossip and he highly suspected she had seen the sketches, he had no proof. If Lydia harbored hopes of an attachment with him, what would she have to gain by making such accusations public? She might be indirectly involved and far from innocent, but Victor found it hard to believe she was capable of such maliciousness. Unlike the perpetrator of *The Muckraker*, Victor wanted to give her the benefit of the doubt—at least until he questioned her.

Burwood sank back into his chair, the defeat on his face heartbreaking. "Then we are at an impasse."

"If you will trust me, I have an idea I would like to pursue on my own. However, I suspect you called me in here to discuss more than the source of the gossip."

"Juliana." Burwood sighed again, softening back to a brother who only wanted the best for his sister, something Victor understood. Deep in thought, the duke toyed with the papers on his desk once more. "I want Juliana to be happy. To have the kind of marriage that I have. One based on love." He raised his eyes to Victor. "Do you love my sister?"

"We barely know each other. I dare say there hasn't been sufficient time for either of us to have developed such feelings." Odd, but he had fallen in love with Adalyn in half the time he'd spent with Juliana. "I like her. Esteem her."

From the expression on the duke's face, Victor's words had fallen flat. Victor couldn't blame Burwood for wanting more for his sister. And he had no idea the courtship Victor had with Juliana was all a pretense. "If I may, sir. Are you familiar with the scandal that sent my sister into hiding in Lincolnshire?"

"You're speaking of the orchestrated compromise with Ashton. What I know of it from Honoria paints your sister as much of a victim as Ashton."

"Her Grace is generous. I won't excuse Cilla, but yes, she was young and malleable, yielding to my mother's machinations."

Head tilted back toward the ceiling, Burwood pinched the bridge of his nose and sighed. "Your point?"

Right. "I have one, I promise. Ashton pleaded with Cilla to release him. He suggested they proceed with the betrothal, but that before the wedding Cilla could cry off, painting him as a cad who had used her."

Burwood's attention snapped back, his gaze spearing Victor. "You're suggesting Juliana do the same."

"If she does not want to marry me, yes. Have her heap the blame on me. Perhaps before then we can discover who is behind these spurious reports and prove them false."

"It's best not to delay the wedding. If Juliana agrees, the banns should be read immediately, which doesn't give you much time."

"I understand, sir. However, I am fully prepared to honor my promise to marry her, if she so wishes. The decision is in her hands."

"Then let us ask her." Burwood rose, rang the bell pull, and instructed Frampton to fetch Juliana.

❦

JULIANA'S STOMACH TWISTED IN A KNOT, WAITING FOR DRAKE, AND possibly Victor, to return. Honoria had excused herself and rushed off to send messages to the League for an emergency meeting, leaving Juliana alone with her mother.

"What's taking them so long?" Juliana lifted a hand to her mouth.

Her mother laid a staying hand on Juliana's arm. "Stop, dearest, or you will chew your nails to stubs. Trust Drake to handle things. I suspect he wants to determine Victor's feelings for you."

Juliana sighed. "But that's just it, Mama. Victor doesn't really want to marry me. I could see it in his eyes. He's asking out of duty because he's a gentleman." Not to mention their courtship was a sham.

"And what do you want? Don't lie to me. I'm familiar with how your face softens whenever you look at Victor. You forget, I was a woman in love long ago."

Remorse squeezed Juliana's chest that her mother referred not to Juliana's father, but to her first husband. "Did you love Papa, too?"

Mother pulled Juliana into her arms. "Of course I did. It was a different kind of love than I had for Henry. Quiet and comfortable, not the tumultuous riot of feelings that nearly tore me apart. But never doubt that I loved Francis. We were friends first and foremost. He was a good man, and we had a wonderful life together."

The words of her father that long ago evening when he'd been in his cups resurfaced. *I know your mother will never love me as I love her. And yet, I don't care.* Would her love for Victor be enough for both of them? Would she settle as her father had?

"If Drake gives his blessing, will you accept Victor's proposal?" Concern shone in her mother's eyes.

"I don't know." Her answer, no more than a whisper, held both hope and despair.

Frampton appeared in the doorway. "His Grace requests you join him and Mr. Pratt in the study, Miss Merrick."

Her mother rose. "I'm coming with you."

Juliana grasped her mother's hand, and together they walked toward Juliana's future.

Drake and Victor rose upon seeing them, the smile forming on Victor's lips not reaching his eyes.

Pain pricked Juliana's heart like a sharp needle.

Drake and Victor exchanged a glance, then Drake said, "I have accepted Mr. Pratt's offer for your hand, Juliana. However, given the circumstances, he and I both agree the choice should ultimately be yours."

"Please sit, Miss Merrick." Victor motioned to the chair he had vacated.

Drake guided Mother to the chair behind his desk, then stood to the side, melting into the shadows. An ominous portent shrouded the room and its occupants, and the pain in Juliana's chest spread like a disease.

Nothing at all like an eager and hopeful bridegroom, Victor stood before her, his face grim. "It grieves me that these heinous reports have placed you in this untenable situation, Miss Merrick. Our courtship has barely begun, and now our hands are forced. I will work diligently to prove these allegations false, but in the meantime, an engagement between us will help quell the wagging tongues. If I fail in righting these wrongs prior to our wedding, you can cry off, painting me as the worst of blackguards and save yourself."

Juliana blinked. "But you're not a blackguard. You've been nothing but gentlemanly and kind."

Victor grimaced, the reaction so brief Juliana could have imagined it. "Sadly, a man can bear the brunt of negative gossip much more easily than a woman, especially a man with a title. You are the more vulnerable of the two of us."

Drake's voice drifted from the corner. "Victor is willing to throw himself on his sword for you, brat."

"Do you want me to cry off?" Juliana hated the tremble in her lips and willed herself not to cry.

"I want what you want. If you wish to proceed with the marriage, I will do my utmost to make you a good husband. What I don't want is to force your hand any more than this culprit has done."

Juliana hardly recognized the man before her. She'd come to know Victor as a passionate man with deep emotions. His proposal reminded her of one of Drake's business agreements. Factual. Emotionless. Cold.

Not at all like the proposal she had dreamed about, with love and emotion shining in Victor's eyes. His heartfelt declaration of adoration vowing to love her for all eternity.

She should say no and save him from sacrificing himself for her. It was the right thing to do—what a loving person *should* do.

"Juliana?" her mother whispered.

Juliana wasn't certain if the option of crying off led to her decision, or if her own selfishness in pretending to be Victor's fiancée propelled her forward.

But she met Victor's eyes and answered, "Yes. I accept your proposal."

His lips curved slightly upward, the sparkle reaching his eyes. "Good. Might I suggest we begin by making a public appearance as a couple? Perhaps Gunter's for an ice, or a stroll in the park?"

Juliana imagined more than a flavored ice would chill her should she show herself on Victor's arm so soon after the tabloid's report. Judgmental stares and whispers behind gloved hands awaited, and she needed to build her courage. Victor was braver than she. Thank goodness she had an excuse. "Perhaps later this afternoon? Honoria is calling an emergency meeting of the League."

Victor's brow furrowed, his gaze bouncing between Juliana and her mother. "The League? You're speaking of the charitable organization? My sister has mentioned it in passing. But I don't understand how it pertains to what happens or why Miss Merrick needs to—"

Drake stepped forward. "He should know, especially considering the possibility he will be family soon."

At the word family, Juliana winced, hating herself that, somehow, she had placed Victor in such an undesirable position.

Mother took the lead. "The London Ladies' League operates under the guise of a charitable organization, yes. But our true purpose is to unmask the person responsible for the scandal sheet that has defamed so many good people. Considering this latest news affects my daughter, she should be in attendance."

Victor's mouth dropped open, and Juliana found even that adorable about him. "Why, that's . . . that's . . . marvelous! May I join?"

The first genuine smile broke across Juliana's lips. "Victor, it's the *Ladies'* League."

Pink formed on the tips of Victor's ears, and the sweet smile he gave her warmed her heart. "Oh. Of course. Ladies only. Then, with your permission, I shall take my leave and call on you later this afternoon."

Juliana rose to escort him out. Once they were alone in the hallway and out of earshot of her family, she whispered, "Did you tell my brother that our courtship was a fraud?"

Victor shook his head. "But I think he suspects something is amiss."

"I'm so sorry to have put you in this position."

Victor stopped, turning toward her. "You have done nothing wrong. It's my carelessness that may have precipitated this debacle."

She winced. That he would call their betrothal a debacle stung, yet she understood he meant no disrespect. However, she found his remark curious. "Carelessness?"

"Yes, there are some sketches. Not of you," he hastened to add. "Our engagement will give me time to investigate and hopefully gather the evidence necessary to prove the allegations false."

Juliana had so many questions, but they would have to wait for a better time.

Frampton waited at the front door, Victor's hat and gloves at the ready.

"I shall call on you again this afternoon. Until then, Miss Merrick."

To her surprise and joy, Victor took her hand in his, bent low, and kissed it.

When Victor had touched her face with his bare fingers several days ago, waves of pleasure had rippled through her body. But that innocent contact to adjust her pose couldn't compare to the deliberate brush of Victor's lips against her skin.

What would happen if he kissed her lips? She'd no doubt swoon and fall against him in a puddle.

And as Victor took his gloves and hat from Frampton and left, Juliana hoped she would soon find out.

Their courtship might be a pretense to Victor, and he no doubt expected her to cry off if they couldn't disprove the horrible rumors, but that didn't mean Juliana wouldn't enjoy every moment of Victor's attention.

Even if her heart eventually paid the price.

CHAPTER 14

Feminine outrage erupted in the drawing room of Drake's London mansion. Seated next to her mother, Juliana wanted to make herself as small as possible until she simply vanished. Not that the ladies of The League weren't supportive. They were furious on her behalf, but Juliana had never been comfortable with so much attention directed at her.

"They've gone too far this time," Miranda said, handing the scandal sheet to Anne, who had arrived later—per usual. Miranda pointed to the paragraphs in question.

The roar settled down to a hum as Anne scanned the contents. Honestly, Juliana was surprised Anne hadn't already read it. She was typically the first to obtain a copy of the spurious paper.

Anne's gaze darted toward Juliana. "Did you really pose nude?"

Miranda rolled her eyes. "Of course she didn't, you ninny."

Anne squared her shoulders. "Just because Charlotte isn't here doesn't mean you have to speak for her in absentia."

Juliana pressed her lips together, fighting the laugh even under the horrible circumstances. No offense to Anne, but the fact that she even knew the word absentia was humorous. Leave it to Anne to add a bit of frivolity to the direst of situations.

Bea pushed her spectacles up her nose and turned toward Juliana. "The question, as I see it, is why has the culprit recently focused their attacks on you? We need to start charting possibilities. For example, we should list people we may have offended who might have a vendetta against us, but who also were privy to the information twisted in this abomination posing as a newspaper." Bea pointed at the copy of *The Muckraker* and shuddered.

"That's an excellent idea, Bea." Honoria rose. "I'll get some paper and a pencil."

Bea gestured for Honoria to sit back down. "No need. My memory is excellent, and I will put something together for the next meeting. I'm also curious why the culprit would mention something so specific as posing unclothed."

Juliana, her mother, and Honoria all exchanged a glance. After Victor's cryptic remark about additional sketches when he left earlier, Juliana discovered Victor had mentioned them to Drake as well but had failed to provide the subject's name.

"They should have all the information." Mother squeezed Juliana's hand and nodded toward the other ladies.

"Mr. Pratt said there are some sketches of another woman who could be mistaken for me. However, he told Drake he is unsure anyone saw them."

"That must be it," Anne said.

"Did Mr. Pratt say who?" Bea removed *The Muckraker* from Anne's grasp, scanning it. "We could confront her to confirm."

Honoria squirmed in her seat, her gaze glued to her folded hands in her lap.

"Honoria?" Miranda's tone reminded Juliana of Mother's censure when Juliana had come in from an especially vigorous ride covered with mud. Miranda really did seem to be filling in for Charlotte.

"I can't imagine it would be her," Honoria said. "She would never pose in such a manner."

"Who? We can't know unless we ask her," Bea said. "Why Laurence has a portrait of me in his—"

"Don't remind me." Miranda gave a little shudder. "However,

my brother is your husband, Bea. It's different. Whomever Victor sketched is not his wife."

Juliana wasn't so naïve as to believe Victor hadn't had encounters with other women, but the idea still stung. She prayed the sketches were simply an artistic endeavor.

Miranda returned her attention to Honoria and softened her tone. "But it would help if we knew."

Honoria gave a little nod, giving in to the pressure from her friends. "Adalyn Lovelace, or I should say Talbot, resembles Juliana a little. More in their coloring than anything."

Anne sat up in her chair. "The American woman? Didn't Mr. Pratt court her?"

What?

Honoria's eyes met Juliana's, the message in them an apology. "He did. But Adalyn did not reciprocate Mr. Pratt's feelings. Adalyn liked him, of course, but Lord Nash was the man who held her affection." A blush rose to Honoria's cheeks, and she averted her gaze from Juliana's scrutiny. Clearly, there was more to the story than Honoria let on.

Air rushed from Juliana's lungs, the information landing like a well-aimed arrow in her chest. Coupled with the fact that the lady in question had married another, Honoria's words, although carefully chosen, twisted the shaft, causing the arrowhead to gouge the wound deeper. Juliana's heart hurt.

For herself, yes. But also for Victor. The sketches explained so much.

"Of course. How could I forget all the commotion at Ashton's ball? Especially since it led to more scandalous reports from that gossip sheet." Miranda pointed to *The Muckraker* in Bea's hands. "The vitriol aimed at you, Honoria, sickened me."

Honoria was involved?

"Regardless," Honoria said, once again meeting Juliana's gaze. "I'm certain Adalyn did not pose for such sketches."

Anne slumped in her chair, her lips pursed in a pout. "And she's in America, so we can't ask her."

Relief washed over Juliana that the woman who possibly held

Victor's heart was an ocean away. "I could ask Victor." Her cheeks flamed at the idea of asking Victor such a sensitive question, but she would do it if it meant debunking the vicious rumor. "But why wouldn't Victor say anything?" she mumbled, giving voice to the thought.

"To protect Adalyn?" Miranda offered.

Bea rolled her eyes at her sister-in-law. "I don't think *The Muckraker's* reach extends to America."

"Drake mentioned that Victor had an idea he wished to pursue. Perhaps that is the reason," Juliana said.

"Now, *that* makes sense," Bea said.

"My suggestion made sense," Miranda said, sounding like a put-upon child.

Bea turned to Juliana. "We love each other, truly."

That time, Miranda rolled her eyes. "I tolerate you for Laurence's sake."

Honoria gave a delicate cough. "Well, shall we get back to the matter at hand? If we could all recount instances where *The Muckraker* directed its attack on us, with attention paid to whomever could have been privy to the information, Bea will catalogue it to identify any common threads. Thank you, Bea, for suggesting it."

As each lady went through the list of grievances against the notorious paper, Juliana's mind drifted. How deep were Victor's feelings for Adalyn Lovelace? Did he love her? Did he *still* love her? And what did it mean that Juliana resembled her?

Before she realized it, Honoria had called the meeting to a close.

Bea rose. "Allow me a few days to compile and analyze this information. Then, if agreeable to all, we can reconvene to discuss my findings."

As everyone filed out, Juliana glanced at the clock on the mantle. Little time remained before Victor returned that afternoon. "Honoria, may we speak in private?"

Concern grew on her mother's face, but she drew Juliana into her arms for an embrace. "All will be well. I can feel it in here." She pressed a hand to her heart.

Although Juliana looked on the bright side most of the time, she wished she had her mother's unfailing optimism. Intuition told her she would need it.

With her mother gone, Juliana turned toward Honoria. "There's something you're not saying about Victor and Miss Lovelace. All things considered, don't you think I deserve to know?"

Honoria sank into her chair, and a sad smile curled her lips. "Am I that transparent?"

Juliana kneeled before her dearest friend and took Honoria's hands in her own. "You are to me. Remember, we practically grew up together." A smile tugged Juliana's lips. "And you're not a very good liar. Now, tell me about Victor and Adalyn. And how were you involved?"

"The summer before Drake's house party, Lord Nash and I were thrown together by decree of our families. We both agreed we were not suited, but in order to give him time to secure funds for an investment and for me to reach my twenty-fifth birthday when Father would release my dowry, we entered a pretend courtship."

Oh! Were pretend courtships common among these people?

"Early in our pretense, Adalyn and her father came for an extended visit with Ashton. The duke had practiced medicine with Dr. Lovelace in America. The attraction between Lord Nash and Adalyn became clear to me, so I"—her gaze dipped to her lap where Juliana clasped their hands together—"I orchestrated some meetings."

Juliana fell back, releasing Honoria's hands and seating herself fully on the floor. Perhaps she didn't know her sister-in-law as well as she'd thought. "You didn't?!"

Honoria's smile turned sly, and she gave a tiny nod.

"But what about Victor?"

"Please believe me. I had no idea Victor's intentions toward Adalyn had become so serious. At the ball Miranda mentioned, he tried to propose to Adalyn, but she rejected him."

"Poor Victor."

Honoria's gaze became unfocused. "The heart wants what it wants."

Somehow, Juliana understood Honoria wasn't only speaking of Victor.

"Do you think Victor still loves her?"

"I don't know. Adalyn wasn't convinced he loved *her* as much as the idea of her." Honoria retook Juliana's hands in hers. "You're concerned because I said you resemble Adalyn?"

Even though her attachment to Victor wasn't real, the question lingered. "Yes." Victor's tender touches, his kiss upon her hand, the softness in his eyes when he looked at her—could they be because he was imagining Adalyn?

"You are your own woman, Juliana. Are there similarities? Yes. But Victor is an honorable man. He's proven that today. He cares for you—*you*, Juliana."

A knock at the door drew their attention to the nurse in the doorway. "Beg your pardon, Your Grace. Lady Kitty is awake."

With a final squeeze to Juliana's hands, Honoria rose. "Trust Victor, Juliana."

Juliana hoped with all her heart she could.

Seated before his father's desk, Victor tried to explain. "As usual, the reports in *The Muckraker* are false. However, to save Miss Merrick's reputation, I have offered for her."

His father nodded, the dark half-moon shadows under his eyes disturbing. "I would expect no less. Any speculation as to why such lurid claims were levied against you and the good lady?"

"There is *something*." Victor trusted his father. "When Mother and Miss Whyte visited a few days ago, I had some sketches of another lady out. I placed them aside, but . . ."

His father's face reddened as he straightened in his chair. "If your mother had anything to do with this, I shall send her back to Lincolnshire forthwith!"

"Calm yourself, Father. I'm formulating a plan. I don't think either Lydia or Mother is directly responsible." At least he prayed his mother wasn't directly responsible. What type of mother would spread gossip that her own son had sketches of an unclothed woman lying about, even if her son was an artist?

Father answered that question, veritably spitting out the words. "Unless she hopes that publicly shaming you will force you to give up on your dreams. After what happened with Priscilla, nothing your mother does surprises me." He shook his head, as if trying to dislodge the disgust rattling in his brain.

"If Mother did have a hand in this, it backfired. Miss Merrick is the last person she wishes to see me wed."

"Hmph. Her brother is a duke. And I happen to like Burwood. He's a very ambitious young man for one so new to the title. I expect we'll see great things from him. You could do much worse than align yourself with his family."

Victor didn't disagree. But . . .

His father interrupted Victor's wandering mind. "Do you care for the girl?"

"I like her very much."

With a nod, his father said, "Then I have something for you." He placed both hands on the desk's surface and pushed up, a quiet moan escaping his lips. When had he needed such assistance?

"Father, are you unwell?"

His father glanced over his shoulder. "Only old bones. Enjoy your youth while you can."

Awareness flashed in Victor's mind of his father's stiff gait, the placement of a hand on his back after rising. When had he grown —old?

Victor had always admired his father, aspired to be like him when the day came and Victor inherited the title. A good man who wielded power justly. However, he had no wish to have those aspirations come to fruition so soon. He wasn't ready to assume the responsibilities of the viscountcy.

"Have you spoken to Ashton? I've heard good things about his methods." Victor failed to mention he'd heard those things from Adalyn, who praised the duke for his forward thinking when treating his patients.

At the large cherry cabinet, his father turned a questioning gaze

Victor's way. "Ashton has better things to do than to coddle a man simply because he's getting older." He reached into the cabinet. "Ah, here it is."

He returned with a small box covered in rich navy-blue leather. "This"—he set the box down in front of Victor—"was my mother's. I was supposed to give it to your mother upon our betrothal." A sheepish expression crept over his father's face. "But I knew she would consider it"—he pursed his lips, searching for the right word —"inadequate. So I bought her an enormous emerald and pearl ring instead."

Smooth leather felt cool against Victor's fingers as he lifted the jewelry box and used his thumb to push up the lid. Delicate and feminine, the ring nestled in a bed of creamy satin. Three small flowers, their petals fashioned from blue enamel, adorned the gold band. Tiny seed pearls sat in the center of each bloom. "Perfetta." The whispered word slipped from Victor's lips. Simple and elegant, it captured Adalyn—Victor froze at the errant thought. *Juliana. Juliana. Juliana.* He mentally repeated her name like a mantra, then snapped the lid closed. "Thank you, Father. I'm sure Miss Merrick will love it."

Pausing, Victor studied his father. He'd never witnessed great love exchanged between his parents, certainly not the passion he desired from a marriage. "I never asked. Why did you marry mother?"

The bark of laughter lightened the lines of his father's face. "Our parents arranged it. It was the way of things back then. For many in society, it still is."

"Do you . . . love Mother?" At that moment, Victor realized his father hadn't asked him that same question, only if he cared for Juliana.

"I love that she gave me two fine children, both of whom I adore and am proud to call mine." His father laughed again. "Although your sister gave me more than a few gray hairs."

Victor couldn't help but grin. "And still does, I imagine. Poor Marbry. The man should be elevated to sainthood."

"You young people and love. I don't understand it, but I do envy you at times." After coming around the desk, his father put a hand on Victor's shoulder. "Now, go to your young lady and give her the ring."

Victor had left the portrait at the duke's that morning, and he decided to leave his paints and brushes at home, devoting the afternoon solely to courting Juliana. He needed to redeem his paltry proposal. With the ring safely tucked inside his coat pocket, he borrowed his father's phaeton and made his way to Pendrake Manor.

Frampton took his hat and gloves. "Miss Merrick is outside in the gardens, sir. If you would follow me."

At the double doors leading to the terrace, Victor stepped out and patted the ring box in his pocket. Juliana sat alone on a bench, reading.

Not wishing to startle her, he kept his voice low. "Juliana?"

She gazed up at him; her blue eyes shimmered with a glassy sheen.

He motioned to the empty spot on the bench beside her. "May I?" At her agreement, he sat. "What is it?"

With her left hand, she swiped at her eyes. "It's silly, really."

"Not to me." He smiled, hoping to encourage her.

She laughed, the sound more like a gurgle of emotion, and completely unlike Lydia's high-pitched, faux ear-splitting giggle. "You say that without knowing what it is."

His smile widened into a grin. "Isn't that what a man is supposed to do for his betrothed?" He nudged her with his elbow. "Now, tell me, and I shall put on my most serious expression."

"This book." Like a lover's caress, her hands ran over the leather binding of the small book. "Well, the story, actually. It's about two sisters who have gone from a life of wealth and comfort to losing their home and security to their older half-brother when their father dies."

"A great misfortune, to be sure."

She shook her head. "I couldn't help but think how lucky I am that I have a kind, caring half-brother who has done his best to provide for me."

Taking a chance, Victor placed his hand over hers and squeezed. "You are deserving of his care, Juliana."

She gave him a tremulous smile. "When I'm not bringing shame to him." She paused, pulling in a breath. "It's not that, though. In the story, a gentleman named Colonel Brandon loves Marianne—the younger sister—but Marianne is enamored with another gentleman named Willoughby."

"And that upsets you?" A strange camaraderie formed with this Colonel Brandon fellow, even though Victor had never read the book.

Tears formed in Juliana's eyes. "I find Colonel Brandon's unrequited affection for Marianne so touching." She swiped at her face. "I fear he is destined for heartbreak."

Victor squeezed her hand again, the feel of skin against skin sending a pleasant sensation through him. "You have a tender heart, Juliana, to care so deeply for a character in a story."

Eyes downcast, she stared at their joined hands. Silence settled between them like an old friend. Comfortable. Familiar. Welcome.

Her gaze lifted, and her blue eyes sought his in question.

"What is it? Something else is troubling you."

She swallowed, the movement in the long column of her throat slow but visible. "Will you tell me about Miss Lovelace? Is she the woman in the sketches?"

Blast.

CHAPTER 15

With everything in her, Juliana wished to rein in her runaway words. To pull them back into her mouth as if they'd never been spoken. Mistake. She had made a horrible mistake. Worse than a mistake, she had trod on sensitive ground and opened a wound by asking Victor about Adalyn.

Victor's horrified expression said it all. Blinking, he pulled back, removing his hand from hers and taking with it all his soothing warmth. "How do you know about Adalyn?" The pain in his voice slashed at her heart even more.

"Please, don't be angry. You mentioned the sketches of a woman similar in appearance, and Honoria thought it might be Miss Lovelace."

He jerked his gaze away, his hands fisting on his thighs. "I'm not angry."

"You are. But please, don't be angry with Honoria. Be angry with me for asking. I had no right to pry."

He laughed, the sound humorless, dry, and brittle. "If you don't have a right to ask, who does?" He exhaled an audible breath, then turned back to her. "I apologize. You took me off guard."

Although facing her, he stared at a spot above her head, as if meeting her gaze directly would make what he had to say even more difficult. "Yes. The sketches are of Miss Lovelace, but they aren't as lurid as that detestable rag purports. And to be clear, she did not pose for them. I drew them from memory—and imagination."

His words did not surprise her, for Juliana had memorized every contour, every line of Victor's face, the sparkle in his eyes, the arch of his brows, the curve of his lips when he smiled, the image forming so clearly that, when alone, she only had to close her eyes to summon it.

"Honoria mentioned Miss Lovelace resembles me. Or I resemble her." Flustered, she hurried to amend her statement. "What I mean to say is, we resemble each other."

His gaze snapped to hers, searching, questioning.

Could he see the insecurity lurking there? With her heart pounding a furious rhythm, she licked her lips and waited.

He nodded. "There is some resemblance; that is true. You both have blond hair, although hers is lighter, more of a silver blond, while yours is golden. Your blue eyes are more cornflower, while hers are cerulean." His brow furrowed, and Juliana realized she had memorized that as well. "Which whoever might have seen the sketches wouldn't have deduced from them, as they are in pencil."

He shrugged, the gesture smooth like flowing liquid. "But there are other differences. The tip of your nose turns up, just a little. Your face is a little fuller—here." Featherlight, like an angel's kiss, he brushed the back of his fingers against her cheeks, and a shiver of pleasure shimmied up her spine. "Innocence and lightness shine in your eyes." He grinned at her. "Especially when you're laughing."

Juliana cherished each word, pulling them close to her heart and holding them in an embrace.

"But a cursory glance, for example, one made in haste, might lead a person to conclude the sketches were of you, especially if my suspicion proves true."

"Then you believe someone *has* seen them?"

"It is a distinct possibility, and something I'm going to investigate. However, I have something very important to do."

"More important than discovering the person behind *The Muckraker?*" she asked, keeping her tone light and teasing.

"At the moment, yes." Reaching into his pocket, he pulled out a small box and opened the lid. "This was my grandmother's. I would be honored if you would wear it as a sign of our betrothal."

Held before her, the box contained the most delightful and whimsical ring Juliana had ever seen. Little blue petals adorned the band with tiny pearls in the center of each flower. She *knew* those flowers. "Forget-me-nots!" Her gaze shot to Victor's.

His lips tipped up, his eyes crinkling at the edges. "Are they?" He plucked the ring from its satiny bed and examined it. "Why they are. Excellent eye, Miss Merrick. Now, if I may have your finger."

Fingers trembling with nervous excitement, she held out her left hand, and Victor slid the ring home. It fit perfectly.

"Do you like it? I can get you something else if—"

Without thinking, Juliana flung herself into Victor's arms, and he let out a small "Oomph."

"I love it, Victor." Tears blurred her vision when she looked up at his surprised expression. What had she done?

Before she could apologize for her utter lack of restraint, his expression softened, and he smiled warmly. "I'm glad."

A tear escaped, trickling down her cheek, and Victor brushed it away with his thumb.

"Now, where shall we go to show the world we will stand up against gossipmongers? I've borrowed my father's phaeton, which sits three comfortably. Would you like to go to Gunter's for ices?"

Wary about facing condemning stares from people in the *ton*, Juliana hesitated, but Victor's gentle touch gave her courage. She could face anything with him by her side. "That would be lovely."

"Perhaps His Grace could accompany us as chaperone. A duke's presence should silence some of the wagging tongues."

Juliana shook her head. "He's left for Lords, and I hate to ask Honoria. My mother, perhaps?"

"If you wish. However, no disrespect to your mother, but I hoped for someone with a little more power."

He had a point. They needed someone strong who could deflect any barbs thrown their way. Immediately, one person came to mind. "I know someone! I'll ask my mother if she will allow me to accompany you alone temporarily."

"Who is it?" Victor's lips tipped up playfully. "The sparkle in your eyes I spoke of earlier is there. You're up to something."

"You'll have to wait. It's a surprise."

Giving her hand a squeeze, he rose. "Very well, go ask your mother. Wear your loveliest bonnet and put on a smile while I have the phaeton brought around."

When Juliana told her mother her idea for a chaperone, her mother hugged her and agreed it was a marvelous choice. "I trust Victor to be a gentleman, and you don't have far to go."

Victor waited outside for Juliana and took her hand to assist her into the vehicle. Climbing next to her, Victor took the reins from the groom. "Where to?"

Juliana could hardly restrain her smile. "Aunt Kitty's."

Victor snapped the ribbons, laughing all the way as they rode down the street.

❧

THE COUNTESS OF GRYFFIN. VICTOR'S ADMIRATION FOR JULIANA grew along with his laugh. His pretend fiancée was not only lovely, she was clever. "We could have walked." He turned toward her and winked.

She wagged a finger at him, her blue eyes dancing merrily. "Ah, you forget we are going to Gunter's. You and I could manage the walk there easily. However, Aunt Kitty could not."

Although plenty of room remained between him and Juliana to adhere to propriety, the phaeton's bench seat wasn't overly large. Yet, the fact that Lady Gryffin's small frame would fit next to them easily was somehow disappointing. The thought dipped in and out of Victor's mind like a darting bird, unsure whether to land or make haste in an escape.

Before he had time to examine it further, he pulled the phaeton up to Lady Gryffin's stately townhouse. After handing the reins to a groom, Victor assisted Juliana down from the vehicle and to the countess's door.

The butler peered down his nose at them. "Who shall I say is calling?"

Didn't the butler recognize Juliana? Victor glanced at her, his gaze catching the uptick in the corner of her mouth.

Victor held out a calling card. "Please tell the countess that Mr. Victor Pratt and Miss Juliana Merrick request the pleasure of her company."

With a blink, the butler took the card and opened the door wider. "Please wait here. I shall see if my lady is receiving."

After they stepped inside and the butler departed, Juliana whispered, "He knows very well who I am. It's a game he likes to play. He even questions Drake as if he's never seen him before. Brilliant idea handing him your card. I think it threw him off entirely."

Down the hall, the countess's voice rose. "Well, show them in, you fool!"

When the butler returned, his haughty manner remained, not appearing the least bit chagrined by his mistress's chastisement. "Follow me."

After leading them to a parlor, the butler bowed and took his leave. The countess's gnarled hand gripped her cane as she rose. "Juliana. Come give your Aunt Kitty a kiss on the cheek." She nodded toward Victor. "Mr. Pratt. We've met before, have we not?"

"Yes, my lady." Victor bowed. "Briefly at Burwood's house party last summer."

"Of course. Of course. My eyes are weak, but I never forget a handsome face." She reseated herself on the sofa and patted the cushion next to it. "What brings you both here? Is it that regrettable report in that rag *The Muckraker*?"

As Juliana settled next to the countess, Victor took the lead, seating himself in a chair across from the ladies. "Partly. Although there is no truth to the accusation that Miss Merrick posed inappropriately, she has accepted my offer of marriage."

"Hmm." The countess studied him, her eyes sharper than she'd indicated. "An honorable young man. Although Juliana is not my niece by blood, her happiness is paramount to me. Do I make myself clear, young man?"

Victor smiled. "Quite. And I assure you, Miss Merrick's happiness is also foremost in my mind."

She waved him off. "But you are not here to get my blessing or permission, I'd wager. Drake would have seen to that, and if he has agreed, then he must set great store by you, Mr. Pratt. Tell me more about this false report. I'm sure my great nephew was less than pleased. How did you explain it to him?"

Victor recounted most of what he knew, explaining he had hopes of uncovering who was behind the presumption that his sketches were of Juliana.

The old woman's eyebrow cocked. "I see. So you have sketches of another lady. Perhaps you are not as honorable as I believed."

Juliana rushed to his defense. "Oh, he is, Aunt Kitty. Victor told me all about the sketches."

Not quite.

"They're not as scandalous as *The Muckraker* makes them out to be," Juliana continued.

Grateful for Juliana's trust in him even though she hadn't seen the sketches, Victor sent her a smile, hoping to convey his appreciation.

The countess gave another *harrumph.* "Well, that much doesn't surprise me. Whoever is responsible for that gossip rag should be drawn and quartered. Has the League made any progress identifying the culprit?"

Victor blinked. "You're aware of the League?" How many women were involved in the enterprise?

The countess glowered at him as if he were a dolt. "Of course."

"Lady Montgomery has recently joined The League, Aunt. She is performing an analysis for us now to identify common threads."

"Odd woman, but brilliant. However, back to my question. Why are you both here?"

Sincere curiosity colored the countess's question, relieving Victor's feelings of inadequacy over his intelligence. "We—that is,

Miss Merrick and I—believe making an appearance in public would help counteract the claims. Having a powerful ally at our sides, one who could silence any further gossip, would be advantageous. Miss Merrick thought of you."

Blue eyes twinkling, the countess grinned. "Wise girl. And where do you propose we make this appearance, Mr. Pratt?"

"How does Gunter's sound, my lady?"

The countess threw back her head and laughed. "Ices to freeze those wagging tongues. Clever, Mr. Pratt. I knew I liked you. I'll call for my carriage."

Victor lifted a hand to halt her as she began to rise. "If you don't mind. I have my father's phaeton that seats three."

Mischief sparked in her eyes, and she appeared years younger. "I haven't ridden in a phaeton in ages." Gnarled hand grasping her cane, she leaned forward. "Do you drive fast?"

"As fast as you wish." Victor grinned at the old woman, catching the tilt of Juliana's lips as well, and an urge to kiss his betrothed floated over him. Perhaps later on their drive back to Pendrake Manor?

Several minutes later, seated on the gig's tall bench, Victor snapped the ribbons guiding the two matched greys down the street toward Berkeley Square. When the countess declared she needed space around her because of her rheumatism, Juliana—wedged between the countess and Victor—scooted closer to Victor. Her thigh pressed against his.

Each time the gig hit a bump, and she brushed against him more fully, Juliana's cheeks colored as she muttered apologies.

Victor admitted the sensation was more than pleasant and suppressed a chuckle at Lady Gryffin's devious expression.

Once they arrived at Gunter's, Victor wasn't certain if he was relieved or sorry. At least they would have the return journey to enjoy the closeness again.

Gunter's was busy on the late afternoon day, and people's curious gazes lifted from their treats as the trio entered the shop. Heads of the patrons bent together as if plotting a conspiracy, their eyes never quite leaving Victor and Juliana.

One glacial stare from Lady Gryffin and they returned to enjoying their ices as if nothing of interest had diverted their attention.

After placing their orders, Victor tipped his head to a table in the corner.

"No, no, dear boy," the countess whispered. "Don't hide. It will only give credence to the lies and the vultures more ammunition." Instead, she moved toward a vacant table in the middle of the room. "This shall serve nicely," she said, loud enough for most of the crowd to hear.

Victor did his best to concentrate on Juliana and Lady Gryffin as they savored their flavored ice, but the spoonful of elderflower ice that had begun to melt in his mouth seemed to become solid, almost choking him when Lydia Whyte entered the shop, accompanied by —of all people—his mother.

"This lavender is quite lovely. I think . . ." The countess's words halted as she gazed up and caught who had snagged Victor's attention.

Juliana, too, had paused in lifting a spoonful of cherry ice to her lips. "What is it?" she whispered before turning her head toward the door.

"If you will both excuse me." Victor placed his serviette next to his dish of elderberry ice and strode toward his mother and Lydia.

Lydia's eyes widened.

His mother stumbled back. "Victor, what are you doing here?"

"Countering the vicious gossip, Mother, while Miss Merrick, Lady Gryffin and I enjoy some ices. The question is, what are you doing here with Miss Whyte?"

His mother straightened, her flashing eyes defiant. "Don't take that tone with me, Victor. After that dreadful report and your insistence to offer for Miss Merrick, Lydia is heartbroken. I'm merely providing support and consolation."

Lydia quickly looked away when Victor turned his attention toward her, her attempt to appear demure and play the victim almost laughable. "Heartbroken indeed. However, I would like a word with Miss Whyte in private, if I may."

His mother stepped in front of Lydia. "Haven't you caused enough scandal with one woman?"

"Very well, stay with her, but may we at least step away from prying eyes?" Victor motioned for the ladies to precede him out the door.

Outside the shop, Victor took Lydia's arm, perhaps a little too roughly, but his normally even-tempered disposition had worn thinner than a poor man's coat. "Wait here, Mother. Miss Whyte and I will remain well in sight as to avoid any semblance of impropriety."

Aside, even out of earshot of his mother, Victor lowered his voice. "I won't mince words, Lydia. Did you look at the sketches that were on my desk?"

Lydia's eyes blinked rapidly, but not in the manner she employed when flirting. "I—I don't know what you're referring to."

"When you accompanied my mother to my studio a few days ago, you were in the room alone for several minutes. Don't lie to me, Lydia, you don't do it well. Did you see the sketches and, more importantly, did you tell anyone?"

Her cheeks flushed red, and once again, she averted her gaze. Yet she remained silent.

"Lydia, I'm not accusing you of anything, but for your information, those sketches were *not* of Miss Merrick. If you had anything to do with spreading that rumor, don't you owe it to her to set it to rights?"

Her eyes snapped to his. "Who was it if not Miss Merrick?"

Barely containing his anger, Victor pulled in a calming breath. "As to who was the subject, that is none of your concern. Artists often draw from imagination." Deliberately softening his tone, he said, "Who did you tell?"

Tears pooled in her eyes, and one trickled down her cheek, but Victor had no desire to wipe it away as he had for Juliana. Lydia *should* be ashamed. "It was only because . . . I worried Miss Merrick was seducing you. I only told her because I thought she could talk some sense into you."

"Who?" The question slipped through gritted teeth.

"Your mother."

Although he expected Lydia's answer, his heart refused to believe his mother would stoop so low as to disgrace her own son. "Who else?" Blindly, he grasped Lydia's arms. "Think, Lydia. Did you say anything, even in passing? Where someone could have overheard? Perhaps a servant who gossips?"

Lydia shook her head, the tears falling freely. "I don't know. You're hurting me."

"Victor!" At his mother's sharp voice, Victor dropped his hands to his side.

Incensed and focused on discovering the truth, he didn't realize both his mother and Lady Gryffin had approached.

"Mr. Pratt, calm yourself," the countess said, her tone much more motherly than that of the woman who had birthed him. "I'm sure Miss Whyte promises to tell you if she recalls anything. Won't you, Miss Whyte?" An almost imperceptible hardness coated the countess's gentle tone when she addressed Lydia. In her state, Victor doubted she'd even noticed it.

"I promise."

The countess took his arm. "Now, come back inside. Your betrothed awaits. And Lady Cartwright, I would suggest you and Miss Whyte collude in another location."

Questions swirled in Victor's mind like a tornado, many of them as destructive. But like the twisting storm, his mind would have to settle before he could parse them out.

"She knows something," he muttered.

The countess nodded. "Hmm. But you won't get it out of her by force." A curious gleam arose in her eyes, and she patted his arm. "Leave that to me."

CHAPTER 16

Juliana sensed the shift in Victor's mood when he and Aunt Kitty returned. She tamped down her disappointment that their outing had been interrupted, finding solace at least that Lady Cartwright and Miss Whyte did not reenter the shop. Still, Aunt Kitty met her questioning glance with one that said *we will discuss it later*.

Curiosity pricked every inch of Juliana's skin, and she was dying to know what had transpired between Victor, his mother, and Lydia Whyte.

Rather than discuss it, Victor suggested they finish their ices and go for a ride in Hyde Park. However, the weather, like Victor's mood, had turned gloomy, and to provide him an excuse, Juliana pointed out Aunt Kitty's rheumatism would suffer should they get caught in the rain.

They rode to Aunt Kitty's in relative silence, and rather than have Victor return her home, Juliana feigned a headache. Aunt Kitty, quick to pick up on Juliana's cues, told Victor she had a remedy and would see Juliana got home safely once her headache abated.

As Victor assisted her down from the carriage, his lips quirked up on one side the way Drake's did when he planned something mischievous. Aunt Kitty disappeared inside her home, and Victor held onto Juliana's hand. "Before you go. I wanted to apologize for ruining our afternoon."

Before she could open her mouth and assure him he had nothing to be sorry about, he placed a finger to her lips. "But I must admit, I'm a little disappointed not to have a few more moments alone with you on our ride back without your aunt. Would it be bold of me to admit I hoped to steal a kiss?"

Her breath hitched in her throat, and her heart hammered in her chest. A kiss. Perhaps she had been hasty feigning a malady. Heat rushed to her cheeks, but lest he misunderstand, she said, "You can't steal what is freely given." She peered around Victor's tall body, dismayed that Aunt Kitty's butler stood at attention in the open doorway. "However, we have an audience."

Following her line of sight, Victor twisted around. When he turned back, he instructed the groom to wait with the phaeton, then grabbed Juliana's hand. "Over here." Victor led Juliana behind a tall shrub at the front of the house, and a wide grin broke across his face. "Now, where were we?"

"You mentioned a kiss. Under the circumstances, a kiss would be most welcome."

He tugged off his hat. A long strand of blond hair broke free from the queue's restraint, the look both disheveled and dashing.

Juliana held her breath as Victor cupped her face with his free hand, then lowered his lips to hers.

She should have breathed, for Victor stole what little air remained in her lungs. Tender, the light brush of his mouth tingled against her skin, the kiss impossibly sweet. When he pulled back and took his delicious heat with him, she wanted to protest, but only a moment passed before he pressed his lips to hers again.

Passion in the second kiss buckled her knees, and she stumbled against him. Still cupping her cheek, he wrapped his other arm around her waist, his hat bumping against her bottom, and kept her upright as her head spun.

Long moments passed before he broke the kiss. "Forgive me," he whispered, his breathing as ragged as hers. Yet, the corners of his mouth tipped up, indicating he wasn't terribly sorry.

And neither was she. "Please don't apologize. It was wonderful."

"I should go." He continued to hold her. "But I don't want to."

Neither did she, but she placed a hand on his chest. "Tomorrow?"

He nodded, then set his hat back on his head with a tap and led her back to the entrance, where Aunt Kitty's butler still waited.

"Until tomorrow." Victor bent and kissed her gloved fingers, his gaze never leaving hers.

She watched him climb into the carriage and drive away, and a contented sigh finally escaped.

"Miss?" the butler called.

When Victor's carriage blended with the others and moved out of sight, Juliana turned and entered Aunt Kitty's.

"Well? What detained you?" The old woman's eyes twinkled with the question as Juliana joined her in the drawing room.

Warmth flooded her cheeks as she remembered Victor's palm pressed tenderly against it. "Victor wanted to say goodbye."

A knowing smile crept across Aunt Kitty's face. "Did he? And how was that goodbye? What you'd hoped for?"

Juliana took a seat next to the countess. Reluctant to share such a precious moment with anyone, even Aunt Kitty, she opted for a simple but truthful answer. "It was. But what happened outside of Gunter's? Why did Victor storm out?"

"I'm not entirely sure, my dear, but people underestimate these old ears of mine. They hear better than those of a bat." She laughed. "Even an old bat. From what I could gather, Victor suspects Miss Whyte knows something about those sketches. I intend to do some of my own investigating. Whatever she knows she's probably discussed with her mother, and Lady Whyte is as big a gossip as Lady Cartwright. Not to mention those two are thick as thieves. No doubt they'd orchestrated a union between that ninnyhammer and Mr. Pratt. As old Willie said, 'Something is rotten in Denmark.'"

"But Aunt, you don't think Victor's mother could have anything to do with that report?" Juliana couldn't even imagine how devastated Victor would be.

"Not intentionally, no." She patted Juliana's hand. "Don't worry your pretty head. Which speaking of, do you really have a headache?"

"No. But it was clear Victor's mind was preoccupied."

"Hmph. He doesn't know what a treasure he has in you, child. But he will if I have anything to say about it. I'll call my carriage to take you home."

At home, Juliana had barely entered the drawing room when her mother asked, "Where is Victor? Did you encounter trouble?"

Before Juliana could recount how Victor's mother and Miss Whyte had upset Victor, Honoria breezed into the drawing room.

"Who would have thought writing invitations would be so exhausting?" Contrary to her words, Honoria appeared energized. Her green eyes sparkled, and she practically vibrated.

Happy to see her sister-in-law so excited, Juliana tilted her head in encouragement. "For the ball?"

"Yes. But Drake and I discussed it before he left for Lords and decided it will be an engagement ball for you and Victor."

"But what about little Kitty?" Juliana asked, not eager to be the center of attention at another ball.

"Kitty will hardly care. She will be sound asleep in her cradle."

Juliana stifled a chuckle when Honoria muttered, "I hope."

Mother nodded her approval. "I think it's a splendid idea, Honoria. We shall show the *ton* that the Merricks and the Pendrakes do not cower in the face of gossip."

Juliana only hoped it wouldn't be as disastrous as her come-out ball.

ON HIS WAY BACK TO RETURN HIS FATHER'S PHAETON, VICTOR'S LIPS tingled from Juliana's kiss. The jolt racing through his body the first time their lips touched had surprised him, urging him to capture her mouth again and again.

A pleasant surprise indeed, and one that promised his betrothal—pretend or not—to Juliana Merrick would be no hardship. In fact, he anticipated their next encounter with great eagerness. Images coalesced in his mind of pausing briefly as he painted her portrait, perhaps again in the orangery. With her mother preoccupied, he would take Juliana's hand, and they would sneak between the lush foliage of the trees where he would steal more of those delicious kisses.

No. Not steal. Freely given. One thing Juliana continued to be was straightforward, and his first impression of her held steady. He liked her honesty, her love for her family, her compassion for others. She didn't participate in idle gossip, especially against other women.

How many times had Victor listened to Lydia ramble on about another woman's poor fashion taste, or someone's freckles from being exposed to the sun, or a disadvantageous match someone had made because of some scandal? Too many, and Lydia's latest tirades had been directed toward Juliana in particular.

But had Juliana ever launched a counterattack, even though she could have found a myriad of things to say about Lydia? In fact, had she ever said an unkind word about anyone? No.

In short, Juliana Merrick was a breath of fresh air.

Trite? Perhaps, but true nonetheless, and Victor found being with his betrothed easy.

At least until that kiss had complicated things.

He would tread carefully as he sorted out his feelings and what exactly Miss Juliana Merrick meant to him.

THOUGHTS OF A QUIET DAY HIDDEN AWAY IN THE DUKE'S ORANGERY and painting Juliana's portrait—and perhaps enjoying more kisses—were dispelled the moment Victor walked through the door at the duke's mansion the next day.

Raucous male laughter arose from deeper inside the home, and Victor glanced at Frampton in question.

"Mr. Beckham and Lady Charlotte have returned, sir. They are with the family in the drawing room."

Victor followed Frampton, noting feminine laughter mingled with the more boisterous male voices. He drank in the scene before him.

Mr. Beckham stood in the center of the room, apparently relaying an amusing story. Juliana wiped at her eyes, but not in sorrow. Radiant, she beamed with joy. The duchess had a hand over her mouth, but the crinkle of her eyes gave her away. The duke slapped at his knee.

Even Lady Charlotte appeared amused. And although her mouth was pressed in a thin line, the corner twitched slightly. But more surprising was the look of affection shining in her eyes as she gazed at her husband. From the reports in *The Muckraker,* their marriage had been due to a compromising situation, but like the false claims against him and Juliana, Victor surmised the accusations against Mr. Beckham and Lady Charlotte had also been exaggerated if not blatantly false.

Victor harbored no ill feelings toward Lady Charlotte. After all, she couldn't be blamed for who her brother was, just like Victor wasn't accountable for his mother's sins. However, her cold demeanor was common knowledge, especially among men of Victor's acquaintance. But from Mr. Beckham's besotted expression as he gazed at his wife, perhaps those accounts, too, had been hyperbolic.

Or . . . the unexpected match had more than favorable consequences.

Interesting.

As if waiting for a pause in the revelry, Frampton finally announced Victor's arrival.

Juliana paused from wiping the tears of laughter from her face and bounded from her seat. "Victor! You just missed the funniest story."

Victor couldn't restrain his own smile as he followed Juliana to the settee. The joy of the happy family before him was contagious. "So I see."

Mr. Beckham grinned. "I can tell it again."

Lady Charlotte groaned. "No. Please don't. Now, sit down, you buffoon. Mr. Pratt has come to call on Juliana. We don't want to run him off."

Juliana patted his arm. "I'll tell you later, but I doubt it will be as humorous as when Simon tells it."

"May I offer belated felicitations on your marriage, Mr. Beckham? Lady Charlotte."

"Call me Simon. We'll be practically family once you marry Juliana. Why, she's like one of my sisters."

Lady Charlotte rolled her eyes. "As if you need more sisters."

Despite the banter between Simon and Lady Charlotte, Victor recognized the love between them. He'd witnessed it between Cilla and Timothy, and Burwood and his duchess. A different kind of love, true, but love, nonetheless.

Love out of what was probably the oddest match in Victor's memory.

His attention returned to Juliana. Would it be possible for love to grow between them should Juliana not cry off? If their kiss was any indication, it certainly appeared promising.

"Should I come back another day to work on your portrait?"

Burwood rose. "Not at all. Simon and I have some business to attend to, and I'm sure Honoria is eager for some time with Lady Charlotte. Ask Frampton for the portrait and set up wherever you wish."

Simon gave his wife a wink. "Are my ears going to burn when you speak to Honoria?"

"Like Rome," Lady Charlotte said, her expression one of dead seriousness.

Simon roared with laughter as he followed the duke from the room.

Once Honoria and Charlotte had left, Victor turned to Juliana and her mother. "Would the orangery suit you both today?"

"I'll leave the location for the two of you to decide. Under the circumstances, you may forgo a chaperone." Mrs. Merrick kissed her daughter on the cheek, then left them alone.

The possibility of more kisses resurrected, but Victor reminded himself of his promise to tread carefully.

After agreeing upon the orangery, Victor set up his easel and prepared his paints while Juliana waited nearby.

Seated on a chair a footman procured, Juliana smoothed the skirts of her sprigged muslin gown. "Should I change into my riding habit?"

Victor glanced up from mixing his paint. "Perhaps later. I can concentrate on the details of your face first. If the weather holds tomorrow, we can ride out to our spot, and I can concentrate on Sunshine's details."

With the paints ready, he adjusted Juliana's pose. As he tilted her head to the correct angle, her gaze anchored on his. His heart lurched at the softness—the trust—within her eyes. Was he worthy of such faith?

Motionless, he stood before her, an unknown force like an invisible hand holding him in place yet tugging him forward, dangerously close to falling within their blue depths.

He jerked his gaze away and returned to the safety of his palette and brushes. Dabbing paint onto one of the brushes, he opted to appear nonchalant. "Her Grace wrote to me about organizing a ball in our honor. I meant to thank her. If I don't see her before I leave, will you convey my gratitude?"

"Of course." Soft as the gaze he'd torn himself from, her voice sounded forlorn in the expanse of the room. "In truth, although Honoria is practically bubbling with excitement, I'm less enthusiastic."

His attention snapped back to her. "Are you having misgivings about our betrothal? Ready to cry off already?" Why did the idea not please him? He adopted a playfully affronted expression. "Am I such a distasteful suitor?"

"Oh, no. That's not what I meant at all." Delicate pink tinged her cheeks, and he wished she could maintain the effect without the inciting embarrassment. "Simply that my last ball was less than successful."

"Ah, but that was my fault, not yours." Or should he say Lydia's?

Which, if Lydia attended, he promised himself he would protect Juliana from any further machinations. "On my honor, I promise not to spill anything on you."

Juliana's lips tipped up slightly, not enough for a full smile, but as if she held a little secret.

"Bella! Don't move. Hold that smile, just like that if you can." Victor worked quickly, capturing Juliana's enigmatic expression. Finished, he stepped back, his hands on his hips, and assessed the result. Warm satisfaction flooded his chest. It was good. Really good, if he did say so himself. That je ne sais quoi he had spoken about to the duke stared back at him, alive on canvas.

"Well? May I see?" Juliana's voice brought him back.

Victor held out his hand, and when she approached, he threaded his fingers with hers. "It's still not finished."

Her intake of breath told him she was pleased. "Oh, Victor. Is that really how you see me?"

How could she not know? "It's how you appear when you aren't worrying about what people think, or when you're trying to fit in. When you're simply . . . you. Unguarded and real."

"How . . . how do you know?" Intensity shimmered in Juliana's eyes, the connection between them unnerving. He suddenly felt unsteady on his feet.

Victor released her hand and began cleaning his brushes. "I studied you." He smiled to himself, then slid a glance back to her. "It's not as nefarious as it sounds. My painting master in Florence told us in order to accurately paint a subject, you must first know them." Victor kept it to himself that Master Giovanni used the word *intimately* lest Juliana misunderstand.

Brushes cleaned, Victor took her hand, and they sat together on a small bench among the lush foliage. "When you're with your family, your face is relaxed, especially here." He traced a finger over her brow between her eyes. "Your smile is carefree and even a little mischievous. Your lips tilt slightly, here." He placed a finger on the corner of her mouth, and an overpowering urge to kiss her followed.

His gaze flicked up to hers, his question asked, and her answer waited. Sliding his hand to cradle her head, he lowered his mouth to hers. Similar to the day before, the same unexpected surge of energy rushed through him. He teased, savored, lost himself in the kiss. Like a breath held too long, he released the name burning in his mind. "Adalyn."

She pulled back, the look of horror on her face hitting him square in the chest.

Juliana. Not Adalyn.

Oh, God, what had he done?

"I'm so sorry. I didn't mean . . ." But the damage was done.

The pain in Juliana's eyes accused and convicted him. Her body stiffened, and her expression grew guarded. Gone was the true Juliana, and in her place was a woman protecting herself.

Thank goodness she didn't cry. He couldn't handle her tears. Instead, she became pensive, staring down at her hands clasped before her. "You loved her. Adalyn. Still love her."

Not a question, but he answered anyway. She deserved the truth. "Yes." Averting his gaze, he swallowed and scrambled for a way to salvage his egregious misstep. "But she is far away. Married to another." A scoundrel of a man, Victor added silently. He would never understand why a woman would choose a blackguard over a man who would cherish her.

"It is a difficult thing to love someone who doesn't return that love."

He wanted to thank her for her understanding, but when he turned toward her, her eyes appeared unfocused, distant, as if she wasn't speaking to him, but stating a fact she herself was well-acquainted with.

His mind stuttered on the realization.

Who had broken Juliana's heart? Whoever the blackguard was, Victor wanted to beat him to a pulp for toying with the feelings of such a lovely young woman. And Victor wasn't a violent man.

Her eyes cleared, and she turned toward him. "Forgive me. I feel another headache developing."

He almost shot from his seat. "Of course. I shall call again tomorrow. Weather and your head permitting, we could go riding to our spot, allowing me to work some more on Sunshine."

Waiting silently while he gathered his paints, brushes, and the canvas, Juliana wore a tremulous smile like a coat of armor, the sparkle that so typically lit her eyes absent.

Victor mumbled an awkward, "Goodbye," then stole from the house like a thief.

CHAPTER 17

For a week and a half, Juliana vacillated between calling off her engagement to Victor and hoping against hope his affection for her would grow. Releasing him was the right thing to do, no matter how much her heart argued against it. But each time she summoned the courage to broach the subject, Victor quickly provided a counterargument.

Three days before the ball, as they strolled through St. James Park, their conversation was no different.

"Victor, our time is running out—"

"We should wait. Lady Miranda is investigating the connection Lady Montgomery found to Lord Middlebury. If we can unmask the perpetrator, we have an excellent chance of restoring your reputation."

"According to Bea, Middlebury does seem to be at the center of numerous reports. But Lady Charlotte doesn't believe he is connected to the scandal leading to her marriage."

"He's still a viable candidate. Middlebury kowtows to Edgerton, so surely he could have received a whiff of the Beckhams' scandal that way. Not to mention your Aunt Kitty said Lady Whyte has tea with him regularly, and Lydia's mother and Middlebury both love gossip. Ours in particular paints Lydia in a sympathetic light."

"I suppose." With only six days to their wedding, Juliana's confidence waned that she would actually be able to cry off at the last minute. And Victor had promised he would marry her if she didn't.

No matter how much she loved him, could she trap him into a marriage when he still loved another? In her mind, that wasn't love at all. It was selfish.

But she couldn't paint Victor as a scoundrel, either. Saying Victor had used her ill would only compound the lie that she didn't want to marry him.

Once again, her mind swung to hope. Hope that by some miracle, Victor would truly see *her* and not an imitation of another woman. Would grow in true affection for *her*.

"Patience, Juliana. The ball may provide an excellent opportunity to expose the scoundrel. If we can do so and prove the allegations against us are fabricated, we can admit the betrothal was a pretense to catch the culprit."

Drake and Simon had concocted a plan to discreetly feed harmless misinformation to those Lady Montgomery had identified in her analysis. "I'm aware of that scheme. Honoria said she sent out additional invitations to all the suspects. Both Lady Charlotte and Lady Montgomery were averse to the idea of inviting Middlebury and Lord Felix, but they understood the necessity."

Victor chuckled. "Mr. Beckham mentioned he planned to indulge in an overabundance of whisky and position himself close to Davies should he find the urge to cast up his accounts."

A reluctant smile tugged at Juliana's lips. "I should like to see that, and I expect Lady Charlotte would as well." The change in Lady Charlotte's demeanor had been nothing short of transformative. Although Juliana didn't know her well, she'd never seen the woman smile as much as she had since their return from their wedding trip to Wiltshire.

Hope poked at the vulnerable spot in Juliana's heart again.

Everything had turned out well for the Beckhams. Could she also have a favorable outcome with Victor? Regardless, she needed to keep a clear head.

When they returned from their walk, Victor lingered at the door. Frampton had long since learned to give them privacy, although, since Victor uttered Adalyn's name, each time he lowered his head to kiss her, Juliana turned her head and stepped away.

Victor exhaled a sigh, and when Juliana met his gaze, she saw hurt rather than anger in his eyes.

"Unless we succeed in our efforts against *The Muckraker* or you cry off, we *will* marry, Juliana. Won't you ever forgive me for my slip and give us a chance?"

How could she tell him she wasn't angry with him? That she wanted nothing more than a chance at love with him, but she needed to protect her own heart?

"I do forgive you, Victor." It was the best she could manage and remain truthful.

He brushed her cheek with the back of his fingers. "Then won't you allow me to kiss you?" His lips tipped up in a playful smile. "I really want to."

Oh, how she wanted him to as well. She dreamed about it every night—until the beautiful image popped like a soap bubble on a strong breeze when Victor whispered Adalyn's name.

"Please?"

Victor's forlorn expression broke through her barrier of self-defense, and she gave the smallest of nods, then prepared herself for the onslaught of sensation and emotions she was certain would follow.

His lips barely brushed hers, and her knees buckled, the anticipation and longing she'd been fighting for nearly two weeks taking its toll.

Victor slipped an arm around her waist, holding her upright and deepening the kiss.

Her chest tightened as she waited for the name that was no doubt on his mind.

But when he broke the kiss, he merely smiled, then kissed the tip of her nose. "Thank you, Juliana. I would say it was worth the wait if I hadn't found the wait interminable."

A laugh bordering on a giggle rose to the surface at his hyperbolic statement, and Juliana pushed him out the door. Closing it, she stood with her back against it and breathed a sigh of relief as well as satisfaction.

Hope nestled down in the crack of her armor and made itself at home.

THE NEXT FEW DAYS PASSED IN A BLUR AS SERVANTS HURRIED ABOUT rearranging furniture and cleaning each room until wood glistened and crystal sparkled. Juliana did her best to stay out of their path, for the most part staying confined to her room, or curled in a chair in the library reading her book.

By the afternoon before the ball, she'd almost reached the end, and things appeared bleak for poor Elinor when Edward Ferrars confirmed his engagement to Lucy Steele. An attachment, he admitted, that was made during the impetuosity of youth. Juliana could feel Edward's regret leaping from the page.

And Marianne fared no better when Willoughby turned out to be a scoundrel and threw her over for the wealthy Miss Grey. *Ugh!* As if money could buy happiness! Juliana almost threw the book against the wall in fury, especially when dear Colonel Brandon adored Marianne to distraction. Why couldn't Marianne see what a good man he was and how much he loved her?

She wasn't certain which sister had the most dire situation.

Juliana almost regretted reading the book, but Honoria encouraged her to continue, promising the ending was well worth it. However, when Marianne became deathly ill, Juliana put the book down. She needed a pleasant diversion and some laughter.

Little Kitty's soft cries drifted from the large parlor, and Juliana rushed in to see if she could offer assistance. Lady Charlotte was doing her best to calm the infant, but her frantic expression had

Simon hurrying to her side and lifting the baby from Charlotte's arms.

"I don't think she likes me," Charlotte muttered.

"Nonsense, pudding cup. Just pretend she's Trifle." Simon kissed his wife on the cheek.

Honoria raised a hand to stifle a laugh, but Juliana had no such compunction and giggled at Simon's odd endearment.

Juliana took a seat next to Honoria. "Do you allow him to call you such ridiculous names, Lady Charlotte?"

"I would gladly show him my displeasure if he weren't holding an innocent babe."

A wide grin spread across Simon's face. "There is method to my madness, my darling."

Within moments, Simon had calmed Kitty, and the child stared up at him in wonder.

Charlotte shot her husband a murderous look. "I think I hate you."

Simon snorted a laugh, disturbing Kitty, who began to wail again.

Frampton appeared at the door. "Your Grace, Lord and Lady Nash Talbot are here to see Lady Charlotte."

"Nash!" Charlotte's surprised expression was almost comical.

Honoria rose and straightened her skirts. "Please show them in, Frampton."

A knot formed in Juliana's stomach. According to Honoria, Adalyn had married Lord Nash. Why were they in England?

On legs that felt as numb as if she'd been riding Sunshine all day, Juliana forced herself to rise. With less than a week until her wedding, the timing couldn't be worse for the previous object of Victor's affections to appear.

A tall, dark-haired man entered the room. He had a dangerous appearance, with his slightly hooked nose and brooding features. In his arms, he held a small child, not much older than little Kitty. His gaze immediately landed on Simon, and his eyebrows quirked over his almost black eyes.

Close behind, a woman and a young girl followed. Both blonde, the woman was taller than most, while the girl was diminutive in stature. Unlike her husband, the woman—Adalyn—smiled warmly as she approached, arms extended toward Honoria.

"My dear friend. How good it is to see you again. You look wonderful. Motherhood suits you, as I knew it would."

Lord Nash glared at Simon, who wore his usual broad smile. "Is this him? The duke?" Lord Nash's gaze never left Simon. "I don't care what your rank is, you had better treat Honoria with love and kindness or you will answer to me."

The grin instantly fading from his face, Simon paled and took a step back.

"No, brother," Lady Charlotte said. "That fine specimen unfortunately belongs to me."

Simon's grin returned. "Oh, buttercup, you called me a fine specimen."

"Did you miss the *unfortunately*?" Although Charlotte's tone was sarcastic, her lips twitched. "Nash, allow me to introduce my husband, Mr. Simon Beckham. Simon, my brother, Lord Nash Talbot."

Lord Nash threw his head back and laughed, the reaction not one Juliana expected given the glares and scowls the man demonstrated so far. "Oh, Lottie. He's perfect for you. But," he said, his glower returning as he nodded toward Kitty in Simon's arms, "it appears the scandalous reports leading to your marriage might have had some bite. Weren't you just married several months ago?"

Honoria released Adalyn's hands and rushed forward. "Lord Nash, this is *my* daughter, Kitty."

"Can I hold her?" the young girl asked.

"*May* I hold her?" Adalyn corrected. "That's up to the duchess."

Feeling superfluous in the midst of the reunion, Juliana wanted to slink away. However, as she muttered an apology and moved toward the door, Honoria, being Honoria, stopped her. "Goodness, where are my manners? Lord Nash Talbot, Lady Nash Talbot, allow me to introduce Drake's sister, Miss Juliana Merrick."

Lord Nash bowed. "Lady Juliana. A pleasure."

Juliana's cheeks heated. "It's just Juliana. Drake is my half-brother."

"Ah, of course. Then I'm simply Nash, and this is my wife, Adalyn. My courtesy honorific is practically useless in America."

"Except when you want to impress someone," Adalyn said, to which Nash's lips quirked.

"I'm Mena." The young girl curtsied, but her blue eyes gleamed with mischief. "And this is my baby brother, Benjamin." Mena tilted her head, studying Juliana. "You look a little like Adalyn."

Heat raced up Juliana's neck and flooded her face.

"Manners, Mena," Adalyn admonished.

"Well, I meant she's pretty."

Mena's compliment did nothing to relieve Juliana's blush. "Thank you, Mena."

"Forgive our adopted daughter, Juliana. For most of her life, Mena lived on the streets, pick-pocketing under the pseudonym of Fingers. That is until my wife took her under her wing. Adalyn can't resist a challenge." Nash grinned.

Somehow, Juliana had the impression Nash wasn't only talking about Mena.

Nash shifted Benjamin to his other arm, not appearing to mind at all when the child patted his father's cheeks. "And where, pray tell, is your husband, Duchess? I was looking forward to meeting the man who finally captured your heart. I need to size him up to make sure he's good enough for you." Although Nash's voice held a note of seriousness, his dark eyes crinkled at the corners.

Honoria lifted Kitty from Simon's arms. "He's at Lords, but we expect him home early. The session is nearly finished, and they've only remained this long because of Prinny's—the king's—ill health."

"Old Prinny is still holding on, eh?" Nash shook his head. "Please forgive the intrusion, Your Grace. After receiving word of Charlotte's marriage, I felt it my brotherly duty to come and meet the man she's decided to torture for the rest of his poor days. We enquired at Edgerton's, but his relic of a butler practically threw us out, saying we would find them both here."

"Ha! See, he understands. I like this fellow, *Lottie*." Simon waggled his eyebrows.

Charlotte glared at them both. "You are both fortunate that I love you."

Honoria cast a quick glance at Juliana, and something in her eyes sought permission. Before Juliana could move close enough to ask what for, Drake strode into the room.

"Frampton told me we have guests."

Juliana waited quietly while Charlotte made the introductions, the whole time sneaking little peeks at Adalyn. The woman wasn't only lovely, but poised, intelligent, and warm. No wonder Victor fell in love with her.

Adalyn cooed over little Kitty and, much to Charlotte's dismay, hugged her new sister-in-law when Simon made the announcement that they, too, were expecting a child next spring.

"We have so much to celebrate," Drake announced. "Juliana and Victor Pratt are to be wed, and you've arrived just in time to attend the ball held in their honor tomorrow evening."

"Oh, that is wonderful news," Adalyn exclaimed. "Felicitations. I'm so happy Mr. Pratt has found someone with whom to share his life."

Juliana squeaked out a tiny, "Thank you." She peered at Nash, who studied her.

"Speaking of the wedding," Simon said. "Why don't we take the future husband out this evening for a final night of freedom? I propose *The Knave of Hearts*. It's a new gambling hell that Drake has yet to visit. Why not join us, Nash? I'd like to get to know my more amiable brother-in-law better. You can share stories of *Lottie* with me so I have something to hold over her."

Charlotte snorted a derisive laugh.

Honoria's gaze darted nervously toward Juliana. "No doubt Lord Nash and Adalyn are exhausted from their journey, Simon."

Nash's gaze remained locked with Juliana's. "The duchess is correct. Exhausted, and we've yet to secure lodgings."

"You must stay here." Simon's gaze darted toward Drake. "If that's agreeable?"

"Of course. There's plenty of room, and Charlotte's family is ours."

"I appreciate the gracious offer, but I must beg off accompanying you gentlemen. No doubt Benjamin will be up all night, and Adalyn becomes as disagreeable as my sister when she doesn't get enough sleep." Nash grinned at his wife.

Simon barked a laugh and received a sound slap to his shoulder from Charlotte.

Once again, Nash's dark eyes met hers, and somehow Juliana knew that *he* knew why Victor was marrying her.

Due to all the preparations and activity at Pendrake Manor for the ball, Victor had stayed away from the duke's home. Instead, he spent his days putting the finishing touches on Juliana's portrait. Stepping back, he assessed his work, pleased that he'd captured the glint in Juliana's eyes, and the enigmatic smile that spoke of secrets worth discovering.

Conflicted when he'd last left her, he tried to use the time to sort out his feelings. Part of him wanted nothing more than to expose the person behind *The Muckraker*, and while that was still true, a small part—no, a part that grew larger by the day—hoped she wouldn't cry off and that, regardless of what happened with *The Muckraker*, she would marry him.

Each time Juliana broached the subject of their impending nuptials, implying she was going to cry off, he'd found a way to stall her.

But she was right about one thing; they were running out of time. The banns had been called the last three Sundays. The wedding itself was set for the following Monday.

He'd ordered wedding clothes, surprised to learn that Mr. Abernathy, the tailor, was Juliana's grandfather. The old man had smiled and patted Victor on the shoulder, pronouncing his approval of Juliana's choice of husband.

"My granddaughter deserves the best. And you, my boy"—the

man wagged a finger at him—"are getting the best. Never forget that. No one has so kind a heart as my Juliana. She would find a way to give you the moon if you asked for it."

And the more Victor learned about Juliana, the more he liked her—the more his affection grew. However, she'd kept him at arm's distance since his egregious slip, and he worried it had cost him any real chance with her.

Abernathy was right. She deserved the best. But was that him? He would do his utmost to make her a good husband, that much he knew. But would he be good enough? Her comment about loving someone who didn't return your love nagged at him. Who in her past had broken her heart?

At that moment, as he stared at her portrait, he wondered if together they could overcome their past demons and find a future together. To build a family—a home—a life. Things he longed for desperately.

Tucking the question away, he turned his attention to some sketches he started of the duke's likeness, should he be so fortunate to gain the duke's approval and permission to continue with portraits for the rest of the family. Pride and hope lifted his spirits as he sketched out ideas for poses.

Victor's head jerked up at the knock on his studio door, and Tierney entered, holding out a letter. "This just arrived, sir. It looks important."

Victor's eyebrows rose at the ducal seal on the back. "It's from Burwood." Victor used a small knife to break the seal.

MR. PRATT
Expect a call from me at eight o'clock this evening.
Burwood

Victor frowned and turned the sheet of paper back and forth. Was that it?

"Sir?" Tierney had the same puzzled look that Victor presumed he himself wore.

Victor glanced at the clock on the mantle. "Make sure this place is immaculate. The Duke of Burwood is paying a call in two hours."

"Is all well, sir?"

Victor shook his head. "An excellent question, Tierney. The contents of this note are most enigmatic—and disconcerting."

When Tierney realized Victor wasn't going to expand on his statement, he raced off, calling for Victor's one maid of all work to get cracking.

Had Juliana decided to cry off and Burwood planned to deliver the news? Or did Burwood have some news about *The Muckraker*?

Victor had little time to dwell on it, and after he peered down at his hands, he marched to the door and called for Tierney to draw him a bath and lay out some fresh clothing. Whatever the duke wanted, Victor would at least present himself as a gentleman.

At five minutes till eight, Tierney wiped the rest of the shaving soap off Victor's face, then removed the bowl with the soapy water, just as a knock sounded on the door to Victor's apartments.

Tierney spun like a top with the bowl, water sloshing over the side.

"Good God, man, he's a duke, not the king." Victor chuckled and motioned for Tierney to place the shaving bowl on the dressing table and go answer the door.

After a quick glance in the looking glass and a tug on his coat, Victor strode from his bedchamber into the small parlor, not certain what to expect.

From the Duke of Burwood's expression, it couldn't be good. Victor couldn't recall if he'd ever seen the man scowl before. Even stranger, next to him, Simon Beckham stared at Tierney, his lips pressed in a thin, straight line.

What the devil had happened?

"Your Grace? To what do I owe the honor? Is Miss Merrick in good health?"

"My sister is in perfect health. I've come regarding your upcoming nuptials."

Victor's stomach tumbled to his feet. *She's cried off.* Rejected twice. With his luck, the only woman who would have him would be Lydia. And didn't that thought make his stomach churn?

The man Victor had come to know as Drake glared at him, appearing extremely ducal as he barked his next question. "Well? What do you say?"

"I . . . I'm not sure what I'm supposed—"

Mr. Beckham broke out in uproarious laughter, bending over as he held his midsection.

What the deuce?

Wiping his eyes, Mr. Beckham straightened. "Oh, well done, Drake. The man looks positively ghastly."

As the duke himself broke out into a huge smile, Victor shook his head. "What is going on?"

"We've come to take you out for a night of enjoyment. Simon has been going on about the new gambling den, *The Knave of Hearts*, and we thought it would be a good chance to get to know you better without women hovering." Looking decidedly less ducal, Burwood cocked his head. "But I did have you going for a minute, didn't I?"

Relieved, but still rather confused, Victor placed a hand on his chest, pleased to find his heart still beating. "You did, sir. I thought you'd come to tell me Miss Merrick has cried off."

"Ye of little faith, Simon. I told you I could pull it off. It was you who almost showed our hand. This was his idea, by the way." Burwood pointed to Mr. Beckham. "But I must say, I'm rather pleased that your distress came from thinking my sister cried off, rather than something I might have discovered about you."

Victor's confusion continued. "You are?"

"Well, of course," Burwood said. "It pleases me that the thought of *not* marrying my sister would cause you heartache." He turned toward Mr. Beckham. "That sounds awful, doesn't it?"

Mr. Beckham slapped the duke on the back. "Yes, but I think Pratt is smart enough to understand your meaning."

Such a strange conversation. Victor braved the question lingering in the back of his mind. "Are you two . . . foxed?"

Mr. Beckham grinned. "Not nearly enough. Now, let's remedy that and be off! On to *The Knave!*"

They ushered Victor out the door and into the duke's waiting carriage.

CHAPTER 18

Later that evening, after Drake and Simon left, chuckling like nodcocks over some prank they planned to play on Victor, Juliana listened politely as Charlotte explained to Nash and Adalyn everything that led up to her marriage to Simon.

When everyone else seemed preoccupied with Charlotte's recounting—and Nash barked a riotous laugh at the part where Simon vomited on their brother—Honoria leaned close and whispered, "Drake had no idea of Victor and Adalyn's history, but I advised him before they left this evening. I asked him to refrain from mentioning Nash and Adalyn's arrival to Victor. If you're uncomfortable having Adalyn and Nash here in the house, I will do my utmost to find a delicate solution. Perhaps I should speak to Adalyn."

Juliana squeezed Honoria's hand. "There is no need for that. They're Charlotte's family, and this is her home now, too. Drake did what any good man should do." Juliana dearly loved her sister-in-law and understood what an uncomfortable position Nash and Adalyn's arrival had placed her in.

Honoria gave her a wan smile. "Have faith in Victor. In his affection for you."

If only she could. But Honoria didn't know about Victor's slip. Ever since the fateful kiss when Victor uttered Adalyn's name, Juliana's faith in capturing Victor's heart had withered. And with Adalyn's arrival, Juliana suspected that when faced again with the woman he loved, Victor would not only allow her to cry off from the wedding—he would welcome it. Juliana would only pale in the comparison.

In moments of weakness, she longed to share her heartache with her mother or Honoria, to unburden her heart and seek their wise counsel. But how could she explain Victor's blunder and not reveal their courtship was a sham? She had promised him to keep their pretense a secret, and she would not betray him.

She would hold her tongue and hope for the best while she prepared for the worst. The ball would decide much. In a little more than a day, she would no doubt have her answer.

Adalyn had taken Benjamin and Mena upstairs for bed, leaving Nash with the ladies. Juliana's mother had a myriad of questions about America, which Nash answered happily. He seemed so very different from Victor. Not only in coloring, with his dark hair and almost black eyes compared to Victor's blond hair and blue eyes, but where Victor practically wore his heart on his sleeve, Nash seemed guarded, as if he were holding in all his emotions.

He had much in common with his sister, Charlotte. And yet, Juliana sensed the man didn't miss a thing, and she especially felt as if he were taking her apart bit by bit and examining her.

The sensation was disconcerting.

Covering her mouth, she yawned. "If you would excuse me, tomorrow is going to be an eventful day. I think I'll retire to my room and continue reading my book."

Nash chuckled. "Another woman who loves to read, like the duchess. What book was it you raved about when I was calling on you?"

"*Pride And Prejudice*," Honoria said.

Charlotte grinned. "An excellent book. Reminiscent of Simon's and my fraught relationship."

"Fraught?" Nash frowned. "The man seems overly agreeable."

He held up his hand, saying with a chuckle, "Never mind. That explains it."

When Juliana rose, Nash did as well. At first, she thought he'd done so as a simple matter of courtesy, but he bowed to Honoria. "I think I shall retire as well. I'll escort you upstairs, Miss Merrick. Good night, Your Grace. Mrs. Merrick. Lottie."

"I shall never forgive you for letting that slip in front of Simon," Charlotte grumbled.

Nash threw back his head in laughter. "After you, Miss Merrick."

They ascended the stairs in silence, Nash with his hands clasped behind his back, his expression pensive.

"You seem deep in thought, Lord Nash."

"Simply Nash, Miss Merrick," he reminded her. "May I speak frankly?"

"Please call me Juliana. I'm having enough difficulty adjusting to my brother being a duke. And I much prefer people be direct."

A small smile curved his lips. "You must appreciate my sister, then."

She couldn't help but smile in return.

"Juliana, if Victor Pratt doesn't see what a treasure he has in you, then he is more of a fool than I took him for."

Juliana's mind stuttered, and blinking, she jerked back. From the way he'd studied her since his arrival, she expected him to comment on her resemblance to his wife, specifically in regard to Victor's attachment. But not that. She wasn't sure if it was more a compliment to her or an insult to Victor.

"I've surprised you. Good to know I haven't lost my touch. It's obvious you're an intelligent young woman. You've noticed your similarity in appearance to my wife. And I suspect you know Mr. Pratt had hopes for an attachment with her several years ago. But let me be clear, Juliana. I don't believe he would have made Adalyn happy. My wife is a physician. She likes to fix broken people, and— unlike myself—Mr. Pratt is not damaged enough. In turn, Adalyn would not have made him happy, and I believe you will. Do you realize your face lights up when someone speaks his name?"

Her cheeks warmed. Was she that transparent?

"If you believe my wife's and my presence will in any way have a negative impact on the ball tomorrow night, say the word and we shall make ourselves scarce."

How could such a dangerous-looking man be so kind and insightful? "To be honest, I would rather know the truth of Victor's feelings."

Nash nodded. "Very well. As I said, Pratt is a fool if he doesn't appreciate you."

At the top of the staircase, he bowed and left her.

And she prayed with her whole heart he was correct.

CONTRARY TO VICTOR'S SUPPOSITION ABOUT THE DUKE'S AND MR. Beckham's state of inebriation, both were lucid during the carriage ride to *The Knave*. However, the duke appeared on the verge of saying something several times before turning away and staring out the carriage window.

What did they have up their sleeves?

"Are you nervous, Pratt?" Mr. Beckham asked.

Victor chuckled. "About going to a gaming hell?"

Mr. Beckham turned toward the duke. "Oh, he's nervous, all right." He then directed his attention back to Victor. "No, you dolt. About marriage. It's not so bad. And it does have some advantages." He wiggled his eyebrows.

The duke shot Mr. Beckham a glare. "Did you forget he's marrying my sister? I don't want to think about *that*."

"Your Grace, I assure you I will treat your sister with the utmost respect."

"Don't 'Your Grace' him this evening, Victor. We're Simon and Drake. Simply three men out for a bit of fun. And don't mind my friend here, it took him forever to—"

The duke, that is Drake, elbowed Simon in the ribs. "Never mind him. And I know what goes on between a man and a woman.

But she's my *sister*, for God's sake." He glared again at Simon, who laughed.

As he had before, Victor thought being a part of the duke's family might be rather enjoyable.

The carriage came to a halt, and the driver lowered the steps. Victor had heard the talk about *The Knave*, but he'd yet to enjoy its attractions himself.

A man the size of a young oak stood at attention at the door.

"Hartley, my good man! How fare you this fine evening?" Simon asked.

The man grunted. Victor swallowed as the man proceeded to look both him and Drake over. "Friends of yours, Beckham?"

"Indeed, and this one in particular has quite a lot of blunt to lose!" Simon patted Drake on the shoulder.

Hartley's face broke into a wide grin, and he pushed the door open with one large paw. "Then, by all means!"

As they stepped past the man, Victor craned his neck back to stare at the fellow. "Are you certain this place is safe?"

His question was answered the moment he returned his gaze inside the building. Elegantly furnished, the establishment almost compared to White's—other than the intermittent shouts of curses or exclamations of triumph peppering the air. One fellow flung his cards across the table at another as Victor and his companions passed.

Recognizable faces peered up and nodded a silent greeting. Lord Harcourt sat at a table with Andrew Weatherby, a cheroot clenched between his teeth as he scooped up his winnings. Other men Victor didn't recognize sat alongside peers and landed gentry. Not as impeccably dressed as their table companions, their groans at losses, or whoops of joy at their wins were no more boisterous than those of the upper-class gentlemen.

"This place is marvelous." Barely audible over the unfiltered conversation and clink of glasses, Drake's words held a touch of wonder.

Victor agreed. "It's like the best of both worlds. Less restrictive than White's, but just as elegant. And safer than *The Devil's Draw*."

Victor shuddered, remembering the one time he had ventured into the gaming hell in the East End. Never again!

Simon grinned. "I told you. Now, come. Here's a table with some vacant seats."

Victor hesitated at the sight of Lord Middlebury seated next to Lord Whyte at the table Simon indicated. "I'm not sure that's a good idea."

Simon winked. "It's perfect; we can begin Operation Catch Gus."

Drake laughed and shook his head. "Is that what you're calling it? That's ridiculous."

Victor frowned. "Who is Gus?"

"He's an enormous brown trout on my father's property. Slippery devil. We've been trying to catch him for years. Much like the culprit of *The Muckraker*. And besides, my wife gave the name for our plans her stamp of approval when I suggested it last night."

Drake chuckled again. "You must have caught her half asleep."

"Caught!" Simon barked a laugh. "Well done, Drake. But Charlotte was in a relaxed state and most agreeable, if you understand my meaning. Now, Drake, why don't you toss out a line and see if we get a bite?"

Lord Whyte gazed up, his eyes widening in surprise, as Victor pulled out the chair next to him. "Don't you have a wedding to prepare for?" the man grumbled. "It's bad enough you broke my daughter's heart. Must you rub salt in the wound by sitting next to me?"

"Our money not good enough for you, Whyte?" Drake seated himself across from Whyte and next to Middlebury.

"Your Grace!" Middlebury began to rise, blubbering something about being honored.

Drake held out a hand, motioning for the man to remain seated. "Don't strain yourself, Middlebury. Goodness knows the owner of this fine establishment wouldn't want a case of apoplexy casting a pall over things."

Simon remained uncharacteristically silent as he sat between Drake and Victor.

A smirk spread across Whyte's face. "The game is speculation, gentlemen. We will play pure, no checking cards even when bidding on a trump card. Markers equal one pound."

Once everyone agreed and purchased markers, Whyte dealt the cards.

Victor's palms grew sweaty. Coming to *The Knave* was a terrible idea. He prayed his normally poor luck at the tables would change.

He lost the first two rounds to Whyte, who seemed exceptionally pleased to take his money. "Perhaps it's best you aren't going to marry Lydia. You'd have her in rags before long. Fortuitous you'll have a rich brother-in-law to support you."

Victor darted a glance toward Drake, who ignored the comment, but lifted his hand in a "calm down" motion. "Speaking of speculation, gentlemen, have you heard the rumors about the king?"

"Something other than his ongoing ill health, Burwood?" Whyte's tone dripped with boredom.

"He's on his deathbed, Whyte. Show some respect," Drake snapped.

Whyte snorted. "For Prinny? He's been a laughingstock for years. Time for someone else to step in, what?"

Middlebury snapped to attention and, unlike Whyte, took the bait. "Is he truly dying, Your Grace?"

Drake leaned in conspiratorially. "Well, don't say you heard this from me, but Ashton, being a physician, may have consulted with the king's private doctors, who don't expect him to last a fortnight. But that's not the biggest concern."

Middlebury folded his large body closer. "No? What then?"

"His brother may refuse the crown upon Prinny's death."

"No?!" Middlebury gasped.

Drake shrugged. "So they say. However, prudence dictates we don't take stock in such gossip."

Victor marveled at the ease with which Drake tossed out the line. He'd never imagined the man, who seemed so straightforward and honest, could be so cunning. It was a perfect tidbit to toss before Middlebury. Although the king was definitely gravely ill—Victor's father had said as much—Drake's addition regarding the possibility of the Duke of Clarence abdicating his rightful claim to the throne was brilliant. Ludicrous enough that no one but a gossipmonger would believe it.

Whyte, on the other hand, chortled in disbelief and tossed in his markers for the next hand.

With no winners after two rounds, the pot grew. When Middlebury dealt the hand, Victor's mind stuttered at the trump-determining card. The Jack of hearts side-eyed them from the center of the table. Victor stared down at his dwindling pile of markers, speculating Middlebury would never sell the card to him for the pittance he had left. He half laughed to himself. Speculation indeed!

"Oh-ho!" Middlebury waved his arms in the air. "This calls for the captain!"

Victor turned to Simon. "Who is the captain?"

"The owner of this fine establishment. It's an additional rule here. Not only does the dealer have to add another marker to the pot, but the captain has to oversee any bidding on the card and then stand as witness while the hand is played out."

A serving girl passed, her arms laden with a tray of drinks. Middlebury pinched her bottom, and the girl yelped, the glasses clinking as they rattled together. Middlebury leered at her. "Fetch the captain, my sweet."

Casting a murderous look over her shoulder, the girl hurried off.

Victor's hands curled into fists. "No need to treat her so disrespectfully simply because she's a working girl, Middlebury."

"Says the man who paints portraits of nude women," Middlebury mumbled.

Victor's chair screeched against the floor as he pushed back and rose. "What did you say?"

Drake jumped to his feet as well. "Careful what you say about my sister."

"Is there a problem here, gentlemen?"

Victor craned his neck up at the man towering over them all.

Arms crossed over his chest, the man was as tall as the human tree at the front door. A wicked silver slash of a scar traveled from his left cheek to his jaw. He glared at Middlebury, but when his gaze shot to Drake, it softened. "Is this man bothering you, Your Grace?"

Drake blinked. "You know who I am?"

"I make it my business to know my clientele. Now, is there a problem?"

Middlebury fawned over the man in his obsequious manner, blubbering his words. "No, Captain, sir. Not at all, sir. We have a Jack as the trump determiner. Just following your rules, Captain, sir."

The captain raised a brown eyebrow, then glanced at the table. Although Victor had never met him prior to that evening, something about the man looked very familiar. "So you do. Very well, proceed with the bidding."

Reluctantly, Victor sat back down, and Drake followed, still shooting a deathly glare at Middlebury.

Whyte bid ten pounds, eliciting a laugh from Middlebury. "You'll have to do better than that. The pot alone is worth forty-six. What about you, Pratt?" He peered over at Victor's pathetic pile of markers. "Pity. It doesn't appear you have enough to appease me."

Simon offered twenty-five pounds, Drake thirty. Middlebury turned both of them down. "I think I shall keep it. Shall we proceed?"

Drake's first card was a ten of clubs. Simon turned up a three of spades and cursed. Victor revealed a measly four of hearts.

He consoled himself that he still had two cards remaining, especially when Whyte flipped up a seven of diamonds.

Still with the high card, Middlebury practically jiggled in his seat as the play skipped to Drake.

Drake revealed an ace of diamonds, and both he and Simon groaned.

"Right color but wrong suit, Burwood," Middlebury said, a note of glee in his voice.

Simon turned up a King of clubs and cursed again.

Victor revealed a two of spades. Wasn't this supposed to be an enjoyable evening? He gazed up at the owner, still puzzling out what about him was so familiar. There was something about his eyes.

Intent on studying the man with his artist's perception, Victor missed Whyte's play, only turning back at the collective groan from his table companions.

The Queen of Hearts smiled prettily at them. Bids were bandied about, while the captain stood like a sentinel over the proceedings. Whyte refused them all.

Reluctantly, Middlebury turned over his first card—a ten of hearts. Drake's hands flew up in frustration with his last card—an eight of clubs. Simon followed his example, using some of the most colorful language Victor had ever heard upon seeing his Queen of diamonds.

Whyte turned toward Victor. "Why don't you allow me to purchase your remaining card and put you out of your misery, Pratt? It will replenish your funds so I can win it back from you during the next few rounds."

Simon shook his head. "Don't do it, Victor. You're overdue to win one, and there are still two cards that can beat him."

Victor's eyes snagged the captain's. "What would you do?"

"I'm only here to oversee, not give advice. However, I would remind you that I run a gambling establishment. Risk is my business."

Victor could swear the man winked.

"Twenty-five pounds, Pratt." Whyte taunted him. "Consider it a wedding gift."

"I think not." Victor squeezed his eyes shut, not wanting to look, then slowly turned the card over.

A collective gasp sounded, and he peeked through one eye, catching sight of the King of Hearts. "Not for sale, gentlemen." He prayed his luck would hold and breathed a sigh of relief as Whyte and Middlebury turned over their remaining cards, none of which were the ace of hearts.

The captain slapped him on the shoulder. "Getting married, eh? Good luck to you!" He turned toward Middlebury. "And you, sir, if I ever hear of you abusing my girls here again, I will throw you out bodily myself." He turned on his heels and, on long legs, strode away.

Pushing his chair back, Drake rose. "If you would excuse me. I want to speak with the captain."

"There's something about the owner that seems familiar," Victor mumbled.

"It's the eyes," Simon said.

Victor nodded.

Whyte grumbled as he picked up his remaining markers to cash in. "I'll leave you two to speculate about the mysterious Captain." He barked a dry laugh over his play on words. "Enjoy your winnings, Pratt. It's about the only luck you'll have once you marry that commoner."

When Simon protested and began to rise, Victor laid a hand on his arm and whispered, "Don't. He's upset because the Whytes had hopes for a match between me and Lydia. But it was never going to happen. Not if I had anything to say about it."

Middlebury also left muttering something about having to attend to something important.

Simon flagged the same serving girl over and ordered drinks. Victor gave her a marker, apologizing for Middlebury's unwelcome advances.

When their drinks arrived, Simon sipped his whisky, his blue eyes studying Victor over the rim of his glass. "Do you love Juliana?"

Victor choked on his drink. "I beg your pardon?"

"It's a simple question. Yes or no. You're about to commit your lifetime to a woman. Do you love her?"

"His Grace has already questioned me about this matter, and I've been as honest as I can be."

"Humor me. Your answer will stay between us."

Victor considered giving him the same answer he gave to Drake. That he liked her, esteemed her, but those words spoken several weeks ago now seemed inadequate. Why was that? He answered as truthfully as he could. "I honestly . . . don't know."

Simon grinned. "A fair answer. Truthful. Which means there is hope." Fingers turning the glass of amber liquid, he peered into it. "I understand you were enamored with another woman some years ago. Might you still be harboring past feelings that are preventing you from embracing what is waiting in the present?"

Victor opened his mouth. Closed it. Opened it again, but the outraged objection didn't come. And here he'd thought Simon Beckham more a man of joviality and frivolity. But the weight of his question stung.

Simon's gaze darted up and over Victor's shoulder. Victor turned, seeing Drake and the captain returning. Both men took a seat at the table.

"Gentlemen," Drake said. "Allow me to introduce my cousin. Miles Grey."

CHAPTER 19

JUNE 25, 1830

After a fitful night's sleep, Juliana forced herself out of bed late the next morning. Birdsong and the sweet smell of late-blooming wisteria drifted in from the open window.

Juliana stretched and rubbed her eyes.

Miss Price cast a smile over her shoulder as she poured fresh water into the washbasin. "Good morning, miss. Did you sleep well? Excited about the ball this evening?"

Before Juliana could answer, Miss Price, always the chatterbox, continued, "Silly question. Of course you are! Now, don't be a slugabed. Let's get you washed and dressed."

For once grateful for the maid's ramblings, Juliana responded and smiled at—what she hoped were—the appropriate times. Truth be told, she hardly comprehended a word Miss Price said. Scenarios which had flitted in and out of her mind most of the night persisted even more vividly once she was fully awake.

How would Victor react upon seeing Adalyn again?

Should she have accepted Nash's offer to refrain from attending?

No. Convinced she had made the right decision, she prepared herself to face the consequences.

Even though Victor had no chance of winning Adalyn, Juliana dreaded witnessing the affection on his face for a woman who was not her. To know he would never gaze at her with such love and devotion would break her heart.

Unlike her father, Juliana didn't want to be the second choice—no matter how much she loved Victor. And make no mistake, she'd come to accept she loved Victor with her whole heart.

Where did that leave her? Marrying another man who would be her second choice?

Why must love be so—so messy?!

As Miss Price brushed and tugged Juliana's hair into submission and chattered on, one word snagged Juliana's attention.

"Cousin? What did you say?"

Hairbrush still clutched in one fist, Miss Price propped her hands on her hips and stared at Juliana in the mirror's reflection. "Are you not listening, miss? Well, I suppose that's your right and all with it being such an exciting day. But I was telling you what I heard from Mr. Dawson."

"About Mr. Dawson's cousin?" Juliana asked, trying to piece together the fragments.

Miss Price huffed. "No, miss. His Grace's cousin. Dawson said His Grace is thrilled, but Mr. Dawson said it's all a little scandalous."

Juliana chuckled. "Dawson seems to have a lot of opinions. What is scandalous about a cousin?"

Although only the two of them were in the room, Miss Price leaned forward and whispered, "Mr. Grey was born on the wrong side of the blanket."

Oh, of course. Drake's Uncle Forbes's son. She'd been so wrapped up in her own thoughts. Her cheeks warmed that it had taken her a moment to make the connection.

"They found him?"

"At the gaming hell." Miss Price lowered her voice once more.

"He *owns* it. Can you imagine?" She shook her head and tsked her apparent disapproval.

"Well, I think that's wonderful. Very enterprising of him."

Mercifully, Miss Price finally finished with Juliana's hair and left. Wandering down to the breakfast room, Juliana stopped short when Adalyn exited the blue parlor.

"Good morning, Juliana. If you would excuse me, I'm told Benjamin is upset about something and refuses to be quieted by anyone except me. I worry Nash and I spoil him."

Juliana muttered, "Of course," as Adalyn raced off in a blur.

Voices echoed from the room Adalyn had just left.

"Are you certain you want to do that, Your Grace?" Nash's deep voice cautioned.

"Why not? He's family."

Curious to learn more about Drake's cousin, Juliana postponed her breakfast and entered the room. "Good morning. Miss Price told me about Mr. Grey. Well, that you'd found him. If she said anything else, I'm afraid I wasn't paying much attention."

The three men, Drake, Simon, and Nash, rose in greeting. Trifle, Charlotte's kitten, who had been curled up in Simon's lap, meowed in protest at being disturbed. Honoria placed her teacup on her saucer and gave a little laugh. "One's mind does drift when Susan begins her nattering."

Once seated next to Honoria, Juliana listened as Drake relayed how they discovered that Miles owned *The Knave of Hearts*.

"We should get special privileges," Simon said and received a glare from Charlotte.

"You already cheat. You're lucky he doesn't throw you out and ban you completely."

"Me?" Simon placed a hand on his heart, his expression one of innocence, eliciting laughs from everyone who knew him well.

Juliana accepted a cup of tea from Honoria. "But how did you find out he is your cousin?"

Drake shook his head. "It's hard to explain. But I had this uncanny sensation that we were connected somehow. And of course, there are his eyes. Amber like mine."

Simon plucked Trifle off his trouser leg and settled her back on his lap. "The first time I saw him, I knew there was something familiar about him. But of course, it was my wedding day, and I was so madly in love, I wasn't thinking clearly."

Charlotte gave an unladylike snort.

Nash straightened. "You went to a gaming hell on your wedding night? And I thought I liked you." He grinned. "But of course, with Charlotte as a bride . . ."

Simon slapped his knee and guffawed.

Drake's expression turned sheepish as his gaze met Juliana's. "I've invited Miles to the ball. I don't know if he will accept; he seemed reluctant. I know I should have asked you, but I'd had a little too much to drink and . . . well . . ."

Juliana turned toward Nash. "You think it's inadvisable?"

Nash shrugged. "Members of the *ton* don't normally accept by-blows at their formal gatherings. Expect some talk, fodder for the scandal sheets."

"It might prove to our advantage," Honoria said. "If Mr. Grey's connection to Drake is revealed within hearing of one of the suspects."

"Good luck trying to catch the culprit of *The Muckraker*," Nash said. "He's as slippery as an eel."

"But what about Mr. Grey?" Juliana frowned. "To use information about him as bait seems cruel."

"Miles doesn't care about his reputation," Drake said. "In fact, he told me it might boost business. His reluctance in attending the ball isn't because he's worried about himself. Victor had some misgivings, and Miles didn't want to ruin your evening, Juliana."

"Victor was concerned?" Sudden warmth flowed like honey through her veins.

Simon nodded. "He said he wanted the evening to be perfect. Said something about making a final change to your portrait and bringing it to unveil this evening as well. Of course, he was feeling a bit full of himself after that win at speculation."

Drake's eyes crinkled at the corners. "Besting both Middlebury and Lord Whyte the way he did made it even better. When Victor turned over that king of hearts, I thought Middlebury's eyes were going to bulge out of his head. And Whyte! The look on his face was almost as good as Stratford's when I revealed I was Burwood. Regardless, Victor understands the importance of unmasking the person behind that scurrilous rag. Middlebury took the bait with greedy jaws last night, even believing the ridiculous part about Clarence refusing the throne, although Whyte saw through it. I doubt he'll pass that information on to his wife or Lydia."

"Which begs the question, who should we target for the bit about the captain?" Simon asked.

Juliana frowned. "Who is the captain?"

"Miles." Drake answered. "He served in the navy like his father. Since gossip involving him relates to our family, perhaps someone who has a direct vendetta against you, Juliana."

"You mean Lydia?"

"Yes," Drake said. "Whyte made a point of stating Victor's and your engagement broke Lydia's heart."

Both Charlotte and Nash barked a laugh, but Charlotte was the one who voiced her disbelief. "Lydia doesn't have a heart."

Simon quirked a dark eyebrow at his wife.

"No comments from you, please. I have a heart. I simply don't parade it around for all to see."

"I know that, my love. It's because it's the softest of hearts and in need of that coat of armor you wear for protection."

Charlotte gave a sharp nod, then lifted a slender finger. "And if anyone in this room repeats that, I will have a narrow list of people to interrogate and seek retribution."

Honoria chuckled into her tea. "I agree with Juliana. Lydia should be the one to hear about Miles. That leaves Lord Felix and Lady Cartwright."

"Leave Felix to me," Nash said. "According to Charlotte, he's aligned himself with my brother and will likely report back anything he hears about me. I can drop some false news about my investments."

"What about Victor's mother?" Juliana hated thinking the woman was behind the awful gossip sheet. "She wouldn't report anything that appeared to harm Victor, even if it involved me, would she?"

Honoria shook her head. "I would hope not. Aurelia's taste in gossip leans more toward inappropriate behavior or unfortunate matches."

Juliana cringed. "Like mine and Victor's?"

Honoria grasped Juliana's hands. "Oh, my dear, I didn't mean to imply you at all. And there was nothing inappropriate about your behavior, nor is your match unfortunate. But I do have an idea and will enlist Lady Montgomery's help."

With their plans in place, the men dispersed to attend to business, and Juliana excused herself to have breakfast.

The piece of toast she nibbled sat like a stone in her stomach. She needed to warn Victor about Adalyn.

A note would not suffice. She wanted—no needed—to see his face when he heard the news. Only then could she be certain of her next course of action. She took a deep breath and another bite of toast, hoping the evening itself didn't end in disaster.

TOO EXCITED TO SLEEP ONCE HE RETURNED TO HIS APARTMENTS, Victor stayed up until the wee hours, making a few small changes to Juliana's portrait.

Finally at dawn, as the rising sun cast stripes of yellow light across his studio, he snuffed out the candles and, with hands on his hips, stood in front of his easel, more than proud of his work.

As he studied Juliana's expression in the portrait, something settled in him he hadn't known was missing. Not the frantic chaos of the past, but something steadier, more solid and real. Peace and surety flowed through him like warm honey.

However, his feelings for Juliana were anything but passionless. The kiss they'd shared where he'd stupidly said Adalyn's name had turned his world upside down. His foolish mind simply had reeled back to Adalyn.

But it wasn't Adalyn who elicited such strong sensations in him.

He'd been so focused on the past, he couldn't see what was right in front of him in the present—offered like a gift of rare price. He couldn't wait to see Juliana and tell her, to beg her to marry him even if they unmasked the perpetrator of *The Muckraker* and disproved the horrendous allegations.

Victor *wanted* to marry her.

Like a brush in his hand, or the perfect color combination, it felt —right.

Tierney knocked and entered, taking one look at Victor and shaking his head. "Sir, have you been up all night? You have a bit of paint splotched on your face and nightshirt."

"Come see, Tierney. Let me know what you think." Victor motioned his valet over and waited for his reaction.

"Oh, sir. I don't know quite what you've done, but I can feel the breeze flowing and that addition here"—Tierney pointed to the one item Victor hoped would convey his feelings for Juliana—"is bloody brilliant."

"Do you think she'll like it?" Odd, how his earlier concern was pleasing the duke, but now he only cared about pleasing Juliana.

"If she doesn't, she's blind. Well done, sir. But you should rest. You have a big night ahead of you."

After eating some toast and tea, Victor strode to his bedchamber on the opposite side of his apartments. He quickly washed, changed his nightshirt, and climbed into bed. Tierney pulled the heavy drapes closed and promised not to disturb him until it was time to prepare for the ball.

Contentment, deep and real, settled on him, and Victor slept more soundly than he had in years.

When Tierney woke him, the sun, hanging low in the sky, cast elongated shadows from the trees outside.

Victor stretched and rose, then pulled off his nightshirt for his bath. He hummed while washing his hair, and Tierney laughed while laying out his evening clothes.

"You're in a fine mood, sir. Not dreading the parson's mousetrap?"

"Not at all. I'm eager to marry Miss Merrick." Not to mention looking forward to the wedding night. But he kept that part to himself.

"Miss Merrick stopped by to see you this afternoon. But as instructed, I told her you didn't wish to be disturbed. You needed your rest, sir."

Victor froze at Tierney's words. "From now on, Tierney, Miss Merrick is the exception."

Tierney had the decency to look sufficiently penitent.

"Did she say what she wanted? Leave a note?" Surely it wasn't to cry off? Not the night of their engagement ball?

"No, sir. She wanted to speak with you directly."

Victor heaved a sigh. What could Juliana have wanted? At least he would see her soon.

Bathed, shaved, and dressed, Victor gathered Juliana's portrait, carefully wrapping it for the unveiling.

His parents' carriage arrived precisely at half-past eight, and Victor hoped his mother would hold her disapproving tongue. Hopes were dashed the moment he climbed into the compartment.

Seated in the forward-facing seat, his mother scowled as Victor settled himself next to his father opposite her. He leaned the portrait of Juliana—encased in its protective covering—against the seat by his mother. "Good evening, Mother. Father."

His mother huffed. "Unless you plan to end this travesty of an engagement, I don't see what's good about."

"Aurelia." Icy warning in his father's tone shot through the carriage compartment. "If you don't keep a civil tongue in your head this evening and at least pretend you are happy with our son's choice of brides, once we arrive at Burwood's, I will send you back home and then to Lincolnshire in the morning. I will not have you ruin this for him. Is that understood?"

Even in the darkness of the carriage, Victor saw his mother pale as she gave a defeated nod.

Ignoring her, his father tilted his head toward the portrait. "Finished?"

"This morning."

"Is it good?"

Victor grinned. "I think so."

"Then it is marvelous; you've always underestimated your gift."

His mother gave a discreet sniff and received another glared warning from his father.

Witnessing the discord between his parents throughout his life, Victor swore he'd never settle for a marriage where he didn't care for and respect his wife, and hopefully, genuinely love her. No matter how many times his mother pushed "acceptable" young ladies in his path, Victor remained resolute. Perhaps, he reflected, it was what had drawn him to Adalyn and yes—he admitted—Juliana, who could not be more different from women like Lydia Whyte. As much as Victor loved his father, a small part of him pitied the man who tried to make the best of a loveless marriage.

Before he could ponder it further, the carriage came to a halt.

Mercifully, the line of waiting carriages in front of the duke's mansion was short as he promised Juliana he would do his utmost to arrive early enough to stand by her side as they greeted guests.

When his father handed his mother down from the carriage, he whispered one word, just loud enough for Victor to hear. "Sheep."

Victor restrained his chuckle and followed his parents inside where Frampton greeted them and took their hats. "Their Graces and Miss Merrick are upstairs."

Victor handed the portrait to Frampton. "Could you place this on an easel in the ballroom? Make sure it remains covered."

"I shall have a footman stationed to guard it."

As he climbed the stairs to the upper floor, Victor imagined Juliana's portrait hanging on the walls next to Drake's ancestors, and pride swelled in his chest. Reaching the top, he scanned the small group of people outside the ballroom.

A few early guests gathered around the duke and duchess, chatting amiably. Where was Juliana?

Upon catching Victor's eye, Drake broke away from the group. "Ah. Here's one of our guests of honor." He shook Victor's hand, a slow grin spreading across his face. "Recovered from last evening?"

"As best I can be. I finished the portrait. Frampton will have it ready for the unveiling in the ballroom."

"Excellent! Now, come join us. Juliana is dawdling but should be here momentarily. Some nonsense about her hair."

Victor bowed before Honoria. "Your Grace. May I take the liberty to say you look lovely this evening?"

Honoria leaned close and touched him lightly on the arm with her fan, which was not annoying in the least. The duchess could give Lydia lessons. "The secret is sleep. Kitty slept for six hours last night."

Watching the duchess, Victor found himself remembering Nanny Malone's broad smile and Irish temper that produced a few educational expletives. Her sunny nature and the way she tucked the blanket tighter even when he protested contrasted sharply with his mother's polished smiles and chilly reception when he and Cilla were brought before her for a few minutes each day.

Thank goodness when Victor was old enough, his father showed more interest, teaching him about estate matters but also how to ride and taking him fishing and hunting. He wanted to emulate his father and hoped that—if he and Juliana were blessed with children—she would be more like Nanny Malone or Honoria than Lady Cartwright.

The duchess's brows dipped ever so slightly. "Mr. Pratt, I should tell you—"

"Here she comes, Victor." The duke tapped him on the arm, and Victor turned.

Stunned. All the air whooshed from his lungs at the sight of Juliana approaching.

Their eyes locked, and Victor's stomach tumbled from the same look of concern he'd witnessed moments before in the duchess's gaze. But he spent no time pondering why, as his mind had locked on Juliana's radiance. A discreet gasp sounded from his right.

His mother's sharp intake of breath became nothing more than a hum in the background. He couldn't tear his eyes away from Juliana. She had eschewed fashion—and what Victor understood as good *ton*—and wore her hair down, flowing in golden waves around her shoulders, and a jolt of pride and elation shot through him. He couldn't wait to see her reaction with the changes he'd made to her portrait.

Soft-blue silk flowed over her body, the lower waistline beckoning his hands to wrap around the nip of her waist and pull her close. Tiny blue flowers, much like those in her betrothal ring, edged the neckline and short puffed sleeves of her gown. Sleeves, Victor was quick to note, which sat low and exposed her shoulders, making way for that glorious hair.

He itched to run his fingers through her golden locks, then considered himself fortunate he had two hands—one for her waist and one for her hair.

She executed a perfect curtsy before him and his parents. "Lord and Lady Cartwright. Mr. Pratt."

Although Victor's tongue had apparently become glued to the roof of his mouth, his father had no difficulty providing the appropriate compliments. "Miss Merrick. You look lovely. My son is a lucky man. Isn't that right, my dear?" His father's endearment held the all-too-familiar note of warning.

"Miss Merrick." His mother curtsied. "That is an . . . unusual choice of coiffure. Are you certain it's wise to deviate so drastically from the appropriate fashion?"

Pink bloomed on Juliana's cheeks, but Victor loved the effect.

"Victor—I mean—Mr. Pratt told me he liked my hair down."

His mother jerked back as if a blow landed, and she turned toward him. "You've seen her with her hair down?"

Finally managing to swallow, Victor pried his tongue loose. "Not like this. This is magnificent."

Juliana held out her gloved hands. "Victor, I need to tell you something."

As he reached for them, eager to have her by his side, his mother gasped again.

What now?

"What is she doing here?"

Victor followed his mother's horrified expression, his heart banging hard against his ribcage.

He blinked, clearing his vision.

Surely, it was his imagination.

Yet, there, she stood, next to the dark-haired man Victor had loathed for two years.

Adalyn.

CHAPTER 20

Exchanging a pleading glance with Honoria, who quickly occupied Victor's parents, Juliana chastised herself for being late. She had spent too much time with her hair, the hot rod Miss Price used to add curls to her typically straight locks taking forever to heat between the applications.

She'd had every intention of alerting Victor about Adalyn and Nash's arrival. To prepare him for the shock of seeing her again.

Victor blinked rapidly, no doubt trying to make sense of things. His gaze darted toward her, and Juliana winced at the pain reflected in his eyes.

Victor's gaze returned to Adalyn, who was whispering something to her husband. "How long?"

Would she ever be the center of an event where it didn't crumble to dust around her? She shook her head, unsure if he meant how long had Adalyn and Nash been in England, or how long had she known about it. Words rushed out even as her throat tightened. "I wanted to tell you. But Drake didn't want to ruin your evening out. Earlier today, I came to your apartments, but Tierney said you had been up all night and left word not to be disturbed."

"When did they arrive?"

"Late yesterday afternoon. They came to see Charlotte. Her marriage. To meet Simon. They didn't know about . . . us."

Why wouldn't he look at her? "Victor, can you forgive me?"

In slow motion, he turned toward her as if reluctant to tear his gaze away from the woman he once loved. Still loved? "Forgive you? For what? Did you bring them here? To remind me of what I lost? Hurt me?"

She swallowed the bile rising in her throat. "No. Of course not. I would never do anything to deliberately hurt you."

"Then let's not discuss it further and do our best to get through this evening."

His words landed with a *clunk* in her heart. Instead of a joyful celebration of their impending union, the evening had devolved into something Victor merely wanted to *get through*. Why must the *ton* insist on saving face and acting if everything was right when clearly it couldn't be more *wrong*? She would never understand them, never fit in.

Having worked some magic on Victor's mother, Honoria squeezed Juliana's hand. "More guests are arriving. We should take our places."

Victor's father, who had been speaking with Drake, met her eyes, and the understanding within them nearly brought her to tears. "Take heart, my dear." He bowed over her hand, then moved aside.

Lady Cartwright was not so gracious, the emptiness in her eyes matching her hollow words of congratulations. "Good luck to you both."

Victor's narrowed gaze slid toward his mother. As she moved before him, he whispered one word, "Sheep," which had her scurrying off.

Victor clearly noticed Juliana's confusion. "I'll explain later. For now, ignore her. My father will keep her in hand."

Early arrivals worked their way through the receiving line and Adalyn grew closer. Juliana's heart drummed hard against her ribcage. Adalyn smiled and gave Juliana's hands a squeeze. "I wish you every happiness, Juliana."

A dull buzzing sounded in her ears, muffling the voices around her. She fought the tunnel of darkness encroaching on her vision. Had she even managed a '*Thank you*'?

Adalyn stepped aside to greet Victor, and although Nash had moved before her, Juliana's attention remained on her betrothed and Adalyn.

"Mr. Pratt." In the same manner as Adalyn did with her, she took Victor's hands in hers. "I'm thrilled you have found someone to share your life with. I wish you every possible happiness."

Victor stared down at his hands entwined with Adalyn's, his expression blank. What was he thinking? A tiny smile formed as his gaze rose to Adalyn's face. "Thank you, Lady Nash. I'm a lucky man to have found Miss Merrick."

Juliana blinked, and the infernal buzzing in her ears lessened.

"Miss Merrick?" Nash's dark eyes bore into her. "You've only to say the word, and we shall make our excuses."

"No, Lord Nash. I am quite well. But thank you." She would *get through* the evening. For Victor.

But she couldn't help but notice Victor's gaze following Adalyn as she moved from the receiving line into the ballroom. And it stung.

"Pratt. May I offer my congratulations?"

Victor muttered a curt, "Thank you," and even shook Nash's hand.

She continued to greet the never-ending line of guests. How many people had Honoria invited? Friendly faces, faces she had never seen before, all blurred together. Each person wished her joy and happiness, notes of sincerity ringing in some and doubt in others.

She cast a glance at Victor as he greeted Lady Miranda, and although he smiled, no sparkle danced in his eyes.

"Well, this must be a turn of events for you." The masculine voice pulled Juliana's attention back to Lord Felix standing before her. Shaking his head, he clucked his tongue in a *tsk-tsk*. "Shame having your intended's former lover show up at your engagement ball. You wouldn't have had that problem had you considered my offer."

"Is there a problem, Miss Merrick?" A man as tall as a giant stood behind Lord Felix.

Sheer shock transformed Lord Felix's face, his eyes widening and jaw dropping as he turned toward the man. "Where did you come from, and what are you doing here?"

Ignoring Lord Felix and with a grace Juliana didn't expect from a man his size, he bowed before her. "Miles Grey, Miss Merrick. His Grace was kind enough to invite me. I had the pleasure of meeting your betrothed last evening." He slid a glance toward Victor. "Permit me to say he's a lucky man."

Imposing as Drake's cousin was—and Juliana would have words with her brother regarding his neglect in preparing her for the sheer enormity of the man—gentleness shone in his eyes. Eyes, Juliana was quick to note, that reminded her exactly of her brother's.

Lord Felix continued to gape at Mr. Grey. "Why on earth would the duke invite *you* to his sister's engagement ball?"

Miles quirked a brow. "Perhaps, because unlike so many of your ilk, His Grace sees value in a man beyond his birthright or occupation. Or perhaps it's simply because he's a decent sort. What I'm wondering is why he invited *you*, Davies?"

Next to her, Victor covered a laugh with a cough, which drew a scowl from Lord Felix. "Take care which skirt you chase, Pratt. I hear Lord Nash is an exceptional shot."

Without a further word, Lord Felix moved into the ballroom.

By some miracle, Juliana managed greeting the remainder of the guests, even Lydia, whose icy words of felicitation could have kept the ratafia chilled all evening.

However, neither Lydia's cold reception nor Lord Felix's insults, or even Lord Middlebury's fascination with her décolletage stung as much as Victor's distance. Although he remained by Juliana's side, from the moment he laid eyes on Adalyn again, it was as if a barrier had dropped firmly into place between them.

Soft music welcomed them as they finally made their way into the ballroom. Golden candlelight lit and warmed the room, reflecting off the crystal bobs of the chandeliers and polished silver wall sconces.

Faces of the guests turned toward them. Some wore genuine smiles, while others, such as Anne Weatherby—who had confided she had practically given up hope in finding a match—appeared perhaps a bit less sincere.

Scattered among the guests of Juliana's personal acquaintance, others she had not met prior to that evening watched in what she could only think of as curiosity or indifference. Lords and ladies of Drake's and Honoria's acquaintance, powerful men Drake had either allied with or argued against in Parliament with names she would never remember, filled the room.

So many more people than had attended her failed come-out ball only months before, the crowd boded even greater disaster and embarrassment should the evening not go well.

Victor squeezed her hand resting on his arm, the first sign of affection since Adalyn's appearance, and even through his glove, Juliana took courage in the warmth of his touch.

"Chin up, Juliana. All will be well."

Oh, how she wanted to believe him.

❧

Victor finally regained his footing after the shock of seeing Adalyn again—there at the betrothal ball in his and Juliana's honor, no less. He had a million questions flooding his mind.

Of course she had come with Nash because of Lady Charlotte's marriage. For one fleeting moment, Victor had wondered if Adalyn had come because of him—to stop his marriage to Juliana. To profess her love for him and admit her foolishness in marrying Nash. He'd fantasized about it for years.

Yet even before he saw Nash's dark head rising in the crowd behind Adalyn, a sharp realization crept into him. Shocking though it admittedly was, seeing Adalyn again failed to stir the feelings he'd been coddling and watering like a dying plant he was desperate to keep alive. Instead, a numbness, like being out in the cold too long without his gloves or hat, replaced the longing ache he'd nurtured for years.

Still as beautiful, as interesting and *different* as she had been, Adalyn hadn't changed. He had—or perhaps his feelings had. Rather than a dream he couldn't have, his heart had turned to a very real woman. One whose kisses sent sparks up his skin and ignited a fire in his soul.

But Adalyn's arrival hadn't only shifted something in him. Juliana's demeanor had changed as well. Had she decided to cry off? Would he forever pine for a woman who didn't want him?

Was he destined to lose women to rogues?

Jealousy had coiled like a serpent in his chest, ready to strike when Davies ogled Juliana's enticing bosom. Middlebury had also directed his attention to Juliana's low-cut gown, and Victor had the urge to plant both men a facer. If only the duke hadn't felt it necessary to invite the two odious men.

Victor promised himself neither would manage a dance with his betrothed. In fact, if it had been permitted, he would have monopolized Juliana's dance card. As they entered the ballroom, he consoled himself that he would make sure to claim one of the waltzes.

Curious onlookers gathered around the covered portrait while a footman stood like a sentinel before it.

"Your brother plans to unveil the portrait to commence the ball."

Juliana beamed up at him, and his heart swelled. "I can't wait to see it now that you've finished. Tierney said you were working on it until early this morning."

He gave her hand another squeeze and pulled her closer to witness the unveiling. "I hope you like it." He would make things right with her, confess his growing feelings to her that very evening. If only he could get her alone for a few minutes.

Drake strode toward the portrait and raised his hands to quiet the crowd. The music ceased, and a hushed silence filled the room. "Lords and ladies, honored guests. Thank you for joining us as we have much to celebrate this evening." Drake stretched out his hand to Honoria, who beamed and threaded her fingers in her husband's. "My duchess and I have not only been blessed with our beautiful daughter, Lady Katherine Abigail Constance Pendrake, but we will also be welcoming another family member with the upcoming wedding of my dear sister, Juliana Merrick, to Mr. Victor Pratt."

Polite applause rose, but not from all. Davies's hands curled by his side. Other less congenial faces joined in Davies's disapproval. Next to her parents, Lydia pouted, waving her fan before her like a weapon. His own mother stood unmoving until his father leaned down and whispered something in her ear, causing her to join in with the others in congratulations.

"In addition to Mr. Pratt joining our family, he has painted Juliana's portrait. A subject which has caused some speculation." Drake's tone grew serious. "False, I might add, as you will now see for yourselves."

Victor steeled himself as Drake pulled aside the velvet cloth, removed the protective cover, and revealed the portrait.

Gasps sounded around the room. Bodies of those closest to the portrait collectively leaned forward as if pulled by a magnetic force. Juliana's hand lifted to her mouth.

"Oh, Victor." Juliana's voice was like a soft caress.

"You like it?"

Her golden hair swished against her shoulders as she shook her head, and a leaden weight dropped in the pit of his stomach.

But when she turned, her eyes glistened. "I love it." She laughed, a lovely melodic sound that sent effervescent bubbles racing through his veins. "I'm so glad I wore my hair down this evening. And here I was complaining because it took Miss Price so long to fix it."

Drake stepped back, assessing the portrait. It was one thing to please Juliana—and admittedly, pleasing her had become a priority —but Victor also longed to impress the duke and win the commission to paint the rest of the family.

He held his breath as Drake spoke. "As you can all see, the only thing about this portrait one might consider scandalous is my sister's beautiful hair lying loose about her shoulders." He chuckled. "Scandalous indeed, but—speaking as her brother, and all of you can agree this evening—so very Juliana. This portrait will be the first of many painted by my soon-to-be brother-in-law. If he is willing to take the commission to paint my mother, wife, daughter, and myself. What say you, Mr. Pratt? Care to take on the rest of the Merrick-Pendrake clan?"

All eyes turned toward Victor. Doubt and even derision reflected in those of people like Davies and Middlebury, but admiration in others', perhaps even a little envy in a few of his friends who'd expressed a desire for an occupation while at Oxford, but who had settled for the idle life of an aristocrat.

"I would be honored, Your Grace. And since we will be family, there will be no payment required."

Muffled laughter floated through the room.

"Now, if Mr. Pratt will escort my sister to the dance floor for the first set, let the ball commence." Drake raised his hand and signaled to the orchestra to begin.

As Victor led her to the dance floor, Juliana gave him a shy smile. He wished the first dance was a waltz, but it was a quadrille. At least he would get to hold her hands and be near her. Completing their square, Drake and Honoria faced them with Simon and Charlotte to their left and the Duke and Duchess of Ashton on their right. Favorable company indeed.

"Remarkable work on Miss Merrick's portrait, Pratt," Ashton said. "Adalyn mentioned what an accomplished artist you were, but I had no idea. We're thinking of having new portraits painted of the boys with their new baby sister if you're interested. It seems we blink, and Edmund and Charles have grown several inches. When you're back from your wedding trip, of course."

"In demand by not one, but two dukes, Pratt. Maybe they'll duke it out." Simon laughed at his own joke.

"See what I must put up with? I deserve a medal." Charlotte gave an exaggerated sigh, but the smile in her voice gave her away.

Other couples gathered as the opening strands of the quadrille rang out. Next to him, Juliana moved through the steps as gracefully as any high-born lady.

Victor wanted to whisk her away somewhere private and confess his feelings, but the moment the dance ended, another gentleman claimed the next set with her.

Stationed by the refreshment table, he watched the man flirt with her, and it took every ounce of his strength not to stride across the room and push the man aside. What was wrong with him? Juliana wasn't some possession to be stolen from under his nose. Yet it galled to see her turn a bright smile toward someone other than him.

"Pratt."

Wrapped in his dark thoughts, Victor startled at the masculine voice of Lord Nash. Victor's stomach churned. "Here to gloat?"

Nash's brows furrowed into a deep V. "About what?" Understanding crossed the churl's face. "Ah. About Adalyn. I doubt the duke would take kindly to your obsession with a married woman when you're betrothed to his sister."

The man was obnoxious. "I'm not obsessed. I'm simply concerned about her. She deserves better than the likes of you."

Nash gave a sharp laugh. "If you expect me to disagree with you, you'll be sorely disappointed. Make no mistake, Pratt, I know how very lucky I am. However, it's curious about the likeness of your intended to my wife. If you're trying to substitute Miss Merrick for Adalyn, I would caution you."

"I am doing no such thing. Miss Merrick is her own person." Even as the words left him, guilt gnawed at him. Hadn't he himself made comparisons? Not to mention his egregious slip when he kissed Juliana and said Adalyn's name.

Nash quirked a dark eyebrow. "Glad you recognize that. I like her. I'd hate to see her get hurt." He sipped a glass of ratafia and made a face. "Damnable sweet drinks at these things."

Although he actually agreed with the man, Victor grunted. "If you don't enjoy it, why did you take a glass?"

Nash's answering insouciant shrug further annoyed him. "Because I wanted to speak with you and pretending to enjoy refreshment provides a good cover."

"Well then, if you're finished lecturing me about how to treat my fiancée, consider your mission accomplished."

Nash barked a harsh laugh. "The whelp has a bite! But, alas, no." Making certain no one else lurked around them, Nash pulled Victor to the side and lowered his voice to a whisper. "Although my concern for Miss Merrick's happiness is genuine, I wanted to pass on a bit of information about an entirely different mission—the one to bring down the scum responsible for that gossip rag."

Victor straightened. "You've been back in the country for what? A day? What could you possibly know?"

Nash sipped the ratafia, his face twisting once again in displeasure. "This stuff really is abominable. No information. I volunteered to lay a trap for Davies. The *worm*, as my sister calls him, accosted her. If he's responsible for that rag, I want to take part in his downfall."

Hot anger bubbled in Victor's veins. "I wanted to be the one to deal with Davies."

"With what information? What do you have to dangle in front of him that wouldn't harm someone you cared about?"

"I would think of something." Even as the words formed, Victor acknowledged the absurdity of his statement. To be effective, each trap should be meticulously planned with precisely the right information for each suspect. He fully expected Nash to laugh in his face.

The man's patient expression surprised him. "I understand your desire to best Davies. Burwood and Mr. Beckham recounted his behavior toward Miss Merrick, as well as my sister. I planned to corner Ashton—with Davies nearby to overhear, of course—and relay some investment advice for his clinic. Why don't you join us?"

"You're going to dupe the duke?"

Nash laughed again. "At one time, my answer would have been a hearty, 'Yes,' but no longer. Harry will be aware of the nature of the information. He wants to see the culprit brought down as much as the rest of us. However, if you wish to take a more primary role, someone needs to slip about Mr. Grey's relationship to Burwood to Miss Whyte. From what I hear, you might have a personal reason to see her brought to task as much as Davies."

Nash had him there. Victor still believed Lydia had seen the sketches of Adalyn. Of course, he wasn't about to tell Nash that bit of speculation. Nash would probably take him out in the back of Pendrake Manor and shoot him dead. "Yes. I'll handle Lydia. But I would like to take part in the other as well. I could give you a signal when Davies was nearby and listening in."

Nash nodded. "Make it unobtrusive and subtle. Perhaps check your pocket watch? I would advise the same tactic on your part. Discuss the information with a trusted source but with Miss Whyte nearby."

"Aunt Kitty would be perfect."

"Then it's settled. I would offer my hand, but that alone would appear suspicious to any prying eyes." Mercifully, the cad put his drink down on the refreshment table and slithered away.

When the current set ended, Victor scanned the dance floor for Juliana, pleased he found her walking toward him. Halfway across the ballroom, Stanley Ludlow, one of Victor's old school chums, stopped her.

When Juliana lowered her head to check her dance card, Victor's heart dropped. Would he never have a moment alone with her? He needed to tell her how he felt. To make sure she understood he wanted nothing more than to proceed with their wedding plans.

But in the meantime, he would make himself useful. With Lydia watching him like a bird of prey, her fan flapping furiously, he gave her a brief smile, then threaded through the crowd to Aunt Kitty.

CHAPTER 21

Juliana cast a longing glance toward Victor as Mr. Ludlow led her back to the dance floor. Her pinching slippers made her long for a seat, but before she could make her excuses, stating she wished to get back to her fiancé, Victor strode across the room toward Aunt Kitty and the other widows seated against the wall.

"Miss Merrick?" Head tilted, Mr. Ludlow peered down at her, his nasally voice sending uncomfortable shivers up her back. He held out his arm. "Shall we?"

As Honoria taught her, Juliana placed a gloved hand on Mr. Ludlow's arm, hoping he wouldn't talk too much during the dance.

Still, according to Honoria, she was expected to converse pleasantly with her dance partner. "Mr. Ludlow, have you known Mr. Pratt long?"

"Ages, my dear lady." He sniffed. Perhaps his vocal tone was due to a cold. The urge to put a greater distance between them became overwhelming. His thin, dull-brown hair sat limp on his head, his sideburns traveling down to his chin. "Vic and I were schoolmates at Eton and later Oxford. Always expected him to marry a diamond of the first water."

The barb stung, but she smiled. Let him think her too stupid to understand the insult. "And were there many ladies of such fine quality available? I'm afraid I don't quite understand the qualifications necessary to be awarded such an accolade."

If the pitying expression on his face wasn't enough, the man proceeded to explain as if she were a simpleton. "Beauty, of course, which I will admit, you're pretty enough. But she must possess good breeding, poise, elegance of form and graceful movement."

He could be describing a horse. "Were any ladies here afforded the honor?"

Mr. Ludlow's thin lips pursed. He then proceeded to critique nearly every woman present, dismissing each with smug authority.

"It would appear you—and by extension, Mr. Pratt—have run out of options."

"Ah. You forget one gem among us. Miss Lydia Whyte."

Lydia? He had to be bamming her.

Mr. Ludlow droned on. "I fully expected the Duke of Burwood to snap her up during his house party. But my, wasn't that the turn of events?"

The man was insufferable. But he was, after all, Victor's friend. Juliana tamped down her annoyance and anger on Drake's behalf. "If you're referring to how my brother was reunited with the love of his life, then I quite agree."

"Well . . . of course. Of course," Mr. Ludlow sputtered, most likely remembering he was dancing with the duke's sister.

Juliana did her best to keep her voice calm and friendly and turned to a less volatile topic. "How have you found the weather, sir?"

Mr. Ludlow blinked twice, then turned his complaints to the unpredictable weather. Mercifully, not long after, the dance ended.

After she executed a perfect curtsy to Mr. Ludlow's less than graceful bow, she hurried off to find a friendly face and prayed another obnoxious gentleman would not stop her and request a dance. She really needed to rest her toes.

Victor's sister, Priscilla, sat at the side of the room, chatting with Lady Montgomery. Two friendly faces! Juliana hurried over as fast as her tender toes would carry her. Both women smiled warmly as they looked up and greeted her.

"Why isn't my brother whisking you around the dance floor, Juliana? Should I have words with him?" Priscilla grinned mischievously and snapped her fan. "Please say yes."

Bea motioned to the empty chair beside her, and Juliana sat, grateful to get off her feet. "Honoria told me I could only have two dances with Victor. Since we opened the ball, I think he's saving the second dance for the waltz."

"Perhaps he's smarter than I gave him credit for. Although he's never been one to strictly abide by the rules."

"An admirable quality," Bea said. "Was that Stanley Ludlow torturing you during the last set, Juliana? He's so dull, he makes wallpaper seem exciting."

Priscilla chortled. "He pursued me for a brief period, but then Mama turned her sights on Ashton."

Bea glared. "I've still not quite forgiven you for that. But for Timothy's sake . . . well."

"Ha! You're one to talk. Staging your own compromise. Although I can't blame you. Middlebury. Ugh!" Priscilla shuddered.

"No one in their right mind could blame me. Middlebury wanted me to get rid of Catpurrnicus! Can you imagine?" Bea asked.

Juliana frowned. "Who?"

"He's my darling cat. Such a sweetheart."

Priscilla laughed. "Not according to Timothy. He calls him a demon. But I've found him delightful."

And as Bea launched into a tale of one of Catpurrnicuss's exploits, for one of the first times since Drake had learned of his inheritance as duke, Juliana felt like she belonged in society.

MAKING RATHER A SHOW OF STRIDING ACROSS THE BALLROOM FOR Lydia's sake, Victor arrived where the Countess of Gryffin sat among the other widows. He executed a deep bow and delivered his most charming smile. "Ladies. Why aren't you beauties dancing?"

The Dowager Countess Easton, who must have been at least one hundred, cackled, eliciting a coughing fit.

The Dowager Countess Brakefield patted her companion on the back and sent Victor a warning glance. "Careful with those empty compliments, dear boy. You'll send one of us to an early grave."

Lady Gryffin gave an almost imperceptible eye-roll. "Early my foot, Gertrude. She's been threatening death ever since her great-niece, married a commoner. What has that been? Eight, nine years?"

Lady Easton laugh-coughed again.

Before things devolved and became unsalvageable, Victor intervened. "Forgive the interruption. Lady Gryffin, would you care to take a turn around the room with me?"

Gnarled fingers curled around the top of her walking stick, Lady Gryffin hoisted herself up from her seat. Victor hurried forward, taking her free arm. She leaned, whispering, "Salvation at last from these ancient crones."

"See who that is dancing with my granddaughter, Kitty, and report back," Lady Easton said, before erupting into another coughing fit.

Several feet from the widows, Victor nodded toward the dancefloor. "There's Lady Miranda now, dancing with Mr. Grey."

Lady Gryffin shook her head. "Well, I certainly won't report that back to the poor dear. She would have an apoplexy on the spot and ruin the entire evening for you. The only reason she comes to these events anymore is in hope Lady Miranda will bring someone up to scratch. At first, at the house party, I thought perhaps Simon posing as Burwood might be a match for her."

She exhaled a heavy sigh, and although Victor's steps were slow, he worried they were still too exhausting for the countess. "Are we walking too fast?"

Her laugh, mercifully cough-free, relieved his mind. "No. Although I appreciate your consideration. It's just . . . if I were fifty, or even forty years younger, I would have given Charlotte a run for her money over that man. Simon Beckham reminds me of someone from my past."

"Your husband?"

She shot him a horrified look. "Heavens, no. Someone my family didn't approve of."

"Then we have that in common."

"You speak of your mother." Understanding in her pale-blue eyes bore through him.

"I don't want to believe she has anything to do with *The Muckraker*, but even my father worries some misguided belief may have led her to do something rash."

"Like spreading the rumors about Juliana's portrait to sully her name in an effort to dissuade you from pursuing her?"

"Yes." Victor glanced over his shoulder. Lydia circled the ballroom several steps behind them, pretending to stop and chat with other guests. He kept his voice low. "You know about our plan to ferret out the culprit?"

"Of course." She laughed. "Although Simon would never be asked to spy for the Crown with that ridiculous name he came up with. Catch Gus, indeed!"

"Lady Gryffin, I'd love your help setting a trap for Miss Whyte. I still believe she's the one who saw the sketches."

Wrapped around his arm, her gloved fingers patted him on the sleeve. Victor was pleased she didn't use her cane. Objects in women's hands became weapons. "Please, dear boy, call me Aunt Kitty. Juliana is as dear to me as any niece." She eyed him warily. "But to your point, I believe you may be right about Miss Whyte. I paid a call on Lady Whyte shortly after our outing to Gunter's. She was in a tizzy, wringing her hands and moaning about things not going the way she'd planned."

Victor stopped short. "Did she say Lydia saw the sketches?"

"No. Although I tried my best to get her to confide in me. Lucretia's protective of her daughter, I will give her that. Simply that she'd hoped you would see the foolishness in courting Juliana and come back to Lydia."

"She's several steps behind us now. Let's move to the vacant corner there and see if she positions herself close enough to overhear."

Aunt Kitty nodded, and he led her to one of the few empty spots in the ballroom. They huddled together with their backs to the crowd. Victor peeked over his shoulder as discreetly as possible. "She's coming over now. Play along."

"Are you certain of this information, Countess? If anyone finds out, it could bring scandal to Burwood. And Lord knows, we don't need any more trouble."

"I'm positive, my boy."

Victor shook his head pretending to clear it from horrifying news. "Miles Grey is Burwood's illegitimate cousin."

What Aunt Kitty said next surprised Victor. She was certainly a crafty old lady. "Ah, but is he illegitimate? That is the question. There were rumors that Forbes married Miles's mother before he left on his last mission." Aunt Kitty followed suit and shook her head, feigning—or perhaps not feigning—sadness. Forbes Pendrake was her nephew, after all. "But he died a hero at the Battle of Trafalgar. So young. Such a waste."

"But what could this mean for Burwood? Will Grey challenge his claim with the College of Arms? Is there proof of a marriage in a church register somewhere?"

Aunt Kitty patted his arm. "Those, my dear boy, are very good questions."

And as Victor turned, he contained his satisfaction at the wide-eyed expression on Lydia's face.

Line cast. Bait taken.

❧

ONCE LYDIA HAD SCURRIED OFF, VICTOR ESCORTED AUNT KITTY back to her seat with the other widows. Noticing Davies lurking around the refreshment table next to the Duke of Ashton, Victor caught Nash's eye as he finished his dance with the Duchess of Ashton. Perfect timing.

Victor pulled out his pocket watch and tilted his head in the direction of their target. As Nash escorted Her Grace back to her husband's side, Victor moved to join them. The natural turn of events couldn't have been more perfect.

Victor bowed before the duke and assumed a position allowing him to discreetly watch Davies from the corner of his eye. "Your Grace. Thank you again for sharing this special night with Miss Merrick and me. We're honored by your presence."

Davies chuffed an obviously derisive laugh.

Perfect. He could hear them clearly.

His back toward Davies, Ashton gave a wink. "How are the investments going, Nash?"

"Not as well as I'd hoped. We've taken on some heavy losses due to labor issues with the railway development. However, I have a new lead here in England that might be of interest to you. You as well, Pratt. Consider it an early wedding gift."

"Oh?" The intrigued tone of Ashton's voice couldn't have been more sincere. "I'm not much of a gambler, as you well know."

"This is no fool's bet. And the proceeds could fund your clinic for years. Although I'd like to keep my investments close to home in America, this is too good to pass up. So I've contacted my old solicitor to handle things for me."

"Pray tell." Ashton lifted a hand in encouragement.

As Nash lowered his voice conspiratorially, Davies inched forward, his face a mask of focused attentiveness. "Excitement is growing with the anticipated opening of the L&MR later this year."

"The Liverpool and Manchester Railway?" Victor asked, genuinely curious as to where Nash was going.

"Exactly," Nash said. "And there has been increasing interest in building a line linking London and Birmingham and also with the L&MR. They're keeping things very hushed at the moment, but I have a contact who is selling shares."

"And do you trust him?" Ashton asked.

Davies edged nearer. Two more paces and Ashton would tread on him.

A gleam appeared in Nash's eyes as they flickered toward Davies doing his utmost to appear interested in his glass of ratafia. "As much as I trust anyone. If I provide his name, you must promise to keep it in strictest confidences, Ashton. You, too, Pratt. They wish to limit new investors to half a dozen, and they're only accepting investors with deep pockets."

"Of course." Ashton nodded. "You have my word."

Victor joined in. "Mine, as well. The information will go no further than the three of us."

With great solemnity, Nash spoke the name, "Harry Hudson." He then jerked his head up as if only then noticing Lord Felix. "What do you want, Davies? This is a private conversation."

"Pardon?" Davies turned, his expression as if Victor and his companions had materialized out of thin air. "Were you saying something to me? I'm afraid I was off in a world of my own." He made a great act of scanning the room. "Ah, I have yet to dance with your betrothed, Pratt. And there she is without a partner for the next set. And for the waltz, no less. If you will excuse me."

Victor's body stiffened. How could he have been so careless to not realize it was time for his next set with Juliana? "Oh, no, you don't, Davies. That dance is mine."

Nash laughed. "You'd better hurry. I see Middlebury approaching as well."

Damn. Victor mumbled a hurried, "Pardon me," as he pushed past several guests to reach Juliana just as the orchestra was striking up the first notes of the waltz.

With a tap to Middlebury's shoulder, Victor wedged his way in front of him. "This dance is mine, Middlebury."

Juliana's lovely blue eyes twinkled as Victor pulled her into his arms. "Thank you for rescuing me. I was worried you'd forgotten."

"Never." He pushed back the guilt, knowing he'd almost done just that.

The playfulness in her smile vanished. "Although I saw you speaking with Lord Nash and the duke. Is all well?"

"Oh, that. Yes. Yes. Nash dropped a bit of information in earshot of Davies, and I was just there to assist."

Her eyes widened. "You're helping Nash?"

"Well, Nash wanted to include me because he knew I had a

personal stake wanting to see Davies brought down after how he treated you. I didn't do much other than give a signal when all the players were in place."

"It sounds like you've made amends with him."

Victor wanted to laugh, but in some respects, perhaps he had. "I'm trying. And he had a point that Davies had done more harm to Lady Charlotte, so Nash wanted some retribution."

"Did he mention something about his investments?"

Victor nodded. "He did, and I would like to ask him if any part of what he said was true. It sounds like an incredible opportunity. But"—he twirled her on the dance floor—"let's not talk about setting traps or dull boring things like investments. Not when I have you in my arms at last."

Juliana's cheeks pinked just as he'd hoped. "If you wish."

"Good. Because right now, I only want to concentrate on you. In fact, I have something important to tell you. Why don't you meet me in the orangery later?"

Her blush deepened. "When?"

"Who is your next set with?"

"I believe Lord Montgomery."

Victor breathed a sigh of relief her next partner wasn't Davies or Middlebury. "Finish the set with him, then wait a few minutes. I'll exit the ballroom first so as not to arouse suspicion."

With Juliana's agreement, Victor focused on the waltz and the feel of Juliana in his arms. His hand pressed against her waist, his other clasping hers in a gentle caress. Even through their gloves and the fabric of her gown, heat traveled from his fingers up his arms, spreading through him to find a resting place in his chest. Like basking under the sun on a warm summer day, comforting warmth reassured him and validated the affection he'd begun to acknowledge for his intended.

He would tell her as much. That their attachment, first a pretense to repair her reputation and dissuade his mother from throwing unmarried women in his path, had—over the course of time—become real.

And as for Adalyn, he would assure Juliana that his past

infatuation had faded into oblivion. He wanted to have her alone when he told her. To have the freedom to express the emotions they both felt. Excitement bubbled in his veins as he imagined Juliana's joy, her kiss, her whispered name on his lips.

Juliana.

Juliana.

Juliana.

"Victor? Victor?"

Juliana's confused gaze coupled with the repeat of his name snapped him out of his lovely daydream, only then noticing the music had stopped.

Curious gazes turned toward them. Smiles and muted laughter followed.

Victor couldn't contain his grin, and he bowed over Juliana's hand, then placed a soft kiss on it, before whispering, "Orangery. After the next set."

He couldn't wait.

CHAPTER 22

As much as Juliana liked Lord Montgomery, she struggled to comprehend what he was saying. Something about an invention he—or was it Bea?—was working on.

Ever since her waltz with Victor, her mind was a muddled mess. Those piercing blue eyes of Victor's scattered her wits to the four winds. Coupled with his suggestion to meet him in the orangery, his whispered words a promise of something deliciously provocative, they rendered her utterly useless on the dance floor.

Luckily, Lord Montgomery didn't mind. Each time she stepped on his foot, he laughed and said she reminded him of Bea. Juliana took that as a compliment.

He smiled warmly as she managed through the steps of the country dance. Keeping his voice low, he said, "My wife tells me there are plans afoot to ferret out the perpetrator of that odious gossip sheet."

She did her best to hold up her end of the conversation and whispered her reply. "That's true. I'm so glad Lady Montgomery has joined The League. She was the one who narrowed down our suspects."

"She *is* brilliant. If anyone can help catch that scoundrel, it's Bea. If you want my opinion, my money is on Middlebury."

"My brother encountered him last evening at *The Knave of Hearts* and enticed him with a bit of false gossip about the king."

Lord Montgomery cocked a brow. "Oh? Any fallacious reports about our monarch could backfire with dire consequences for the one reporting such falsehoods." His eyes gleamed with mischief. "Although I can't say I would be brokenhearted to see that churl brought to his knees. But what about your brother?"

"He promised he couched the rumor as just that—speculation, and if necessary, he will deny it. Drake said sometimes it's good to be a duke."

Lord Montgomery gave a hearty laugh. "If he has any doubts, please relay to His Grace how much I like him." He gave her a wink. "And it's good to have two dukes as friends. If there is anything I can do to assist in your endeavors to catch this rat, you have only to ask."

Once the dance ended and Lord Montgomery returned her to the side of the ballroom, Juliana glanced around for Victor. She gave a little shudder when her gaze landed on Lord Felix and he raised a glass of champagne in salute. Scanning further, Juliana found Victor stationed near the entrance, talking to Mr. Ludlow. When he peered over and caught her eye, her heart beat against her ribcage with giddy anticipation, only to increase both in speed and intensity when Victor slipped from the ballroom.

She heeded his instructions and waited five minutes, then carefully, so as not to attract attention, wove her way toward the doorway. What should have been simple—and would have been had she not been one of the main parties being honored—proved to be a challenge.

People stopped to wish her joy again. Several gentlemen asked if she still had availability on her dance card. Five more minutes passed.

Almost there. I'm coming, Victor.

With the ballroom's doorway inches away, she jerked back when Lord Felix's body appeared from the hallway and blocked her exit.

Hadn't he been by the refreshment table?

"In a hurry, Miss Merrick?"

"As a matter of fact, I am, sir. If you would kindly move."

He stood steadfast.

She tried to go around him, but as she stepped to the side, he did as well.

"I say, Davies, let the lady pass," Mr. Grey's commanding voice distracted Lord Felix enough for Juliana to skirt past him and escape into the hallway.

Modulated anger echoed behind her from Lord Felix's protests. But she didn't care. A rendezvous with Victor awaited!

VICTOR BREATHED IN THE FRESH SCENT OF LUSH FOLIAGE AND CITRUS mixed with the pungent aroma of fresh earth in the pots and plant beds. The orangery boasted multiple orange trees, of course, but also lemon and pomegranate trees, along with succulents and fragrant flowers in colorful varieties, literally bursting with life. Faint illumination from the waxing crescent moon and flickering candles bounced off strategically placed mirrors used to reflect the light toward the growing plants. Branches of the trees and plants created eerie shadows in the dim lighting.

Memory of his egregious slip when he'd kissed Juliana crashed back in tumultuous waves. Perhaps the orangery hadn't been the best choice to confess his feelings. Would she doubt his sincerity, thinking he only used her as a substitute for Adalyn?

He'd only just arrived, and she promised to wait a few minutes. Perhaps if he left immediately, he would chance upon her and direct her to another place?

Soft footfalls against the tile flooring and the rustle of leaves surprised him. Was she so eager to meet him she had not waited as he instructed? Taking a deep breath, he turned to greet her. At the flash of dark-blue fabric, the genuine smile tugging his lips vanished, and his eyes narrowed in confusion. Had someone else followed him, or had another couple stolen away for a secluded interlude?

"Mr. Pratt? Victor?" The feminine voice, although not Juliana's, was uncomfortably familiar.

Adalyn stepped from the lush foliage, and he breathed a small sigh of relief. At least it wasn't Lydia. Adalyn's smile, though genuine, seemed tentative, and Victor's momentary relief dissipated.

Tension, like a taut bow, stretched between them.

"Lady Nash. Or do you go by Mrs. Talbot?"

"Adalyn will be just fine. We're still friends, I hope."

Friends. The word sent him back to that awful night when, on the verge of proposing, Adalyn had quickly stopped him. Prepared to risk scandal for her, he'd never felt so crushed.

But at that moment, as he met her gaze directly, none of the anguish, none of the rejection he'd felt that night surfaced. No ache of longing squeezed his chest. He admired her, liked her. But he didn't love her any longer.

Did he ever know her well enough to truly love her?

He rather thought not.

"Of course we're friends."

"Forgive me for following you. I wished to speak with you in private."

Whatever could she want? Best to find out quickly. He didn't want to offend her, but he needed her to leave. But how could he tell her he'd planned an assignation with Juliana? Not that Adalyn would spread any gossip, but something in him wished to protect Juliana at all costs.

"Is there a problem?"

She glanced over her shoulder behind her. "That depends."

His brow tightened. "I don't understand."

"Nash feels our presence here might be a problem for you."

Nash. Would he forever carry that scoundrel around his neck like a millstone? "In what way?"

Streams of candlelight refracted from the mirrors illuminated her face, enough that he saw her cheeks darken.

"Nash seems to be under the impression that you still carry a tendre for me, especially considering Miss Merrick's and my resemblance to each other."

"He said as much to me earlier this evening, and I have assured him that is not the case." The uncomfortable guilt gnawing at him earlier eased when he realized, although his attachment with Juliana had started out as a pretense, it had become very real to him, and the feelings binding him to Adalyn had not only loosened, but had fallen away entirely, freeing him to give his heart to Juliana without condition.

He cared for Adalyn, but as a friend, which, in her wisdom, she had recognized years ago. "Are you happy with Nash?"

"I know it's probably not what you want to hear, but yes. I'm incredibly happy. He's a good man, Victor, although he'd be the first to deny it. And he's a wonderful father to our Benjamin and Mena."

"I'm happy to hear it." Surprisingly, Victor meant every word. Although he never understood why she chose the rake over him, he was glad she had. Especially if the scoundrel made her happy.

She stepped closer and took his hands in hers. "And I'm so glad you found someone to love you as you deserve. Juliana is a lovely girl, and she adores you."

Victor's mind reeled at Adalyn's words. *She does?*

"I truly wish you all the happiness in the world, Victor."

Unexpectedly, she wrapped her arms around his shoulders in an embrace and kissed his cheek.

No trill of sensation tripped up his spine, no desire to pull her closer flowed through him, nothing except for the comfortable warmth he felt for a friend.

About to make his excuses so he could find Juliana, he startled and jerked his head up at the feminine gasp mere feet from them.

Juliana wanted to lift her skirts to her knees and run like the wind to the orangery to find Victor, but people filled the house, some of whom wandered the hall from the retiring room, card room, or small parlors. And as they had in the ballroom, they stopped to extend their felicitations.

Finally, a break in the throng lay ahead, and once she turned the corner, she should find no more impediments. Her corset dug into her ribs and restricted her breathing, and around the corner, she placed a hand against the wall and paused momentarily to pull air into her lungs.

Blood pounded in her ears. And as she inhaled a deep breath, the scent of cigar smoke and brandy mixed with sandalwood made her spin around.

How had she not heard him behind her?

"You're a hard woman to keep up with. Generates all sorts of ideas in a man's mind." Lord Felix smirked as he raked his gaze over her.

She had no time for this fool. "Perhaps, *my lord,*" she laced the honorific with as much vitriol as she could muster, "it's because I have no wish to remain in your company. Now, if you would excuse me."

When she turned, he grabbed her arm, and his fingers dug painfully into her flesh. "Now. Now. Don't be like that. Why don't we have a friendly *private* little chat."

"You have nothing to say that I wish to hear."

"Are you certain about that? What if I told you as you were rushing off to meet your betrothed, he was already having a tryst with another woman?"

"I would say, sir, that you are a liar."

"Ah, but am I? Curious what he was up to, I followed your betrothed when he left the ballroom. Imagine my surprise to see him with the woman he courted several years ago. Being a gentleman, I left the two alone to their liaison. Instead, I rushed back to inform you of your intended's betrayal."

Adalyn? Lord Felix must be mistaken, at least as to the purpose of the meeting.

"Mrs. Talbot and Mr. Pratt are friends, nothing more."

He tsked, shaking his head as if she were a simpleton. "Then why not have their conversation in the ballroom? Why meet in secret?"

A knot formed in her stomach, tight and painful. But why would Victor ask her to meet him in the orangery if he had planned a tryst with Adalyn? She would catch Lord Felix in his lie. "And where, pray tell, sir, did you witness this alleged tryst?"

"In the orangery, which I must admit was brilliant on Pratt's part. Being able to hide amid all that greenery. A stroke of genius."

The knot twisted. But Lord Felix's accusation still didn't make sense.

As if she were a child who had just discovered there was no Father Christmas, the pity, cold and harsh on his face, made her want to retch.

"Oh, my dear girl. You're wondering why. Permit me to explain. Many a man has evaded the parson's mousetrap by allowing his intended to witness an indiscretion before their marriage." He shrugged as if it were a trifle. "And if the woman chooses to look the other way, so much the better for the man to continue with his mistress after the wedding."

"Victor isn't like that." She spat the words at him, wanting to believe them. Needing to believe them.

He shrugged again. "Suit yourself. I merely wished to save you the pain of witnessing it first-hand. Now you can cry off and maintain your dignity. Or . . ." He turned to peer into the empty parlor on their right. "You can get even. With me. How convenient there is a vacant room just waiting for us."

"You're a madman, and I'm done listening to you." With all her strength, she pushed against him hard enough to throw him off balance. She spun around, ready to escape, but he recovered quickly and grabbed her by the arms again.

His leer made her skin crawl even as his fingers pinched her upper arms tighter. Her stomach roiled. She may have been an innocent, but she was reared on a grand estate and watched her brother tend to horses. Wild and dangerous, Lord Felix's eyes reminded her of a stallion's brought to mount a fecund mare.

She gritted her teeth. "Take. Your. Hands. Off. Me. This. Instant."

He pursed his lips, as if considering her demand. "I think . . . not." Releasing his grip on one arm, he trailed the fingers of his free hand down her cheek. "The country girl posing as an aristocrat. Tell me, how many men have you taken to your bed, sweet? Hmm? Some bumbling country oafs, no doubt. How would you like a man experienced with women?"

The gall!

"Miss Merrick, is this man bothering you?" The question was like an angel song from heaven, only spoken in a deep male voice.

Lord Felix turned and, upon seeing Miles Grey approaching, dropped his hands from Juliana's arms.

Wasting no time, Juliana called over her shoulder as she raced away toward the orangery. "Thank you, Mr. Grey."

CHAPTER 23

Victor jerk backed, heart pounding like a runaway horse's hooves on cobbles. His face heated, but it was Lydia's wide eyes that burned through him.

"This isn't what it appears to be." As soon as the words had flown from his mouth, Victor understood the absurdity of them. Whenever someone insisted something wasn't what it appeared, it meant it was *exactly* as it appeared.

Adalyn took a step toward Lydia. "Allow me to explain."

Lydia straightened her shoulders as if she hadn't been the one eavesdropping. "And why should I believe you?! You who came between Lord Nash and Lady Honoria—I mean Her Grace. Although goodness knows what she saw in him. Good riddance is what I say. And does your husband know you are cavorting with the soon-to-be-bridegroom?"

"We are not cavorting!" Victor's hands clenched at his sides. Of all people, it would have to be Lydia.

Lydia's gaze darted between Adalyn and him, a sudden understanding crossing her typically clueless countenance. She raised a hand to her mouth. "Oh! It was her! Not Miss Merrick, wasn't it? Those sketches. And to think I had pinned my hopes on you at one time, Mr. Pratt."

Words scrambled in his mind. What could he say? How could he defend himself?

His only hope to explain that Adalyn's kiss was an innocent exchange between friends before Lydia ran off and conveyed the news to all who would listen slipped from his fingers. Adalyn brought him to his senses.

Her lovely brow creased. "What sketches, Victor?"

"Scandalous sketches of a woman with too much décolletage exposed. A woman who looks suspiciously like Miss Merrick—or you." Lydia appeared proud to relay that bit of information and cause more damage.

Victor tried his best to ignore Adalyn's horrified expression. "And just how would you know who the woman looked like and how she was dressed, Lydia? Unless, of course, you had seen the drawings yourself."

Lydia's mouth moved soundlessly, finally managing a few stumbled words. "Well . . . I . . . that is . . . it's what *The Muckraker* reported."

"If memory serves, *The Muckraker* simply said the woman was in a state of undress, nothing about her bosom being exposed. Admit it, Lydia, you rummaged around on my desk and saw those sketches."

Lydia's face reddened, and Victor pressed forward, although he doubted his next accusation. "And *you* are the perpetrator of that horrible gossip rag."

From the corner of his eye, he saw Adalyn's focus shift to Lydia.

"No. No." Lydia shook her head so furiously, strands of her well-crafted coiffure broke loose. "I mean, yes, I saw the drawings." She stepped forward, reaching for Victor, but he pulled back. "I only wanted to admire them. You're so talented, Victor."

"Stop the flattery, Lydia. Admit your guilt fully, and we shall be done with this."

"I'm not responsible for what's in that scandal sheet. I may have mentioned seeing the drawings to someone, but—"

"Who?" This time Victor moved forward, his hands still clenched at his sides. He needed to control himself when every part of him wanted to grab Lydia and shake the truth from her.

"M-my mother. I was upset about them. I thought if Mother could talk to your mother and dissuade you from sullying yourself with a commoner—"

Adalyn asked the question forming in Victor's mind. "You planned to blackmail Mr. Pratt?"

"You make it sound sordid."

"Blackmail is sordid, Lydia," Victor said.

"We only thought to use it as leverage to get you to realize how associating with those beneath you could damage your own reputation. How was I supposed to know *The Muckraker* would report it before we could speak with you directly? Then you went and offered for Miss Merrick!"

Adalyn faced him, hurt in her eyes like a knife slicing through him. He would have to make amends with her later. "Do you believe her? That she's not responsible for spreading such rumors in print?"

Drawing a hand down his face, he exhaled a heavy sigh. "I do. Only because Lydia isn't bright enough to write the rag."

"I beg your pardon!" Lydia squared her shoulders, clearly affronted.

Victor ignored her. "However, that doesn't mean she's not involved in some other way. And I intend to find out how."

A soft, feminine voice called from the entrance to the orangery. "Victor?"

In all the commotion, Victor had forgotten that Juliana was supposed to meet him.

"We're over here, Miss Merrick." Lydia's smirk sent a chill skirting up Victor's spine.

Her cheeks rosy as if from exertion, Juliana came to an abrupt halt, and her gaze darted between Victor, Adalyn, and Lydia, landing back on Adalyn with a *thud*.

"You are a little too late, Miss Merrick," Lydia crowed. "But if I were you, I would give serious thought to your upcoming nuptials. It would appear your betrothed isn't quite sure who is his fiancée." She sauntered off, flicking a devious look over her shoulder as she passed Juliana.

Adalyn approached Juliana. "Miss Merrick, are you unwell? You appear flushed."

Juliana's gaze remained fixed on him. "I'm quite well, thank you. However, I would like to speak with Victor in private if I may?"

"Of course." With a final look of apology, Adalyn slipped from the orangery.

Silence engulfed them. Finally alone with Juliana, Victor shifted uncomfortably under her scrutiny, and his neckcloth suddenly became overly tight. Their rendezvous was not at all what he'd planned.

So many questions raced through his mind. Would Lydia refrain from revealing to others what she thought she'd witnessed? Would he lose any further commission from Burwood? Could he salvage things with Juliana?

Most questions would have to wait, for Juliana addressed the most important one.

Pain, sharp and visceral from her gaze stabbed at his heart, her eyes bright but unblinking. "Is it true?"

Unsure what she expected when she burst into the orangery, Juliana had hoped for the best, to find Victor alone and waiting for her. But the guilty look on his face as he stood next to Adalyn coupled with Lydia's self-satisfied smirk appeared to confirm Lord Felix's accusations. Nausea fought its way up her throat, and she forced it down.

Rather than exhibiting confusion at her question or asking for clarification, Victor seemed to understand exactly what she meant.

"No." Spoken with such confidence, she held onto his denial as if it were a lifeline.

"Why was Adalyn here?"

Victor's gaze, which up to that point, had been direct and open, traveled to the side, and her heart dropped.

"She wanted to wish me happiness."

"Hadn't she already done so in the reception line?"

A few leaves had fallen to the tile flooring, and Victor's feet rustled against them as he shifted his position. "She asked if her presence created a problem for me—for us."

Ah. "Lord Nash asked me the same question last night."

Victor's gaze jerked back to hers. "What did you tell him?"

"That if it was a problem, I would rather learn the truth of your feelings before the wedding than after." Despite Victor's adamant denial, doubt niggled at her. "Is it a problem? Is that what Lydia meant by saying you were confused about who was your fiancée?"

"She misunderstood something she saw."

"What, Victor? What did she see?"

"A kiss." Victor stepped forward, his foot landing on a dried leaf, the crunch mimicking the breaking of her heart. "But it's not what you think."

The room tilted, and her knees grew weak. "Not what I think? Do you mean like when you said Adalyn's name after kissing me?" She shook her head, trying to clear it. "Why would you ask me to meet you here if you were meeting Adalyn? Were Lord Felix and Miss Whyte right? If you wanted me to cry off, why not just ask me? I never wanted to tie you to a marriage you didn't want, Victor. My reputation be damned. All you had to do was say the word."

"That's not what I want. In fact, I—what do you mean Lord Felix? What does Davies have to do with this?"

"He accosted me in the hall on my way to see you. He told me you were here with Adalyn." She shook her head. "I didn't want to believe him, but it appears he was right."

"Accosted you? Did he harm you?" He took another step forward. "I will strangle him with my bare hands if he—"

She held out a hand. "Stop. Please, don't come any closer. I need to think. Let's get through the evening—as you said. Then, in the morning, I'll tell Drake the wedding is off."

On shaky legs, she stumbled from the orangery. Tears blurred her vision as she hurried down the hallway, desperate to get away—anywhere but where Victor was.

Voices drifted ahead as she grew closer to the ballroom. Anxious to avoid confrontation, she ducked into another room and closed the door. Time would help her get her tears under control before returning to the ballroom. Nausea crept up her throat again. She turned the scene over in her mind again and again, like a jagged stone she couldn't stop touching. Adalyn's face, Victor's fierce denial, Lydia's glee—each one another blow. Would Victor really be so cruel as to orchestrate a scene in order for her to witness a tryst between him and Adalyn? It didn't make sense.

But Victor admitted to a kiss. Did Victor kiss Adalyn, or did Adalyn kiss Victor? But why would Adalyn kiss Victor? In seeing him again, had she realized she had deeper feelings for him than she believed? By all accounts, she appeared to be happy with her marriage. To love Lord Nash.

Oh, poor Nash! What would he do? She'd heard tales about his marksmanship. Would he challenge Victor to a duel of honor?

Juliana paced the floor. *Think. Think.*

She felt herself slipping into Drake's pattern of second guessing and worst-case scenarios. "Stop," she muttered to herself. No matter what the explanation, one clear path lay ahead of her. She would release Victor with an open heart. The clock on the mantle struck half past midnight, and everyone would be gathering for supper.

After wiping away her tears, she cracked open the door, poked her head out, and listened. No voices rose from any of the rooms, and the hallway was clear. With deliberate steps, she strode back to the ballroom, her head held high. She would not embarrass Drake or Honoria by making a scene.

Catching her eye, Drake hurried over to her. "Where have you been?" No anger laced his words, and she recognized the worry in his eyes.

"I needed some air. Where is Victor?"

"Over speaking with Lord Nash and his wife."

Juliana's gaze jerked toward where Drake indicated. Nash didn't appear to be on the verge of murder. But what did it mean?

Drake pulled her attention back. His amber eyes studied her. "Victor seemed upset when he came back into the ballroom. And frankly, you do as well. Don't lie to me, Juliana. Did something happen?"

"I don't want to ruin the evening, Drake. I promise I will tell you when the ball is over."

He gave her a stern, brotherly look. "Very well. But I don't like it. Now, Victor is coming over to escort you to supper."

Muted conversation swirled around her, the words indiscernible as Victor approached, his expression pleading. She forced a smile, and behind it, everything hurt, like a mask pressed tightly to her face.

He bowed to Drake, then extended his arm to her. "May I escort you into supper, Miss Merrick?"

"Of course." Slipping her hand onto his arm, she forced a painful smile to her lips, the effort Herculean. Regardless of what had transpired, she would put on a brave front.

And hide her broken heart.

❦

WITH A HEAVY HEART, VICTOR HAD TRUDGED BACK TO THE ballroom after Juliana left him standing hopeless and alone. His plan to tell Juliana of his growing affection and honest desire for their marriage spoiled by an innocent kiss, as if someone had splashed paint over the Mona Lisa, turning something beautiful into something ugly.

Adalyn promised to do what she could to make it right. Nash, to Victor's astonishment, was understanding, saying he trusted in Adalyn's love. Although, he did make an off-handed comment about going a round or two with Victor at Gentleman Jackson's Boxing Academy.

But at the moment, as he escorted Juliana into the massive dining hall, Victor ached to see her grace him with a genuine smile—the one that made her eyes sparkle. He leaned down and whispered, "Juliana, I need to explain."

Straight ahead, her gaze never faltered. "Not now, Victor. People could overhear."

She was right, of course. They needed to discuss what happened out of view and earshot of anyone else.

Supper was an exercise in discomfort. Seated across from Victor, Lord Middlebury prattled like an old hen, going on and on about the king's ill health. Next to Juliana, Miles Grey chatted with Juliana's mother, although Victor couldn't discern the conversation. Across from Mrs. Merrick, Victor's mother dipped her spoon into the turtle soup and glared daggers at the other woman.

But his mother's glower couldn't compare to Davies' scowl. He practically simmered with suppressed anger next to Lydia, who at that moment leaned over to whisper something into Stanley Ludlow's ear.

Ludlow's eyes widened as they shot to Victor.

The entire dinner party was seated on a powder keg ready to blow. The only question remaining was who would light the match?

"Your mother tells me you love to ride, Miss Merrick," Mr. Grey said.

"Yes, sir." Juliana stirred her soup aimlessly, her answer to Mr. Grey's question polite, but brief.

Victor leaned forward, peering around Juliana. "She's an accomplished horsewoman, sir. I dare say she could outride me."

A tiny smile ghosted Juliana's lips. "Thank you, Mr. Pratt. But you exaggerate my skill."

"I'm more at home on a ship than a horse," Mr. Grey said.

"Perhaps you could visit my brother at his country home in Dorset. I'm sure Drake would be happy to teach you to ride."

Mr. Grey chuckled. "I know how. I just prefer the ocean. But thank you for the invitation. It is most generous."

Watching their interaction, Lydia leaned over to Ludlow again, this time, her gaze trained on Mr. Grey.

Drat. The more Lydia spread what she'd overheard about Mr. Grey, the less likely it would be to pinpoint the culprit behind *The Muckraker.* To prove his point, Ludlow leaned over, whispering to Lord Harcourt.

Luckily, Harcourt's affronted expression meant—at least for the time being—the gossip chain had been cut short. He and

Ludlow exchanged a few apparently heated words before Harcourt turned his attention to Lady Stratford on his left. Whatever Harcourt said, it most likely wasn't about Miles Grey as Lady Stratford tittered much like a young debutante, the color in her cheeks rising.

Victor leaned toward Juliana. "Her Grace's father better mind his wife. Harcourt is flirting with her."

Juliana's mouth hung open. "No!" She swung her gaze toward the older pair. "Honoria's mother is so proper. I wonder what he said." When Juliana turned back, her smile beamed.

To see her happy warmed his heart. He had to make things right between them.

Then she seemed to remember what had transpired earlier, and her smile faded, taking her warmth with it.

"Juliana, please let me explain."

Sudden awareness arose that Middlebury, who had been slurping his soup rather loudly, had stilled, his large body tilting closer.

Juliana gave a subtle shake of her head. "If you mean about delaying our wedding trip, please don't give it another thought. We can discuss it later."

Goodness, but she was a quick thinker.

Gently, he placed his hand on top of hers and gave it a tiny squeeze as he mouthed the words, *Thank you.*

She slid her hand out from under his, and he resisted the urge to take it back. He couldn't press her, but damn if he didn't need to set things straight.

He scooped up another spoonful of soup, doing his best to sound nonchalant. "If I'm not mistaken, there is one more waltz after supper."

Barely perceptible, she winced. Was she so angry, find him so reprehensible, she wished to avoid any contact with him whatsoever?

"You are correct. However, since it is the last dance of the evening, if you find yourself in need of a respite, only say the word."

"I would never be too tired to dance with you, Juliana." He prayed the sincerity of his words were evident.

After an hour, the interminably long supper drew to a close, and as the women departed for the ladies' retiring room to refresh themselves, Victor waited for Juliana in the ballroom.

"Something is wrong, Pratt. Tell me what it is." Burwood's voice, although commanding, wasn't harsh.

Victor glanced around, not exactly pleased they were alone as he'd hoped to evade the duke's question using the excuse they could be overheard. "Something happened—although innocent—that upset Juliana."

"Go on."

"Lady Nash wished me well and kissed me. I promise you, it was in friendship only."

"And yet, my wife tells me you held a tendre for the lady several years ago. Courted her, in fact. Is it possible your feelings remain the same?"

Victor shook his head. "I assure you, sir. Whatever affection I held for Lady Nash is in the past."

"And where did this innocent kiss occur, might I ask? Surely, not in public?"

How could he tell Drake he had been waiting for Juliana? However, lying wouldn't help his cause. "In the orangery, sir."

The duke's eyebrows hitched. "Quite a distance from the ballroom. And both Lady Nash and my sister came upon you there by accident?"

Although reared as a steward's son and a groom, the man was shrewd. "Lady Nash followed me. As I told Juliana, Lady Nash wished to ensure everything between us was in the past."

"And my sister? Was that by chance?"

Victor's throat tightened. "No, sir. I asked her to meet me there."

"Alone?"

"Yes."

"Do I want to know why?"

Bitter and dry, a hollow chuckle rose in Victor's throat and caught. *Yes and no.* Victor couldn't tell the man his relationship with Juliana, although now very real to him, had started as a pretense. Burwood would have his head for using his sister. Victor formed his answer carefully. "Nothing improper. I wanted to tell her something —personal—in private."

Rightness wrapped around Victor like a warm blanket. Only when faced with Adalyn again and realizing how shallow his love for her had been compared to what he felt for Juliana did he understand the depth of his feelings. What he felt for Juliana was more than growing affection. When he had least expected it, had love taken root?

Lips pressed together in a tight line, Drake appeared deep in thought—and those thoughts were unreadable on the man's face.

Like a man waiting for a judge's sentence, Victor sucked in a breath.

"I should object to you arranging a liaison with my sister, but considering your honesty and the fact that you are already betrothed, I will turn a blind eye. However, your problem remains. Could you not explain to Juliana?"

"Believe me, I tried. I'm ashamed to say she has reasons for doubting me."

Drake nodded. "Because of your previous association with the lady in question. Yes. I can see that. And yet, she hasn't broken the engagement, so there is hope."

"She didn't want to make a scene. She plans to end our betrothal in the morning."

"Then, Pratt, I would say you have some work to do before daybreak."

As the ladies drifted in from the retiring room, Drake patted him on the shoulder and went to join his wife.

And Victor hoped he would have enough time.

CHAPTER 24

S upper had been sheer torture. Seated next to Victor, Juliana wanted to enjoy his nearness, the gentle touch of his hand on hers, the smiles, the pleading look in his blue eyes. And yet, she couldn't, not when she had little faith in his true affection for her.

Excited voices surrounded her in the ladies' retiring room, and she tried desperately to block them out. A fierce debate raged in her mind. She had two choices.

Take what little Victor would offer her and be grateful for the crumbs, knowing she might never be first in his heart.

Or give him up, hoping someday she would find someone else to fill the void Victor left. And what then? Would that man be second best in her heart? How would that be fair to him?

Her Papa's words rang in her head. *Love takes no prisoners, and there are few survivors.*

If no one could win, what was the point?

Somewhere, deep in the recesses of her usually rational mind, the answer lurked. But she was simply too emotional to allow it to dig its way to the surface.

She wanted to give in, to say it didn't matter.

But it did.

"Juliana?"

Juliana gazed up at the soft, feminine voice, and swallowed down the lump in her throat at the sight of Adalyn.

"May I?" Adalyn motioned to the vacant spot on the settee.

Oh, God. How could she do this now? She schooled her features and nodded.

Most of the other women were occupied in conversation, resting their feet, or having their maids repair their coiffures.

Adalyn kept her voice low. "Please allow me to explain."

"It's not necessary, really."

"Oh, but it is. What happened between Victor and me was innocent, and I alone initiated it. I took Victor by complete surprise, and my only desire was to express my joy that he found someone so wonderful to share his life with."

"Regardless of your explanation, Victor's heart doesn't belong to me." Juliana fought back the tears.

Adalyn's gaze swept the room, confirming no one was paying them heed, and she leaned closer. "You're wrong, Juliana. And if you think his heart belongs to me, that is also untrue. Allow him to explain and tell you how he feels."

She patted Juliana's hand and rose. "Now, I believe I have a dance with my husband, who, for a man his size, is remarkably light on his feet."

Could it be true? The kiss had been innocent? But even so, it didn't mean Victor's affections had changed.

Did it?

Wild thoughts like unruly children shouted for attention and rendered rational thinking impossible.

"Juliana," Honoria's voice jolted her back. "It's time to return." Her brow crinkled with concern. "What is it? You seemed so quiet at supper."

Ladies made their way from the retiring room to rejoin the festivities, but if she confided in Honoria, she would lose the last bit of control she clung to with desperate fingers. She pressed a hand to her stomach, as if that would somehow calm the nausea churning within. "It's nothing. Just the excitement of the evening."

A troubled furrow creased Honoria's brow, and she threw Juliana a dubious glance. "Very well."

Juliana rose and allowed Honoria to wrap an arm around her waist as they returned to the ballroom.

Across the room, Victor peered over from where he stood by Drake. As always, the mere sight of him sent her heart hammering in her chest, and she had to calibrate to his presence.

Drake peeled off and approached Honoria. Left alone, Victor froze her with his gaze, his eyes locked with hers so fiercely, she fought to pull in a breath.

"Miss Merrick?"

Juliana turned toward the masculine voice. "Mr. Grey." She returned a curtsy to his bow.

"I believe the next dance is ours." Out of place for such an imposing man, his gentle voice calmed her.

"Thank you again for your intervention with Lord Felix."

"If he threatened you in any way, your brother should know. As it was, I had a few strong words with him, but it's best to keep your distance if possible."

As he led her to the dance floor, she forced a wan smile and placed a hand on his arm. "Of that you need not worry. I intend to avoid Lord Felix at all costs."

"That's wise. Otherwise, you might end up with more than bruises on your arm."

Her gaze darted to her upper arm where Lord Felix had dug his fingers into her flesh, finding faint purple marks forming.

"You seemed in a great hurry, although I cannot blame you. I trust all is well."

Kindness radiated in his eyes as she craned her neck to meet his gaze. He meant well, but how could she respond when at that moment nothing was *well*? "Forgive me for my rudeness in rushing off without properly thanking you earlier."

"Think nothing of it. And forgive me if I've overstepped."

During the country dance, she did her best to make polite small talk. "Have you enjoyed the evening, sir?"

A smile teased his lips. "As much as a man like me can. Your brother is most gracious, as is Her Grace. He did well in choosing her for his wife."

"Do you know of their story, sir?"

He shook his head. "Only what I've read in the scandal sheets, and I don't put much store in those rags."

"Drake has loved Honoria for ages. Ever since he was groom for Lord Stratford when they were not much more than children. It's rare to find such a love."

"Indeed." He canted his head, studying her. "It's fortunate for them things worked out as they did, and he inherited the title. Not all are so lucky."

Affronted, Juliana pulled back. "If you're insinuating that Honoria only married him because he inherited, you are mistaken, sir."

"Forgive me. I've overstepped yet again. I simply meant that his title makes their marriage more acceptable to society."

She couldn't argue his point. Wasn't her betrothal to Victor—pretend though it was—proof of that? At least where his mother and others were concerned? Not all well-wishes she'd received that evening were heartfelt and genuine. Regardless of her brother's lofty title and position within the aristocracy, she was a commoner, and many considered her beneath Victor.

As heir to a viscountcy, Victor would be expected to take his rightful place among the *ton*. Would her common birth, her lack of noble blood, cause him difficulty? Would he grow to resent her?

From what she had learned about Victor, he had no great political ambition. But would that change after he inherited and was faced with the responsibilities of his title? As a young man, was it easy to defy society without understanding the stakes involved?

If he truly loved her, Juliana had little doubt their marriage *could* work. Together, they would face any difficulties that arose. But without love . . . no matter how much she loved him, if he didn't return her love, pressure from society might be one obstacle too many.

One more argument as to why she couldn't, in good conscience, marry Victor.

The music came to an abrupt halt, and dancers stopped mid-step on the dance floor. Everyone turned toward the orchestra on the dais, curious to see what had happened.

Solemn-faced, Drake clutched a piece of parchment in one hand as he waved the guests to silence. "My lords and ladies. I've just received distressing news. The king is dead."

Hushed murmurs traveled through the throng as people digested the news.

Next to Juliana, Mr. Grey stood motionless, his face unreadable.

Although the king, who many had only thought of as Prinny, was not well loved, he had still been their king.

Some gasped, hands over their mouths, while others seemed to accept the news as unremarkable. Lord Middlebury waddled over to Lord Felix and muttered something in his ear.

Drake held up his hands again. "As much as it pains me, I suggest everyone return home to mourn our sovereign in private. I thank you all for coming. I wish this evening had not ended on such a sad note. May our new king live long and prosper. Long live the king."

"Long live the king," the crowd replied.

In hushed silence, the crowd dispersed, and Juliana's gaze landed on Victor.

As selfish as it was, she was grateful the sad news had put an end to the evening.

Selfishly, Victor silently thanked Prinny for putting an end to the evening. What had started as a joyful celebration had turned maudlin in so many respects. He needed to speak with Juliana alone, and he'd had little hope of doing so among the throng of people. With a quick word to his parents, he instructed them to go home without him. He would hire a hackney.

Across the ballroom, Juliana stood next to Mr. Grey, her face—like most—a mask of disbelief and sadness.

The question was: did Juliana mourn the king or was Victor

responsible for her distress? He refused to examine it further, for deep inside, he knew the answer.

When she turned to look at him, their eyes locked. He stood rooted in place, his mind begging his feet to move. Slowly, as the crowd thinned, he took the first laboring steps, his legs leaden. One opportunity to convince Juliana he truly cared and wished to proceed with their marriage awaited him.

He could not bungle it.

Mr. Grey remained staunchly at her side like a bulwark impeding Victor's progress.

"Might I have a private word with Miss Merrick, Mr. Grey?"

The giant of a man quirked an eyebrow at Juliana. "You should tell him about the incident in the hallway."

After that enigmatic comment, Mr. Grey bowed to Juliana, gave Victor a nod, then left.

Victor frowned. "What incident in the hallway? What is he talking about?"

"Miss Whyte wasn't the only one to see you and Adalyn together. When I was on my way to meet you, Lord Felix stopped me in the hallway to tell me about it. I didn't want to believe it, and we argued."

Fear gripped Victor, and his head pounded. His gaze dropped to where Juliana hugged herself, covering her arm. As gently as he could, he tugged her hand away, revealing distinct fingerprints. Fear morphed into rage, and the pounding in his head worsened. "I will kill him."

He spun on his heel and frantically searched the remaining guests for Davies.

"He's already gone."

Juliana's soft voice brought him back to earth, and he turned back to her.

"He left with Middlebury right after Drake's announcement."

Torn, Victor wanted to race after Davies, find him, and beat him to a pulp. But he also needed to mend things with Juliana. And given that she planned to break their engagement in a few hours, Victor knew his priorities.

"I'll deal with him later. You're more important. Please allow me to explain."

Her lips, which he so wanted to kiss, pressed together in a razor-thin line. "If you want to tell me the kiss was innocent, I believe you."

"You do?" He wanted to shout *Huzzah* from the rooftops. "That's wonderful. Then you'll still marry me?"

"No."

How could one simple word destroy him? What was it about balls and women rejecting him? If he never had to attend another ball in his life, it would be too soon.

"I don't understand. If you believe me, then why won't you marry me?" A shock of realization hit him hard, the force of which, if physical, would have knocked him over. She didn't love him. Was that it?

Bracing himself, he waited for her answer, prepared to tell her to give him time. That they would grow to love each other. That he was on his way already.

Her gaze darted to the side, and her formerly pinched lips parted.

Why wouldn't she answer?

"My refusal has nothing to do with what did or didn't happen between you and Adalyn," she finally said.

Her answer did nothing to clear his confusion. "Then what?"

"It's about you and me, Victor. I want a marriage based on mutual love. Unfashionable though it may be. Perhaps everyone is right, and my commoner blood has distorted my thinking. But marrying because of scandal or to further one's fortune or status is something I don't understand."

Victor swallowed her words like a bitter pill. "But that's what I want as well."

Her tremulous smile nearly broke his heart. "I know. And that's why I release you with a free heart to find someone to love as much as they love you." She leaned up and kissed him on the cheek, the action reminding him of what had precipitated the whole fiasco. "Goodbye, Victor."

Numb, Victor watched her leave, his gaze locked on her until the blue of her gown disappeared at the doorway. His chest felt hollow, as if she'd scooped out his insides and taken them with her. Adalyn's rejection of him, although devastating at the time, couldn't compare to the despair gripping him at that moment—the word *Goodbye* landing with a *thud* in the void where his heart used to be.

The orchestra had finished putting away their instruments and, one-by-one, quietly filed out.

Alone in the empty ballroom, Victor told himself he should go. But he couldn't. Leaving would mean it was over. Finished. That he had given up. The thought unbearable.

Nash appeared at the entrance, his dark eyes boring into Victor. Even if Victor hadn't been the only person in the room, he had a feeling Nash had purposely sought him out.

The churl strode toward him, his long legs eating up the length of the ballroom in a trice.

"Here to shoot me or escort me out?" In no mood to waste time, Victor snapped the question. Odd, but he would prefer the former to the latter.

Nash's dark chuckle did nothing to alleviate Victor's nerves. "Neither. I passed Juliana on the staircase. Since she was in tears, I thought you could use this." Nash handed him a flask.

Victor snatched it and gulped down the liquor. Whisky—an excellent quality, Victor hated to admit—seared his throat and dulled the razor edge of his thoughts.

"Slow down. If you plan to win her back, it won't do to get yourself foxed." Nash pulled the flask from Victor's fingers.

"Give it back." Victor reached for it, but Nash held it above his head.

"First we talk, then you drink."

Victor eyed him suspiciously. "Why?"

"Do you want my help or not?"

Victor continued to glare at him. Why couldn't the man just leave him to his misery? "You? Help? How?"

"First, tell me. Do you love her?"

"Adalyn? No, I swear."

Nash rolled his dark eyes. "No, you dolt. Juliana."

"I . . ." The feelings he'd been struggling with came into focus. Different from what he'd felt for Adalyn, the affection he held for Juliana was less self-serving and more the desire to give. To want her happiness. He supposed that's why her words had hit him so hard. How could he ask her to commit to a marriage to a man she didn't love? She would be miserable. Even if he—Lord, he *did* love her.

"Yes."

"Are you sure? Because you don't sound sure."

God, how he hated Nash.

"I do. I do love her." Victor hung his head. "But she doesn't love me."

"Christ, you really are a dolt. Of course she loves you, man. Are you blind as well as stupid?"

Head still down, Victor swung it side-to-side. "No. She practically said as much."

"What exactly did she say, you fool? The exact words. Try to remember."

He didn't want to remember. They hurt too much. But if it meant getting rid of Nash. Well. "She said . . . she wanted a marriage based on mutual love. Wanted me to find someone to love as much as they loved me."

"Blind, deaf, and dumb." Nash tsked. "Love is wasted on young fools."

His head felt like it weighed ten stone, but he lifted it to meet Nash's taunt. "Just challenge me and get it over with. I won't fight back."

"Let me put this to you as clearly as I can. Are you listening?"

Victor wanted to spit in his eye.

"If Juliana said she wanted *you* to love someone as much as they loved you, that was her way of telling you she loves you but thinks you don't love her. Have you ever told her you loved her?"

"Well, no. Not in so many words." Especially considering he'd just realized it himself. Lord, he *was* a dolt.

One dark eyebrow hitched, Nash's look spoke volumes.

"Very well. No. Not in any words. I was going to tell her of my growing affection tonight before everything went to hell." Part of what Nash had said finally registered in Victor's addled mind. "Wait. Did you say Juliana loves me?"

"Ah, thank goodness. I thought I would have to give you a piece of my mind, and I worried that, being in need of it, you wouldn't give it back."

"There is no need to insult me. Do you really think she loves me?"

"Anyone with eyes can see it."

"But she thinks I don't love her?"

"The boy is catching up. So what are you going to do about it?"

"I need to tell her. Right now!" Victor skirted around Nash, fully intending to find Juliana.

Nash grabbed him by the arms. "Not so fast. You need a plan, something that will sweep her off her feet. You can't simply go running off half-cocked." Nash laughed, apparently finding humor in his last words.

Victor folded his arms over his chest. "I'm listening."

"You need to give her every reason to marry you. Not just tell her you love her. Show her. Do you understand me?"

Victor narrowed his eyes. "You want me to seduce her?"

Nash waved a dismissive hand. "Don't think of it like that. Think of it as expressing your love."

"And how do you expect me to do that? Just march upstairs to her bedroom?"

"Of course not. The servants would see you. Make a show about leaving for Frampton or the night porter—whoever is stationed at the front door. Then wait thirty minutes and come around to the back of the house. I'll be waiting."

"Why on earth should I trust you?"

"Because I've been a lovesick pup myself once."

And as he left Pendrake Manor, taking his hat and gloves from Frampton and telling him to relay his thanks to the duke and duchess, Victor hoped trusting Nash Talbot wasn't the biggest mistake of his life.

CHAPTER 25

Alone in her bedchamber, Juliana stared out the window into the dark night. The sliver of the crescent moon barely illuminated the terrace and gardens in the back of Pendrake Manor. Eerie shadows cast from swaying tree branches danced against the ground. The devastated look on Victor's face haunted her.

Had she made an enormous mistake?

Should she have confessed her love and risked her heart? Accepted what Victor was able to give? Find contentment as her father had?

Why was love so hard?

A soft knock sounded. "Juliana, it's Drake. May I come in?"

With bare feet, she padded to the door and opened it to let him in.

"Perhaps you and Honoria should give up hosting balls in my honor. It would appear they always end in disaster." She forced a weak smile.

He followed her to the bed and sat next to her. "You are not responsible for the king's death, brat." The teasing nickname held no bite. "That's not why I wanted to speak with you. Victor told me something happened in the orangery and that you intend to end your betrothal."

"Oh." Air whooshed from her lungs.

Drake stared straight ahead as he spoke. "Don't tell me it's because you don't love him. I have eyes, and I know what it's like to be in love."

She couldn't lie to him. Not Drake, who had caught her in every childish fib. And loving Victor was so much more than breaking mother's favorite vase. "I do love him. With all my heart. But Victor doesn't love me. His heart still belongs to another."

Drake's head jerked toward her. "Are you certain? Because when he spoke with me, he assured me his feelings for Lady Nash are in the past, and he vowed to do everything he could to mend things with you."

Taking a deep breath, Juliana prepared to tell Drake everything. "What you don't know is our whole courtship is a farce, and he only proposed to save my honor."

Drake listened patiently as she explained how Victor had offered to repair her reputation with the *ton* while at the same time avoiding his mother's matchmaking machinations, and along the way she had fallen in love with him. "So you see, for Victor it was all pretend, but he's too honorable to go back on his word."

The gentle smile Drake gave her was one she remembered as a girl. One that said, *You silly goose.*

"And why is it so impossible for Victor to have also fallen in love? For it to have become real for him as well? You're a wonderful girl, Juliana."

"A girl who's a commoner. He's in line to inherit. What type of viscountess would I be? Would the *ton* shun him because of me?"

"I can't argue with that. Not when class differences separated Honoria and me. But when she didn't know I was a duke, she still chose me. From what I know of him, I don't think Victor cares much about the views of society. If he loves you, your parentage won't matter."

Hadn't she considered the same argument earlier? "But how can I be sure?"

Drake sighed. "I suppose a cynical man would say we can't ever be certain. My stubbornness in believing Honoria wouldn't choose me over her family almost cost me the woman I adore. She felt she had to prove in no uncertain terms she chose me and wanted to marry me with or without her father's approval."

"How?"

Drake's lips quirked in that half-smile Honoria always went on and on about, and his cheeks darkened.

Juliana grabbed his arm. "You're blushing. Is it something scandalous?"

"You must never tell anyone. Promise me."

Oh, it was scandalous! She shook his arm. "I promise. Now, tell me. Tell me."

"The night of the house party's ball, she came to my room."

"So that's why she wanted to know where it was."

Drake's eyes widened. "You were the one who told her?! I always thought it was Simon, although he denied it."

"She told me she wanted to leave you a note. That sly fox."

"She can be quite resourceful, for certain. And persuasive."

"Drake, you two—didn't?"

"Let's just say she convinced me beyond a shadow of a doubt of her commitment to me."

"I don't see how this applies to Victor and me. It's not like he's going to come sneaking into my room in the middle of the night to confess his undying love."

A deep chuckle rose from her brother. "He'd better not. But there are two days until the wedding. If he calls tomorrow, which I expect he will, talk to him and listen to what he has to say. Don't throw love away, Juliana. It's worth the risk."

He rose from the bed and kissed her on the top of her head. "Now, get some sleep. I'll need to go in to Lords early tomorrow because of the king, but Honoria and Mother will be here if you need them."

As the door closed with a soft *snick*, Juliana thought about her brother's words. Were they so different from what her father tried to tell her? Even if love took no prisoners, was it worth the risk?

She drifted back to her niggling question. *If no one could win, what was the point?*

The answer floated to the surface. Maybe it wasn't about winning or losing, but simply loving, and unconditional love itself was the point.

She strode back to the window and opened it. A cool, early summer breeze drifted in, fluttering the curtains and bringing with it the sweet scent of lilacs. Movement on the terrace below caught her eye, and she squinted into the dark. A figure, a man, stalked along the terrace. Her body tensed, and she prepared to go to the bell pull and alert a footman they had an intruder. A burst of light illuminated the face of Lord Nash as he lit a cheroot and lazed against the terrace railing. Grateful no predator lurked in the shadows, she breathed a sigh of relief and relaxed.

VICTOR WANDERED THE NEIGHBORHOOD BY THE DUKE'S MANSION, checking his watch every few minutes. A few times, when a constable making his rounds strolled by, he ducked behind nearby shrubbery. No need to be asked all sorts of questions about why he was out on foot skulking around the homes in Mayfair so late at night. What was he to say? I'm waiting to return to the Duke of Burwood's and win back the woman I love?

Ha!

Not likely.

Peeking out from a yew that poked him viciously in the eye, Victor confirmed the street was clear and emerged from his hiding place. Twenty-nine minutes had elapsed according to his watch, and he slipped it into his waistcoat pocket and strode back to Pendrake Manor.

Dim light shone in several upstairs windows, and using the stealth of an assassin, Victor crept around the back of the house. Where was Nash?

Faint orange light glowed on the terrace. Careful not to trip,

Victor climbed the steps and found Nash leaning casually against the railing, a cheroot dangling from his fingers.

"What kept you?" He took a long drag on the cheroot, the orange tip growing brighter.

"I'm not late. You said thirty minutes."

Nash blew out a trail of smoke and gave a deep-throated laugh. "I didn't expect you to wait the whole time. Figured you be eager to win back ye fair maiden."

"Are we going to stand here arguing or are you going to tell me how you plan to sneak me inside without the servants seeing? If we take the servants' stairway, we're bound to be discovered."

"Oh, you're not going inside the customary way through a door. Remember, the goal is to sweep Miss Merrick off her feet. To perform a daring feat to win her over so she throws herself into your arms."

"Then how the hell am I . . ." Words stuck in Victor's throat as Nash stepped away from the railing and pointed to a window on the third floor.

"That's Miss Merrick's bedroom. Fortunately for you, she opens her window to let in the breeze. Also, fortunately for you, it isn't raining."

Momentarily setting aside the fact that said window was on the third floor, Victor addressed the most pressing question. He knew the man was a rake, but this was beyond the pale. "And how do *you* know that's Juliana's window? If you've done anything—"

"Relax. I'm a happily married man. However, Her Grace has requested I smoke outside, and I enjoy the cool evening breeze here on the terrace. I happened to notice Miss Merrick at her window."

Fists clenched at his sides, Victor clamped down his anger and addressed the next question. "And how am I to get up there? Grow wings and fly?"

When Nash rolled his eyes, Victor wanted to plant him a facer.

"How do you think? Climb."

Victor craned his neck—up, up, up the expanse of the building to the third-floor window that held all his hopes. "If I fall, I'll kill myself."

"Then don't fall. And the fall won't likely kill you. You'll simply break a leg and if not set properly, the infection will kill you. However, both my wife and Ashton are excellent physicians. They could amputate and save your life."

"Ha. Ha."

"Think about it. A man so desperate to confess his love, to beg his lady's forgiveness, he's willing to scale the highest mountain to reach her. What woman wouldn't swoon over that? She'll be so overcome, she'll practically rip your clothes from your body to have her way with you."

"How in the hell did Adalyn ever fall in love with you?"

"Leave my wife out of this. I could still shoot you for those sketches."

Victor gulped. He knew about the sketches? "About that—"

"Survive tonight and hand them over to me, and we'll discuss it no further."

Victor nodded and gazed in trepidation at the open window again. Stationed strategically apart, the windows had sills that could provide a hand and foothold. Crevices between bricks, although small, could allow him to get a toehold.

Nash took another pull from his cheroot, then blew it out, the smoke forming circles. "You do know how to climb?"

"Of course I know how to climb." Victor glared at him. It had been years, but he and Priscilla had run amok climbing trees on their father's estate in Lincolnshire as children. But walls of homes weren't trees, and he wasn't a boy any longer. "I'm deciding how to start. The first window is at least eight feet off the ground."

Nash threw his cheroot on the ground and crushed it out with the toe of his shoe. "I'll give you a leg up." Nash laced his fingers together to form a foothold. "Take your gloves off."

"But my hands. That brick is rough."

Straightening, Nash gave him an icy glare. "Those aren't your leather riding gloves. Satin is slippery. What do you care about more, your artist's fingers or that woman upstairs?"

Eyes narrowed at his nemesis, Victor held his tongue. With more force than necessary, he tugged off his gloves and shoved them in his pocket. "I wish I had my boots on instead of these dancing slippers."

"Quit your grumbling." Nash laced his fingers together again, and Victor reluctantly placed his foot in the cup. "Ready? On the count of three."

Victor nodded, and on the three count, Nash boosted him into the air. Surprised by the man's strength, Victor grasped the window ledge and, digging his toes into the small crevices between bricks, gained enough purchase to pull himself up.

Elation energized him. "I did it!"

"Quiet." Nash's whisper drifted up in the still night. "Do you want to be discovered before you make it to the top?"

Victor couldn't be certain, but it sounded like Nash mumbled *imbecile.*

Ivy clung to the walls, and when Victor reached for his next handhold, his fingers wrapped around a vine and pulled it loose. "Ouch!" The damn thing knocked off his hat and scratched him. Muttering a few curses, he worked his way up to the next window.

Although the stone sills around the windows were smooth, the same grooves and crevices of the brick he used for his climb's purchase dug into his skin. Almost at the next window, his foot slipped as he tried to get a toehold, and his shoe fell off, landing with a *thud* below him.

Tempted to look down, he resisted and pressed forward. The cotton of his stocking snagged on the rough brick as his toes dug into the tiny notch, and he held on for dear life.

After catching his breath, he contemplated his next move. Thankfully, in between the windows, smaller ledges protruded out, allowing him to maneuver up to the next level.

"Almost there," he muttered to himself in encouragement even as his fingers screamed in agony. The open window beckoned him to safety—and Juliana. With a move that surprised even him, he leaped up, grabbed the ledge, and pulled himself up.

He darted the quickest of glances below. Nash had vanished.

"Churl." Victor swung a leg over the window sill and summarily fell with an ungraceful *plop* onto the floor.

"Juliana?" At least he prayed to God it was Juliana's bedroom. It would be just like Nash to send him to Burwood's room, where the duke would no doubt take a pistol to his head in a trice.

Grateful to be on solid ground, he squinted into the dark room, and as he straightened himself off the floor, rustling sounds came from the bed.

Tremulous, a soft feminine voice followed. "Who's there?"

"Juliana? Don't be alarmed. It's me. Victor."

CHAPTER 26

"Churl."

Juliana stirred at the scraping sound at her window. Motionless in her bed, she held her breath. Perhaps she had dreamed it.

A sharp *thud* followed the man's single word. "Juliana?" the man asked, the voice familiar.

Her heart rammed hard against her ribcage. She sat up in bed and tried to tamp down the fear rising in her throat. "Who's there?"

"Juliana? Don't be alarmed. It's me. Victor."

Victor? She scrambled from the bed and lit the lamp on her bedside table.

Still not certain she wasn't dreaming, she rubbed her eyes.

"Victor, what are you doing here?" He looked a fright. What appeared to be an ivy leaf was stuck in his hair. An ugly red scrape slashed across his right cheek, and he was missing a shoe.

"I had to see you."

"In the middle of the night? And how did you get in here?" Her gaze darted to the open window.

"I climbed up."

He sounded extraordinarily proud.

She rushed forward to get a closer look at him. Other than the scratch, disheveled clothing, and missing footwear, he seemed no worse for wear. She plucked the leaf out of his hair. "What were you thinking? You could have been killed."

"Nash assured me I would only break a leg. And even if I did fall to my death, it would have been worth it, because I realized I don't want to live without you."

She blinked. *What?* Victor's two odd statements warred for attention. The weight of the second required more time to digest, so she addressed the first. "Nash? He knew?"

"It was his idea."

Prepared to deliver a few harsh words to Lord Nash, she rushed to the window and peered down. No one remained on the terrace below. "He's not there."

"The churl left me as I climbed up. You would think he'd be keen to watch me fall and break my neck."

She turned back around, right into Victor. His hands wrapped around her waist. He was impossibly close. Heat from his fingers seared through her thin nightrail. The hard planes of his chest pressing against her breasts made her dizzy.

"Steady." His breath brushed against her upturned face as she looked deep into his eyes. Their gazes held, the moment stretching between them taut and fragile. Silence enveloped them with only their ragged breathing filling the void.

She needed to think, and she couldn't with him so near. Giving a gentle push against his solid chest, she stepped back to give her body and her mind space. His arms slipped from her waist and dropped to his side.

"Please, Juliana." He reached for her again, and she held up a hand. The dejected look on his face broke her heart.

"Why? Why would it be worth risking your life?"

"Because I love you."

Her mind stuttered to a halt. "No. You think you love me because I remind you of Adalyn."

His shoulders slumped. "I know that's what you think, but it's not true. Tonight, seeing Adalyn again made everything clear. Yes, it was a shock, but more than that, I realized that I loved a person who only existed in my imagination. Not the real Adalyn. I think I loved what she represented. Someone different from the society misses of the *ton*. Independent and determined. But I didn't really know *her*. I'm ashamed to say I saw her as a way to rebel against society's constraints, especially my mother."

A sudden chill raced through her. "But isn't it the same with me? Your mother doesn't approve. And what about when you take your father's place as viscount? Regardless of Drake's title, I'm still a commoner."

"I realize it looks that way, and I hate to admit, it was one of the things that attracted me to you initially. But then . . . then I got to know you. Learn about your own hopes and dreams. Watched your heroic rescue of Eva Somersby. How you support me in my passion for the arts. Your kindness and generosity to everyone around you, no matter their station in life. That's the kind of woman I want by my side. I should have said something sooner. Should have been more direct. Instead, I presumed you were crying off because you didn't love me. Do you love me, Juliana?"

"I . . . I do." Tears blurred her vision. Everything in her wanted to believe their marriage could work.

He stepped closer and took her hands. "Then it's settled. You'll marry me?"

"I want to. More than anything."

Light filtered across his face, and, in a blink, the joy in his eyes transformed into a question. "I sense a 'but' in your answer. Have I waited too long? Am I too late?"

"It's not that."

"Then what?"

"You say you were attracted to both Adalyn and me because we represented a way to rebel against society. But what if that same reason drives us apart? One day, in the distant future, you will be Viscount Cartwright. What will society say if you have a wife born of commoners? Drake's grandfather disowned his own son because he married my mother, the daughter of a tailor. I am the granddaughter of a tailor, Victor. My father was a steward. I have no aristocratic blood. What if the *ton* shuns me and possibly our children?"

"Do you really think I give a damn about what society thinks?"

"You should. You have a responsibility. Don't think I don't understand. I've seen the burden Drake carries. Thank goodness he has Honoria, the daughter of a marquess. She was reared for the aristocratic life. What do I know about running a grand house, or hosting parties for society?"

He squeezed her hands. "Have you forgotten how many people attended the ball in our honor this evening? Your brother is a powerful man. We have friends, Juliana. Good friends who accept you. Petty people who wouldn't accept us are not worth our time. And you're an intelligent woman. You can learn all the facets of running a home. You would have help—a housekeeper, butler, servants."

"Those are skills, but it won't change who I am inside. It's more than learning the rules of etiquette. Members of society have an innate confidence, an elegance—even superiority—that can't be taught. I'll never be one of them. Never fit in."

He shook his head, the smile tipping his lips—indulgent. "Juliana, haven't you heard what I've said? I don't want you to be like them. Even *I* don't want to be like them. I know who you are. Free from artifice. Authentic. Different, yes, but I love you for who are, just the way you are."

Everything he said was true. She couldn't deny it. Pondering his words, for the first time since Drake had assumed his role as duke, she felt comfortable in her own skin.

"You really love me?" It seemed too wonderful to be true.

He cupped her face with his hand, his thumb running gently over her cheek. "With all my heart. I know I've given you reason to doubt, but I would give anything to show you just how much I love you. Do you want me to climb down and back up again?"

She answered him with a laugh.

"No? Very well. But if you promise to marry me, I will spend the rest of my life proving my love."

Risk. Wasn't all of life a risk? What guarantee did anyone have? Love, even if it was fleeting, was worth the risk.

"I do love you, Victor, and I believe you. Believe *in* you."

"And you'll marry me?" The expectation, the hope, written across his face tugged at her heart.

"Yes," she whispered.

"Thank God." His eyes drifted shut, and he tugged her to him.

The space between them whispered away, leaving only the gentle scrape of his evening clothes against her silk nightrail.

Holding her in his arms, he lowered his head and kissed her. Lightly at first, a soft brush of lips against lips, he deepened the kiss as she surrendered, feeling the love he professed with each press of his mouth to hers.

One of his hands left her waist and cradled the back of her head, his fingers tangling in the locks of her hair. Over and over, he kissed her, the delicious sensation of his mouth on hers driving all rational thought from her mind until they were both panting and breathless. When he rested his forehead against hers, he exhaled a contented sigh. "I could do this all night. But I should leave and let you get some sleep. Promise you'll marry me? You won't change your mind?"

Her heart ached at the pleading in his eyes. She couldn't blame him if he doubted her. "Yes. I mean no. I mean, yes, I'll marry you."

"Good." He kissed her forehead and turned toward the window.

Impulsively, she grabbed his arm. "You can't go out the window! You'll fall."

"I can't fall. We're getting married in two days." His jest did nothing to relieve her worry. "Just don't change your mind again."

"Let me check the hall." The door creaked as she cracked it open and peeked outside. Footsteps echoed up the stairs. She quickly closed the door. "You can't go out that way either."

With tenderness that melted her heart, he ran his fingertips over her lips. "What do you suggest?"

Juliana's thoughts drifted back to her conversation with Drake earlier that evening. Although he didn't admit it in so many words, Juliana understood his implication. To prove her love and commitment to Drake, Honoria had given herself to him the night of the house party ball.

Clasping his hand to her face, Juliana made a decision. She could prove her love and commitment to Victor that very night. "Don't go. Stay the rest of the night with me. I'll figure out a way to sneak you from the house early in the morning before the servants rise."

Heat from his gaze scorched her. "If you insist."

VICTOR NEVER IMAGINED JULIANA WOULD INVITE HIM TO SPEND THE night with her, even if Nash had implied she would swoon into his arms from his heroics of climbing three stories to her window. But at that moment, as she stood before him—the light from the lamp shining through her nightrail and outlining her figure—he could think of nothing else but making love to her.

Yet, he couldn't presume that's what she meant. An escritoire with a delicate chair sat against the wall, and a settee too small even for a woman to stretch out, much less for a man his size, was at the foot of the four-poster bed. He supposed he could sleep on the floor. "May I borrow one of your pillows?"

Vertical lines formed between her eyes, and he wished to smooth them away with a kiss. "Why?"

Pointing to the floor, he answered. "To sleep."

Cheeks darkening, she gave him a shy smile. "There are plenty of pillows on my bed. When I asked you to spend the night with me, I meant . . ."

"You want us to make love?"

So soft, he barely heard her reply as her gaze darted to the lush Aubusson carpet. "Yes."

Wrapped up in the marvel of the woman before him, Victor remained silent and relished the moment. The gravity of Juliana's offer wasn't lost on him. In giving herself to him before marriage, she would not only prove her love, but her promise to marry him.

When he didn't respond, her gaze shot back to his. "Unless you don't want to."

"Oh, I want to. I want to very much." With the back of his fingers, he traced the delicate curve of her cheek and relished in the velvet softness of her skin. "I didn't do you justice."

She blinked. "What do you mean?"

"Your portrait. I believed it to be good, but I realize now it doesn't compare to you in this moment. The blush of your cheeks, the glow of love in your eyes, the way your lips part as if ready to whisper words of longing. Why didn't I see it before? Nash was right. I'm a blind dolt."

"See what?"

"How much you love me. I want you to see that love in me, too, Juliana."

She took his hand, still stroking her face and kissed the palm. Her eyes widened. "Your hands! And your poor face. You're hurt."

Tugging his arm, she led him to the chair by the escritoire. "Sit."

A chuckle rumbled his chest at her assertiveness. "As you wish."

At the washbasin, she dipped in a cloth and wrung it out. "Let me see your hands."

Palms up, he laid his hands on his thighs. Abrasions, red but not deep, marked his palms and fingers from the rough brick of the outside wall.

With tenderness that made his chest ache, she knelt at his feet and dabbed at the lash on his face the ivy branch left, then cleaned his hands. "I should have done something sooner. Thank goodness they're not any worse. Your hands are precious."

As she fussed over him, he wanted to give her the same loving attention. To cradle her with so much love and care, she would never doubt his feelings for her.

Satisfied the scrapes were clean, she rose and stepped to her dressing table. "I have some salve that will help with the healing." Back at his feet, she dabbed the soothing salve on his face and hands. She grinned up at him. "Sometimes I ride without my gloves."

"Such a rebel." He grinned back at her.

Her laugh, bright and airy, did more to heal him than the salve she applied. Mischief glinted in her eyes. "It's one of the reasons you love me, is it not?"

"One of the many. True." He pulled her hands away from their ministrations, and rising, pulled her to her feet. "That's enough. I need another type of medicine."

"Oh?"

"Medicine for the heart." Drawing her close, he kissed her— slow and deep, and the world beyond her ceased to exist. "Much better," he whispered against her lips. "It's working." Long and leisurely, the intensity of the kiss increased as he savored her sweet lips, and when she opened for him, he teased her with his tongue, pleased when she met him stroke for stroke.

He tangled his fingers in her hair, silk-smooth and warm, and drew her closer with each kiss, unable to get enough of her. Breathless, he pulled back and lightly kissed her nose. "You set me off balance, Juliana."

Hazy with her own desire, her gaze lifted to meet his, her parted lips a vivid vestige of their kisses. "I won't say I'm sorry."

A soft laugh escaped. "Nor do I wish you to. But I fear you aren't thinking clearly as well. Are you certain this is what you want?" His body begged her to say yes, but his mind prepared to respect her wishes if she changed her mind.

"I'm quite certain. I trust you, Victor. Trust in your love."

Sweeter words had never reached his ears. "I will do my utmost to make it enjoyable for you. Do you know what transpires?"

Her laugh unsettled him. "Victor. Remember, I wish to breed horses. One does not embark on that endeavor without understanding the process."

"Well, it's a little different for people, but you have a point; the basic idea is the same."

Her gaze held his as she unbuttoned his coat, then slipped her hands up and under the front, sliding it off his shoulders. Instead of allowing it to drop onto the floor, she folded it neatly and set it on the chair he had vacated.

He pulled her back into his arms, and lavished kisses down her neck, nibbling on her ear, which, to his delight, made her sigh with pleasure. When she reached for the buttons of his waistcoat, he stopped her. "Allow me."

With lightning speed, he shed the rest with practiced ease, leaving only his trousers.

The expression of keen interest on her face encouraged him. She wasn't frightened, but he wanted to slow things down. "More kisses are in order." Over and over, he captured her sweet mouth with his, loving how she responded.

As he trailed his lips down her throat, she arched into him, pressing her hips into his. He groaned with need. *Slow down.*

And yet, every sigh from her sent him closer to the edge. His hand traveled up from her waist to brush the underside of her breast. Her breath hitched, her body curving instinctively into his touch. He teased her nipple with his thumb, then lowered his mouth to suckle through the soft fabric of her nightgown.

Her fingers raked his scalp, pulling his long hair loose from the restraining queue, her passion matching his.

"Juliana," he whispered, knowing another name would never pass his lips in such moments ever again. "I want you so much, my sweet, sweet Juliana."

He lifted her into his arms and laid her on the bed. "God . . . you're exquisite. Così bella." He gazed down at her. She lay before him, more breathtaking than any painted Madonna— radiant with quiet trust shining in her eyes. He pulled in a steadying breath, then climbed up beside her.

Emotion rushed through him. He was no novice at lovemaking, but being with Juliana was momentous.

She drew idle patterns through the fine hair on his chest. "Kiss me, Victor."

His heart hammered against his sternum, and he worried she would feel it. He placed a gentle kiss at the soft area at her throat, then followed the curve of her neck. Her pulse fluttered beneath his lips, and he smiled with satisfaction that he affected her as much as she affected him. He trailed kisses along her jaw, finally capturing her mouth again, and she moaned into his.

Once again, he sought her reassurance. "Tell me again this is what you want."

"More than anything," she murmured, her breath warm and seductive against the corner of his mouth.

CHAPTER 27

Fire burned within Juliana, Victor's every touch sending sparks and igniting flames of passion. How many nights had she fantasized about being in Victor's arms? Of him whispering words of love and desire? Too many, and yet, not enough.

And none of them compared to reality. For not the first time that evening she wondered if she were dreaming, but Victor's kisses, his caresses, never felt as wonderful in her dreams or fantasies as they did in that moment. And when he spoke what she presumed was Italian, her stomach did little flips.

When she pressed her hand against the hard planes of his chest, her fingers drifting through the dusting of hair, his heart pounded against her palm. His nipple peaked, growing hard, as she ran her finger around it, and he gave a soft moan.

"Kiss me, Victor."

He obeyed, his lips driving her wild as he traveled up her throat to nibble her ear, before capturing her mouth. Her own heart pummeled her ribcage in punishing beats.

When he pulled away, she chased his lips.

"Are you certain this is what you want, Juliana?"

Mind reeling from the sensations flowing through her, she pulled herself together enough to answer, "More than anything." Nothing in her life had ever been truer.

"May I remove this?" Victor tugged on the silky ribbon at the neck of her nightrail. Tenderness in his eyes stoked the ever-growing fire in her.

Unable to form the simple word, she nodded.

He smiled, and—his eyes never leaving hers—he made quick work of the three ties, then pulled the gown from her shoulders. He peppered kisses across her shoulders, and she inhaled his scent—warm cardamom and woodsy sandalwood, with the faintest touch of turpentine. As he continued to tug her gown down her body, his lips traced every inch of newly exposed skin.

She slipped her arms from the sleeves, allowing him to pull the garment down and reveal her breasts.

Kneeling beside her on the bed, he sat back on his heels and stared down at her. "Even more beautiful than I imagined."

At the sight of him, something tender and fierce unfurled inside of her, as though her heart recognized its home. His long hair flowing free curtained his face, the defined muscles of his shoulders and arms bunching with restrained strength. For an artist, he was no stranger to taking care of his body. Tentatively, she stretched her hand up and ran her fingers over the ripple of muscles on his abdomen to where a fine line of dark blond hair trailed from his navel and disappeared beneath the waistband of his trousers.

Her gaze drifted lower, where the taut fabric of his trousers left little to the imagination. When she dropped her hand to touch him, his eyelids shuttered, and he sucked in a harsh breath.

Emboldened by his response, she rubbed him harder.

He pressed his hand against hers, halting her ministrations. "You keep that up, and I'll spend in my trousers." Raspy and raw, his voice strained with effort as he spoke. "And unless you stop me, I really want to be inside you."

Her own voice husky with desire, she said, "I don't want to stop you."

"Bene—good." He leaned down, his hand rising to cup her face. His thumb skimmed her cheek as he pressed his lips to hers in an endless kiss. Soft, slow, and deep, each caress of his mouth on hers melted into the next, the gentle scrape of stubble a contrast to the silken glide of his lips.

With the same careful attention, he cupped her breast and teased her nipple to a hard peak with his thumb much as she had done to him—the sensation glorious.

Yet, when he dipped his head to her breast, it paled in comparison, and she arched off the bed, her fingers sliding hungrily through his hair. "Oh!"

He continued to suckle, and her mind blanked. She was only feeling, the heavy aching need building low in her abdomen ever growing and insistent.

"Lift your hips for me, cara mia." His soft command brought her temporarily back to Earth.

When she obeyed, he slipped the nightrail off her completely and tossed it aside.

His gaze drifted over her—slow and deliberate—like a tender caress. "After we're married, I want to paint you just like this."

Heat scorched her cheeks and bloomed on the underside of her skin, setting her ablaze.

He smiled, slow and easy, and the look eased her embarrassment. "For my eyes only, of course."

A thrill of naughtiness tripped up her spine, and she gave a languorous stretch, the rustle of sheets accenting the silence that enveloped them like a cocoon.

His smile widened. "You, my dear Juliana, are a temptress."

Like a powerful cat, he reclined beside her and resumed his kisses.

"Won't you remove your trousers?" Throat so parched, her voice cracked like dry paper.

"My trousers are the one thing keeping me from ravishing you like a man possessed, and I want you to find your pleasure first."

When he lowered his hand to tease her between her legs, she cried out and clung to his shoulders with a punishing grip. "Oh!" The aching need grew almost unbearable, and she arched into his touch.

"Oh, Juliana," he whispered, his voice thick with wonder.

Each kiss became more passionate, and as their tongues tangled in a frenetic dance, he inserted one finger while, with his thumb, he rubbed little circles over the sensitive spot between her legs, driving her wild. Movement of his fingers matched that of his tongue—swirling, probing, driving her to the brink of madness.

Pressure built within her as he continued his sweet torture, and she drew closer to the precipice of pleasure. When he broke their kiss and instead suckled at her breast once more, her mind shattered into a million glorious little sparks of light, and she fell into a sublime oblivion.

"Oh, God! Victor!"

He quickly silenced her cries of ecstasy with a kiss until the waves of her release eased. Never before had she experienced such a sense of abandon and decadent rapture.

Boneless with bliss, her limbs melted onto the mattress, as though she had become only sensation and breath. Satisfaction flowed through her like warm honey. When his kisses ended with a quick peck on her nose, she gazed at him with wonder. "You really love me." All doubt dissipated when she saw the evidence in his eyes.

Tenderness in his gaze mixed with passion as the circle of blue expanded, leaving only a small rim around the black of his pupil. "I do. And because I do, I really should leave now and save the rest for our wedding night."

After another deep kiss, Victor started to rise from the bed, but Juliana grabbed his arm. "I don't want to wait. I want to assure you that I will marry you."

He turned back toward her. "I trust you, Juliana. You don't have to prove anything to me."

Concern crinkled the corners of his eyes, and she loved him all the more for it. But it was more than wanting to prove her commitment, she truly wanted to make love with him. "And I trust you. Please, don't stop. I want you, Victor."

Long moments stretched between them as he gazed down at her, then with a quick nod, he rose from the bed and removed his trousers.

Goodness! Her breath caught and heat flared in her cheeks. None of her fantasies had prepared her for the reality of him.

He gave her a sly grin. "If you're used to horses, I'm not nearly as impressive."

She laughed, the sound echoing through the room, and he climbed up next to her and placed an index finger on her lips.

"Shush. Someone will hear us." His grin widened. "But I hope you weren't laughing at me."

"Never. You are magnificent." She pulled him down for a lingering kiss. "Now, where were we?"

WHERE, INDEED? WHEN VICTOR CRADLED AND TILTED JULIANA'S head to the perfect angle for the kiss, his body pulsed with energy. The way she responded to him, her trust, her belief in him, had each nerve ending sizzling with life. Every point of contact between them created a thrum of awareness. Sweet and slightly spicy, the warm scent of her skin wrapped around him like a promise. He could so easily get caught up in his own desires.

Yet he paused, thinking of her. "I understand there will be some initial pain, but only the first time, and I will do my best to be gentle and make it enjoyable for you."

She threaded her fingers through his hair. "I trust you."

Her skin felt like silk as he traced his hands over the expanse of her abdomen and cupped her breast. Her nails raked against his scalp, the sensation generating gooseflesh along his arms.

"Open for me, tesoro mio." The words fitting, she was his treasure more precious than gold. He nudged her legs apart, and she complied, instinctively bending them at the knees. As he positioned himself at her entrance, he whispered, "Ti adoro. I adore you, Juliana. Only you. Never doubt it." With excruciating slowness, he pushed forward as her body yielded to his. God, she welcomed him so exquisitely, every inch of her drawing him in, testing his control to its limits. But he needed to go slow, to be careful for her.

As he met resistance, he gritted his teeth and prepared for the moment he dreaded. His voice a gravelly rasp of need, he said, "Wrap your legs around me, amore mio."

When she did, and he pressed forward, she sucked in a breath, the moment he breached her maidenhead clear from the wince of pain on her face.

He stilled. His arms shook, and his heart hammered in his chest as need built to a crescendo. Every muscle in his body screamed for release, but he held still, anchored by the sight of her beneath him. It broke his heart to know he'd hurt her. "Is the pain—very bad?" He choked on the question, not sure he wanted the answer.

"Not t-terribly bad." But the crack in her voice belied her words.

"I won't move until you tell me." God knows how he would manage, but he would. For her.

Her eyes shimmered, and a tear pooled in the corners.

"Oh, God. It's horrible, isn't it? I'm so sorry, Juliana."

She shook her head. "It's not pain—it's that I love you so much my heart can't contain it."

And as he gazed down at her, he saw the love in her eyes. He heard it in her words. Felt it as she stilled his shaking arms with her soft touch. Tasted it in the sweetness of her kisses. Even the air between them—thick with heat and longing—was scented with her desire. Every sense evidenced her love for him.

She loved *him*! Not his name or future, but the man he tried so hard to be. Who he uniquely was.

The realization overwhelmed him.

She was his, and he was hers. They were one. Not only in that precious, glorious moment, but for the rest of their lives.

He would wait forever if he had to; Juliana was worth it.

Luckily for him, forever wasn't necessary.

"I'm better now if you want to move."

Thank God.

Moving slowly at first, his strokes tentative, he studied her face and searched for any sign of discomfort, grateful when he found none.

After a few minutes, he picked up his pace, and soon she moved with him in a steady rhythm.

Her eyes drew dusky, and a soft moan escaped her parted lips, rosy and swollen from their kisses. She stroked his shoulders, the tender slide of her fingers against his skin setting him aflame.

He braced himself on one forearm and, with his other hand, reached between them to touch the swollen nub between her legs.

Her hips bucked against him, and she gave another moan. "Oh, God. Yes."

Oh, how he wanted to make her come again. "That's it, cuore mio. Don't think. Just feel." His heart nearly burst with love for her. His beautiful Juliana. He would spend the rest of his days adoring her.

He increased his pace, and she met him thrust for thrust.

Her legs began trembling, then she fell apart in his arms. Her muscles clenching around him felt incredible. Not just the physical sensation, but the joy flowing through him for how much Juliana loved him.

Her expression softened, lips parted and brows drawn tight, every line of her face etched with feeling as she cried out in ecstasy; he looked forward to witnessing it for years to come.

"I love you, Victor." Imbued with so much love, her words seemed almost unnecessary.

Yet, they pushed him over the edge he'd been teetering on, and he kissed her long and hard to stifle his own shouts of passion as he spilled into her.

Whatever walls he'd once held between them crumbled—nothing remained he hadn't given her.

Deep, soul-reaching satisfaction settled inside him as he collapsed on top of her. Perhaps a little late, he answered back, "I love you, too."

Outside, the distant hoot of an owl broke the silence, reminding him time still moved even though everything inside the room had shifted.

Not wishing to crush her, he slid off her. Pulling her to his side, he nuzzled against her neck and nibbled on the shell of her ear. Her skin still glowed with the heat of their joining, her pulse a flutter beneath his lips.

"Mmm," she murmured dreamily.

"In three days, you will be mine forever," he whispered.

"Two days; it's already Saturday."

"Even better." He fought the sleep threatening to take him under. It had been an eventful evening. The warmth of Juliana's body curled next to his only furthered his wish to drift off.

A knock, sharp and insistent, startled him. How long had he drifted off? He bolted upright. "Someone's at your door, Juliana!"

CHAPTER 28

"Wake up, Juliana. Someone's at your door." Victor's voice shook Juliana from the most wonderful dream. Or was she still dreaming?

With groggy eyes, she stared into Victor's panicked face.

The hushed voice of a man followed a knock at her door. "Miss Merrick. Wake up."

She scrambled from the bed and threw on her dressing gown, holding the ends tight around her to cover her nakedness. When she cracked open the door, Nash peered at her, then quickly averted his eyes.

"Forgive my asking, Miss Merrick, but is Mr. Pratt with you?"

Oh, dear God. They'd been found out. But wait, Victor said Nash witnessed him climbing up to her window. Heat rushed up her neck and burned her cheeks.

Before she could answer, Victor's body pressed against hers. "I'm here, Nash. What do you want?"

"Get dressed and follow me. It's almost five, and the servants will be rising soon. And you dropped this." Nash held Victor's missing shoe as he slipped his hand through the crack in the door. "Now hurry. We don't have time to waste."

While Juliana stood helplessly at the door, Victor grabbed his shoe and rushed off to gather his clothing.

She forced down the lump forming in her throat. "Are you going to tell my brother?"

Nash gave a soft chuckle. "Did Pratt grovel enough to redeem himself? Are you going to marry him?"

If only Nash knew just how well Victor had redeemed himself. Then again, from the smirk on Nash's face, perhaps he did. "Yes."

"Then even if I were the type to rush to your brother—which I am not—I wouldn't. Now tell your young man to hurry. I'll wait out here for him."

With a strangled, "Thank you," Juliana closed the door.

Victor had already slipped on his shirt and trousers. His waistcoat remained unbuttoned, and he shoved his bare feet into his shoes, stuffing his stockings into his pocket. "My coat? Where did I leave my bloody coat?" He spun in a circle like a child's top.

"Over there." She pointed to the chair where she'd laid it mere hours ago.

Looking devilishly handsome in his state of dishabille, Victor pulled her into his arms. "Good night, my love." A smile tipped his lips. "Or should I say, good morning. I shall call on you later today. For now, get some sleep and dream of me." He kissed her long and hard until another persistent knock sounded.

"Pratt. Hurry."

As he walked to the door, he held onto her hand, their arms outstretched until only their fingertips touched. "I love you," he whispered as he slipped through the door and closed it with a *click*.

Rooted in place, she stared at the door, still in a daze from everything that had transpired.

Victor loved her!

Had made love to her.

And it had been glorious. Twirling like a ballerina, she danced across the floor, then came to an abrupt stop. An uncomfortable thought slipped into her mind, and freeing herself from her stupor, she raced back to the bed and threw back the counterpane and sheets. The smear of red condemned her.

She chewed on her bottom lip. *Think. Think.* Could she blame it on her courses? She just had them a little over a week ago, recalling how she'd been grateful her lovely new ballgown wouldn't be stained.

When she grabbed a cloth to try to wash it away, the cloth itself was tinged with blood. Victor's blood from the scratches on his face and hands. After rinsing the cloth in cold water, she tried to dab at the stain on the bed, only then seeing pinkish traces from Victor's wounds on the pillow and higher up on the sheets.

Resigned to the fact that she'd never be able to explain it adequately, she prayed that Miss Price would keep her secret.

And if not, she prayed Drake would remember his own indiscretion and not kill Victor.

For she dearly wished to marry him.

⚜

VICTOR WANTED TO WIPE THE SMIRK OFF NASH'S FACE AS HE followed the churl through the quiet house.

"You dropped this as well." Nash handed Victor his hat the vine branch had knocked off during his fateful climb.

Victor grunted a "Thank you."

"What's that?" Nash held a hand to his ear and gave a deep chuckle.

"Thank you," Victor said, still reluctant to put much feeling into the words.

"From the appearance of things, you *should* be thanking me. Profusely. I'd venture you had a very good evening. Miss Merrick certainly had a glow about her."

"If you so much as speak a word—"

"Relax, Pratt. I'm the last person to judge."

When they reached the end of the hallway, Nash held out his hand and peered around the corner. Soft shuffling from below drifted up the staircase. Nash held a finger to his lips then continued watching for an opportunity to descend.

Victor's heart pounded in his chest. If he were caught, what would Burwood do? Of course Victor had no qualms about marrying Juliana; he wanted that more than anything. But he surely didn't want to die. And the duke had been a decorated soldier in the cavalry.

After an interminable length of time, Nash motioned him forward, and the only time Victor remembered going down the stairs faster was when he slid down the railing as a boy. Of course that ended with a severe reprimand from Nanny while Cilla giggled furiously.

Dim light shone in the entrance of the grand home, and Victor breathed a sigh of relief as they arrived unnoticed and unscathed.

As Nash opened the door, a maid appeared and stopped short, her mouth gaping open as her gaze darted between Nash and Victor.

Victor stared down at his hastily dressed body, his waistcoat and coat unbuttoned and hanging loosely around him, his neckcloth haphazardly tied. No doubt his hair looked a fright. In his haste, he'd forgotten to find the ribbon with which to secure it.

"You've seen nothing," Nash said to the maid and ushered Victor out the door. "Don't worry about her. I'll slip a few coins her way and explain you were lost and looking for directions."

"Do you really think she'll believe that? You realize I'm a frequent caller here."

"A caller who is going to marry the duke's sister." Nash stopped and stared. "You *are* going to marry her, aren't you?"

"Of course, I'm going to marry her. I would marry her even if we hadn't—" *Damnation.* He'd almost blurted the truth out to that blackguard.

Nash laughed again. "Despite what you think, Pratt, I know what goes on between a man and a woman, especially when he emerges from her bedchamber looking like something the cat dragged in. Now, I hailed a hackney for you and told him to wait several houses up the street. Go." With a push, Nash sent Victor off.

Victor popped his hat on, gave it a little tap, and raced off to the waiting hackney. The driver didn't bat an eye as Victor gave his address and hopped inside. He sank against the worn squabs of the coach and closed his eyes.

Juliana loved him! Gave herself to him.

And it was glorious.

He lifted his hand to his face and inhaled deeply, Juliana's alluring mix of jasmine and ginger recalling the memories of her in his arms.

The carriage jolted to a halt in front of his bachelor apartments, and he climbed out, grateful to be home, but already missing Juliana. For the small amount of sleep he had—which truthfully had been nothing—he felt remarkably alert as he entered his apartments and headed toward his bedroom.

Slumped in a chair, Tierney snored loudly, and with a snort, startled awake. "Sir! You're home. I was so worried when you didn't arrive. Have you heard the news?" He leapt to his feet then came to an abrupt halt. "You're injured! What happened?"

"I'm fine. Minor scratches. And if you're speaking about the king's death, yes. Burwood announced it at the ball when the news arrived. Now, I need sleep. Please don't disturb me." His bed beckoned, but he turned back, almost running into Tierney, who had been right on his heels. "Except if Miss Merrick comes. Then wake me immediately."

Victor voiced no protest as Tierney untied his cravat—clucking his tongue in disapproval—and removed his coat and waistcoat.

As Tierney moved to hang up his coat, he pulled out the stockings Victor had shoved into his pocket. "Sir?" His gaze shot to Victor's feet.

"It's best not to ask." Victor waved him off. "I can finish the rest. Wake me around noon; I'll take a bath then."

With a final questioning glance, Tierney bowed and closed the door behind him, leaving Victor blessedly alone. He collapsed into bed and hoped to dream about his wonderful night with Juliana.

He had indeed been enjoying a wonderfully erotic dream about Juliana when Tierney's annoying voice pulled him from his slumber.

"Sir! Sir!"

Victor pulled the pillow over his head. "What is it? Don't tell me it's noon already." Lord, it felt like he'd only just fallen asleep.

"It's close, sir. But that's not why I woke you."

"Then what the devil is it?" As his mind rose to consciousness, Victor remembered the one reason he told Tierney to disturb him. He bolted upright in bed. "Is Juliana here?"

"No, sir." Tierney had the gall to look chagrined. "It's this. I thought it best not to wait." In his shaking hand, Tierney held out *The Muckraker*, and Victor's stomach dropped.

❧

UNABLE TO SLEEP AFTER VICTOR LEFT, JULIANA WASHED, SHIVERING from the cold water. After she'd dressed, she pulled the stained sheets from the bed and crumpled them up to cover the evidence. If the maid collected others along with hers, perhaps no one would tie the blood to her. A faint hope at best, but a hope, nonetheless.

She occupied her mind with her book. For the last few weeks, she had put the story of the two sisters aside, unwilling to read about their heartbreak on top of facing her own.

How quickly things had changed for her, and she picked up the book in hopes that things would work out for Elinor and Marianne just as beautifully. Enthralled by the story right as Edward enlightened Marianne that he was unmarried and how Lucy Steele had married his brother, Robert, and not him, Juliana glanced up at the quick knock at her door.

"Come in," she answered, doing her best to keep her annoyance from her voice.

"I expected you to still be sleeping, miss. But here you are, already dressed." Miss Price breezed into the room and stopped short at the sight of the bedclothes piled on the floor. "What happened here?"

"I—um—spilled something. Could you ask a maid to put them with the rest of the laundry?"

From Miss Price's expression, she clearly had her doubts about Juliana's veracity, but she nodded and gathered the linens and placed them outside the door. Hands on her hips, Miss Price scrutinized Juliana. "Allow me to dress your hair."

Juliana had brushed it and tied it at her neck with a ribbon—the very ribbon that had fallen from Victor's hair. "I prefer to wear it like this, Miss Price. Victor likes it down."

A smile crossed Miss Price's lips. "So everything is fine with your young man, then? Last evening when I prepared you for bed after the ball, you seemed preoccupied. I couldn't help but wonder if you two had had a tiff."

"It's true; I was worried. But I've—um—realized my imagination was getting away from me."

With a quick squeeze to Juliana's shoulder, Miss Price said, "Good. I'm glad to hear it. Her Grace has already had breakfast and has requested to see you as soon as possible."

Juliana's mind reeled. What could Honoria want that was of such importance? "Is my brother with her?"

"No, miss. His Grace left the house earlier. Sad news about the king, but not surprising."

Oh, of course. Perhaps there were some protocols she needed to learn when a monarch died and that's what Honoria wanted. A twinge of guilt twisted in Juliana's stomach that she'd been so happy when the country would be draped in mourning.

Unbidden, dread tripped up her spine. She swallowed the lump forming in her throat. "Miss Price. My wedding is in two days. Will it be delayed due to the king's death?" Goodness, what if she was with child? How long would she and Victor have to wait?

Pursing her lips, Miss Price shook her head. "I don't know for certain. But if so, I expect you would only have to wait a few months. Now, don't dilly-dally. Her Grace is waiting." With that, Miss Price exited.

A few months! So much could happen in a few months. Her hand drifted to her abdomen. Would she bring more embarrassment and scandal to her family? After gathering her wits, and taking a few deep breaths, Juliana found Honoria in the morning room. "Miss Price said you wished to see me."

Seated at the escritoire by the window, Honoria peered up and gave Juliana a soft smile. "Did you get any sleep at all?"

Goodness. How should she answer that? "Very little, I'm afraid."

Honoria rose and moved to the sofa, patting the cushion beside her. "Come."

When Juliana obeyed, Honoria took Juliana's hands in hers. "Drake told me what happened in the orangery between Victor and Adalyn, and Adalyn confirmed it. It was innocent, Juliana. I encouraged Drake to speak with you last night. Did it help? Have you decided about the wedding?"

"Yes. I've decided to marry Victor."

Honoria threw a hand to her heart. "Oh, thank goodness. I hope you don't mind, but Drake told me everything. We don't keep secrets from each other any longer. I believe with all my heart that, although it may have started as a pretense, Victor truly loves you."

Juliana couldn't help but smile. "He does."

Pulling her into a hug, Honoria said, "Drake will be so pleased his talk helped."

Juliana didn't have the heart—or the courage—to tell her sister-in-law that, although Drake had given her much to think about, it was Victor's bravado of stealing in through her window and his tender lovemaking that convinced her. She pulled back. "But Honoria, will we be able to proceed with the wedding as planned because of the king's death? We won't have to wait, will we?"

"Not long, dear. Drake should find out some details about the funeral soon. Perhaps ten days or two weeks. I was just writing to the vicar when you came in. I wasn't certain whether I should ask him to postpone the wedding or cancel it."

Two weeks! Well, it was certainly better than two months.

"Don't worry, dear. The time will pass quickly, and I'm sure Victor will call upon you every day." Mischief twinkled in Honoria's eyes. "We may even allow you both a little time alone together."

Tendrils of heat crept up Juliana's neck. Honoria had no idea that her generosity was a bit late. That horse had already left the stables.

Honoria must have interpreted Juliana's embarrassment

differently. "Has your mother explained things to you, my dear? Let me assure you, it is quite wonderful when two people love each other. Not that Victor would take advantage before your wedding."

The heat intensified, scorching Juliana's cheeks. "I'm aware of what happens."

Pink bloomed on Honoria's cheeks as well. "Good."

Frampton arrived at the door and broke the uncomfortable moment. "Your Grace. I apologize for interrupting. I believe you should see this."

Honoria motioned him forward and plucked the rectangular paper from the silver salver.

The Muckraker!

As Honoria scanned the contents, her hand rose to her throat. "Oh, dear."

"What is it?" Juliana scooted closer and craned her neck to get a glimpse of the horrible scandal sheet.

"It mentions the king's death, of course." A frown creased Honoria's brow. "But it says the Duke of Clarence is rumored to abdicate and refuse the crown but questions the source."

"You're not upset about that, are you? What else does it say?" Juliana gave a little tug to Honoria's arm.

"There is quite a lot about last night's ball." Honoria's gaze shot to Juliana, an apology lurking in the green depths of her eyes.

"Tell me."

Nodding, Honoria read.

"Last night, the Duke of Burwood hosted an engagement ball for his sister and Mr. Victor Pratt, which proved to be most eventful. Among the guests was a Mr. Miles Grey, the proprietor of the gaming hell, The Knave of Hearts. *As if the attendance of such an unsavory character wasn't enough, it has reached this reporter's ears that the said Mr. Grey is actually the illegitimate cousin of the duke himself! As if the* ton *needed another reason to snub the upstart newcomer.*

"The information about Mr. Grey was not the only on dit this reporter received. I have it on good authority from an eyewitness that Mr. Pratt was caught in flagrante delicto with another woman in the duke's very own orangery. One wonders if the wedding will proceed as planned. Of course, it should be no surprise, as Mr. Pratt already compromised his intended, leading to their forced

engagement. It would appear that Mr. Pratt wishes to have his cake and eat it, too. This reporter is curious to see if they disregard mourning etiquette and proceed with the wedding in two days."

Juliana balled her hands into fists on her lap. "The eyewitness mentioned has to be Lydia Whyte. But Victor doesn't believe she's the one responsible for the rag."

"I would agree. Although Lydia can be a bit, shall we say, scatterbrained, I can't imagine her being so organized to compile this—tripe."

"But Honoria, she must either know who is responsible or she at least spread the gossip about Miles to whomever is."

"Oh, that's an excellent point, Juliana. Perhaps we should call a meeting of the League."

Full of energy that amazed Juliana, Honoria jumped up and crossed to the escritoire, penning notes to Bea, Miranda, and Anne.

Alone on the sofa, Juliana gathered her racing thoughts, her gaze fixed on the discarded scandal sheet. Once again, *The Muckraker* had launched a vicious attack, but the League would rise to meet it. Would it be enough?

The wedding would be delayed—barely a fortnight, if they were lucky—but the damage from the gossip rag might linger longer than black crepe on a sleeve.

Still, Victor loved her. He had said so with words and proved it with action.

She touched the silky ribbon in her hair, the one that had once tied back his own, and drew in a steadying breath.

Whatever lay ahead—mourning, scandal, or delay—she would not face it alone.

And that, at last, was enough.

CHAPTER 29

Victor's skull throbbed, and he snapped the reins of his curricle, urging the horse forward. Lack of sleep exacerbated his already foul mood after reading the reports in that atrocity, *The Muckraker.*

Although he'd held little hope Lydia would remain silent about what she'd witnessed in Burwood's orangery, Victor at least thought the news about the king's death would overshadow any idle gossip. However, the king had been ill for so long, it was hardly a surprise to learn of his demise. It would have served Victor better had his death been sudden and unexpected. Callous? Possibly.

As it stood, the news of the king had scarcely earned a few sentences in the scandal sheet, although Victor noted the perpetrator included the false information about the new king refusing the crown, although the *reporter* didn't put much credence in the possibility. Like Lydia, Middlebury must have spread the rumor to the perpetrator—unless he truly believed the rumor about the Duke of Clarence to be false and intended to throw them off his scent.

Could Middlebury be that clever? Victor had his doubts.

Every bit of gossip intentionally dispensed was included in the rag, save but one.

Missing from the pernicious paper was the information Nash leaked about his bad turn of fortune and possible new investment opportunity.

Odd. But perhaps—not. Maybe Nash was mistaken about Davies having a vendetta against him.

With another snap to the reins, Victor urged the mount faster. He needed to see Juliana, to reassure her all would be well. The memory of her silken skin, her whispered words of love, the promises they exchanged encased him in happiness.

But his cocoon of contentment shattered when, an hour earlier, Tierney had wrapped the black mourning band around Victor's arm. "No doubt you will have to postpone the wedding until after the funeral." Tierney's words had splashed over Victor like ice water.

Damn. Right.

Victor's morbid thoughts continued with the hope that the king's long illness would have prompted advanced plans for a speedy funeral. Of course, he could whisk Juliana away to Gretna Green, but it would only provide more fodder for the rumor mills.

They would simply have to wait. The question remained—how long?

After what seemed an eternity, he pulled his curricle up to Pendrake Manor, threw the reins to a young groom waiting at the entrance, and climbed down.

Black mourning crape draped the front door and framed a black laurel wreath hanging in its center. Moments after Victor knocked, Frampton greeted him, a similar black band wrapped around his upper arm. "Mr. Pratt. Follow me." Even Frampton's curt instruction carried a somber weight.

More black crape draped the windows and railings of the staircase, transforming the cheerful atmosphere from the previous night's ball to one of a house in mourning.

In the drawing room, Juliana peered up from where she sat on the sofa, her fair skin appearing even paler against the black bombazine, and her shiny, golden blond hair a stark contrast of color against the drab, unadorned gown.

Juliana sprang from the sofa. "Victor!" Hands outstretched, she raced toward him.

Oh, how he longed to pull her into his arms for a deliciously slow kiss. But alas, he'd have to wait. Juliana's mother and the duchess rose in greeting, both dressed in the same horrible black. A black widow's cap replaced the pretty lace one Mrs. Merrick usually wore, and even the duchess covered her lovely red hair.

He bowed. "Your Grace. Mrs. Merrick." An incongruous smile tugged his lips. "Miss Merrick."

Juliana took his hands in hers, the softness of them reminding him how they had played against his bare chest and teased down his abdomen. Had it truly been only hours?

He coughed, clearing his tightening throat. "Have you seen *The Muckraker?*"

Juliana nodded. "I'm so sorry, Victor."

He blinked. "Sorry? Whatever for? The person who wrote this despicable tripe is the one who should be sorry. And whenever I find out who it is—"

Juliana placed a hand on his chest, and it calmed him. "I meant I'm so sorry for what it said about you. It was cruel and unjust."

"That scandal sheet has never been anything but cruel and unjust," the duchess said. "I truly believe whoever it is derives joy from hurting people." She shook her head. "What kind of person does that?"

"Jealous, spiteful people who are unsatisfied with their own lives, no doubt," Mrs. Merrick said.

Victor marveled at his good fortune at finding Juliana. Not only did he love her with his whole heart, and she loved him in return, but he was marrying into a family with kind, compassionate, and wise women. Unlike his own mother. "Your mother has a point. The culprit seems to have a vendetta against certain members of the *ton.* The question is—why? What have I, you, or your family done to them?"

Juliana pulled Victor over to the sofa. "That's exactly what The

League is working on. Lady Montgomery has been analyzing—what she calls—the data."

"It doesn't help narrow things down when all the people we leaked information to are the biggest gossips of the *ton*." He shook his head.

Silence settled over them, and the clock struck half past one when the duchess broke it. "Juliana and I were discussing Lydia Whyte. I hate to speak ill of anyone, but I understand she had set her cap for you, Victor. She could harbor ill feelings toward Juliana and wish to punish you both."

During his drive over, Victor had those very same thoughts, and after leaving Juliana, he intended to pay a call on Lydia. "Since we are all in a state of shock over the king's death, let's not discuss such unpleasantness, but rather turn the conversation to our upcoming wedding."

The duke's voice drifted into the room moments before he did. "And tell Mr. Beckham I wish to speak with him," he called over his shoulder to Frampton. Attention fully on the drawing room, he said, "Ah, good. I'm glad you're here, Victor. I've just come from Lords. The king's funeral will be July 15." He turned toward Juliana. "The question is, what have you decided, Juliana? Will there still be a wedding?"

Juliana gave Victor an apologetic smile. "Drake left early this morning for Lords. He's unaware of my decision."

The duchess tilted her head. "Which begs the question, Juliana. From Victor's last statement, he seemed confident there would be a wedding. But according to Drake, when he left you last night in your bedroom, you were still deciding. Can you explain, Mr. Pratt?"

Everyone's attention turned toward Victor, and the duke's eyes narrowed to slits. "Yes, can you explain that?"

"Well—um—I—"

"I sent Victor a note early this morning after I rose, informing him I had given it much thought and wished to proceed with our plans." The words spilled from Juliana's lips. Her hands twisted in her lap, the movement attracting her brother's keen eye. Catching her in the lie, perhaps?

"A note? So if I ask Frampton, he will confirm this?"

"Good afternoon, everyone." Nash strode into the room. "I trust everyone slept well." His dark eyes danced with amusement when he glanced at Victor.

The churl. Muscles in Victor's neck tensed. Surely, he wouldn't expose them? He claimed to like Juliana, but as for his feelings for Victor—well.

Nash folded his tall body in a chair and leisurely crossed one foot across his opposing knee. "Did I hear something about a note for Mr. Pratt?"

The duchess handed Nash a cup of tea. "Yes. Juliana said she sent a note to Mr. Pratt informing him she decided to marry him."

After taking an annoyingly slow sip, Nash nodded. "Miss Merrick seemed especially anxious to deliver it. I happened to be up early, so I attended to the task myself. I believe one of your maids saw me around five this morning."

The cool liar didn't blink an eye. Hopefully, no one would question the maid. Or if they did, Nash had paid her to forget she'd also seen Victor sneaking out of the house. Nash turned toward Juliana. "Did that put your mind at ease so you were able to get some sleep?"

Relief washed over Juliana's face. "Not much. I was up and dressed before Miss Price came in to wake me. Have you seen *The Muckraker*?"

"Adalyn read it to me," Nash answered. "Ugly business. I noticed they didn't name my wife as the woman you were with in the orangery, Pratt. Wise move on their part, although it doesn't keep me from wanting to hunt them down and wring their necks."

The duchess paled. "All things considered, and although I understand your desire to seek retribution, it might be prudent not to say such things aloud in less friendly company."

Nash barked a laugh. An odd reaction from a man accused of strangling a woman to death a few years before. "Fair point, Your Grace." Nash took another sip of his tea, his expression thoughtful. "Unless I missed something, it doesn't provide any indication of the culprit's identity."

Juliana's shoulders slumped. "No."

An idea itched the back of Victor's mind. "There was no mention of what you shared with Ashton, Nash. I'd hoped Davies was involved."

"Or he plans to keep the information about the new opportunity to himself, and reporting my alleged bad fortune would tip his hand. I'd keep an eye on him if I were you."

Longing to discuss something more joyful, Victor brought the subject back to what mattered most, and, turning to the duchess, he took Juliana's hand in his. "How soon after the funeral can Juliana and I marry?"

"I think the following Monday would be acceptable. The fifteenth is on a Thursday. We could plan for Friday, but it would be advisable to not appear in too great a rush. Also, if most of the *ton* remain in Town for the funeral, it would be wise to give them a few days to depart for their country homes. The fewer remaining to spread gossip, the better."

With that settled, although not especially to Victor's satisfaction, he rose. "I should take my leave."

Juliana rose with him. "I'll see you out."

After Victor requested for his curricle to be brought around, he waited for Frampton to leave, then he pulled Juliana into his arms and whispered, "I'll need to thank Nash. I was certain your brother had found us out."

He kissed her as long and passionately as possible before Frampton returned. "I'm sorry we have to wait so long before the wedding."

"I am, too." She sighed and sagged into him, her cheek pressed against his chest. She felt so incredibly right in his arms.

A smile fought its way to his lips. How had he not noticed how her hair was tied back before? Without untying it, he gave the dark-blue ribbon a little tug. "This looks familiar."

The giggle vibrated against his chest. "I couldn't resist. It made me feel close to you. However, Miss Price did question me regarding where it came from."

With his forefinger, he lifted her chin for another quick kiss. "I have something important to do, but I will call upon you tomorrow. Weather permitting, perhaps we can go for a ride."

"I'd love that, although I don't have a black riding habit."

"The king's death is so inconvenient."

Her smile lit up his world. "More for him than anyone, I would imagine."

After bidding Juliana goodbye, he climbed into his curricle, one destination on his mind—Lord and Lady Whyte's. He intended to have a harsh word with Lydia.

Juliana fingered the thin ribbon, a warm buttery sensation flowing through her stomach as she remembered threading her hands through Victor's long hair the night before. The ribbon more than tied her hair back; it linked her to the man she loved. The man she would marry. He'd left only moments earlier, but she missed him already.

A masculine cough sounded behind her, and she spun to find Nash. Leaning against the wall, he studied her. "I had hoped to catch Pratt before he left, but I waited to give you two a bit of privacy."

The warmth she experienced moments before increased and traveled from her stomach up her neck to her cheeks. "He wanted to relay his thanks for corroborating my story about the note."

Nash straightened, making him appear even more intimidating. "He can thank me by giving me the sketches he drew of my wife, which should be no problem since he's finally rid himself of that schoolboy infatuation and found a real love of his own."

During the ball the previous evening, Juliana had heard whispers about Nash. The rumors painted a dark picture of a man not to be trusted. Yet, the little she'd come to know of him discounted that notion entirely. Nash had proven to be a trusted confidant and friend.

Although, at the time, her head had spun from Victor's kisses, something in his last words inched to the surface and settled uneasily in her chest. "Nash, Victor said he had something important to attend to. He didn't say what, but there was a cold look in his eyes that was so unlike him. You don't think he'll do anything rash, do you?"

"You're speaking about the report in *The Muckraker*?"

"Yes. It's clear that Lydia took some part in things as she was the witness in the orangery, not to mention the information about Mr. Grey."

Nash pondered it for a moment. "Other than some reprimanding words, I doubt it. Pratt isn't the type of man to harm a woman. And it may be something completely unrelated. Perhaps he intends to purchase a special wedding gift for you." The smile on Nash's lips didn't quite reach his eyes, and Juliana wondered if the last suggestion was more to placate her than provide a reason for Victor's errand.

CHAPTER 30

Rather than calm him, the drive to the Whytes' had only increased Victor's ire toward Lydia. The horse neighed in protest as he pulled the curricle to a stop in front of the townhouse and threw the reins to a groom.

He may have pounded on the front door a little too forcefully, for when the Whytes' butler answered, the censorious expression on the man's face held all the disapproval of a disappointed father. "May I help you, sir?"

"It's imperative I speak with Miss Whyte." Victor stuck out his calling card, although, since Victor had been a frequent caller at the residence, the butler hardly needed it.

The butler pulled it from Victor's outstretched hand with a *snap*. "I shall enquire if the young lady is at home. Wait here, please." He motioned toward the entrance, then closed the door behind them.

Victor tapped the side of his leg in impatience, knowing full well that any butler worth his salt would know precisely who was home and who was not. Of course, it could mean that Lydia might refuse to see him.

He used the time wisely and took deep breaths to calm himself. It would do no good to question Lydia if he frightened her. No, he would play the game her way—with sweetness and flattery.

Ready to give up, Victor jerked to attention at the returning butler. "Follow me, sir."

After giving the butler his hat and gloves, Victor followed him to a side parlor, where Lydia perched on a settee, her mother on a chair next to her daughter. He gave the smallest bow possible while still remaining polite. "Ladies. Thank you for seeing me."

Lady Whyte scowled in greeting as she rose. "Mr. Pratt. Given the reports of *The Muckraker*, I should not allow any conversation between you and my daughter. However, Lydia insisted she speak with you." She motioned to the vacant spot on the settee next to Lydia, and Victor reluctantly sat.

"That's precisely what I wished to speak about, Lady Whyte. The reports regarding the purported events in the Duke of Burwood's orangery are greatly exaggerated. Nothing untoward happened between me and the lady in question."

"Are you calling my daughter a liar, sir?"

Ah, so she's aware it was Lydia who was the *witness*. "Not at all, madam. I'm well aware Miss Whyte witnessed me in the orangery. However, what I'm saying is she merely misinterpreted what happened."

Using the smile that Cilla christened his *lady killer*, Victor turned toward Lydia. "Miss Whyte. I understand what a shock it must have been to see me alone with a woman last night, but I assure you what you witnessed was completely innocent. Lady Nash Talbot and I are good friends, nothing more, and she wished me joy in my upcoming marriage to Miss Merrick."

Lydia darted a glance toward her mother. "And do your wedding plans remain as they were?"

Oh, so that was Lydia's game. She no doubt held hope that Juliana had broken things off, and by all accounts, it had appeared that way, even to Victor. Adopting his most solemn expression, he decided to play into Lydia's hands. "I'm afraid not." Not a complete untruth. The wedding date had indeed changed, but he would allow Lydia to interpret his answer as she willed.

And exactly as he expected, Lydia took the bait. "Oh, I'm so sorry to hear this, Mr. Pratt." She pressed a hand to her heart in mock sympathy, but no one could mistake the gleam of glee in her eyes. "You must be heartbroken."

"Indeed. It is quite difficult. But that's why I've come here, Miss Whyte. If you could help me with identifying who is responsible for the reports, I would be eternally grateful. Do you remember whom you might have told? Besides your dear mother, that is."

Once again, Lydia's gaze swept to Lady Whyte.

"I'm asking you, Lydia, not your mother."

Lady Whyte glowered. "Sir, you have not been given permission to address my daughter by her Christian name."

"I beg your pardon, but as you can certainly understand, the report in *The Muckraker* is most damaging on many accounts. Even if I cannot persuade Miss Merrick to marry me in two days, perhaps I can convince the author of the false report to write a retraction and salvage my own reputation. Then I will try to heal my broken heart, perhaps with someone else." He exhaled a heavy sigh, shaking his head pitifully and only partially ashamed of his prevarication.

He could almost feel the atmosphere in the room shift to his favor.

"Well, I can't be certain who might have overheard. I was so upset, you understand."

She was upset? Victor restrained the urge to roll his eyes. "Of course. But if you could, please try."

"Mr. Pratt," Lady Whyte said. "While we understand your predicament, I'm afraid this is most distressing to my poor Lydia. If you would allow her to gather her thoughts without the pressure of your presence, perhaps something will come to mind." She rose, informing Victor, in no uncertain terms, the call was at an end.

"Of course. Write to me if you think of anything. And perhaps once this is all behind us, I might be permitted to call upon you again, Miss Whyte. With your permission, of course, Lady Whyte."

The glint in the woman's eye answered his question. "We shall see, Mr. Pratt."

With that, Victor left, hoping beyond hope Lydia's desire to get her hooks into him would loosen her tongue and reveal the identity of the scoundrel behind *The Muckraker*.

Juliana turned the last page of her book and sighed, grateful not only Elinor and Marianne had found their true loves, but that she had as well. Just as Elinor would support Edward in his desire to become a simple country pastor, she would support Victor's passion for art. And if he so desired to eventually pursue a career in politics once he had become Viscount Cartwright, and with Honoria's guidance, she would do her utmost to learn the ways of society.

Stepping outside her room, she decided to take a stroll in the garden and escape the maudlin atmosphere the black crape and somber expressions of the servants created.

Diffused sunshine greeted her as the sun sank low in the sky, and she relished the warmth on her skin, remembering the heat Victor's touch elicited. Although the prize roses that lined the winding path were beautiful, Juliana gravitated toward the hydrangeas; their vivid blue color reminded her of Victor's incredible eyes. She brushed a hand against the lacy flowers and sighed.

"Pardon me, miss."

Juliana spun around toward the child's voice, expecting to see Nash and Adalyn's ward, Mena.

Stretching out a grimy hand, a boy of about eight or ten stood before her. His dirty face broke into a grin, revealing a missing tooth. "You're Juliana, ain't ya? The man said to look for a lady with blond hair. Says I was to give this to ya."

Juliana plucked the folded paper from the boy's fingers. "How did you get in here?" Heavy wrought-iron fencing closed off the garden from the surrounding homes and mews in the back. Drake, with his constant worry, had ensured the gate leading to the mews remained locked, with the keys only entrusted to loyal servants.

The boy puffed up his thin chest. "'Tweren't nothin'. I squeezed through the bars. Lucky I was to see ya. Didn't fancy going up to the door of this big 'ouse none." He gave a little shiver.

Sealed with a blob of wax without an imprint, the letter was written in an unfamiliar hand. She broke the seal and read.

Your man is lying to you. Come to the back entrance of The Knave of Hearts *at quarter past ten tonight to learn the truth. Come alone.*
   A friend

"You said a man gave this to you? Do you know who he was?"

The boy shook his head. "Never seen 'im before. Just gave me two shillings to bring it to the Duke of Burwood's 'ouse and give it to a lady named Juliana."

"What did he look like?"

"Like everybody else."

"Juliana?" Drake's voice drifted into the garden. "Are you out here?"

She turned and stepped around the curve in the garden path, tucking the letter into the folds of her skirt. "Yes. I'm here."

"Mother wants to see you."

"I'll be right there." When Drake ducked back into the house, Juliana hurried back to where she'd left the boy, only to find him gone.

Doubt snaked through her veins and coiled in her mind. Could she be as foolish as Marianne when she trusted in Willoughby's love? Although Willoughby said he truly loved Marianne, he traded that love for financial security. With the help of Drake's connections as duke, would Victor use her to further his artistic ambitions?

She forced the doubt aside. Victor wouldn't lie to her. Not after what they'd shared the night before. Pulling the letter out from the folds of her gown, she stared at the signature.

A friend

As if a friend would ask her to come alone to a gaming hell at night! She wasn't a newly foaled filly. However, that didn't mean she would disregard the letter entirely. There was more to the cryptic message than met the eye. Suspicion niggled at her mind, whispering it had something to do with *The Muckraker.*

She needed a plan.

With determined steps, she marched back into the house, calling forward the girl who defied the rules of propriety to protect who and what she loved.

Later that evening, in his studio, Victor leaned back in the chair at his desk and admired the sketches he'd made of Juliana. He could draw her from memory now; the curve of her cheek, the slight upturn of lips when she gifted him with her enigmatic smile, the sparkle in her cornflower blue eyes. Careful not to draw anything that would be considered scandalous, he kept the sketch confined to her face. But once they were married—well, as he'd told her—he had a lot of plans for when they were in private and wouldn't have to answer to any judgmental gossip.

In addition to his sketches of Juliana, he'd drawn some of her mother—that's if Burwood hadn't changed his mind about commissioning Victor to paint portraits of the rest of the family. It had dawned on him how much the two women looked alike, giving Victor an idea what Juliana would look like in her forties. But more than Juliana's pretty face, Victor knew his future bride would be a kind and thoughtful wife and mother, one her children would run to for comfort. One who would encourage them to pursue their dreams.

And if the *ton* never accepted her, so be it. He never wanted a career in politics anyway. He closed his eyes and envisioned the life ahead of them.

Idyllic lazy days spent painting while Juliana worked with her horses. Their children gathered about them in the evenings. Their eyes would meet and the connection between them would sizzle with electricity.

Naturally, she would read the glint of seduction in his eyes, and after calling the nanny to mind the children, he would lead her to their bedchamber where they would—

"Sir, beg pardon. This was just delivered, and it's marked urgent."

Victor's eyes darted open, frustrated to have such a pleasant daydream interrupted at such a moment. He plucked the missive from the tray and glanced at the vaguely familiar handwriting. Flurries of tension built in his chest as he broke the unadorned seal and read.

Mr. Pratt,

If you wish to discover the identity of the person behind The Muckraker, *come to the back entrance of* The Knave of Hearts *at ten this evening. Be certain to come alone.*

X

Victor's gaze shot to Tierney. "Who delivered this?"

"A street urchin, sir. I sent him to Cook to be fed."

Grabbing his pencil and a sketchpad, Victor bolted from his seat and headed for the door. "Good. Hopefully, he's still there."

In the small kitchen, the boy Tierney mentioned sat stuffing his dirty face with some bread, meat, and cheese. The lad gazed up, his cheeks puffed up like a squirrel's pouch, and his eyes widened.

Not wishing to scare him off, Victor smiled and lifted the letter. "Thank you for delivering this. Can you tell me who gave it to you?"

With an audible gulp, the boy swallowed, and Victor hoped he wouldn't choke himself. "A man. Said to keep it secret. Give me two shillings, 'e did."

"Can you describe him?"

The boy shrugged his thin shoulders. His coat was worn and threadbare. Bony knees poked through the holes in his too-short breeches.

Compassion flooded Victor's heart, and he took a seat next to the boy. "Did the man threaten you?"

The boy shoved another piece of cheese into his mouth as if someone would snatch it away, then shook his head and mumbled, "Nah."

"Was he old or young?"

"Old."

Now they were getting somewhere.

"Like you." The boy grinned.

Unable to resist the chuckle, Victor said. "So, about my age, then? Not old and wrinkled with gray hair?"

The lad swallowed again. "Wha' do ya want me to answer first?"

Right. "He was about as old as me?"

With a nod, the boy shoved the remaining piece of meat into his mouth.

"Was he dressed like me?" Victor waved a hand in front of his superfine coat, silk waistcoat, and—thanks to Tierney—his expertly tied neckcloth.

"Fancy-like, you mean? Nah."

Not a gentleman, then. Pencil poised above his sketchpad, Victor asked, "What was the shape of his face? Round, square, oblong?"

"Wha's oblong?"

Victor drew the shape on his paper. "Like this?"

Mouth full of bread, the boy pointed a dirty finger at the paper. "Yeah, tha's it."

"What about his eyes?"

"Kind of rheumy and squinty."

"Good. Good."

Victor continued to sketch, and with more prompting, had what the boy said was a good likeness of the man.

"Did the man who gave you the letter write it?"

"How's I to know? He just give it to me and told me where to bring it."

The excitement bubbling in Victor's veins fizzled out like flat champagne. Of course, the perpetrator wouldn't be careless enough to reveal himself to the messenger. No doubt he'd paid someone to give it to the boy. At least the sketch was a starting point.

"What's your name, boy?"

"Lucas. But people call me Luke."

"Do you have parents?"

Luke snorted. "O'course, I got parents. Don't be daft. How'd you think I got here? Stork?" The boy snorted again.

What cheek! "I mean, are they alive?"

"Mum is. Who knows where my da is. Mum says he's a no-good son-of-a—"

Victor held up his hand. "Stop. There's a lady present."

It was Cook's turn to snort a laugh.

Victor pulled some coins from his pocket and held out two crowns. Luke's eyes widened, and he reached a grimy hand toward the fortune.

Victor pulled it back. "You mother doesn't drink, does she?"

Eyes still glued to the coins, Luke shook his head.

"Tell her this is for food and some new clothes for you." Victor released the coins to Luke's greedy grasp, then turned toward his cook. "Prepare a bundle of some more food for Luke before you send him on his way."

"Thank you, sir." Luke's blue eyes clouded with tears, and he hastily brushed them away.

"If you find out any more information about who gave you the letter, come see me."

Luke gave a vigorous nod before turning his attention toward Cook.

Not to be discouraged, perhaps Victor would discover the identity of the culprit before the night was out.

CHAPTER 31

Juliana's mind whirled from the note the street urchin delivered. She'd be foolish to go alone, but she couldn't in good conscience ignore it. She needed an accomplice for what she had planned, and she supposed Nash was the most well-equipped for the position, if only she could get him alone.

Her opportunity arose shortly before supper, when she encountered him in the hallway, requesting his help before Drake had appeared.

Nash raised a dark eyebrow, and she whispered, "I'll explain later."

After supper, the family had gathered in the small drawing room and discussed the last few days' events. Juliana shifted in her seat next to Honoria and—for what seemed like the hundredth time— slid a glance toward the clock.

At nine, Adalyn had excused herself to put Benjamin and Mena to bed, stating, as she seemed exceptionally tired as of late, she would follow them.

When the clock chimed half past nine, Juliana took a cue from Adalyn and feigned a yawn accompanied by an exaggerated stretch as Drake described some of the preparations for the king's funeral.

"Am I boring you, Jules?" Drake grinned at her.

"Pardon me. But with the excitement of the ball last night, I didn't sleep well."

Lord Nash sputtered into his glass of brandy, then covered it with a cough. "Strong but good, Burwood."

Juliana caught Nash's eye and rose.

He laid the glass down on the table next to him. "However, I agree with your sister. Perhaps we should all retire early this evening. I think I'll join my wife. May I escort you upstairs, Miss Merrick?"

Juliana gratefully accepted, praying he remembered and still meant to help.

Once they were ascending the stairs, Nash asked, "You seemed concerned about the time, Miss Merrick. I noticed you glancing at the clock all evening. Is the help you require from me time sensitive?"

"It is. I received an anonymous note signed 'A friend,' instructing me to come to the back entrance of *The Knave of Hearts* at quarter past ten tonight. The person implied Victor was either hiding something from me or lying about something. They said to come alone."

"Ah. And you suspect a trap of some sort?"

"Possibly. But even if it's not, I'm not fool enough to think a woman can go out at night behind a gaming hell unprotected."

"You want me to accompany you?"

"Yes. No. Not exactly. They said to come alone, so it must at least appear no one is with me. Obviously, I couldn't ask Drake, as he would forbid me to go. However . . ."

Nash held up his hand. "Say no more. Although I'm inclined to agree with your brother. Even if I'm discreetly with you and stay out of sight, there's no guarantee this person won't harm you." His dark eyes studied her, probing for what, she couldn't say. "If I'm to agree to this hare-brained scheme, you must promise me to do exactly as I tell you. No arguments. I owe a large debt to the duchess, and I couldn't live with myself if something happened to someone she loved on my watch."

She nodded, her crossed fingers hidden in the folds of her gown.

"Very well. Our biggest challenge will be sneaking out of this house unnoticed. It's still early enough that most people won't be abed, especially servants. When we arrive at the meeting place, if I detect the slightest hint of danger, I will signal you with a low whistle, and you must promise to run as fast as you can toward me. Do I have your word?"

Juliana swallowed the lump clogging her throat. "Yes."

"Very well." Nash's icy tone indicated he didn't quite believe her, and she cursed herself for the poor liar she was. "That gown won't do. Do you have something more sensible to change into? Nothing with lacey sleeves or ribbons to grab hold of, not so heavy of a fabric so you can run."

"My summer riding habit."

"Good. Change as quickly as you can. We don't have much time. I'm going to create a diversion, then I'll come get you."

Giving a quick nod to Nash, Juliana slipped into her room. She had mere minutes to transform into someone else entirely. Someone bold enough to sneak out into the London night and brave whatever awaited behind *The Knave of Hearts*. As she scrambled to locate her half-boots, she startled at the soft knock at her door. Nash couldn't expect her to be ready so soon. She hadn't even removed her gown.

The door creaked open, and Miss Price poked her head in. "Why didn't you ring for me, miss? Lord Nash came downstairs and mentioned you were ready to retire."

What a dilemma. Although she could use assistance removing the elegant gown she had on for supper, Juliana could hardly request to change into her riding habit. "I have a terrible headache. I was just going to get out of this gown and corset and then climb into bed."

Miss Price tsked and made quick work of removing Juliana's gown and corset. When she pulled a soft cotton nightgown from the clothespress, Juliana shook her head.

"No need. I'm fine like this." Juliana made a show of climbing into bed and slipping beneath the covers, sighing loudly.

"Well, I suppose your chemise is close enough to a nightgown."

Miss Price's disapproving tone belied her words. "Will there be anything else?"

"No, thank you. And please let everyone know not to disturb me."

The moment Miss Price left and the door clicked shut, Juliana bolted from the bed and retrieved her riding habit. In addition to affording her the ability to ride astride, it was easy to put on without assistance. She had just slid her foot into her remaining half-boot when another knock sounded. That time, no one opened the door and peeked inside. She stilled, holding her breath.

"Miss Merrick?" Deep but quiet, Nash's voice shook her from her paralysis.

Shoelace loose and dragging next to her, Juliana raced to the door and flung it open.

"Ready?" Assessing her, his gaze traveled down her body. "Good. Sensible. But you've forgotten something." He knelt down and tied the remaining shoelace. "Can't have you tripping and breaking your neck now."

The tenderness of the action threw Juliana off guard. With a wife and children, was she asking too much of him? Putting him at unnecessary risk?

"What about Adalyn? Will she keep this secret?"

Nash gazed up with those dark eyes, and Juliana couldn't think of a person more opposite in appearance to Victor. Yet he was the man Adalyn chose, or perhaps who her heart chose, because Juliana believed she had little control over what her own heart wanted. And at that moment, Juliana gave a little prayer of thanks, that the two men were so different.

"Adalyn is already in bed, and I expect her to sleep through the night. She won't even know I'm gone."

"How are we going to leave the house?"

Nash rose and towered over her. "Servants' staircase. When I spoke to Miss Price, I sent the rest of them on a merry chase to look for a pair of missing boots. I can be rather harsh and demanding when I need to be. Learned that from my father and brother.

However, I'm afraid I scared the poor scullery maid so badly, she might still be cowering in the corner of the kitchen."

"How long do we have? Did you find a good hiding place for the boots?"

His chuckle held a slightly devious tone. "The boots I described don't exist. They should be searching for hours. Now, come." He motioned for her to follow him toward the door leading down through the servants' entrance at the end of the hallway.

After cracking open the door, Nash held out a hand, signaling her to wait as he walked partway down. For a big man, he moved stealthily, his feet barely making a sound against the wooden steps.

"It's clear," his whispered account drifted up, and, taking a deep breath, she stepped out and closed the door behind her.

When they reached the bottom, once again, Nash held up his hand, then put a finger to his lips.

She jolted when she heard his voice boom. "What are you still doing here? Why aren't you looking for my boots?!"

A quivering girl's voice answered. "I'm sorry, milord. I—I—I'll go right now."

In front of Juliana, Nash's body filled the entry of the staircase, preventing the terrified servant from rushing up past him. A few seconds later, he motioned Juliana forward and into the kitchen.

Juliana scanned the vacant room. "Where did she go?"

"She headed toward the larder. Hurry! We can't count on her hiding there long." He opened the back door and practically pushed Juliana from the house.

When she headed toward the mews, Nash grabbed her arm. "Can't take one of your brother's carriages. Someone might alert him."

Thank goodness for Nash. Clearly, she wasn't suited for subterfuge.

Juliana followed Nash along the side of the house where he instructed her to wait once more. Nervous tension coiled in her belly as precious moments ticked by.

After what seemed an eternity, Nash appeared and led her to a hired hackney coach waiting several homes away.

Seated across from him, Juliana marveled at how calm he appeared. "What time is it?"

He pulled out his pocket watch. "Five till ten. I instructed the driver to let me out several buildings away before depositing you at the gaming hell. Remember what you promised me. At the slightest sign of trouble, run toward me and don't look back."

She nodded and prayed it wouldn't be necessary.

AT TWENTY TO TEN THAT EVENING, AND AFTER A FINAL ARGUMENT with Tierney about accompanying him, Victor boarded a hackney carriage to meet the anonymous letter writer at *The Knave of Hearts*.

Although it wouldn't change anything about his plans to marry Juliana, unmasking the culprit and bringing them to justice would make a wonderful and unique wedding gift for his bride.

Victor stared out the window into the night as the carriage moved along the city's streets. Darkened windowpanes of shops and vacant streets announced the late hour. Gas lamps burned low, casting ominous shadows against the empty pavement. Black wreaths hung from doorways out of respect for the king's death. Heat from the day dissipated, and an odd chill settled against his face. Fog hung low, obscuring his vision and providing a moody atmosphere on his journey.

When the carriage halted in front of *The Knave of Hearts*, Victor shivered, but not because of the cold. Was it folly to answer the call of an anonymous correspondence? An odd tingling of his skin crept over him as if death breathed down his neck, and he raised his hand to tap on the carriage roof and tell the driver to take him back home. Withdrawing his hand, he brushed it off as silly superstition and chided himself for his lack of courage and overly dramatic nature.

He would see this through. For Juliana. For himself. For all who had been harmed by *The Muckraker*.

Victor stepped from the carriage a determined man.

"Place is closed," the driver said, as if it weren't obvious from the lack of light and activity within.

Victor ignored him and strode toward the back entrance. The narrow passage was deserted with only the scurrying of what must have been rodents seeking a morsel of food. Pulling out his pocket watch, Victor checked the time. Three to ten. The hackney had made good time.

Light from a window on the building's uppermost floor caught Victor's attention, and it seemed out of place from the otherwise darkened gaming hell. A silhouette of a man passed in front and stopped as if he were gazing down at the back street below.

Victor pressed his body closer to the wall, then relaxed at the scrape of a window being opened. Whoever it was probably only wished to let in the cooler night air. Still, he wondered if the person was his mysterious correspondent.

Horses' hooves clipping against the cobbles slowed, and the scrape of carriage wheels came to a stop.

Victor peered down the back street's dark passageway toward the sound of the halting carriage, and his heart kicked up its pace as a figure appeared. He blinked, clearing his vision, his mind not making sense of what his eyes saw.

A woman approached. Was she mad? Was *he* mad?

"Who's there?" he called out.

"Victor? It's me. Lydia."

Lydia? What the blazes?

She appeared to be alone, which made even less sense. "Lydia, were you the one who summoned me? Do you know who's responsible for *The Muckraker*?"

Dressed in black, Lydia almost melted into the dark shadows. Her gaze darted nervously around her as she stepped closer. "Why is it so important to you, Victor? Is it because of the gossip about you and Lady Nash in the orangery?"

Victor sucked in a calming breath. How could she not even consider the harm the paper had done to others? "Among other things."

"I could retract my statement, explain that it was all a

misunderstanding and what I saw was a simple exchange between friends."

"Then do it. Why call me to a deserted passageway at night?"

"Will you promise not to resume your betrothal to Miss Merrick if I do?"

His patience worn thin as the cloth he used to clean his brushes, he gritted his teeth to restrain himself from grabbing her arms and giving her a good shake. "And return to courting you?"

"We are a good match, Victor."

"By whose standards? Yours?" Definitely not by his. They would make each other miserable in less than a year.

Still, she flinched at the vitriol in his voice, and shame flared in his chest. Raised to be a gentleman, he prided himself on respecting women. But Lydia pushed him to the limit.

"What if I told you if you don't, you will put Miss Merrick's life in danger?"

Hair prickled on his neck at her threat. Was she truly that desperate to sink her hooks into him? Losing all his restraint, he took her by the arms. "What do you mean? How?"

"Please, Victor, you're hurting me."

Her cries had the desired effect, and he dropped his hands to his sides. If Lydia was telling the truth, how could he jeopardize Juliana's life? "Tell me what you know, and I'll consider your ultimatum."

"The person responsible for *The Muckraker* has a vendetta against the Duke of Burwood and his family."

When he opened his mouth, she shook her head. "If you're going to ask, 'Why,' I don't know."

Terror tightened his throat, and he choked out his words. "Who is it, Lydia? For the love of God, tell me."

It may have been the shadows playing across her face, but Lydia's expression contorted, changing her normally pleasant appearance to something ghoulish. "I can't. Not if I value my own life."

"Hello?" a woman's voice called behind him—a voice he had grown to not only recognize, but love.

He spun around, momentarily forgetting the importance of his mission to seek information about *The Muckraker*.

"Juliana. What are you doing here?"

Without warning, Lydia stepped from behind and threw herself at him, draping her body against his. "Oh, no! We've been discovered, Victor!"

Sheer reflex had his arms going around her waist to keep them both from falling off balance.

Juliana's gaze darted between him and Lydia.

Not again!

Juliana could hardly believe her eyes as she stepped into the dark passageway behind *The Knave of Hearts*. She moved closer, but there was no mistaking the man with long blond hair tied back in a queue. What was Lydia doing with Victor?

As soon as the thought entered her mind, Lydia dispelled it when she brazenly threw herself into Victor's arms.

Even in the dim lighting, Victor's horrified expression spoke volumes.

A "friend" indeed!

Victor pushed Lydia from his arms. "Juliana, this isn't what it appears to be."

She had no need for his explanation, as the truth of the matter was crystal clear. "Are you the *friend* who summoned me here, Lydia?"

Lydia scuttled backward. "I don't know what you're talking about. I'm as surprised to see you here as you no doubt are to see me."

Victor took a step forward, his eyes curious but pleading. "Someone summoned you as well?"

Juliana's attention remained on Lydia as she answered Victor. "I received a note from *a friend* stating you were lying to me and if I wanted to learn the truth to come here—alone."

"Juliana, cara mia, if you think there is anything between Lydia and me, I swear—"

"I know there isn't, Victor. But it's what Lydia wants me to believe; isn't it? But why here? Why not stage some compromise in a safer location?"

"Truly, I didn't send a note to you, Juliana. I'll admit I sent a letter to Victor, but I was instructed what to say."

"By whom? The culprit responsible for *The Muckraker?!*" Rage shook in Victor's voice.

"I can't tell; I told you," Lydia screeched.

Juliana's mind whirled to put the pieces together. Was Victor there in hopes of unmasking the perpetrator?

"Can't or won't?" Victor insisted.

Lydia shook her head, and a tear, whether real or forced, Juliana had no idea, rolled down her cheek.

"But if you didn't send me the note, who did? And why?"

"They must have sent it. They said . . . said . . . that if I followed . . . instructions . . . Victor would be mine. That . . . I wouldn't have to . . . worry about . . . you any longer." Lydia choked out the words in between sobs.

Although the night was still warm, an ominous quality of Lydia's words chilled Juliana. "What on earth does that mean?"

Victor turned imploring eyes toward her. "Lydia said something about your life being in danger. I don't like this at all. We should leave." Victor directed his attention to Lydia, his voice chipped ice. "If this person has threatened you as well, it would be wise to tell us who it is. We can protect you."

Lydia shifted, her face a mask of fear, and, shaking her head, darted her gaze behind her in the direction she had come.

Juliana followed Lydia's line of sight. A figure moved into the passageway, tall and lean, their face in shadows. Juliana's throat constricted as she said, "Someone's there!"

Victor took a step forward, but the crack of a shot rang out in the still of the night. Victor reversed direction and lunged toward her, his heavy body pulling Juliana down to the ground and landing on top of her.

A warm sticky liquid coated her hand trapped between their bodies. Alarm prickled the skin on her neck at the metallic smell of blood.

Victor slid off her and stumbled to his feet. "Lydia?"

But Lydia had vanished into the night, along with the assailant.

When Victor offered to assist her up, he grasped her hand, and his eyes widened. "Dear God, you're hurt."

The blood she smelled was not only on her hand but on her riding habit. Yet, other than a stitch in her side, she didn't feel any pain. "I don't think it's me." Frantically, she scanned Victor's body, cursing the dim lighting. A dark stain spread across his waistcoat.

Heavy footsteps raced in their direction, and Nash appeared. "I heard a gunshot. Are you injured, Miss Merrick?"

She shook her head. "It's Victor."

Victor frowned at Nash, then peered down at the rapidly spreading blood.

"Victor?" she whispered, her voice cracking.

His eyes wide, he crumpled before her.

CHAPTER 32

Fear, ugly and unrelenting, clawed up Juliana's throat at the sight of Victor lying on the cold ground. She fell to the pavement next to him, her hands trembling as she reached for Victor's face. "Victor! Victor! Can you hear me?!"

Nash crouched beside her and placed two fingers on the side of Victor's neck. "He's alive. Probably passed out from either the pain or shock."

A door slammed, and pounding from another pair of feet drew their attention. Juliana tore her gaze from Victor as Mr. Grey rushed from the building.

"I heard a shot. What the hell happened?" Mr. Grey's gaze jerked from Nash to Juliana, utter surprise widening his amber eyes. "Does your brother know you're here?"

Before she could answer, Nash interceded. "Now's not the time, Grey. Pratt needs a doctor. No offense to my wife, but all things considered, going back to Burwood's will only raise more alarm. Find Ashton. He's the best. I'm going after the culprit. Where did the shot come from, Miss Merrick?"

Juliana pointed a shaky finger down the shadowy passage, and Nash raced off without a backward glance.

Dropping to his knees, Mr. Grey pulled open Victor's coat, then unbuttoned his bloody waistcoat. Blood bloomed like a living creature, vivid against Victor's once-pristine white linen shirt.

"We need to get him inside." Mr. Grey rose, ran back to the building, and yanked open the door. "Hartley, come down here!" His voice bellowed in the eerie night.

"Which one?" a man called back.

"Both of you!"

Two enormous men exited, their appearance strikingly similar. As they took stock in the situation, one of them said, "Are you hurt, miss? You have blood all over you." His voice was surprisingly gentle for a man his size and appearance.

She shook her head. "It's Victor's blood. He used his body as a shield and fell on top of me."

"Probably saved your life," Mr. Grey said. "And now we need to save his. I'll have someone ride and find Ashton."

Juliana grasped his arm, purpose flowing through her like wildfire. "Let me go. I know where he lives. And I have to do something, or I'll go mad with worry."

"Hartley One, go to the mews and have a horse readied, then come right back and we'll get Mr. Pratt inside." Mr. Grey turned a gentle gaze toward her. "You'll have to ride astride, but from what I've read in the scandal sheets, that won't be a problem."

Thank God she'd worn her riding habit. She leaned over Victor and, with trembling fingers, smoothed back a lock of his blond hair. "You reckless, brave man. Don't you dare die on me, Victor. I love you. Fight with all your strength and live." When she placed a gentle kiss on his lips, Victor's eyelids fluttered, then opened.

Her breath caught. For a moment, the world receded to only his eyes, unfocused and full of pain—but alive.

As he looked up at her, a faint smile tipped his lips, and he lifted his hand to cup her face. "Cara mia. Per te vivrò." His hand fell limply back to the ground, and he groaned in pain.

"Save your strength, and don't try to talk, Victor. I'm going to get a doctor to help you."

"Not Adalyn. Nash wouldn't like it," Victor moaned.

She caressed his beautiful face. "No. Not Adalyn. Ashton. But you must be strong until I return. Mr. Grey will take care of you."

She kissed him again, struggling to hold back the tears. She had to be strong—for Victor.

Hartley—she'd already forgotten which one—returned with a horse, saddled and ready.

Mr. Grey helped her mount the horse, a gelding several hands higher than Sunshine. For a moment, she watched as the three men picked up Victor and took him inside. Then she kicked the horse into action, grateful it was late at night and the streets were empty. She bent low over the neck of the horse, reminiscent of how she had ridden on Rotten Row to help little Eva Somersby.

However, this time, although her heart pounded furiously in her chest and matched the pounding of the horses' hooves, the urgency seemed even greater. A thought flashed through her mind of Colonel Brandon rushing to retrieve Mrs. Dashwood as Mariane lay so deathly ill. She prayed her story would have the same happy outcome, then pressed forward to her destination.

In front of Ashton's residence, she vaulted from the horse, and after haphazardly tying the reins to an iron gate, rushed up to the duke's door. Tension coiled in her chest, and she pounded her fists on the solid wood as if her life depended on it. No, not her life, Victor's.

Light still shone from the front windows, and she breathed a sigh of relief that at least someone was still up. After what seemed like an eternity, the door opened.

The butler Burrows's eyes widened with surprise and then alarm as he took in her blood-stained riding habit and gloves. "Miss Merrick, are you injured? I shall fetch His Grace." He motioned her inside and sent a footman to find Ashton.

With no time to argue with the old gentleman, Juliana allowed him to lead her to a chair while she waited and dearly hoped the duke had not already retired for the night.

Muffled voices and footsteps drew her attention to the long staircase leading to the upper floors as the duke rushed toward her.

Without a neckcloth, his shirt hung open at the neck, and his hair was mussed as if he'd been running his hands through it.

She bolted from the chair toward him. "Your Grace, you must come!"

He made no complaint about the intrusion. His hazel eyes were serious as he raked his gaze over her in a medical assessment. "Peter said you were injured." Lifting her bloody hands, he examined them, then frowned. "Whose blood is this, Miss Merrick?"

"Victor's. Please, you must come immediately. He's been shot."

"Where is he?"

"At *The Knave of Hearts*."

A blond eyebrow hitched. "You were with him? At this time of night? Is anyone else with you? Anyone else hurt?"

"Please, Your Grace. I'll answer all your questions later. But there is no time to waste."

"Burrows, have my carriage readied."

Forgetting all propriety, Juliana grabbed the duke's arm and reiterated. "There is no time. It will be faster on horseback."

"You rode here—alone?"

"I did, Your Grace."

His lips curved in an unexpected, slow grin. "Reckless, but impressive." Ashton nodded toward Burrows, who instructed a footman to run to the mews and have the duke's horse saddled. Another footman handed the duke his medical bag.

Precious minutes ticked by as they waited for Ashton's mount to be readied, and she relayed the events of the evening as best she could.

Horses ready, the duke helped her into the saddle of the borrowed horse, then mounted his own. "Lead the way, Miss Merrick."

Pleased the duke was such an accomplished rider, Juliana pushed her horse to the limit, the duke following closely behind. Upon reaching *The Knave of Hearts*, both jumped from their saddles.

One of the enormous men waited outside the back entrance and ushered them inside.

"Up here," the other giant called from a balcony above them.

Ashton took the lead. His medical bag clutched in his fist, he bounded up the stairs as if he were ten years younger.

Hartley—one, two, she couldn't be sure—pointed to a room.

Juliana sucked in a breath at Victor's ghostly appearance. The soft glow of lamplight illuminated what the dark shadows of the back passageway had hidden. Stripped to his waist, Victor lay on the bed, pale as death, eyes closed, while Mr. Grey pressed a cloth—dark with blood—to Victor's side.

Nash leaned against a wall, arms crossed and brow furrowed as he watched the tableau before him.

As they entered the room, Ashton's gaze snapped momentarily to Nash. "Did you do this?"

"Don't tell me you're putting credence in those rags now, Harry. For once, I'm innocent. And although I tried to catch the culprit, he slipped from my fingers."

"Hmm." Ashton muttered, returning his attention to Victor. "Putting pressure on it. Good, Grey."

Mr. Grey stepped aside so Ashton could examine Victor, his voice tense as he said, "Bullet went through him. I packed the wound on his back with a cloth, which appears to be where the bullet entered, but the bleeding . . ." He shot Juliana an apologetic glance.

Dizzy, Juliana grabbed a nearby table for support, the edges of her vision growing dim and her knees giving way from under her. For the first time since everything had happened, a sharp pain lanced at her side.

Nash rushed over and led her to a chair.

Ashton and Mr. Grey's voices grew distant. "The question is, Grey. If Pratt shielded Miss Merrick's body, and the bullet went through from back to front, how did it miss her?"

The last thing Juliana remembered was Nash saying, "It didn't."

VICTOR WAS IN HELL. FIRE LICKED HIM FROM THE INSIDE OUT, searing muscle and bone. His throat burned, but he forced out the one word that mattered— "Juliana"—before blissful darkness swallowed him whole.

Finally, after what seemed an eternity—for what was hell but ceaseless torture—his insides cooled. His eyelids felt glued together and as heavy as lead. Yet he forced them open.

Blurred figures formed in front of him. "Pratt. Do you know who I am?"

The man's voice was familiar, and Victor struggled to focus his vision, recognizing the duke. "Ashton," he croaked out, then added, "water."

The duke disappeared from Victor's view, then returned and held a glass to Victor's lips. "Just a sip."

A sip?! Parched, Victor wanted to drink an ocean, yet he obeyed. Cool and soothing, the tiny bit of water slipped down his throat like a balm. "Juliana? Is she safe?"

"She's recovering at Burwood's."

Recovering?! The word hit like a blade. Pain slashed through Victor's side as he surged upright. "She's injured? I thought . . ."

Ashton grasped Victor's shoulders and pushed him back onto the bed. "Easy. You'll pull your stitches. We all thought the bullet had missed her. Thanks to you, I might add. But it exited you and nicked her side. It's a minor flesh wound, and Dr. Somersby is taking excellent care of her."

Juliana's home? Victor blinked, his vision slowly sharpening on the unfamiliar room around him—the flocked wallpaper, the soft flicker of lamplight, muffled voices outside the walls. "Where am I?"

Ashton lifted the water to Victor's lips and allowed him to take another sip. "At *The Knave*. I advised Mr. Grey that you were in no condition to be moved."

Even Victor's arms felt limp and useless, but using all his willpower, he grabbed Ashton's forearm. "I need to see her. To make sure with my own eyes she's going to be all right."

"That's not possible at the moment. But someone is here to see you. Shall I send them in?"

The only person Victor wanted to see was Juliana, but perhaps whoever was there could give him more information. "Very well."

Ashton opened the door. "Do not upset him." The sternness in the duke's voice made Victor lift his head to see who was there, and he quickly second guessed his permission as his mother strode in. Thank goodness Father and Cilla were with her.

His mother held a handkerchief to her bosom. "Victor! Victor! We've been waiting for days to see you. What were you thinking doing something so foolish?"

Days?

"Lady Cartwright, I warned you. If you don't restrain yourself, I will remove you." Ashton's tone brooked no argument.

"Aurelia!" his father said. "What our son has done is nothing short of heroic. He saved his betrothed's life! And if you do not behave, I will send you back to Lincolnshire."

Through his murky haze, Victor thought Priscilla uttered something that sounded like *Baa.*

"Father, have you seen Juliana?"

Cilla took his hand, giving it a squeeze. "I have, Victor. She wants to come see you, but Burwood is livid about what happened."

"Mother said it's been days. How long?" Victor jerked his gaze toward Ashton, who stood to the side, apparently ready to remove Victor's mother at a moment's notice.

"Only three. You've been in and out of consciousness. You had a fever. No internal damage, but I kept you here to watch for infection. I've applied a poultice of honey to the wounds and dressed them."

"Honey?!" His mother screeched and feigned a swoon, and that time Victor was certain Cilla bleated like a sheep.

Ashton nodded. "That was Dr. Somersby's idea. The Romani have been using it for years. There are natural properties to the honey that draw out the infection. We've had great success with it. And Victor's fever seems to finally have broken."

Victor turned toward Cilla, the only woman in the room he could trust. "And you promise Juliana isn't seriously injured?" He swallowed, his throat tight with emotion. "Does she still want to marry me?"

"More than anything, Victor. But you need to get better first."

She leaned close and whispered in his ear. "For your wedding night."

He chuckled, the action sending a sharp pain in his side. "Damn it, Cilla. That hurt."

His mother waved the handkerchief in front of her as if she had been the feverish one. "Victor! Your language."

"If you will pardon us." Taking her by the arm, Victor's father led his wife from the room. "Our son has every reason and right to curse, Aurelia!"

Ashton stepped forward, removed his pocket watch, and lifted Victor's other hand to take his pulse. "I'm glad your father intervened. I was about ready to do so myself." Finished, he slipped his watch back in his pocket. "Better. Steady and strong. You had us worried for a while."

"When can I see Juliana?"

Ashton smiled. A good sign, certainly? "That will depend on the duke. As your sister said, he's furious you put his sister in such danger."

"But I didn't know she was going to be there. I swear. Surely, she's told him that?"

Ashton patted Victor's arm. "I suspect he knows you're innocent and did everything you could to protect her. He'll come around, I'm sure. Now, rest. If you continue to improve, I'll see about transporting you back home."

Cilla kissed him lightly on the cheek and preceded Ashton from the room.

Victor allowed his heavy eyelids to fall shut. He needed his strength so he could go to Juliana, to plead with Burwood, to throw himself on his mercy.

He needed to see her. Not just for reassurance—but because life without her no longer made sense.

Three days after the horrific events at the back of *The Knave*, the League gathered in the parlor of Pendrake Manor.

Reclined on a sofa and propped up with a pillow, Juliana bit her lip, fighting back the lightning flash of pain from the two-inch-long slash in her side every time she moved.

"Ladies, Ladies!" Honoria rarely raised her voice, but the outrage the group expressed became palpable.

Bea pushed up her spectacles. A tiny dot of ink marred the tip of her nose. "Thank you, Honoria. Now, as I was saying, based on the last two editions of the abomination posing as a newspaper, I believe we can narrow down our suspects to Lord Edgerton and Lord Middlebury."

"My *brother*?" Charlotte asked. "How in the world did you come up with that ludicrous idea? And what about Lydia Whyte? Considering what happened to Mr. Pratt and Juliana, we can't rule her out."

Anne, who had been unusually quiet, raised her hand.

Charlotte stared at her, dumfounded. "Who are you, and what have you done with Anne?"

Anne lifted her chin. "I didn't want to interrupt, although you do seem to be in better spirits since your marriage. I wanted to agree with you. Lydia is a schemer."

Juliana pushed against the sofa with her elbows, hissing at the pain in her stitches and drawing Honoria's attention. "Although I agree with Lady Charlotte and Anne to some extent, I don't believe Lydia is the mastermind. Involved somehow and knows something, yes. But if you had seen the fear on her face when Victor and I pressed her for more information on the perpetrator's identity, it would erase any doubt she is responsible."

"Lydia is an accomplished liar," Miranda said. "I don't think we can discount her completely."

"Perhaps not completely. But she wasn't the one who shot Victor," Juliana said.

"Lydia couldn't shoot an effigy of Prinny two feet from her," Aunt Kitty said. "She could have enlisted someone to do her dirty work. And don't forget, the target most likely was you, Juliana."

"You think the perpetrator and the assailant are one and the same?" Charlotte asked.

"I think it's possible." Juliana winced, her eyes watering, as she attempted to sit up farther.

Honoria raced over to Juliana's side and straightened her pillow. "Drake tried to get answers from Lydia, but the Whytes left for their estate in Derbyshire the day after the incident. I suspect their swift departure accounts for the paucity of details in the report. Reporting her own presence at the gaming hell would spark scandal. Whoever was responsible for *The Muckraker* either wasn't privy to the information or had their own reasons for restraint."

True. Although the scandal sheets reported the shocking turn of events that evening at *The Knave*, wherein Mr. Victor Pratt had been shot by an unknown assailant, there had been no mention of Juliana —or Lydia Whyte—at all. Even *The Muckraker* had been uncharacteristically silent regarding the situation, merely stating they believed Victor had been the victim in a failed robbery attempt and was expected to survive.

Charlotte nodded as if they had their answer. "Well, Lydia

certainly wouldn't want her name connected to what happened. And innocent people don't run away."

"Very well," Bea said. "We shall include Miss Whyte. But as to my reasons for Edgerton—and I do beg your pardon, Lady Charlotte—but your brother is a sneaksby and a . . . a johnny-bum."

"Bea!" Juliana laughed, exacerbating the pain in her side.

"Well, I'm sorry, but he is. I could say worse, but, well . . ."

Honoria adjusted Juliana's pillow again. "But why would Edgerton write about his own brother and sister? *The Muckraker* attacked both Nash and Charlotte."

"Edgerton has no love for our brother," Charlotte admitted. "Nash told me Roland has been ashamed of him for years." She shook her head. "But I can't forget the reports implicating Nash for the murder of Lady Worthington, and would Roland stoop that low?"

"He might to remove suspicion from himself," Anne said.

Everyone's eyes widened at Anne's statement.

"An excellent point," Bea said. "And one I was going to make. As for you, Charlotte, didn't Edgerton pressure you to marry Lord Felix?"

"Yes, but I don't see why shaming me with gossip . . ." Charlotte's eyes widened. "Oh. Punishment because my refusal thwarted his plans. Roland said something about forming an alliance in Lords with Felix's father, Lord Scarborough. An alliance against the proposed reforms."

Bea held up a finger. "Reforms led by Burwood, Ashton, and Stratford. And if I understood you correctly, Juliana, Lydia said the perpetrator had a vendetta against Burwood and his family, which would include Honoria's father, Lord Stratford."

Aunt Kitty pounded her cane on the floor. "By God, they're right about you, Lady Montgomery. You have a brilliant mind. And if what you're suggesting is true, I want to help bring the scoundrel down."

Honoria returned to her seat. "I believe we all do, Aunt Kitty. But Bea, you also mentioned Lord Middlebury. Do you really think he could be responsible?"

"Not directly, perhaps, but as Juliana suggested with Miss Whyte, I believe he's involved in some way. Perhaps, unwittingly, but we must remember Edgerton hasn't been present for many of the events leading to *The Muckraker's* reports. However, Middlebury is his toady and could have kept him informed."

A memory rose to the surface. "The day little Eva Somersby's horse was spooked, we passed Edgerton and his family, and Middlebury was with them."

"As was Lord Felix," Honoria said. "I don't think we can rule him out, either."

Bea sighed. "If only so many of our traps from the ball weren't included in *The Muckraker* we could narrow it down further. If everyone agrees that Miss Whyte and Lord Middlebury might only be pawns, that leaves Edgerton and possibly Lord Felix. I think we should concentrate our efforts on Lord Edgerton first."

"We need a plan," Miranda said.

Juliana nodded. "And proof."

PROPPED UP IN BED WITH TWO LARGE PILLOWS, VICTOR TRACED A pencil over the rough paper and created a likeness of Juliana. He'd awoken from a restless sleep and requested the rudimentary supplies from Mr. Grey. If he couldn't see Juliana in person, he did the next best thing and drew her.

Light from the late afternoon sun filtered in through the window, and Victor imagined Juliana standing before him as she would on their wedding day, her golden hair shining as the rays of light played across its long strands. She would wear her hair down of course, as she had the night of their engagement ball. Or maybe she would deign to wear it fashioned up to avoid any further whiff of scandal. Then, when they were alone, he would take his time, unpinning and releasing each glorious strand. Either way, he couldn't wait to run his fingers through it.

He closed his eyes and sighed. If only he could see her, hear her voice, kiss her, he would recover much more quickly.

A knock sounded, and Mr. Grey stuck his head around the door. "Someone's here to see you."

"If it's my mother again, please tell her I'm sleeping."

"It's the Duke of Burwood."

Victor sat up straighter and braced himself. "Show him in."

Drake strode in—every inch the duke. From the expression on his face, Victor doubted he would be allowed to continue calling the duke by his Christian name.

Victor pushed down the fear hammering at his heart. "Your Grace, forgive me for not rising."

Without a word, Burwood took a seat on a chair near Victor's bedside.

"May I enquire as to Miss Merrick's health?"

Burwood continued to stare at him.

Victor resisted the urge to squirm, took a few—inconspicuous—breaths, and waited until his patience had worn out. "Your Grace?"

"I'm trying to decide whether to strangle you and finish the job the assassin started or thank you for saving my sister's life."

A smile tugged at Victor's lips. "I'd prefer the latter. But please, sir. If you choose to finish me off, allow me to see Juliana one last time."

Burwood's gaze dropped to the sketches in Victor's hand. "Juliana told me everything."

Everything? Victor wisely refrained from asking questions, save but one.

"What did she say?"

"She admitted that she received a summons by an anonymous source to come here alone. Nash may join you on my list of people to deal with. He put my sister at great risk. It's not how I expect a guest in my home to behave."

Victor snorted a laugh. "I don't think Lord Nash cares much for propriety or rules. And as much as it galls me to admit this, I think he accompanied her for protection."

"Hmm. Perhaps. And Juliana admitted when she requested his assistance, he was reluctant." Burwood paused, as if considering how to proceed. "She told me Miss Whyte was there in an attempt to convince Juliana your intentions toward her were dishonorable."

"Has anyone spoken to Lydia?"

Burwood shook his head. "She and her family have left London for their estate in Derbyshire. I've sent a message demanding an explanation, but I don't hold out much hope of a believable answer. As for the marksman, Nash said he disappeared like a puff of smoke, as if he never existed. However, I'm wondering if he was aiming for you or Juliana."

Something niggled at the back of Victor's mind. More to himself than the duke, Victor said, "Lydia said something about putting Juliana's life in danger if I didn't comply with her wishes."

"Which were?"

"As far as Lydia knew, Juliana and I had ended our betrothal—which was a lie. She offered to state she had been mistaken about what she witnessed in the orangery with Lady Nash—as long as I didn't mend things with Juliana. Instead, she wanted me to resume courting her."

"But why threaten Juliana if she thought you had broken your engagement?"

"She said the person responsible for *The Muckraker* has a personal vendetta against you."

The duke reeled back in the chair. "Me? Did she say why?"

Victor shook his head. "She said she couldn't reveal any more if she valued her life. Before I could ask more questions, Juliana arrived."

Pensive, his brow furrowed and his gaze far away, Burwood sat in ominous silence.

After what seemed like several minutes, Victor plucked up his courage. "Sir? You will allow me to marry Juliana, won't you?"

"I shouldn't. Not after what happened. But I suppose I have no choice."

Tension squeezing Victor's chest eased, then his mind latched on to the last part of the duke's statement. "What do you mean?"

Rising, the duke ran a hand through his hair. "My sister begged me. Told me she had to marry you."

Victor gulped down the stubborn knot that had formed in his throat. While technically it was true since Victor had ruined her, he wasn't fool enough to admit that to the duke. "I beg your pardon?"

"Did something happen between you and my sister, Mr. Pratt? After the ball, she confided in me that, for you, your courtship and engagement had been a pretense. She was fully prepared to let you go. Yet the next day, before she'd even spoken to you, she was not only willing to marry you, but eager. Although I had a heartfelt brother-to-sister talk with her, I doubt my words alone swayed her."

Victor swallowed again. Why would that lump not go down?

"And to be honest, she had a glow about her the next day. One I remember well from Honoria. I shared something—personal—with Juliana, and I wonder if it encouraged her to do something similar."

Oh, God.

Burwood held up his hand. "I don't want to know. If what I suspect is true, I'd rather have you marry Juliana than have to kill you. I'll bring Juliana to see you when you've moved back to your own apartments. This isn't a fit place for her."

When the duke reached for the doorknob, Victor found his voice. "Your Grace?"

Turning back, Burwood's expression was like steel. "Yes?"

"When I offered for Juliana, you asked me if I loved her. In truth, I didn't then. I liked her, esteemed her, but I didn't love her."

The duke's expression softened. "And now?"

"I love Juliana with my whole heart. I would die for her, Your Grace."

"Call me Drake." He tapped his hat into place and smiled. "And I believe you almost did."

CHAPTER 34

Victor stared down the long nave of St. James's Church, eyes locked on the doors leading to the narthex. He didn't dare blink and miss Juliana's entrance.

He'd already taken stock of the sparse crowd in attendance for the wedding. His father sat in one of the front pews next to Cilla and Timothy. After one complaint too many from his mother about Victor's bride, his father sent her back to Lincolnshire—indefinitely.

In his mother's absence, Victor admitted his father's health improved, and a spring returned to his step. For many reasons, it was a great relief to Victor. Not only did he love his father, but he was in no rush to assume the duties of viscount. Drake had commissioned Victor to paint portraits of the rest of the family, both individually and in toto. After his and Juliana's wedding trip, of course.

On the other side of the nave, Victor's future mother-in-law sat in the front pew next to Honoria. It would be such a pleasure to have such kind and supportive women in his and Juliana's lives.

Drake had written to the Whytes in Derbyshire and received no response, not that it surprised either of them. But Drake promised not to let it go. Lord Whyte had to return to London for the winter session of Parliament.

And at that moment, Lydia had been the farthest thing from Victor's mind.

"Breathe, Pratt." Nash's deep voice threatened to pull his attention away, but Victor resisted.

It had been an odd decision asking Lord Nash Talbot to stand up with him, and although Cilla had suggested Timothy, Victor owed a great deal to Nash.

Not only had the man spared Victor from a disastrous match, but he'd had an active hand in Victor securing Juliana's love. Although Victor wasn't quite sure he'd ever forgive Nash for bringing Juliana to *The Knave of Hearts* that fateful night.

Still, the men had made a sort of peace, and when Victor finally handed over the sketches of Adalyn to her husband, Nash deemed them an excellent likeness—though missing a small beauty mark high on Adalyn's left breast. And although Nash professed to have every confidence in his wife's virtue, he stated he found it comforting that the revealing sketches were merely from Victor's imagination.

It had only been a month since he'd been shot, but once the king's funeral had passed, Victor insisted he was recovered enough for the wedding. There had been no need to rush, as Juliana confided she wasn't with child, but Victor couldn't wait to make her his bride. So Ashton had tightly wrapped Victor's still healing wounds and told him to avoid any unnecessary exertion.

Like breathing, apparently. The deep breaths Victor pulled into his lungs to calm his jittery nerves sent a shock of pain through him, and Nash gripped Victor's arm to steady him.

"How the hell you think you're going to get through a wedding, much less a wedding night, is beyond me."

Victor shot him a menacing glare, but just as quickly remembered he should be watching for Juliana's entrance and returned his attention to the entryway.

And as the doors swung open, his breath hitched at the sight of his bride, and he barely registered the twinge that pulsed in his midsection.

Wearing a shimmering pearlescent gown of soft pink, Juliana floated down the aisle on her brother's arm as if on a cloud. Locks of her golden hair flowed over her shoulders and framed her face, the image of her burned in his mind forever.

Juliana's gaze lowered as Drake placed her hand in Victor's. Crescent lashes feathered against her pink-colored cheeks. And when she raised her eyes to meet his, he sucked in another breath, not even caring about the pain. The love he saw shining in the cornflower-blue depths nearly knocked him off his feet. How could he have missed it for so long?

He did his utmost to convey the same adoration, awed she'd ever been his to lose. "Tesoro mio." His treasure, and he would cherish her for the rest of his days.

Juliana's tremulous smile sent his heart racing, and although he knew the importance of the ceremony, and he repeated his vows flawlessly, as far as he was concerned, Juliana had become his—his wife, his life—on the wonderful night they'd spent together. The words they exchanged in front of the vicar simply confirmed it.

Everything Juliana hoped for stood before her—personified in Victor Pratt. A man who not only accepted her hopes and dreams—but championed them. Who had greater ambitions than an idle life for himself. Who loved her as she was. And as they pledged themselves to each other, she felt his love for her deep in her bones. He'd put his own life before hers.

Although he looked resplendent in his dark gray coat and silver waistcoat adorned with red roses at the points, pain etched the corners of his eyes when he moved, and Juliana longed to urge the vicar to make haste so Victor could sit. Everyone—Ashton, Victor's father, Drake, Priscilla, even Juliana—urged him to wait another month or two to heal. But Victor would have none of it.

He'd given her a devious smile, saying, "With our luck, I can't take any chances of losing you."

She'd acquiesced, realizing once they'd married, it would be so much easier for her to take care of him and fuss over him as she wished.

When the vicar finally pronounced them man and wife, she wanted to throw herself into his arms and cover his face with kisses, something Victor clearly guessed, judging from the mischief in his blue eyes. But she behaved like a proper lady should and refrained from creating any more scandal.

However, after exiting the church, and in front of their family and close friends, Victor pulled her into his arms. "Finally."

At first a soft brush of lips, the kiss grew hungry, and Victor removed one hand from her waist and cupped her face, tilting her head just so. Thank goodness his other arm remained wrapped around her when her knees buckled. She would never tire of Victor's kisses.

"Ahem." The male voice broke through her haze of pleasure.

Breaking the kiss, Victor chuckled. "I may have become carried away." But his grin indicated he wasn't the least bit sorry.

She peered around him to find Drake gaping at them. Aunt Kitty elbowed him in the ribs, and Honoria gave them a nod of approval. Simon grinned, and even Charlotte's lips twitched. Mother dabbed at her eyes with her handkerchief. Dr. Marbry wrapped his arm around Priscilla and tugged her close, while Lord Cartwright smiled warmly. Adalyn leaned her head on Nash's shoulder.

Their family. Hers and Victor's.

Victor brushed aside a tear which had trickled down her cheek. "Tears, cara mia?"

"Of happiness." She gave a small poke to his chest. "But I want to learn Italian so I know what you're saying."

"That can be arranged." He drew her in for another long, luxurious kiss, and all thoughts of foreign languages vanished.

EPILOGUE

FLORENCE, ITALY—DECEMBER 1830

From the marble balcony of their apartments overlooking the city, Juliana leaned into the cool morning air. Below, Florence stirred awake with the faint sounds of hooves clattering on stone and wood smoke curling into the pale sky. The first blush of sunlight glinted off the terracotta tiles of Il Duomo.

The domed cathedral reminded her a little of St. Paul's in London. She exhaled slowly, pressing a hand to the balustrade. For the first time since their magical wedding trip, the quiet weight of homesickness swept over her.

They decided to travel the entire route by sea rather than sail from London to Belgium and complete the journey by land. Having gone to Italy for his own wedding trip, as his physician, Ashton suggested traveling by ship was preferable to spending long days trapped inside a jostling coach as he and the duchess had. Ashton, however, admitted he'd been averse to the sea voyage due to his propensity for seasickness.

The long voyage by ship had given Victor's wounds time to heal completely—that and the undivided attention and care he received from Juliana.

"You are fussing over me like I'm an infant." He'd grinned at her, letting her know he loved every moment of it.

"There isn't much else to do on this ship."

At which point he pulled her onto his lap and kept her busy for hours.

Florence—or Firenze, as the Italians called it—had been a dream. On golden sunlit afternoons, Victor had led her down narrow cobbled streets, his hand warm around hers as he pointed out sun-dappled fountains and the tucked-away atelier of his old painting master. The man had spoken animatedly about how Victor was his favorite and best student and kissed her cheeks, saying, "Bellissima!"

It had been wonderful, but she sighed. This day, above all others, she missed her family.

Behind her, bed linens rustled, followed by soft footfalls. Victor wrapped his arms around her waist and pulled her against his hard chest. "Mmm. Come back to bed, amore mio."

She rested her head against him, breathing in his scent. "Dopo." Her Italian, although not nearly as proficient as his, had improved as she immersed herself in the rich, romantic language.

Burying his face in her hair, he chuckled, the sound rumbling in his chest against her back. "Not later. Now. It's Christmas morning, and I want to give you a gift."

She fought back the grin. "Oh? What type of gift might that be?"

His laugh, full and throaty, indicated his mind traveled in the same direction as hers. But he surprised her when he said, "Not that. Although I can definitely arrange that. Now, come."

He spun her around and tugged her hand as he led her back to the bed. "Close your eyes, and don't peek."

She giggled. "You shouldn't say that when you're naked. How can I help myself?" Yet, she obeyed and sat silently on the large four-poster bed.

Sounds of Victor moving about the room and a drawer opening tempted her to crack one eye open, but she resisted.

"Hold out your hands."

"I'm afraid to. Once, Drake gave me a toad."

Warm breath brushed against her neck. "It's not a toad. I promise."

Featherlight, the paper he placed atop her upturned hands skimmed the surface as light as a kiss. *What?*

Victor waited a beat before saying, "Go ahead. Open your eyes and read."

The wax that had sealed the letter was already broken, and she read the contents, confused how a letter from Drake could contain a gift. Pleasantries were exchanged with Drake waxing on about Kitty's amazing ability to say "Dada" and enquiring how they were enjoying Italy. Then her gaze snagged and froze on the following:

Per your request, I have secured three excellent mares and an exceptional stallion from Tattersall's, all of them from the best bloodlines. The stallion's name is Victory. A fitting name, no? We shall settle the cost upon your return home.

Give Juliana my love.

Dumbstruck, her throat closed around the sudden swell of emotion. Juliana blinked back the tears. One hand journeyed up to cover her mouth, while the letter trembled in the other. The words on the page blurred, searing into heart.

Victor sat beside her. "For your horse breeding enterprise. I'll admit, three mares aren't nearly enough, but we don't want to wear Victory out too soon. And if—"

Juliana threw herself into Victor's arms and smothered his face with kisses.

"Oomph." In between kisses, Victor managed to ask, "So you like it?"

"I love it. But where will we keep them? Not in London?"

"Your brother said we could keep them on his estate in Dorset for the time being. At least until—well, I inherit. I didn't think you would want to travel up to Lincolnshire to work with them. Not only is it far from your brother, but my mother is there."

She gazed at the man who understood her so well. "You've thought of everything."

He plucked the letter from her grasp, set it aside, then took both of her hands in his. "I want you to know how much I support your dreams, just as you've supported mine. If you like, I can purchase some land by your brother's estate so you can be close to him and breed the horses there."

Arms wrapped around his neck, she grinned at him. She was going to wait, but what better time than then? "I have a gift for you, too."

JULIANA'S RESPONSE TO HIS GIFT WOULD HAVE BEEN MORE THAN sufficient, but Victor wondered when she would have found time to go shopping without him. They'd spent almost every single moment together, both awake and sleeping. Their time together in Florence had flown by, yet over the last few weeks, he sensed a longing in her. She hid it well, but he had become well versed in her moods during the five months since their marriage, and he admitted their time in Italy was coming to an end.

"That's not necessary, tesoro mio. Everything I ever wanted is right here in my arms."

"Well, I'm afraid I can't return this gift, but you will have to wait to receive it."

"Is it back home like your horses?"

A pink blush covered her cheeks. "No. But it will take some time to arrive."

"How long?"

"Victor! Don't you really have any idea what I'm trying to tell you?"

He blinked. Then barked a laugh. "Are you calling me a dolt?"

In answer, she placed his hand on her abdomen. "Your gift is in here."

Stunned with the realization, he blinked, his mouth dropping open, then slapped a hand over his eyes. "Good God, I *am* a dolt."

In hindsight, he wondered why she hadn't become pregnant sooner. Although, it had taken Cilla and Timothy years, so he excused himself for his obtuseness. "A child? Truly?"

She nodded, her eyes shimmering once again with tears. "Are you happy?"

"No. Estatico." His fingers hovered, then settled reverently against the soft rise beneath her nightrail. The world seemed to hush around them with quiet promise. "When?"

"Late June or early July, I think. Do you want a boy or a girl?"

"I can't decide. Can we have one of each?"

Juliana's eyes grew wide. "At the same time?"

Lord, but she made him laugh. "Amore mio. I will tell you what my father said to Cilla upon her announcement. A healthy child is all that matters." He placed a soft kiss where their child was growing inside her. "And you, of course. Now that I've found you, I couldn't bear to lose you."

He pulled her onto his lap for a long, sensuous kiss. Reluctantly, he broke the kiss. "I've sensed your restlessness—your longing for home, and that you miss your family, amore mio. But traveling in winter would be treacherous either across the Alps or by sea." He placed another kiss on her abdomen. "We have precious cargo to protect. Will you be heartbroken if we have to wait until spring? I promise I'll get you home before the baby arrives."

She wrapped her arms around his neck. "As long as I have you."

"Sempre," he whispered before lying her back on the bed and showing her how much she really did mean to him.

Would you like a peek into Victor and Juliana's future? Scan the QR code on the next page and sign up to my newsletter and receive a bonus scene with a peek seven years into their future as a thank you welcome gift. In addition, there will be fun contests, book news, and subscriber only extras. You may unsubscribe at any time. No hard feelings.

If you enjoyed the book, why not let other readers know by leaving an honest review?

AUTHOR NOTES

Researching when writing historical romance is not only necessary but can often be fun and enlightening. It can also be frustrating and tedious.

As with every book, there are certain events, character traits, and occupations that require me to dig just a little deeper to provide a solid basis of truth to the narrative.

This book was no different. Going in of course, I knew Victor was an aspiring artist, particularly a painter. So naturally I researched painting techniques as well as famous or important painters of his day (especially portraitists).

The painters mentioned when Victor has his interview with Burwood (Drake) were real people. Thomas Lawrence, considered portraitist of kings, (1769-1830) was an English portrait painter and the fourth president of the Royal Academy.

The Scottish painter Victor recognizes as painting the portrait of Drake's father, Henry, (although not named) is based on Henry Raeburn (1756-1823). It was noted that Raeburn's portraits captured the *je nais se quoi* quality Victor speaks about, his portraits speaking about the subjects and their interests. He also made no preliminary sketches of his subjects, although not always ending in the best result.

Even though I went down a bit of a rabbit hole learning about painting techniques, I used very little about what I learned in the finished novel. But no effort in learning is wasted (or so I tell myself).

However, even the best planning can have gaps. As my critique partners barreled through this in record time, Lisa asked how Victor was going to transport the canvas with wet paint.

My reaction was: 😳 😵 😬 which led to some impromptu research. What I (thankfully) found as a solution was a makeshift pochade carrier Victor could have easily created using another canvas with small pieces of wood glued around the frame that would create a gap or spacer between the back of the blank canvas and the wet canvas. Whew. I hope I described it clearly enough that you could envision it.

Another bit of impromptu research and help from my critique partner, Amy, came when I was writing Victor and Juliana's engagement ball, which occurs the night before King George IV dies.

I realized that because George IV was so ill months before his death in June of 1830, he would not be presiding over any debutante's presentations. In fact, I discovered he spent almost the entire time of 1830 until his death at Windsor. So he wasn't even in London.

Instead (thank you, Amy) I learned that his brother and successor, Prince William, the Duke of Clarence, presided over presentations with his wife, Princess Adelaide. So I had to make some minor adjustments in my manuscript.

Another odd research item, which led me down a rabbit hole even farther than (probably) necessary was the development of the railway system in England. This led me to a little nugget that Nash uses to dangle in front of Felix about a lucrative investment. Nash gives a name of Harry Hudson as his contact for purchasing shares. I am still patting myself on the back for this. In truth there was a railway promoter by the name of George Hudson (1800-1871), called the "railway king" of Britain, controlling nearly 30% of the rail track operating in Britain before some scandalous revelations forced him out of office. The "twist" here for those who have read *The Hope Clinic* series, and especially Harry's (The Duke of Ashton) book is that Harry's twin brother, who predeceases him, is named George. I kind of like that play on the Harry/George theme. There was great speculation over the railway and fortunes could be made or lost in a heartbeat. No spoilers, but keep an eye out for this small plot line to surface again in the last book of the series.

Speaking of Speculation, (goodness), I spent an inordinate amount of time trying to understand the game and the little nuances that it could have. My critique partners assured me that even if they weren't familiar with the game, they could follow the basics to understand what was happening. I sure hope so. I know it can be confusing. Speculation was a popular game of the time and was somewhat similar to Whist. Characters in Jane Austen's *Mansfield Park* are seen playing Speculation.

As for Jane Austen, the tie-in for this book, *Sense and Sensibility*, is fairly loose. But I hope you can see some similarities. I realized (oddly) that Juliana is very much an Elinor character, putting needs of others before her own, and Victor is very much a Marianne character, all dramatics and emotions. But I also realized that Juliana would not only relate to Elinor, but to Colonel Brandon in his deep, secret love for Marianne. I still sigh over Alan Rickman's portrayal of him in the 1995 Ang Lee adaptation. I hope you find these little tie-ins enjoyable. I certainly love revisiting Miss Austen's books and re-watching the film adaptations.

If you haven't seen it, another good adaptation is the 2008 BBC mini-series. The 2008 version holds the truest to the book, and I do love Dan Stevens as Edward Ferrars. His portrayal of Edward holds truer to the book (in my opinion). It's enjoyable, and I've watched it several times, but the acting (especially by Emma Thompson and Alan Rickman) tips the scales to the 1995 version (in my opinion).

Speaking of character tie-ins, I hope you can see the similarities between Lydia Whyte and Lucy Steele. Schemers, both of them. Amy, one of my critique partners wondered if I had plans to redeem her and give Lydia her own book, because in Amy's words,

"I never know with you." LOL! At this time, there are no plans for a book for her—but don't rule out redemption.

There are some definite clues in the book as to the identity and the motive of the perpetrator of *The Muckraker*. I expect savvy readers will figure out who it is, but I don't think they'll necessarily know the "whys" behind it all. It's going to be a bit of a twist.

So stay tuned, and I will try to get this next book out much sooner than a year from now.

ALSO BY TRISHA MESSMER

❦

The Hope Clinic Series
No Ordinary Love (Prequel Novella)
The Reluctant Duke's Dilemma
A Doctor For Lady Denby
Healing The Viscount's Heart
Saving Miss Pratt
Redeeming Lord Nash

❦

The London Ladies' League
A Duke In The Rough
Every Rake Has A Silver Lining
A Picture Is Worth A Thousand Heirs
Don't Get Your Viscount In A Twist (coming soon)
The Lady Takes It All (coming in 2026)

❦

Contemporary Romance
Different World Series
The Bottom Line
The Eyre Liszt
Look With Your Heart

ABOUT THE AUTHOR

Trisha Messmer had a million stories rattling around in her brain. (Well, maybe a million is an exaggeration but there were a lot). Always loving the written word, she enjoyed any chance she had to compose something, whether it be for a college paper or just a plain old email. One day as she was speaking with her daughter about the latest adventure going on in her mind, her daughter said, "Mom, why don't you write them down." And so it began. Several stories later, she finally allowed someone, other than her daughter, to read them.

After that brave (and very scary) step, she decided not to keep them to herself any longer, so here we are.

She hopes you enjoy her musings as much as she enjoyed writing them. If they make you smile, sigh, hope, and chuckle or even cry at times, it was worth it.

Born in St. Louis, Missouri, Trisha graduated from the University of Missouri – St. Louis with a degree in Psychology. Trisha's day job as a product instructor for a software company allowed her to travel all over the country meeting interesting people and seeing interesting places, some of which inspired ideas for her stories. A hopeless (or hopeful) romantic, Trisha currently resides in the great Northwest.

www.ingramcontent.com/pod-product-compliance
Lightning Source LLC
Chambersburg PA
CBHW020237010826
48973CB00006B/1557